Angela Fournier

Adventure Thriller Series

Book One

Tabula Rasa

John F Russo

Angela Fournier - Tabula Rasa

John F. Russo

Join John's fictional novel debut

The Perplexity of Engram
(A futuristic fable)

Enjoy **Angela Fournier**
Adventure Thriller series
in
Tabula Rasa – Book One
Darkness After Midnight – Book Two
Compromised Interests – Book Three
Le Journal – *A Novella* – Book Four

Other titles in this series coming soon!
Whiteburn – Book Five
(including excerpts from Le Journal)

Books2Read:
https://books2read.com?ap/8prE7z/John-F-Russo
Instagram: @johnfrussoauthor
Website: johnfrussoauthor.com

Disclaimer and Copyright

Sale of this book without a front cover may be unauthorized. If this book is coverless, it may have been reported to the publisher as "unsold or destroyed" and neither the author nor the publisher may have received payment for it.

Angela Fournier — Adventure Thriller Series Book One - Tabula Rasa is a work of fiction. Names, characters, businesses, organizations, places, events and incidents are the products of the author's imagination or are used fictitiously. Any resemblance to actual events, locales, or persons, living or dead, is entirely coincidental.

E-book ISBN-13: 978-1-7346457-3-6

Paperback ISBN-13: 978-1-7346457-2-9

Dedicated Always

to

My loving wife, Lori Russo

And

Our Family & Friends

Acknowledgements:

Thank you to my wife, Lori for her continuous input and endearing support. A special thank you to my proof readers for their guidance: Patricia, Laurie and Tricia.

And with much gratitude to my friend, Tom Cuba, who diligently edited the 2020 version.

Vuitton™, McQueen™, Glock™, Bose™, Air France™, The Roof Garden—Peninsula Beverly Hills™

'Bound to You' ©Christina Aguilera

With most artwork, the artist is not truly happy until he makes that one last brush stroke. With the continued Angela Fournier series, a few added brush strokes needed to be added to this, the latest version 2026.

Thank you, Karen Russo, my Vegas connection, for sharing your insightfulness on viewing my author's copy.

I want to sincerely thank my editor, Malory Wood, of The Missing Ink LLC for her diligent work, her comments, and her friendship.

FB: /themissinginkwritingservices

IG: @themissinginkllc

LinkedIn: /the-missing-ink-writing-services

Content

Act I

Strength   1

Act II

Angela, Remembering Her Past   99
Newspaper Note   156

Act III

Brutal Force   333

The Author   366
Interesting Facts   367

From the Author

There are many reasons why someone would choose to disappear without a trace. We will never know that illusive 'why' because there is no way of categorizing them without the liberated giving up their anonymity.

Introduction

A young Gloria suffered the heartache of losing her father when she was nine years old. Her mother was unable to adjust and settled for a dubious suitor. His abusive nature complicated Gloria's idealism of how a man should behave—with respect.

Her plan was to escape. A terrifying accident in the uninhabited White Mountains of New Hampshire led to her savior, a mountain man, Gilles Fournier, who had suffered the injustice of also losing someone very dear to him. Together, they mended their hearts, but Gloria's steel-clad wall would remain with her until she met another injured soul many years later.

Arriving in L.A., Gloria cast a new identity—Angela Fournier was born. Dissatisfied with her treatment and forced profession by Rev. M., an opportunity turned into friendship and a new mentor, George Stanza. Separately, they weaved the thread of suspense that revenged injustice and set Angela onto her life's course and destiny.

Angela Fournier - Tabula Rasa

Escaping her assassin, Angela mounted her make-shift bridge, precariously made out of an abandon roof-top aviary. She slithered on her stomach across the eighteen-foot span between the buildings, only looking down once at the sixty-foot drop and her certain demise if she failed. The twisted wire securing the boards bared their teeth as she attempted to slide over them, peeling back her exposed skin leaving three rows of dripping blood. She screamed through her gritting teeth. If she survived this, would she still manage to stay alive?

Act I

Strength

The late autumn evening swelled with a symphony of sounds as the stroking of crickets' forewings reached its crescendo until all went quiet—and then, the mellowed croak from a muttering frog engaged the players once more. The full October moon had reappeared from behind the dense rain clouds, casting a bluish-ring as it surrounded a seemingly lifeless farmhouse. The cold metal structure of an aging vehicle reflected the moon's glare into slim spires disappearing in the deep shadows. And a modest breeze toyed with the remaining leaves deposited to the ground from the grand oak tree that stood proudly next to the farmhouse. The small encircling veranda's roof shared its glow from a dim light that escaped from a window up above.

The room was cozy and neatly arranged with its humble furnishings. The walls were sparsely adorned by photographs of past years while in contrast, well-dressed stuffed animals resided at the head of the bed. The moonlight peeked through the window and added to the illumination of a pretty mid-teen girl, Gloria Jackson. Sitting on the floor with tears swelling in her eyes, she tucked her blonde hair behind her ear and gazed at a small-framed picture of a man in a white Navy uniform. The inscription read: *'To my little Angel, Love you, Daddy'*. The picture was spread across the fourth and fifth pages of an opened diary that rest in her lap.

Dear Diary, June 20th: Today was the saddest day in my short nine years of living that I hope I will never have to see or do again. You see, my friend, when Daddy gave you to me three months ago for my birthday to write my most secretive feelings, I don't think he had this in mind.

Today as I stared out the tinted side window of a big black car, I saw a long, winding path that was dotted with miniature mosque-shaped buildings, mingled with smaller brightly polished stone monuments, engraved with unknown names and dates. The car we were following finally came to a stop, and as six men appeared in front of our car, they opened the back of what they called a hearse, exposing a polished wooden coffin. I looked at Mom only briefly as I could not keep my eyes off that box. My mother stepped out first with the assistance of a man in uniform holding his white-gloved hand out for her. She went without any protest. I was summoned next but hesitated with their unknown formalities because I was afraid to step out. I didn't want to leave. I knew this would be the end and I would never be able to see my father again. I was crying, my friend. I couldn't stop.

My mother whispered something to the soldier who then stepped to the side. She calmly told me to come and stand by her. She said she needed me. She was wearing a black hat, a black dress, which she also made me wear, and black gloves. Mother never wore black, and when this hand covered in black came through the opened back door to gather me, something final like a cold chill seemed to rush over my body. I took her hand tightly and together we walked through the crowd of people.

There were different kinds of people standing in military uniforms, like Daddy had, with medals and ribbons pinned to their chests. Mr. Nankichi was there in his best blue suit; JT, Dad's business partner was dressed pretty nice too, and his wife, RoAnn, looked very sad. She usually is very sparkly and loves showing me exciting things she has seen or bought. I like her. She always has time for me even when I ask her, as she says, "grown-up" questions. Mom says I am too smart for my britches.

The man in the white gown with a purple sash seemed friendly to everyone. He started talking after we all gathered at Daddy's shiny box. It is called a coffin and I don't know why; Daddy isn't here to ask. The man talked like he knew Daddy, calling him an able sailor, a leader in our community, and a faithful husband, and then he looked right at me when he said, "...and father of a beautiful, intelligent daughter." I have never met him. How does he know who I am? But I started to cry again uncontrollably and didn't hear anything else he said.

Gloria slowly turned the page of her cherished childhood diary. Tears welled in her eyes and she shuddered just like it happened yesterday.

Dear Diary, August 8th: I am so sorry for not writing anything in the last couple of years. Losing Daddy has been really hard on me and Mom. I had that dream again of watching myself running in a field of flowers. Mom says that it is natural after a tragedy. This man Steve that took over one of Daddy's stores in Carroll has been driving down here to see Mommy. I don't like him. He looks at me funny. Mom and I had a big argument today. This guy wants to marry her and move us up to his farm near some town I have never heard of. I screamed at her and said that I didn't want to leave Daddy—we wouldn't be able to visit him. And all she could say was, 'We must move on. Daddy can't look after us anymore. We need to do this, baby.' I hate it when she calls me *baby* in that tone.

Gloria flipped to a new page in her book.

Dear Diary, October 24th: It seems I am always apologizing for not writing to you more often. It has been almost five years since when I first started to tell you my story. Today I am sitting in my room reading you, looking at pictures of my dad and my best friend, Carol. I have to write this down. Recently, I've started calling Mom, Elizabeth, and I truly believe she has lost it. Her jerk of a husband, Steve, has been no help. In fact, he is a lecherous pig.

Gloria looked up at the picture of her and Carol and started to write once again.

Last month, Carol and I had our pictures taken at the school by this photographer that was drooling all over Carol. She flashed her pretty blues at him, and took off her sweater, revealing, well let's say, I was getting flushed. Her darkened areolas were somewhat showing through her almost sheer blouse. She gave the sweater to me because she knows I love that sweater. She then softly asked him if he could snap a few of just the two of us, together. You could almost see the wheels turning in his mind. He asked her if she had done any modeling. Now, Dear Diary, I have to tell you, Carol is very, very pretty. Her skin is like silk and her long dark hair is like a calling card to play with. On the occasional sleepover at her house, I brushed her hair for hours as we talked. And not to forget, she has long legs, and her breasts have developed well beyond mine. She is pretty much perfect, but best of all, she is my best friend; we tell each other everything.

After the pictures, he gave Carol his business card and said he would be in touch. I could tell she was interested in the possibilities as well. We gathered our things and went back to our lockers. I was still wearing Carol's sweater, so as we walked through the halls, the guys were whistling and making comments. I have only known these guys a year or so, whereas Carol has been raised with most of them and she just shrugged off their comments with a swish of her hair and "You wish." She is so cool.

I told her that Elizabeth could wash the sweater before giving it back to her. Carol thought it wasn't necessary, but I insisted. It is such a pretty sweater. I know my father would have bought me one just like it.

Carol then said, "I wish I had met your father. He sounds like a very nice man. By the way, how is fuck-head treating you?"

I said, "Still the same. He calls me a little whore when Elizabeth isn't around."

"You told your mom, right?"

"Yeah, but she wouldn't believe me. Then he came in as we were talking and told Ma that I was at that story telling age, when young girls' hormones rage like wild horses."

"He compared you to a wild horse? And she believed him?"

"I guess so. She just doesn't want to be left out in the cold again," I said. We gathered our things out of the locker and headed out the doors.

The sun in September has a magical warmth to it; it makes you want to do things. The guys were hanging out in the parking lot and as we walked by, they continued with their childish banter. I think they think it is foreplay. We kept walking and Carol asked how Mom was doing. I told her she hasn't been too good lately. I think that jerk is suffocating her mind. She just sits there and stares off into space. Then Carol, always inspiring, said, "Hey Gloria, I've got a great idea. Why don't you come down to the arcade with me? The rest of the gang will be down there. It'll be fun. You can get better acquainted with those other jerks so they don't get under your skin."

I said, "No, I don't think so. I'll catch hell if I'm not home to help Elizabeth with getting supper."

"Fuck that old bastard. You gotta live. We are not babies anymore. You need to have some fun. Christ, you're fifteen years old and have never been kissed." Carol has a flair for over-dramatizing things.

"Well..."

"Come on. There's Rodney. We can hitch a ride with him." Carol can also be very convincing.

"No, Carol. I'll come, but let's walk and talk," I insisted.

Carol gave me a big smile and then started to talk like Humphrey Bogart, "O.K., sweetheart, let's go."

She is so crazy. So arm in arm, we headed to town, past the 18th century church with its towering steeple, past the John Deere dealership, and to the steps of the

6

once Regis drugstore to the now flashy 'Arcade'. As we walked under the flashing sign, we could see through the large windows. Rodney jumped up and rushed over to the door to hold it open for us. Well, I should say, Carol. I think his motivation was purely imaginative as he delighted in seeing Carol's image, I could tell. Our friends were already packed into two booths, some half-draped over the backs, spilling into the next. They were all laughing and joking amongst themselves listening to the new release by The Pussycat Dolls *Don't Cha*.

Carol rewarded Rodney with a compliment, "Thank you, Rodney. You are a true gentleman. Obviously, the only one in here." No one responded.

"Pleasure is all mine, Carol," replied Rodney as his friends also enjoyed the slight vision as the sun outlined Carol's breasts through her sheer blouse. She didn't notice or didn't say anything.

"See, I told you they are not all bad," insisted Carol. "Come on," she coaxed, "let's play that archaic King Kong pinball game."

"I don't know how to play," I was embarrassed to admit.

"It's ancient!" said Carol, somewhat surprised I had never played. "Come, I will show you."

Carol rummaged through her backpack for some change, found a dollar's worth of quarters and inserted them; the backboard lit up. I stood to the side so Carol could show me the nuances of the game.

I couldn't help but think of one of the times I stayed at Carol's when we had a conversation about her wanting to run away. So I asked her again.

"So you have run away from home three times?" I said a bit shyly, I might add.

"Yeah." She struck the flippers one more time. "I was six the first time, twelve, and then thirteen. I would have made it the last time except I got lost in the woods. I had to find a road. Stupid me, I should have brought a compass." Carol started to laugh, and then added, "But, I don't know how to read one anyway."

We both laughed at Carol's remark and as her time was up, I took the controls. With encouragement from Carol, bells clinked and clanked until a low *Bing-Bong* determined a victory over King Kong. I couldn't believe it. Must have been beginner's luck. We threw our arms up in triumph and bounced and hugged each other. Next, Carol wanted to stop at the photo booth. We made funny faces, distorted faces, tongues sticking out, and then one just smiling. *Flash... flash... flash*.

"Let's do another round!" insisted Carol as she inserted two more dollars into the machine.

"What are you doing?" I said to her more than embarrassed behind the curtain.

"Shhh," Carol softly whispered loosening her blouse. "Don't let the guys hear you," instructed Carol. "Give me your hands. Now cup my breasts, now smile." Flash. "Kiss me." Flash. "Oh, kiss me again." Flash.

I hold the key to you, my Dear Diary. Don't let anyone read this. I was flabbergasted! I stood still. My eyes must have been as wide as saucers and I was not sure what to say or do. Carol took me by surprise, but what a surprise! I had often wondered what Carol would feel like. Would she feel different than me, the same? She was soft. I just stood there. Carol quickly straightened her top, we gathered our pictures, and left the booth, that beautiful little booth behind. I must have had at least a hint of a glow and I was uncertain if any of our friends noticed my rouged cheeks. Looking back now, what else did I leave behind? At the counter, we agree to rip our intimate moment in half, each getting the other's to hold onto forever. We shared a cola float until I realized what time it was and panicked. I asked Rodney if he minded giving me a ride home. He said, "No problem."

By the time we got to our lane, the sun had all but disappeared. I jumped out of his truck before he even came to a complete stop, not like in drivers ed. As I was running to the door, I could hear him drive off, so I knew they heard inside as well. When I opened the kitchen door, Ma was sitting at the table. She looked up at me with tears in her eyes—from behind, jerkoff Steve came out of the bathroom, pulling up his suspenders over his undershirt. Nice! Not! He started in on me.

"Well, looky here. The little whore finally came home to grace our presence."

I knew he had been drinking, because he only called me that when Ma wasn't around.

"Was that Prince Charming who's driving off?" he said, slobbering as he spoke.

I remained still. I kept looking at Ma who sat like a stone, and then back to this poor excuse of a human being. He made rude gestures with his hands, pawing at his undershirt, and said, "So, was he pawing at those little titties of yours, tugging at your pink panties?"

I lost it. I screamed at him, "You filthy, disgusting pig!" I remember raising my hand like I was going to punch him but he stepped back, either in surprise by my reaction or he has probably had to do it before. Anyway, the bastard stopped my swing and slapped me to the ground. I could tell Ma was not too pleased either as she jumped up yelling.

"No, Stephen, no! Please God, no!"

He shouted at her, "Shut up you old bag. I'm speaking to your whoring daughter."

I had hit the floor hard and he bust open my lip—but I was not finished. "I'm glad I'm not your daughter, you bastard!"

He was in a rage. He stepped over to me and gave me a swift kick in my upper thigh. It hurt so damn bad but I wasn't going to give him the satisfaction knowing he hurt me. I started to crawl to the stairs. My leg was throbbing.

He yelled at me, "That's it, tramp! Crawl to your room. And don't come down until you are ready to apologize to me and your mother!"

With the help of the banister, I managed to stand on one leg and slowly made my way up the stairs. I could feel the tears starting to swell but I held them back so he couldn't see. I was not going to give him the pleasure.

I heard him say to Ma, "That little bitch of yours. How could you have a daughter like her, and bring her into my house." And then I heard him hit Ma, and then, "Don't ever raise your voice to me again when I am disciplining your kid."

I plunged through my bedroom door and collapsed onto my bed, sobbing, kicking, and punching.

"I hate him!" I screamed. "I hate him!" That's when I decided I had to make a decision. Good night, Dear Diary.

After documenting that memory in her diary from only a month earlier, Gloria wiped the tears from her eyes; a memory she will never forget—written or not. No man will hit her again. She replaced Carol and her school picture back onto the nightstand. She removed the photo of her father and her from its frame and together with the ripped picture of

Carol and her, she placed them into her diary. Adding a reassuring nod and a wink to her stuffed friends, she then took a quick glance at the remaining photos as she shouldered her bag and climbed out the window onto the metal roof of the veranda.

With a dampened step, she crossed the roof cautiously until she reached an outstretched limb from the giant oak. Clearing the span of the roof, she made the last swoop, landing on the softness of the rain-soaked ground. She paused momentarily and gazed upward; the moonlight accented the tears that were trickling down her face. She picked herself up and started down the laneway towards freedom and the unknown of the night.

Weigh Station

Business had been slow. Even though the rains had subsided for now, no one could predict the chancy weather through the mountain pass that lay just west of the weigh station. Rick, a balding man—but with a younger look than his receding hairline might have indicated—looked up from his TV and saw his old friend, Pete, pulling in with his rig. The eighteen-wheel tanker stopped on the scales. Pete stepped out wearing a bombardier jacket and ball cap with a PR Trucking insignia. He stood about six feet tall, had a slight build for his height, and a weathered face. He entered the depot where Rick was already filling out the bill of lading.

"Hi ya, Pete. You got a full load today," stated Rick as he charted the weights on his paperwork.

"Yeah, heatin' oil from Canada," informed Pete for Rick's paperwork. "How's the wife and kids doin'?"

"Hey, you know the old story. She complains when she doesn't get it and then cries we'll wake the babies. I suggested I could put a sock in her mouth, but she didn't see the humor in that."

"Haha, it sounds like you got your hands full."

"Yeah, but I wouldn't give them up for the world." He paused. "You better be careful tonight. You know the problems they've been having down around Frenchman Creek, don't ya?"

"Ah, listen, Rick, 'Old Betsy' and I have been through some scrapes before and have made out just fine. I know her every whim or should I say whine."

"Maybe, old buddy, but be careful, nonetheless. I've heard there was speculation of possible washouts up there due to the heavy rains we've been getting."

"I will, my friend. See ya in a couple of days." Pete bid his farewell as he threw his collar up to protect himself from the increased wind. He climbed into his 'Old Betsy', clicked his belts, and released his air brakes. Idling to the road's edge, he turned east and started off down the road. On his radio, he picked up the tail end of a missing child watch advisory.

"*Once again for the third time this week, the search in Cascade County for a young girl, Gloria Jackson, has been called off due to the inclement weather. Her whereabouts are still uncertain, and as the Sheriff's office states:* 'We do not suspect foul play at this time.' *They declined to release any additional information until all have been questioned.*"

The tank truck roared off into the distance leaving a spray of moisture lingering in the illumination of the truck's taillights.

Disheartened

The rhythmic crunching of breaking branches kept in step to the limber, hurried figure of young Gloria whose silhouette contrasted against the bleak background of dried leaves that nestled in the underbrush waiting for winter's blanket of snow. Running with the same determination as she had learned from her cross-country running coach, her breathing felt slightly elevated but she thought that was normal, considering her circumstances. She checked her pulse against her watch, momentarily lifting her eyes from her path, when all of a sudden, she faltered on the ridge and lost her balance, propelling her down a steep riverbank.

Tumbling, she tried to grasp onto anything she could. Clawing at the earth—screaming, she plummeted downward, plowing through dried weeds and dead branches to the riverbed below. Scratched and dirty-faced, Gloria came to a harsh stop against a hefty rock, which lay only inches from the flowing waters. Lying face down in the sand, Gloria coughed and spit out the mud and grass mixture that violated her during her terrifying fall. Painfully, lifting herself up, she propped herself against the very rock that indented her body.

Disheartened, pride as bruised as her body, wet, and tired, she looked at her torn and blood-soaked clothes. Sitting for a moment, frustrated, she eyed the hill she would now have to re-climb. She knew she must remain strong—she couldn't go back to that hell. Opening up her backpack, Gloria pulled out a clean sweater and another pair of jeans. Getting up slowly, she removed her jacket, her mud-torn blouse, and her ripped jeans. Gathering her blouse in a ball, she soaked it in the frigid river and attempted to clean the mud from her face and the blood from her hands and knees.

Talking over the rush of the river, she tried to console herself. "Look," she huffed, "...at the bright side." She breathed in deeply, "...at least I didn't fall into the river." She spit out more dirt.

Tossing her battered clothes into the river, she picked up her backpack and searched for her compass. Thankful it survived the fall, she set it on the rock and finished dressing while eyeing the direction of the needle. She had to make a decision, either back up the hill or tread along the river's edge as far as she could. Adjusting her pack, she stepped from rock to rock and then onto more solid ground. A weathered trail imprinted with animal hooves paralleled the river.

I hope this will lead to an easier path rather than straight uphill, she thought. *Maybe I can find a sign or something once I'm on the road again.*

Her friend, Carol, had given Gloria a lot of information unwittingly, and now it was up to her to perfect her escape where Carol failed. Gloria had planned for over a month; studied maps, bought a compass, and gathered what she thought she would need without the watchful eye of her stepfather becoming suspicious. As long as there was cold beer in the fridge, he could care less about anything else, including her mother.

One day, I will rescue her. I will care for her as Daddy did; I will love her. And that creep, well, he will get what he deserves, that I promise. These last few years have been a living hell. He will not go unpunished for what he has done to me or the misery he has put my mother through all these years. Favoring her leg, her nightmares tugged at her to push on.

Rose's Café

The light of the day had given way to the evening's heavy rain-bearing clouds, which were delivering a deluge upon the roadways. Gloria had managed to stay dry under a bridge before the next round of rains came. She was cold, and although she wouldn't admit it to herself, she was scared. Her mind wandered to the thought of hot soup, even to the point of licking her lips. She estimated that after being a week on the run, she was at least 100 miles from home. If there was a search for her still going on, that distance would be in her favor—she hoped.

Gloria stepped out from under her hideout to face the cold rains. Just down the road, she saw a pinkish neon sign radiating 'Rose's Café'. The traffic was minimal. Her detection would be slim, but out of precaution, she stayed close to the tree line. Coming from the opposite direction, she spotted a semi-truck heading towards her. Ducking out of sight, she watched as it turned into the café's parking lot. The driver parked the semi perfectly for her needs; blocking any view of the café from her hidden vantage point.

Inside the café, Rose, a bountiful woman with a very pretty face, peered out the window as she heard the rumble and noticed the unmistakable insignia of PR Trucking. It slowed and hissed as it came to a stop. Pete jumped out of the cab. Precariously running to avoid deepening puddles, he stepped into the café with a stamping of feet and a swat from his ball cap.

"Nice entrance dance, Pete," Rose said sarcastically. She stood from her stool and moseyed over toward the coffee stand.

"Hi to you too, Rose. Sure is getting nasty out there; it's not fit for man or beast!"

"So what the hell you doin' out there, crazy man?"

"Just came to see your pretty face, Rose," replied Pete, letting the *crazy man* reference lay.

"One of these days, Pete, I might surprise you and jump into your rig and say, 'Take me out of here!'" She laughed.

"Being a crazy man, I'd be obliged to do so, Rose."

"Haha, good comeback. But even I know you're just saying that because you love my coffee."

"You do have the best coffee, no doubt. And your pie is pretty darn good too," said Pete.

Rose stood beside her coffee machine and measured a precise amount of freshly ground beans and dumped it into her filter basket. She then reached for a glass jar, opened it, scooped up a tablespoon of Chicory, and place it into the mix. She then added a pinch of salt, re-inserted the filter basket into the coffee maker, and turned it on.

"Yeah, that's me; win a man's heart through his stomach." Rose reached for an empty cup that was sitting on the ledge near the pass-through window. "The State Troopers phoned and told me to tell my customers that are heading east to stay put. I guess the bridge at Frenchman Creek is out."

"You're kidding! Not more than half an hour ago, I crossed over that bridge."

Rose stepped to Pete with cup in hand and poured him a fresh serving of her famous brew. He swung his leg over the stool at the counter-side and placed his jacket on the one next to him.

"Can I get you anything to eat?"

Pete reached for the menu from behind the condiment stand, but hesitated. He knew everything on it by heart. Instead, he asked Rose, "What's your special?"

Humorously, Rose replied, "If it was closer to closing time, my suggestion would be me."

A smile flashed on Pete's face and a chuckle escaped. "Haha, my sleeper is clean and available, darling."

"I'm givin' ya fair warning, mister. One of these days I will sell this place, and then take to the wind to wherever she pleases."

"You'll never sell this place. Where would you go to find a place where you can harass your customers?"

"There is life to live, my friend. It's not always about money," said Rose. "You want the meatloaf?"

"Love your meatloaf," he said as he blew at the edge of his cup before sipping its salubrious flavor.

Rose returned the carafe back to the burner and slipped into the kitchen. Through the pass-through, she asked, "Vegetables, mashed potatoes with gravy?"

"Need you ask? I tell ya, Rose, if I would've hit that washout after coming out of that blind curve, and with what I'm carrying, I would have lit up the sky. You'd see the fireworks from here," stated Pete.

. . .

Gloria watched, steadfast in the pouring rain. The driver was obviously not stopping for a quick coffee-to-go. She crept closer through the brush, waiting for that precise moment to cross the roadway. Looking to the left and to the right—she darted. Taking refuge beside the rear tire of the bulk loader, she noticed another vehicle slowed. Its roof-mounted lights sent a chill down Gloria's already cold spine. She ran and jumped onto the semi's passenger running board.

From inside the café, the flash of headlights glared through the windows and as the lights dimmed, the driver's door opened to display a friendly star. Pete recognized Trooper James' 4x4 right away.

Outside battling the rain, Gloria hung on tight to the large mirrors and held her breath to avoid the condensation from rising above the cab and giving her away. Trooper James dodged the puddles and jumped onto the small cement sidewalk. He entered the café, but not before a flash of lightning illuminated the parking lot and a crack of thunder boomed.

Taking a well deserve breath, that hot bowl of soup was now out of the question with the State Trooper inside. Her mind recalculated the situation. Patiently, Gloria waited for the next lightning strike. If she opened the semi's door in the darkness, the interior light would certainly have given her away. The storm was right above her. Multiple flashes and tremendous cracks jostled for control. Finally, a jolt of lightning and a loud crack shared the night sky. Gloria opened the passenger side door and slid in. *What now?* She thought, looking around the cab in a panic, she accidentally nudged the curtain behind her.

A bed! How nice would that be to crawl into? And without further hesitation, she slipped through the curtain and curled up in the warm blankets. Lying down, her tears mingled with her rain-soaked face. Her body relaxed and her eyelids reluctantly gave in to her exhaustion. She fell asleep.

. . .

As Gloria enjoyed the comfort of Pete's sleeper, her friend Carol, with her father at her side, was at the local police station. Sheriff Turner was questioning Carol about Gloria's whereabouts. Carol, looking at the Sheriff, couldn't get her friend's nickname for him out of her mind: 'Turner the Sterner'. His daughter, Carol's friend, told her that her dad was extremely strict with her, so strict that she always brought an extra set of clothes with her to school.

Carol imagined, *If he only knew how wild she was, he would go ballistic and probably shoot everyone she's been with.*

"Look, Sheriff, it's late. Carol has told you everything she knows," insisted her father.

Carol's father moved behind her as she sat in a chair facing the rugged Sheriff. Slouched over his desk with his hands clasped together, the Sheriff stared at the teenager.

"Carol, you and Gloria Jackson, from what we have gathered, are best friends. She must have said something to you. Have you left anything out? Possibly a conversation you had...anything?"

"Sheriff, I've told you everything. I want Gloria found too." Breaking down in tears, she added, "Why don't you ask that bastard what he did to Gloria?"

"Who's that, Carol?"

Jumping up in a rage, she leaned forward on the Sheriff's desk, and said, "Her stepfather, Steve! Ask him... ask him that filthy pig!"

Carol's father placed his arms around her to comfort his daughter. "It's okay, honey. The Sheriff is just doing his job. We'll find Gloria; she'll be all right, wait and see."

Turning to the Sheriff, he said, "We're going home now, Sheriff. It's up to you and your men to find her. As far as I'm concerned, you have everything Carol knows. Come on, baby, let's go home."

Carol and her father took leave, sidestepping a deputy that was poised to enter the sheriff's office. The sheriff, only acknowledging the deputy with a nod, swung around in his chair and looked out the window at the pouring rain while tapping his knuckles with a pencil.

"That little bitch has her father fooled. She's been more trouble than a Friday night drunk at Kitchen's Bar. She has put us through enough searches. I know she knows something... something."

"Do you want me to press her some more?" asked the deputy.

"No, we'll let her be for the time being. Have you heard anything derogatory about Steve? Will this rain ever stop?"

The Washout

Pete, with a full stomach, bid his farewell to Rose and Trooper James. It was time to continue his journey. The rains hadn't let up, but that was no excuse—he needed to get his load to the supply depot before morning. He had done this drive on numerous occasions without any problems. One time, a near white-out with an accumulation of two feet of snow had fallen and he still made it through the pass on time. A little rain storm wasn't going to ruin his reputation.

Pete climbed back into the cab and shut the door. It was nice and cozy inside from leaving the engine running while he was having a bite to eat. He reached over and with a little adjustment to his favorite country radio station, he turned on the wipers, blew his horn for Rose, and off he went, disappearing into the darkness of the cloud-covered night.

. . .

The roadway was especially dark that night, so with a flip of a switch, on came the bumper-mounted extra high-intensity fog lamps. The wipers could barely keep up clearing the rain from the windshield, so he decided to slow down, clutch in, shift, the engine revved momentarily, then slowed. He had plenty of time still; there was no sense rushing to be first in line at the gate. It wouldn't open until six in the morning, and besides, he was the only scheduled delivery that he knew of. Safety was on his mind that night. Well, that and Rose. *What a sweet lady,* he thought. He figured he might be ten years her senior, but if she didn't mind the age difference, hell, he was all over it. She had a great sense of humor but could also out-cuss any of his trucker friends—and he had seen her do it. Shaking his head, Pete thought, *What a gal!*

The rains lashed at the semi's windshield as the highway's blackness awoke to the piercing halogen lights and then faded back to that blackening void behind him. Each curve highlighted a new beginning as the rig forged through along the blacktop. At times, the white dotted lines just disappeared. Pete down shifted again, and then again; the first incline approached before the twin bridges. His rig shuddered as each gear found its spot. It chugged up the steep hillside leaving the creek below harnessed in the arms of obscurity.

"Come on, girl. This country isn't new to ya. Just up this hill, a couple of switch backs, the twin bridges, and then home free," commanded Pete out loud.

The eighteen-wheel tanker topped the crest of the incline and leveled for a short distance before gradually descending. The right front tire straddled the edge of the roadway as it rounded the first curve, the rain relentlessly beaded down. Ahead, the headlights illuminated a posted sign announcing a sharp 'S' curve; water splashed its surface as the tanker flashed by. Pete turned the steering wheel; the lights glared off the first of two bridges. *Rumble–rumble*, the wooden boards slapped the tires as the spray of water dripped off the side rails to the dark depths below. Again, Pete turned the steering wheel, this time in the other direction. He geared down, a grind, a double clutch, in it went, and once more, he downshifted as the tachometer's needle jumped.

As the halogens lit the upcoming bridge and surrounding hillside, he could see a massive up-rooted tree rushing down in a torrent of mud and debris. It smashed into the small two-lane bridge before him. Slamming on the brakes, he downshifted once more and watched as the bridge started to tumble. The tanker locked up and started to go into a controlled, sideways slide. Out of the sleeper, Gloria screamed. Startled, Pete looked back. His foot slipped off of the brake pedal. He re-focused back on the road, pumping the brakes, but too late. The rig floated in suspension before the shattered metal of the bridge pierced the skin of the tanker. With a platinum spray of streaking sparks, the fluid ignited with a whoosh of a bang. The force dislodged the tanker from its locking pin on the cab and hurled it down into the swollen creek in a fireball. The cab, with its engine growling, landed on the opposite side of the now void. It bounced, twisting side to side as the front tires screeched on the wet pavement. The back tires spun in the muddy hillside trying to gain traction. The forward thrust was too much. It crashed sideways into a giant fir tree, bending the rig into a 'V', which then propelled Gloria through the ripped-off passenger door. Raising her hands instinctively to protect herself, she slammed into the tree and tumbled past it down the hillside. Pete was thrown to the side of his door jamb and smashed his head on the steel-lined headliner—eyes rolled back in a daze.

The truck idled in the mud, steam escaping from its twisted hood, and then, slipping head over heel, it flipped like a rag doll. It plunged down the bank taking anything and everything with it that stood in its path. Small trees snapped, embedding themselves in the undercarriage. Mud spun from the rig's giant tires causing massive ruts indented into the hillside's face. The cab finally came to rest fifty feet from the fireball, caught on a boulder just before the swollen river. The driver's door sprung open and a bloodied arm fell out. The engine chugged and clunked off in a hiss of escaping steam—a front tire spun in defiance.

Gloria lay still only ten feet from the resting rig; suspended in abyssal pain, the depth of which she had never felt before. All around her, noise crackled. Finally—dizzy, wincing in agony—Gloria forced herself to raise her head. She felt the warmth of blood trickling down her cold cheek from the gash above her left eye and her tattered wrist, raw, embedded with bark and moss, hung like a wet sock.

The blazing tanker had lit up the creek bed as Gloria attempted to focus on the light through her blurred vision. Metal was strewn everywhere. Holding her arm, trembling, she somewhat steadied herself, stood, and made her way to the twisted cab. When she saw the driver's arm protruding from the wreckage, she let out a gasp!

In the oil-soaked grass, she found her backpack and Pete's leather jacket huddled together. Bending down, wavering, she rested her arm on her knee—wrist dangling, and slowly gathered the things that had fallen out of her backpack. Draping the bombardier jacket over her shoulders, and while she was bent over, she picked up the slightly burnt picture of her and Carol from the smoldering grass. Patting it dry as best she could, she returned it to the safe haven inside her journal. Standing, she turned and as she passed by the cab, she paused and momentarily out-stretched her hand, but was afraid to touch the driver to see if he was still alive. Fearful of being discovered, and then forced to returned to her home, she staggered, trying to gather her senses, and painfully walked away from this nightmare. Disappearing into the stormy blackness, she left behind the smoldering wreckage.

Sanctuary

As the light of the next day revealed her whereabouts amidst the dense forest, Gloria strained to straighten her aching body. The cold ground had given her pounding head some relief—her wrist, not so much. Propping herself up, back against a fallen oak tree, she forced her legs to lift her upright. She looked back from where she had been and imagined she had walked miles from the fiery wreckage.

Her blonde hair, caked in reddish-brown mud was plastered to her forehead, and with one eye closed and the other barely functioning, she wearily trudged towards a faint noise in the obscure distance. Underbrush pawed at her as she moved from one tree to the next, ten feet at a time, she zigzagged to their command as they offered their strength for her support. Forward, she hoped.

The rain had turned into a wet-snow mixture and the ground began to accept the accumulation as she slipped over fallen trees and downed branches. Persistently, she carried on without concern for her tattered body. She was cold, tired, beaten, and wet. Nothing could have prepared her for these conditions. She was determined in her mind; her body would have to endure the pain for her salvation.

Lumbering along, the dismal hours were not kind. She had fallen more than she had advanced. The chatter that she heard, however, was becoming familiar, a sound she knew, a cackling she thought—like chickens. The briars scratched at her already bloodied hands and untethered twigs lashed at her face as they attempted to alleviate her backpack from her side. She pulled with all her remaining strength to hang onto her only possessions as she forged through.

Not too far off in a slight clearing, she spotted what she believed to be her reprieve; a fenced-in chicken coop. It was dry on the inside, escaping the imposing weather by its over-extended roof. *Sanctuary*, she thought. The chickens paid her no mind as she closed in. Within reach, she slipped and fell, and before she could grasp the fence to brace her fall, her knees hit the cold ground hard. She lay there for a moment while she gathered her last bit of strength. With one eye swollen shut, she looked up in a blur and spotted what she was looking for. Reaching, she unlatched the clasp and struggled to roll in under the protection provided by the roof, away from the now-amassing heavier snow. A few chickens cackled but without fear, only petty annoyance.

With her uninjured hand, she fetched several eggs as she had done many times before and cracked them open to suck up the nourishment inside. She lay there, exhausted, in the warmth of the straw as the chickens pecked beside her.

Drifting into unconsciousness, she imagined her body floating through the air, cradled in the warmth of her father's arms.

Something of Interest

The barricades were set up and police yellow caution tape was draped from tree to tree to cordon off the accident scene. Flares fizzled out as the morning light showcased the abundance of heavier new snow. Fire trucks, police cars, an ambulance, and of course, camera crews, awaited the rescue of Pete Rogers from the depths below. Twisted metal and the stink of burning rubber attested to the previous night's horror.

High above the wreckage on Highway 302, Rose waited anxiously for news from the rescue crew. Safety lines switched back and forth with pulleys suspended from trees; a wire safety stretcher carefully descended down the hillside. A rescuer acknowledged over his two-way radio that Pete was alive but unconscious; although, it would take some time to cut him out of the wreckage. Rose breathed a sigh of relief, but she suspected Pete was not out of the woods yet. Escaped diesel fuel had made it difficult to use anything that would produce sparks. The 'Jaws of Life' was sent down via a pulley system to help in the rescue mission. Camera crews documented every intense moment.

At the site of the first impact, a state trooper and his tracking dog found long strands of blonde hair embedded in the bark of a tree. He bagged it and quickly communicated with his commander as the news cameraman zoomed in on the anxiousness of the tracking dog. Police and state troopers below intensely started to comb the area in search of something else. They were unaware Pete had a traveler with him, according to Rose's earlier statement. The news anchor, Neil Warren, pestered the commander with questions.

"Sir, what did your trooper just find over there?"

"I cannot comment now. We are not sure what he found or what it may imply."

"Commander, I thought I heard your trooper say, 'Long blonde hair'. Is that correct?" Warren pushed.

"Look, stand back. All I will say at this time is, there is a new development."

Neil turned to his cameraman and said, "Joel, get me in the shot with the trooper and his dog tracking over there."

Joel reset his camera and nodded to Neil to begin.

"This is Eye Witness News on the scene of a horrific accident that happened last night as one of the bridges at Salmon Falls was washed out and took a tanker truck with it. The driver, as we are told, is alive but unconscious. The rescue teams are busy cutting the wreckage from around him but are hampered by the possibility of an explosion by leaking fuel. But as you can see over my shoulder, there appears to be something else of interest, which has not been made public at this time. We will continue to follow the action here on Highway 302. I am Neil Warren, Channel 12 TV News, Whitefield."

"Dex is getting confused with all the footprints over here," stated the trooper to his commander. "I'll take him down to the wreckage. Maybe he can pick up a scent there. This heavier, thicker snow is making it very difficult."

"Okay, Al, and go to channel 8. I want to keep this private. We don't need anybody else tracking all over this scene," instructed the commander. "And Al, give the bag to Trooper Marshall when you get down there."

"Yes, sir."

Neil Warren watched from the other side of the creek as Trooper Allen and his dog, Dex, slipped and slid their way down to the wreckage.

"Joel, follow that trooper and his dog. Let's see what they find," said Warren.

Gilles Fournier

The smell of something cooking mixed with a hint of smoke filled her senses as Gloria tried to open her eyes. A large bandage that wrapped around her head and crossed one eye prevented her from focusing properly. A stone fireplace blazed with the sound of crackling pine as it warmed the room. She mustered a stir; she hurt—everywhere. She was draped in multiple blankets and as she spread open her covers, she discovered she was wearing a large man's flannel shirt. It appeared to engulf her all the way down to her wrapped knees. Her bandaged hands imprisoned all with only escaping fingertips showing, each hidden in the long sleeves. Gloria brought them to her nose. She sensed the same pine smell. Her feet had over-sized wool socks and as she slowly maneuvered the shirt to her waist, she was relieved to see she still had panties on. Looking around the room, she realized it must be a hunting cabin. She wondered, *But who, or why, and how did I get here?*

The large, wooden door in front of her swung open and a flash of cold air rushed in, followed by a giant of a man with a long beard and steel-grey eyes. He was dressed in an animal fur coat and carrying a recently deceased rabbit. Gloria jumped out of bed in pure adrenaline, looked down at the dangling rabbit, and screamed, "Where am I? What have you done? Where are my clothes!?"

Calmly, the old Frenchman, Gilles Fournier, began to explain in his broken English.

"Dans ma cabine," he said waving his hands in denial of any wrongdoing. "Gilles no touch." He pointed to her clothes drying on a wooden rack. "Vos garments um... hang."

The trauma of her past events and her painful, bandaged head had Gloria dizzy, and as the adrenaline lessened, she wavered. Gilles quickly lurched forward and grabbed her, preventing her from collapsing onto the floor. He gently put her back into her bed.

"Your head is still very sore, non?"

"Yes, I...I need to leave," demanded Gloria as she weakly struggled with Gilles' grasp.

"You cannot. The bump on your head gives you much pain. Ton poignet est cassé. You no fit to travel. I no hurt you. Rest and get better," instructed Gilles.

Gloria looked closer at her left wrist and realized it had been immobilized.

"Who are you? How long have I been here?"

"I am Gilles Fournier. I live here for thirty years. I have made some fresh stew for you. You take some to get well," he insisted.

"No. How long have *I* been here? Here in your cabin?"

"One week that I found you in chicken coup."

Gloria reluctantly gave in and Gilles relaxed his grip.

"You will eat. You are skin and bone, and then you will rest some more. The snow has make it dangerous to go out. Very deep, easy to lose footing."

Gilles rewrapped the blankets around her. He felt her forehead; her fever had not quite broken. Returning to his frothing pot, he dished out some of his freshly made stew, returned to Gloria's side, and tempted her with his concoction.

"What is it?" she asked.

"Vegetables, potatoes, and rabbit," he proudly declared.

"Rabbit?"

"It tastes like chicken," said Gilles. "Here, eat. You will feel better."

Gloria accepted Gilles' kindness. The stew was surprisingly good. Each spoonful offered by Gilles warmed her insides. But still she was uneasy. She was anxious to know how she got into his shirt; especially since she was not wearing her bra. *He must have taken it off when he wrapped my bruised body. He better not be like my stepfather.*

She could not argue with him, not now; she was too weak. Gilles sensed that the young girl had had enough stew and placed the half-emptied bowl on the table. He eased her back down in the bed, fluffed her pillow, and laid her feverish head carefully to the side. She drifted back to sleep. *Tomorrow*, she thought.

The snowfall had been heavy and constant since Gloria's arrival, twenty-four inches blanketing everything it touched. All visible footsteps had been long buried, erasing any evidence of Gloria's struggle through the forest. The rising smoke from the fireplace was the only indication that life lived behind the mud-packed log walls.

Gloria Awakens

The snow had drifted to the bottom of the plastic-covered glass windows. Only the early morning footsteps of Gilles leaving the cabin appeared in the deep snow and then disappeared into the thick forest beyond. Everything was quiet with the exception of the occasional branch breaking under the weight of the snow. It was a postcard wonderland nestled in the deep woods of the White Mountains.

The heavy door of the cabin, a barrier to danger but this time, a protectant to the mystery inside, safely kept its visitor from the cold and harshness of winter's reality. Gloria slowly awoke to an empty room. She gradually swung her legs off of the cot and shakily stood up. Her newly washed and folded clothes lay next to the fading fire. On top was a note that read:

"Please, Missy, add wood to fire to keep you warm. I trap for three days and return. You check your head bandage and refresh cut with bottle on shelf with cross bones. Eat more stew to get you strong." It was signed, *Gilles*.

Feeling the area around her throbbing bulge, it was obvious to her that she was in no state to be wandering around in the wilderness. The bandage, she noticed, had absorbed much of the nasty fluid from her wound, and as she slowly unwrapped the binding, the last wrap pulled at her skin. She winced with the pain, and voiced, "AHUMPH!" Breathing deeply, she took the medicine off the shelf, doused a cloth with its liquid, and gently patted her wound. The liquid was cool and refreshing, not at all what she had imagined or what she had anticipated to withstand.

She wondered, *Who was this gentle giant? Her savior? A medicine man, a relic from a different century?* Gloria wrapped a clean bandage around her head and as she did, she noticed on top of her folded clothes was the picture of her father.

The Bond of Winter

The winter had passed quicker than Gloria could have imagined. Her broken wrist had mended as well as her many bruises, but the cut over her eye would leave a visible reminder. She and Gilles had become close friends—telling each other stories, some filled with laughter, others filled with tears. Gilles had a family of deer that let him, and him only, approach them without fear. He talked to them and they seemed to listen. They were his friends and they would be safe from anyone who might approach.

One late spring day, Gilles, in his old beater of a truck, went to a small outpost, which was mostly visited by other trappers and a handful of Cowasucks that settled in the non-reservation area. He said his trappings had been good and now, it was time to settle up with the trading post. Gloria had no idea trading in this manner still existed. She had read about it in history books at school, but never thought she would be part of anything like this. It was as if she had walked through an imaginary door into another world. If it weren't for the scar on her forehead, she would have declared herself insane and the reality would be, she was imagining everything while sitting quietly in her padded white room.

Gloria had added some womanly touches to the little cabin and insisted that Gilles bathe at least once a week. With the melting of snow, a seasonal river had been tapped by Gilles to provide cold spring water. Through a series of dug-out trees as vessels, a small flow of water was diverted to just behind his cabin. There, it drained into a stone-lined pool, and excess flowed to his rows of newly-planted crops.

Gloria knew that behind those steel-grey eyes was a hurting man. Gilles had told her a story that during a holiday from France, his beautiful wife Claire and he had been in a serious auto accident, which claimed her life and their unborn baby.

He hadn't shared much detail of the accident but he had said that he never returned to France. Instead, he became a recluse in the middle of nowhere. Gloria was his first guest in a very long time.

Gilles had constructed a look-out on top of a knoll not far from his main cabin that overlooked an expansive valley. He called it *Claire's Sanctuary* for its beauty and for the gift of life's constant renewal. He believed Claire lived in that valley protecting all new life, whatever that might be. He did not trap in that valley as he held it sacred to his heart. Gloria thought that Gilles, at one time, might have been a man of respect, but now chose to be a man of simple means. She sensed he still held on to his strong emotional ties to the one he loved.

He treated Gloria with respect and said more than once that if he had a daughter, he would want her to be just like her. She loved him for his kindness and everything he shared with her. He was a light for her new beginning, but they both knew, her days were numbered at the cabin as she had more life to live.

Standing at the knoll as the sun was starting to set, she saw Gilles' truck come down the only road. She flashed a smile and could not wait to share her experience of holding newly hatched hawks. The mother had obviously been killed as one day she had not returned and had left her nest abandoned and at risk. Gloria and Gilles checked it every day and secured it from harm's way. So now it was up to Gloria to feed the chicks until they could manage for themselves. She would not leave until they could survive on their own. She promised.

As Gilles' truck came to a stop and the dust cleared, she noticed him having trouble balancing boxes and brightly colored bags.

"Where have you been?" she inquired as a stern mother might.

"I know you have not said anything but we both know you will be traveling again soon. So I could not let you go in the rags in which you arrived in. These are for you," graciously offered Gilles.

Gloria's eyes swelled with tears as she threw her arms around Gilles. He struggled not to drop any boxes.

"You are such a kind man. I will always love and cherish you," cried Gloria.

"Well, you better let go and give me a hand with these before I drop them," insisted Gilles, stumbling on his words.

They went inside and placed the gifts on the table. Gloria declared that it seemed just like Christmas when her dad was alive. Gilles smiled as he handed them to her one by one, while Gloria meticulously separated each piece from its wrapping. She placed each garment up to her for Gilles' approval and waited for a yay or nay. They were all yay. Gloria went behind her privacy blanket and slipped into the skirt with an embroidered hem and put on the white silk top. She stepped out. Gilles choked and as Gloria slowly spun, his eyes misted over.

"You are as beautiful as my beloved Claire," he shared. Gloria rushed to his side and held on to her big burly man as he fought the sniffles. "You make me proud, Gloria, to see you like this. I know you are my little angel. Now promise me, make yourself proud whatever road you may walk down."

"I will, Gilles, I will. I will never forget you and all you have taught me. I will be strong," declared Gloria.

The two held each other as a father and daughter might.

Endearing Love

Gloria stayed true to her promise of caring for the young hawks before she decided on an exact date of departure. Finally, that day arrived. It was an emotional day for everyone and everyone came out to say goodbye. As if Gilles had summoned his family of deer, they showed up with two new fawns; the male's antlers had grown proudly. He nudged Gloria with his nose. Her hawks, Jettie and Claire, soared above them, watched every move she made and squealed as if they were calling her name. She knew she had to leave, and leaving this backwoods paradise proved to be more difficult than leaving her mother and friends. But she was determined to right a wrong and make a place in her changing world.

Gilles put a suitcase in the back of his pickup as Gloria took one last look at their little cabin, the sprouting vegetable garden, and the dust rising from the chicken coup. The brood also seemed to acknowledge her intent to leave them. A squeal from above reassured her decision as she cranked down on the door handle and hopped into the cab. She looked at Gilles with anxious anticipation. He flashed a quick, reassuring smile and started the truck. Her fairytale was coming to an end; however, this experience would be with her forever.

The less traveled, overgrown dirt road just west of the cornfield was strewn with fallen branches, which Gilles cleared by hand with the aid of a honed machete. Gloria, sitting comfortably in the driver's seat, edged the manual shift truck through the clearings. The old trail was in disrepair, but a handy exit if there would be a need to vacate the cabin in case of emergency. A forest fire, at any time, could compromise his usual path of entry and exit. Other than Gilles, maybe one or two of the old Cowasuck trappers knew of this trail's existence. It had been said that it led to the valley of life, where the families—long ago massacred by the white warriors—were able to walk in peace. This tale sat well with Gilles as he had buried Claire in this sacred land. He believed his beloved Claire's spirit had made peace and had settled into the tranquility of the valley.

Gilles returned to the truck and Gloria slid over to the passenger seat. He glanced at her. He was proud of Gloria but saddened to see her go. Their connection had warmed his heart and refreshed it from a mere beating annoyance, to once again be filled with love. He thanked the souls and great spirits for this time he had shared with Gloria. He will never forget his only experience of having a daughter.

The exit to the main highway was a combination of abandoned mining roads, stone-lined creek beds, and a wooden bridge that trestled over the dilapidated railroad tracks. Although his truck was old, it still had the horsepower to maneuver where Gilles wanted to go. With a few head-bumping knolls, they finally rested on Highway 112 and headed south through the old, covered bridge to Conway.

Here, Gloria was to catch a bus in front of the Mobil gas station for the long, winding road to Portsmouth. One last visit to her father's grave before she resumed her trek to her ultimate destination—Los Angeles. Dreams of tall palm trees waving in the breeze, star-studded venues dotting Rodeo Drive, and the lure of movie magic had captured her many hours alone in her childhood room. She had refused money offered to her by Gilles as this was her adventure that she needed to pursue on her own and at her expense. Although, she laughed at this decision because without Gilles, she still would be buried in a snow drift somewhere. As they pushed on down the road, high in the sky past the tall pines soared two red-tailed hawks following their direction.

Gilles pulled to the curb across the street from the coach service. Gloria hopped out of the pickup and casually crossed the street. The station was a relic from decades ago and was in need of repair but in an hour, it wouldn't matter; her life would start anew. With her long blonde hair flowing in the wind, she wisped it to the side and stuffed her change in her front pocket. Her ticket was held tight in her hand as she approached the waiting pickup.

Stepping out of the pickup, Gilles forced a smile, and asked, "Are you all set, Missy?"

"Got it!" she said waving it in the air. "A one-way to Portsmouth, and then onto Boston. I can purchase a ticket from Boston to Chicago, then Memphis through to Albuquerque to Los Angeles."

"How long of a ride?" inquired Gilles.

"Depending on my connections and whether or not I take the express, it could be eight days," informed Gloria. "Lots of time to reflect."

"Don't let your past control your future... but learn from it. You have grown considerably in the last few months. Don't shy away from your intuition; you have a strong will much like my Claire. You will survive. But remember, I will always be here for you," said Gilles.

"I will. I don't know how to thank you. I mean for everything... looking after my stubborn butt, buying me clothes, teaching me what matters. I ..."

Gloria wrapped her arms around Gilles. "You are my true friend."

"And you, mine. You are my family." Gilles eased his embrace just enough to slide his hand into his jacket pocket, and pulled out a letter. He handed it to Gloria.

"Please, my little angel, do not open this until you feel the time is right."

Stepping back, Gloria accepted the letter. "What's in it? When will I know that the time is right?"

"It is for you, and you will know. Accept it as the truth and my wish for you. You better get along; the bus doesn't stop long here. You take care of yourself," he said, handing Gloria her suitcase.

With suitcase in one hand and her ticket in the other, Gloria crossed the road and as she stood nose to nose with the bus, she looked back at Gilles and shouted out, "I love you, Gilles Fournier!"

Gilles, misting at the eyes, replied with a hearty, "I love you too." Under his breath, he said, "My Angel."

Gloria boarded the bus and as she walked back to her seat, Gilles, standing outside of his truck, threw a big kiss to Gloria and then with a tight fist, crossed his heart.

She sank into her seat and wiped the tears running down her face. Looking up through the tinted window, Gloria watched as her friends circled above.

Portsmouth And Beyond

Gloria's fondest memories as a young girl were in Portsmouth. Her mother had given birth to her during the time her father was stationed at the Navy base in Kittery, Maine. When her father left the Navy, they moved to Portsmouth where he started a hardware business. He and his partner were successful in this venture and opened other co-owned stores in many areas.

The cemetery grounds were as she remembered. The winding roads with headstones lining the pathways seemed to lead to that final row that her father rested in. She politely asked the cab driver to wait while she said her goodbyes.

"Daddy, I have missed you so. You were meant to be more than a song in my heart, and more than a passing light that guides my way." After placing flowers on his gravestone, she bravely walked back to the waiting cab.

. . .

The stated 'one day, four hour' trip from Boston to Chicago ended up more like two days. They stopped to change drivers and then made a series of requested stops from the passengers to stretch their legs and gather food at the highway service stations. The mountains looked beautiful with their white-capped peaks and the crystal-clear runoff that flowed over different outreaches. She had a different appreciation of what was beyond her glass window and padded seat. Her thoughts were on Gilles and what an amazing man he was. He never gave up on her when she was struggling with her decision to continue with her journey. He knew what it was like to lose loved ones and how it could change your whole perspective by living without them.

The sun came up, the road stretched on, and the night fell. The early morning lights of Chicago shone with flickering intensity as the darkness fell to the rising sun once again. The traffic was still in its infancy as the bus passed the University of Illinois before turning into its terminal. Finally, the bus came to rest. Gloria was exhausted. She badly needed a shower. After exiting the bus, she gathered her suitcase and went inside the terminal to check the bus schedule. She had an all-day wait as she did not want to end up in Memphis at 2:00 in the morning. So the next departure time wasn't until 9:00 p.m. arriving at almost 7:00 a.m. She paid her $27 dollars, gathered her things, and went into the restroom to wash up.

The restroom was bleak as she imagined every bus station to be. Gloria placed her suitcase next to the cleanest sink and from the top compartment of the suitcase, she pulled out a cloth. Gilles had suggested she pack a cloth as he knew what it was like to travel a great distance. Claire had always liked to freshen up in between stop-overs.

"Aaahhh!" she said in appreciation as she wiped her face and draped the cold cloth around her neck.

"Feel good, honey?" said an elderly grey-haired woman bespectacled with tortoiseshell-rimmed glasses.

"Yes, thank you."

"You traveling far?" inquired the woman.

"Yes, and you?"

"Going to Iowa to see my grandbabies. I hate flying. Although the accommodations aren't much and it takes longer, I would rather stare out the windows of a bus and look at the scenery than see clouds."

"Yes, it is nice to see the vastness of our country to open one's eyes," said Gloria.

"My husband died a year ago after fifty-one years of marriage. I am lost without him. He was my lover, my friend who always took care of me. Never a bad word between us. I wish you to be as happy as we were, my dear. Never take anything for granted. Love your man as tomorrow does come when you least expect it," said the older woman.

"I will, and thank you for sharing. I know it is hard to lose someone close."

Muttering to herself, the elderly woman left Gloria at the wash basin. Raising a hand, she haphazardly waved as she exited and said, "Goodbye, my dear, God be with you."

Gloria thought of her mother. *Was putting up with that creep worth not being alone? It is sad to see this poor old lady but she had 51 years of happiness; my mother has only a distant memory of my father.*

Just then, two teen girls—probably her age, she thought—with ripped fishnets, blue jean shorts, red streaks in their hair, and nose and eyebrow rings bounced into the restroom. Their black eye-shadowed eyes lazily gazed at Gloria and then the two girls shrieked with laughter as they pounded open a stall's door. Together they stepped in, oblivious to life itself.

"Hold my bag, bitch. I need to pee...baaaadly," proclaimed one out loud.

"Me too. Open your legs," loudly voiced the other.

Gloria gathered her things and quickly left the two to their own demise.

This is going to be a long day, thought Gloria as she returned to the waiting area.

Gloria scanned the room and noticed half-empty vending machines gracing one end of the room, and to the left of them, the elderly woman muttering to herself. She sat alone in a middle seat, shuffling papers. Several families sat close together surrounding their baggage like a human fortress. Others moved about aimlessly picking up pamphlets, scanning the pictures but not really reading what was printed on them.

Gloria picked a corner where she was able to stuff her suitcase between the bench and wall and still keep an eye on the undesirable cast. She remembered while taking a film class at school, an Italian director who searched out, from the general populace, the most bizarre characters for his movies. *He needed to come in here,* she thought. *He would have lots to choose from*. The two girls from the restroom stumbled back into the waiting area and sprawled out on a bench. They talked in circles without making any sense but laughed at each other's remarks.

So sad, what a waste of life, Gloria thought. *Where is that book Gilles gave me?*

Bus to Memphis

The afternoon went slowly with passengers arriving and others departing like a pixilation of bodies standing still but moving without motion. Gloria reveled in the thought when

40

Carol and she had made a short film with friends jumping through a water sprinkler. They had set the 16mm movie camera to shoot two frames at a time, then moved their friends ahead a few feet and then shot two more frames. When they had completed the film, it looked like the first silent film movies made in Hollywood. She laughed inwardly imagining the patrons of the bus station doing exactly that. It helped pass the time.

Finally, the station master called boarding at 8:40 p.m. for Gate 8 to Memphis departing at 9:00 p.m. Gloria put a magazine down and left it for the next wayward passenger, retrieved her suitcase, and headed to the staging platform. There were only a handful of people leaving that night for Memphis. Perhaps she would be able to get some sleep on the bus. She didn't dare in the waiting room. *Too many weirdos*, she thought.

Gloria handed her suitcase to the porter, who gave her a receipt, and then she had her ticket verified by the bus driver before she was allowed to board the bus. She took a seat midway down on the driver's side and looked around. There was a closet of a washroom at the back where a young couple with a small baby shared the bench seat. He looked military, with short hair. She still had pimples but the baby was cute, and better yet, quiet. Two elderly men sat in separate seats across from each other, while a woman at least 30 years old and wearing enough make-up to start her own business line sat across from her. A couple of young guys wearing jeans, cowboy boots, and studded shirts completed this set of travelers.

When Gloria had checked her bag, she had noticed two guitar cases placed to the side. Arriving in the nick of time, a handsome, young black fellow sat on the aisle one seat up on the opposite side. He was nicely dressed—looked like a university student. He had thick medical books resting on his lap. He flipped his light on to continue to read from a marked page.

Another interesting gathering, she thought. *Maybe I can get some rest.*

She collected a blanket and pillow from the upper compartment and nestled in for the night's drive.

Hypnotized by the drone of the engine, she didn't start to stir until the sun broke over the mountains and warmed her face. The medical student had books resting on his chest now and his arm hung, fingers dangling near the floor. She could hear the little baby behind her making laughing sounds as he looked around at his sleeping parents and the obvious shadows dancing off of the seats' trim as the sun came up. The made-up woman had smeared lipstick across her face; such a pretty sight first thing in the morning. Just as Gloria stretched, the bus driver announced, *"Forty-five minutes until Memphis terminal."* The others began to stir to his announcement. Even though the sun was still low in the sky, it warmed her face so much so that she had to slouch to the side to get out of its rays.

Next time, she thought as she scanned her schedule, *I better sit on the other side of the bus. Although, going west from here, I shouldn't feel the heat radiating from the window.*

Pulling in, the bus hissed to a stop at the Memphis terminal. All were told to gather their baggage as this bus's schedule had terminated. Another ticket would be required to continue from the Memphis terminal to their intended destinations. Gloria's next bus did not leave until 4:15 p.m.— another full day of sitting around. One of the young guitar players who had been gazing at Gloria approached her.

"Mornin'. Y'all stayin' in Memphis?"

"Ah, no. I'm traveling through," she replied.

"That's too bad. I was gonna ask if ya wanna join us down at Ali's. We gotta set down there at 3 till 7."

"Yes, I'm sorry I'll miss hearing you. Maybe next time."

Tipping his hat, he said, "Well thank ya then. Hava safe trip."

"Um, excuse me," Gloria said, pausing briefly as he turned to her. "Thank you for being so kind."

"Yes, ma'am, good day to ya."

Wow, a gentleman among the thickets, she thought. *How sweet.*

Gloria's stomach was growling. She was so hungry, she felt she could eat a bear. Putting her suitcase into a terminal locker, she strolled across the street to a local restaurant, enjoying the chance to move about and stretch her legs in the sunshine. A long journey of reflection on her time spent with Gilles was both exhilarating and practical. With his love, her freedom felt sweeter. *Yes, sweet freedom.*

Life Carries On

He stood tall with the aid of his cane against the blue-coral sea backdrop. The breeze was light as it played with the white and mauve shears draped over bamboo poles. He waited patiently with the minister at the island resort's beach as he knew she would be soon walking down the orchid-lined path to his side. His life had changed within a flash and then, a long recovery, but Pete Rogers welcomed the many hours Rose spent by his side, encouraging him to take that first step. Months of rehab in salt-water baths, weight training, and two surgeries had him now standing and waiting for his bride-to-be.

Rose was right, money was not the pathway to happiness; however, with his insurance money and her café sold, they had plenty of money to travel or just sit somewhere holding each other's hand. It was a miracle he was alive but what weighed on his mind, at times, was the thought of that young girl who they never found. At least they knew her identity to be that of the missing girl from the DNA they had matched with the hair strands found at the site. Her mother was devastated when they interviewed her on TV. There was another pretty girl sitting beside her holding her hand, sobbing just as hard. The father displayed little reaction, which Pete thought strange. He was probably so grief-stricken, he wasn't able to express any feelings. So sad.

Pete flashed a smile and erased that memory as his lady rounded the corner and proceeded towards him. She looked fabulous. He knew he always wanted her, and today they would be legally together. What could be more magical than an island wedding with his feet in the warm white sand, marrying his dream lady? Nothing. He was so happy.

Notes to Diary

Dear Diary: The one-day, 18-hour, and 35-minute bus trip seemed to drag on; especially through Texas. Some places were so desolate and yet, people actually lived there. I could not believe it. Dust was everywhere, which muted even the brightest of colors. Phoenix wasn't much better, although you could see mountains in the background. The bus driver said we just missed being swallowed up by a freak dust storm called a Haboob.

Los Angeles was a maze of slow-moving freeways. I have never seen so many cars just sitting, not going anywhere, and people doing everything from shaving, reading the paper, and women putting on make-up in their cars. And of course, they were all eating something from the fast food chains. The air... you could barely breathe! And I want to live here? We just pulled into the station, I will write more soon, I promise.

PS: I had that dream again. I looked like I was talking to myself as I watched.

Reverend Michaels Meets Angela

The bus pulled into its docking station and the bus driver announced over the P.A. system, *"Los Angeles bus terminal...7th Street."* The engine died down and the driver opened the door. He continued with his rehearsed announcement. *"Don't forget your belongings you might have stored overhead!"*

The passengers that they had picked up along the way didn't seem as polite to Gloria as the Memphis people. They all crammed to be first out and first to retrieve their luggage. She got jostled around like a bob on a fishing lure. Finally, she got her chance to get her lone suitcase. She had to push her way through the crowds of waiting families and screaming kids to actually catch a glimpse of the exit.

The swinging doors were dashed from her sight as she was carried to the street by the whirlwind herd. Pushed to the side, her suitcase was knocked out of her hand and spilled out over the street. No one stopped to help. Taxi cabs zoomed by. One ran over one of her shirts leaving a tire track of dried dirt down the front of it.

From across the street, a man wearing black pants and a black shirt with a white collar exited a white-stretched Cadillac. He had noticed the young girl's predicament and came to her rescue. Gloria hadn't noticed him as she continued to retrieve her belongings.

"Excuse me, Miss. May I be of assistance?" the man asked.

Gloria was startled.

"It's okay. I've got it!" shouted Gloria in frustration.

"Allow me, my child. My God would be displeased with me if I did not lift a helping hand."

Gloria looked up at the stranger.

"Oh! Sorry, Father, I didn't realize you were a man of the cloth... but I am fine."

"My name is Reverend Michaels." He held out his hand in a friendly gesture. "Are you hungry? It must have been a long bus ride. I know a little restaurant around the corner. Come... let me buy you something to eat. A sort of an apology for my brethren's rudeness."

Gloria stopped for a moment. The reverend flashed a big friendly smile.

"Well... okay, but only if it is not too far. And if we can walk," insisted Gloria.

"I know Los Angeles gets a bad rap, but are all Easterners that mistrustin'?"

"How did you know I'm from the east coast?" asked Gloria.

"Your accent, my child. Not hard to pin-point out here," replied the reverend. "What's your name?"

Gloria hesitated once again. Gilles had warned her of big city promises and predatory sharks lurking in the shadows. *What was my name? Everyone who had loved me called me their little angel...RoAnn, my father, and Gilles only days ago.* She quickly recovered with an answer after seeing yet another sign, a travel advertisement in the bus station window: *"Welcome to the City of Angels."*

"Angela," she replied.

"Well, isn't that a blessed name. Shall we go then, Angela?"

The two rounded a corner and walked halfway up the block until the reverend motioned to a doorway. The restaurant was a crowded greasy spoon, with every type of derelict slurping coffee from the cup without even lifting it to their lips. The clientele looked like they just came from a disaster movie set.

Gloria scanned the diner. *I guess my education starts here,* she exhaled a deep breath. Tightly hanging onto her suitcase, she felt the cold stares eyeing her up and down.

"Come over here, Angel. I have a reserved table here. I do my best work for God out of this booth."

Two questionable ladies were sitting at the table and as soon as they saw Reverend Michaels, they gathered their things and left.

"Are the ladies not part of your congregation, Father? Why do they need to get up just for us?" questioned Gloria. "There is plenty of room."

"No, no, my child. You misunderstand the situation. They were just making sure no one mistook the Lord's generosity and helped themselves without consideration for others. Not all accept my help," informed Reverend Michaels.

They sat down and Gloria pushed her suitcase against the wall.

"It's Angela, not Angel."

"Yes, of course, pardon me. It is a righteous slip, as you are an angel of God."

"Why do you call this the Lord's table?"

"You have a very inquisitive mind, my child. I like that."

"Well?" confronted Gloria. Gilles' words echoed in her young mind.

"Because everything I give is free. As the Lord... food for the starving, money for the needy, clothes for the less fortunate, shelter for the displaced, and prayer for the anguished at heart."

"And those two women?" asked Gloria.

"They are part of my flock. The Lord does not discriminate against those who have fallen from the grace of the church, or for what they do as a chosen profession to survive as they learn their destined path."

"So you do not belong to a church?" she asked, trying to understand Reverend Michael's message.

"I have a shelter where all denominations are welcomed, where we pray and ask forgiveness, where we share the blame of society without shame or question."

A waitress stepped up to the table and took their order. Gloria wondered about the sanitation of the kitchen and what she would actually be eating.

"Are you staying with relatives while here in L.A.?" asked the reverend making for small talk.

"No," Gloria stated matter-of-factly.

"Where will you stay then?"

"I'm going to the YWCA on Wilshire Boulevard."

"That is quite the distance from here. May I suggest a room at my shelter until you get better acquainted with L.A.?" invited the reverend.

"How much?" asked Gloria.

"Haha. I told you, Angela, everything I have is free. You will probably be asked to help out occasionally, just to keep the shelter clean and ready for lost souls who might not have the resources as you."

"Where is it located from here?"

"Just a slow, leisurely walk. Only a few blocks away," said the reverend motioning to the direction. "Come, if you don't like it, you can leave in the morning."

Gloria pushed her hamburger aside after only a few bites of the tasteless food. Grease sloshed from the plate. The two got up and headed out of the diner.

As they strolled along the concrete sidewalk, Reverend Michaels shared some high points of the area. "Within a short walking distance, there are all sorts of things to see. We have the Fashion District, the Los Angeles Music Center, Little Tokyo, and Chinatown beyond that. Do you like baseball? Just on the other side of Chinatown is Dodger Stadium. See, Angela, there is lots for a girl to do around here."

Carrying Gloria's suitcase, Reverend Michaels continued to talk about the developing area around them and his hope for the future. He was passionately persuasive. As they walked, the white Cadillac slowly followed.

Is It My Time?

Gloria had noticed over the course of several passing months on her walks that the old warehouse-laden street had been turned into low-income housing projects. A street over, a couple of stripped-down cars sat on top of cement blocks. But in this one-block stretch, Reverend Michaels saw to it that garbage was cleaned up in front of his shelter. Three blocks to the east, railway tracks dotted the backscape, just before they ran into the Los Angeles River.

On this one particular day, one of the girls, Sheri, who was wearing a loose-fitting negligee with black teased hair and smoking a cigarette on the steps of the shelter, spotted Reverend Michaels' white Cadillac as it rounded the corner. She quickly moved inside. Gloria was on the second floor and had just backed out of the end washroom with a mop and bucket in hand.

"Well, Angie, how do you like the favor of Reverend Michaels? He surely has been placed on this earth as one of God's messengers."

"It's Angela," insisted Gloria. She disliked this woman intensely and hoped Sheri's attitude would not destroy her limited vision of life while being harnessed at the shelter. Gloria wiped the last bit of floor. She put the mop back into the bucket and turned to look at the woman.

"I see Reverend M. is taking good care of you too," replied Gloria with as much implied sarcasm.

"You little bitch..." The woman flicked her cigarette onto the floor next to Gloria's feet. "...your turn will come, honey. You'll be on your back soon enough. Reverend M. will see to that. Nothing is free," sneered Sheri, bitterly expressing her opinion.

Gloria felt a slow burn flushing her face. She tightened her grip on the mop handle. Her friend, Irma, had warned her about Sheri's attitude. Just then, the main door nudged open and a figure entered. The door closed with a defined click as footsteps started to ascend the stairs. The woman, Sheri, scampered to her room and closed her door. When Reverend Michaels reached the upper step of the second floor, he saw Angela standing by a bucket of dirty water.

"Angela, just the person I wanted to see. Please, put down that mop and come downstairs."

Gloria was hesitant and stared at him with the words of Sheri swirling in her head.

"What? Come with," politely asked the reverend.

She stood firm. Reverend Michaels noticed her hesitation. He walked over and took the mop out of her hand.

"Please, come downstairs, child, I have something for you."

He turned and started down the stairs. Gloria stared at Sheri's door as she passed by following Rev. M's direction. The reverend's office was nicely decorated, unlike the bareness of most of the rooms, although he encouraged the ladies to decorate in a tasteful manner. She stood at his doorway.

"Come, child, look what I got you."

Gloria knew Rev. M. was doing his best at being nice to her, but she wondered at his motivation after hearing stories from the other girls at the shelter. Sheri didn't paint a very rosy picture either. The others were more hopeful.

Standing staunch in the doorway, Gloria asked, "What is it?"

"What's the matter? Come in... I won't bite," said Reverend Michaels, jesting. "I have something for you."

Gloria slowly walked over to his lavish desk. He bent down and from behind his desk, he pulled up multiple, beautifully-wrapped presents.

"I got these for you," he said with a deceptive grin.

"Why?"

"Why? Because you deserve them. Look at all the hard work you have been doing around here these last...what...five or six months. This place has never looked so good. Everyone is saying so. You have a gift for decorating. Please, come... look at these," insisted the reverend, reveling in his stylish selection.

Gloria gently pulled the ribbon off as she had done with Gilles and as a little girl with her father. It seemed to her to heighten the surprise and prolong the excitement. Reverend Michaels went behind Gloria and started to massage her shoulders. She shrugged. He backed off. A beautiful dress lay between the sheer sheets of paper. She picked it up and held it at arm's length. Excitedly, Reverend Michaels ripped open the other packages so she could see the waiting treasures. Without hesitation or approval from Gloria, he pulled out a sequin-laced wrap and placed it about her shoulders.

"Beautiful," he said admiringly, not waiting again for a reaction from Gloria. "That dress will look divine on you. Now go change. We are going out to dinner. I want you to meet some friends of mine."

"I can't," she stated.

"Pardon?"

"I can't accept these clothes. They cost way more than my little bit of work around here. I can't accept them."

"But? I don't understand. These are beautiful; you'll look like a movie star," he said, astounded at her defensiveness.

"But they are not me. I am not a movie star."

"Not with that attitude. Listen..." He paused. He took a breath and continued in a sincere, soft voice, "...it's simple. You are a very beautiful girl who needs a break in life. Please let me help you achieve this for you."

He started to pile the boxes into Gloria's arms and gently turned her to the door.

"Now, please go change and get Irma to help you with your hair and make-up. My friends are very influential. They will be able to help you see the stars of Hollywood," reassured the reverend.

Gloria trudged up the stairs to her room. She felt betrayed, reticent to speak her mind, and angry all at the same time, but she was not so naïve. It seemed others knew of this day before she did. And they tried their best to prepare her—emotionally. Irma, a lady of color and Gloria's closest friend, gave her a big smile as she entered her room. At one time, Irma worked as a make-up artist for one of the major studios but got hooked on drugs and was blacklisted. She had Gloria looking like a starlet within an hour. She looked stunning!

"You look super fine, child. Rev. M. will be pleased. Now you do what he says. You'll be all right, you listen, child."

Irma gave Gloria a hug.

"Now go. Rev. M. will be waiting. You'll be fine."

Gloria looked at her reflection in the mirror. She didn't recognize this person that stared back at her. Her face glowed, even hypnotizing—but her eyes reflected fear. She touched her soft skin between the deep 'V' of her dress. This 'Angela' was as beautiful as her dear friend Carol. This small-town girl had grown up. She released her hold on Irma and looked straight into Irma's eyes.

"Is this it, Irma? Is it my time?"

Angela turned and left all things Gloria behind. Irma plopped down on the bed, put her head into her hands, and tried to fight back the tears.

Her Night and Mr. C.

Reverend Michaels was waiting in the foyer for Angela. As she walked down the stairs and he caught her face in the hall light, he let out a gasp. "Oh my! My child, you look simply divine. Tonight will be your night, I promise."

Angela looked at Rev. M and his expensive-looking suit, "You look very nice yourself, Rever..."

Reverend Michaels cut her short.

"Please, tonight why don't you just call me Mister Michaels or even better, Anthony."

"Is Anthony your real name?" asked Angela.

"It doesn't matter if one chooses a name different than his own because everyone will still know them by that name," responded Reverend Michaels rather rationally.

Partially puzzled at his unexpected answer, she paused and then added with a slight smile, "I guess you are right." She thought of her own situation.

Anthony Michaels opened the shelter's door to their view of the waiting Cadillac parked at the curb out front. Its wide open door offered an invitation to relax in its luxury. A tall, heavy man dressed in a chauffeur's suit wearing black gloves stood to the side. As Angela passed, he acknowledged her with a slight, kind smile and an outstretched hand.

"Ma'am, may I offer assistance?" the big man said.

She accepted graciously and looked into his dark brown, almost black eyes. He had an Italian accent and a rugged face, but his demeanor seemed genuine. She had to pick up her skintight, Luis Vuitton-wannabe light green low-cut dress in order to step inside the car. He steadied her. Once inside, he stepped aside for Reverend Michaels. He closed the door with a soft click. Champagne had been poured while soft soulful music played. She had never tasted champagne, but once before she had had a sip of beer that her stepfather forced on her as a practical joke.

She had never sat in the luxury of a limousine. *How could Reverend Michaels afford such a vehicle, basically doing the 'Lord's work' as he called it? A mysterious man indeed!* Reverend Michaels offered Angela her glass and he clinked the glasses together.

"To you, my dear... and to your night. Let this be a night of enchantment for both of us," toasted Reverend Michaels.

Angela was not quite sure how to take it or what he meant. She did as Irma told her—listen!

As she looked out of the tinted side window, she noticed the driver took them down a street called Alameda and then turned onto 1st Street, where Reverend Michaels pointed out a building where he said the Oscars were held. The driver seemed to make several round-a-bouts and then they entered a ramp declaring '101'. The traffic was busy but the driver cruised down the outside lane as if he owned it. The ride was glamorous as compared to the bus ride she had endured almost six months prior. The driver got off at a street called Sunset Blvd., as the sign announced, and then he turned up Vine. Reverend Michaels constantly pointed out points of interest that sparked young Angela's imagination. They finally turned onto Hollywood Boulevard. The traffic crawled along at a snail's pace, but the sidewalks were bustling with people— helter-skelter in all directions, many of them taking pictures of each other against famous Hollywood landmarks.

Reverend Michaels made an enticing suggestion to Angela. "Would you like to see Mann's Chinese Theatre? And then just down from there is the Hollywood Walk of Fame."

"Yes!" screamed the young woman with delight. This is why she came to L.A. *Finally!*

Gloria had been down on herself for the situation that she had gotten herself into. And without much positive guidance, she had kept to herself, other than Irma. But even Irma had a line to toe. Extravagant spending on unnecessary fantasies had to wait. But dressed as she was, Angela was going to take every advantage she could get away with. It was her time.

The driver pulled alongside the over-crowded sidewalk to let her out. The star-gazing fans watched the white limousine and the emerging 'must be' starlet. In their zealousness, they snapped her picture and raced to her side carrying pieces of magazines, tour maps, and anything else for her to autograph. Angela at first was apprehensive, but Reverend Michaels encouraged her to let them believe what they wanted. He whispered to her, "When they go back to Minnesota, they will tell all their friends about the movie starlet they met. You are just helping their fantasy."

Angela was beaming. She had never received attention like this before; however, in Reverend Michaels' mind, he only saw her potential. After the Walk of Fame, the driver once again whisked them off. Down Santa Monica Boulevard they headed until they arrived in Beverly Hills.

The concierge rushed out of The Peninsula-Beverly Hills and with a white-gloved hand, opened the door of the stretched Cadillac. The driver, in a flash, was waiting for Angela at her opened door. The concierge stepped back but maintained a polite and courteous smile. Angela accepted the driver's hand, and once again, she relied on his steadiness to support her as she stepped out.

"Thank you...?" she paused inquisitively, wondering and waiting for his name.

"Joseph."

"Thank you again, Joseph," politely addressed Angela.

Joseph was a mystery man to Angela. She had seen him from an upper window of the shelter but had never been introduced to him. She was happy to make his acquaintance.

He nodded without saying a word. Reverend Michaels, after stepping out, put Angela's arm into his as they were escorted by the concierge through the inviting open doors of the luxurious hotel. Inside, they were greeted by Roland, the head Maître D'.

"Good evening, Mr. Michaels. We have your reservation for four at 'The Roof Garden' as you requested. Please follow me, sir."

"Have our guests arrived?" asked Reverend Michaels.

"They are in the smoking lounge. I will send them up after we seat you and your lady," said Roland.

The Los Angeles air was clear, and as Angela looked up at the star-filled sky, their random twinkling light seemed to add reassurance to the decisions she would probably have to make that night. She noticed as they were guided through that there were a few young ladies, like her, maybe a little older, sitting at tables with older gentlemen. They were laughing and absorbed in the conversation with the one in front of them. They were dressed to the nines with flashy jewelry, stylish hair, and flawless make-up. They looked happy to be there.

Roland held the chair for Angela while she sat down, and when he was assured of the appropriate table by Reverend Michaels, he was passed a folded acknowledgement.

"Thank you, sir. I will send the gentlemen up promptly."

"Thank you, Roland," said Reverend Michaels.

Roland paused and whispered something into a waiter's ear; he immediately rushed over to Reverend Michaels and started to pour the chilled champagne reserved at their table.

The Roof Garden's Maître D' arrived shortly after with the two gentlemen and escorted them to their waiting guests. Reverend Michaels stood out of respect. Angela remained seated.

"Tony, good to see you again," said one of the men with an outstretched hand. "This is my partner, Julius from Argentina... and you must be the adorable lady we have been hearing about," said the man with a glistening, sun-bright smile. He held out his hand and waited for a name.

"Angela," she replied confidently with the years of someone older.

"It is our pleasure to meet you."

The two men sat down and the waiter came over to fill their glasses. A toast fashionably underlined their conversation as Angela watched the other young ladies. She studied their mannerisms, and smiled as they did—not too much but just enough. She flipped her hair.

"Have you been in L.A. long?" asked the man who Angela thought looked like a walking commercial for Colgate—Mr. C, she decided to call him.

"Not long, about six months, wouldn't you say Anthony?" replied Angela with a gloating stare.

"Yes, I would say close to that," pleasantly answered Reverend Michaels.

"And how did you meet?" asked Mr. C.

Angela thought that a strange question as she assumed he knew everything about her already.

"I was in travel," she explained with a matter-of-fact inflection.

"Very good," said Julius. "I love the experience of traveling, whether in my country or abroad. It stimulates one's mind. Would you not say, Angela?"

"I am not sure if it is the traveling or the spending of money, which stimulates one's mind," she said as she threw her hair back as she and Carol had done many times while roll playing in drama class.

The gentlemen laughed at her comment. "Well said," commented Julius. And another clink of glasses circled the table in acceptance. Angela placed the glass to her lips and replaced it without actually taking a sip. Her lipstick made its impression.

"You said she had a spunky nature but I would say charming and truthful," laughed Mr. C.

"I don't believe you have given me the pleasure of your name, sir?" said Angela, keeping in step with her demeanor of the evening.

"Blair, young lady. You can call me, Blair."

"Is there another you prefer?" inquired Angela half-joking.

"Ahahah!" laughed Blair. "Not just charming but witty as well."

Looking directly at Mr. C., Angela said with immense maturity, "So gentlemen, I know Anthony did not spend this much money just to hear my charming ways. What are we doing here?"

"We are in movies, Angela. We are looking for our next star. Would that be you?" said Blair bluntly.

"Depends on your genre of movies," replied Angela.

They all paused as the waiter delivered their dinner.

"We take pride in our productions and have won many awards at the adult industry conventions held in Vegas. We now have joined up with Julius and his production company in Argentina to give our films more of a storyline with international flair."

"And how much do your stars make for a movie?" asked Angela, deeply hoping none of this would go beyond that night.

"Depending on their demand, status, and specialty. Some, a grand or more," stated Blair.

"What's your format?" she asked. *Why did I ask that? They'll see right through me. Specialty? Oh God, Irma!*

"We used to shoot the same as the big boys, 16mm but it got too costly so now we have gone to 3/4" Beta. We have cut out the cost of the film, the special care in transporting and canning, the developing, and on and on. Beta can be transferred from the camera to our editing machines, re-mastered and then transferred directly to DVD/CD or streaming. The industry is constantly changing. Digital has taken over the world and soon, the consumer will have miniature cameras mounted inconspicuously in heavy-framed glasses, which will be able to capture high-quality images. We have to be on top of all new advances to make a profit," said Blair.

"We are looking for amateurs that we can bring up the ladder to increase their visibility and recognition. Every guy wants to fantasize about his neighbor becoming a porn star. It's like, 'I knew her when' syndrome," added Julius.

"And you believe I have the girl-next-door quality?"

"Well, we would have to dress you down. Not as you look tonight," flattered Blair.

"Is that a double entendre?" Angela joked.

"Ahahah, you are quite the kidder, aren't you?"

"I like to laugh with my friends but never at them," she declared.

"Well, Tony, you didn't tell us we had a wildcat. I think we can do business, a very profitable business for all of us," said Blair.

"She does have surprising wit. Let us talk tonight and we will give you an answer tomorrow," said Anthony.

"Sounds good, Tony." The two men excused themselves as their business dealings had been concluded. Blair offered his hand and Angela placed hers into his. He bent to her eye level and kissed the back of it.

"Until tomorrow, lovely lady. Your answer better be yes. I know we can make you a star and I look forward to getting better acquainted with you." Angela smiled charmingly at Blair's attempt at flirting.

The two men took leave. As soon as they were out of sight, Reverend Michaels grabbed Angela's arm and leaned into her.

"What was that all about? What were you thinking? You said you weren't an actress. If you weren't role playing, then you are a damn fine liar. This is business, not some childish game. You are playing with fire, young lady. Remember that," flared Reverend Michaels.

Angela, refusing to let anyone spoil her night retorted, "He disrespected you and me!" Quietly but forcefully, she continued, "He knew everything about me as you had already told him. That's why he wanted to meet me, a girl with no home. He wanted me to melt, to blend into his dream. That's not mine! I am no actress, but his phony sun-bright smile just irked me."

"Yes, well... " He restrained himself. This was no place for his temper to be on display for others to see. He was in control, not some snotty kid fresh out of diapers. If Blair would back out of their deal, he would implement plan B.

Their drive back to the shelter was solemn. Angela sat relaxed in the cushy seat staring out the window. She felt satisfied that she had won the first round.

Joseph watched her in the rearview mirror.

The Seduction of Angela

Angela tried talking with Reverend Michaels after the due date for their reply to Mr. C's proposal. Anthony told her, "They said, 'Although you are obviously beautiful, you would be too hard to work with'—not hungry enough for what they wanted. A dead end." He left it at that.

It had been a month since Angela and Rev. M. last spoke. When he finally approached her, he had another beautiful dress accompanied by a pair of stiletto shoes. He was not so gracious in handing them to her this time. He had a more forceful way when he insisted that she look her best.

Irma, once again, did her magic—not that Angela needed reconstruction but after Irma's touches, her face was flawless. Even better than the first time.

"Irma, you need to have your own shop where the rich ladies can be pampered as you make them into darling divas. Maybe Beverly Hills on Rodeo Drive," Angela said as she repositioned herself to admire her reflection in the mirror.

"Child, you need to see the light. There are no black ladies doing make-up on white women. Especially Beverly Hills, and even more so Rodeo Drive," informed Irma as she moved about Angela dabbing here and there appreciating her own accomplished style. "Stand up, child. Let me look at you."

Angela stood. She stepped out from in front of the mirror so Irma could get a better overall view. Angela's spaghetti-strapped crimson dress was low cut with a built-in push-up bra separated by two gold chains. A diamond cut-out hoovered her naval and stopped just above her pantie line.

"You better take care tonight. Rev. M. wasn't too happy with your last performance." Irma spun her slowly around. "He can be a Jekyll and Hyde, Missy. I don't want to cover up bruises..."

. . .

Joseph dropped Reverend Michaels and Angela off at a different restaurant, and as it seemed to Angela, it did not have quite the same ambiance as 'The Roof Garden'. Although, she thought, the atmosphere seemed more charged with louder table talk and boisterous laughing. The Maître D' welcomed them with a friendly smile.

"Mr. Michaels, sir. So good to see you. I have your private room ready, and your guests are waiting inside."

The Maître D' partially opened a curtain but only enough so they could pass without revealing who waited inside. Angela stepped through.

"You will have Peter tonight, sir, as you requested."

"Thank you." Reverend Michaels passed a gratuity to the Maître D' and stepped inside joining his friends. The Maître D' closed the curtain behind him.

An older, distinguished gentleman with dark greying hair, sat with his back to the wall. His white tuxedo jacket with black pants complimented his mature stature. He was accompanied by a vivacious red-haired woman wearing a slinky sapphire-colored dress with a unique gold cherub pinned to the shirring at the shoulder. A revealing open V-front dared to her navel and as she moved, her supple breasts caressed the pleated material that flowed to her waist. The custom-made dress then stretched across her hips to an open-front slit revealing tanned inner thighs. Angela noticed, as the lady sat at the edge of her chair, that the back of the dress was sculpted down to her tailbone barely covering her rounded butt.

"Anthony," acknowledged the gentleman, John Arnold, who stood and offered his hand in friendship. "It has been too long." Looking at Angela, he said, "Let me introduce you to Sophia."

Sophia smiled very politely and Reverend Michaels introduced Angela to the stunning couple. Mr. Arnold raised his hand to Angela's hand and gently kissed the back of it.

"So beautiful! Please sit here," said John Arnold as he released Angela's hand and pulled out the chair next to Sophia.

"How are you doing, Sophia?" asked Reverend Michaels in a familiar tone.

"Very well, Anthony." She turned her gaze to Angela and said, "I can't thank Anthony enough for introducing John and me to each other. It is coming up to four years that we have been together."

"Has it really been that long?" said Reverend Michaels.

"Yes, Anthony, can you believe it? Never been happier, right Phi, my love?" added John adjusting his heavy-rimmed glasses.

"Baby, you know you do it for me," sensually replied Sophia, blowing him a kiss.

"Well, let's toast to the beautiful ladies and a fun-filled night," said John. Angela's mind was swirling with 'what ifs'. She smiled as she shyly raised her glass and glanced over to Sophia. Angela followed Sophia's lead.

Their glasses clinked with a high tinging sound. "To a fun-filled night!" they shared with Angela being the last to chime in.

Sophia, looking at Angela, couldn't wait to praise her husband. "John is a connoisseur of fine wines. He likes to add devilish decadent morsels to the cuisine that simply enhance the wine's flavor."

"Really?" Angela said. *Really?... Is that all you can say? I am so out of my league. What am I doing here?*

"She flatters me so. I hope you do not mind me taking the liberty to order tonight's fare. Let me explain. Each wine has its own unique blend depending on region, harvest time, weather conditions and of course, vintner. I have started with a lighter bouquet with appropriate delicacies and then we will see from there, depending on our desires," John revealed.

"Sounds fabulous," blurted out Reverend Michaels.

"Another toast my friends to such lovely company and... to a glor...iii...ous night ahead!" said John in a dramatic voice with a wave of the hand, and an actor's bow.

Angela still struggling with her new identity caught herself in a lost memory as she envisioned her father calling her.

"Yes, to friends and the night," echoed Reverend Michaels.

Angela could barely keep her eyes off Sophia and was compelled to sneak a side glance each time Sophia moved. Her flowing draped top revealed her aroused nipples and rounded breasts. The men shared a semi-private conversation while leaving the two ladies to chat amongst themselves. Angela was not sure if it was the wine, but she made a remark to Sophia.

"You are wearing a beautiful dress. I'm sorry if I stare..."

Sophia, wanting to put Angela at ease, cut Angela off and said, "I'm flattered. Don't be shy... I'm not. John likes it when I wear these daring dresses. It is great for our sex life."

Smiling, she nudged Angela and as she did, her dress drifted apart again.

"Phew... I think this wine is already getting to me," Angela said shyly.

Picking up a flat cracker with an oil, mushroom, and red pepper pate, Sophia placed it to Angela's lips.

"Here, don't wait for them. Eat something."

Angela opened her mouth, her tongue dallied—eagerly waiting for Sophia's advances. She allowed Angela to taste the oil dripping from the cracker as she teased her senses. Sophia turned to face her. Angela breathed in her perfume. She smelt wonderful. Her lips were full and red—delightfully edible. Her nails were perfectly manicured. She was so beautiful and best of all, she was nice. Angela felt an immediate closeness to her, even after just meeting Sophia an hour earlier. Angela's recent combative attitude—too quick to judge based on appearances alone—was quickly vanishing. The ease of their conversation had them laughing and being silly with one another, something she had not felt since being with her friend Carol a lifetime ago.

The next bottle of wine was accompanied by a full service of different delicacies. John filled the new glasses with a slightly deeper red and they toasted again. Angela hesitated so she could watch Sophia peek out.

John caught her gaze and adjusted his glasses. "Do you like what you see, Angela?"

"I'm... I'm sorry, but I..."

Sophia lifted Angela's hand from the table and placed it inside her dress. Angela felt an uncontrollable urge flush her body. Her hand lingered on Sophia's breast. Angela's fingers explored Sophia's protruding nipples as if no one else was in the room. Just the two of them as it was in the photo booth with Carol. Sophia let out a sigh. Angela quickly removed her hand, embarrassed.

"I am so sorry, I don't know what got into me," said Angela trying to explain her responsiveness to Sophia's gesture. Beads of perspiration formed above Angela's lips.

"No apology necessary, Angela. It felt nice. I liked your touch," reassured Sophia.

"We are all friends here, Angela. What happens behind these curtains stays behind these curtains," said John jokingly, then added, "Like Vegas."

They all laughed and clinked their glasses to the finish of that bottle of wine. Peter brought in another bottle and another full service; this time, it was a little more substantial. John instructed that the deeper the red, the heartier of delicacies it could endure without fracking the bouquet or your pallet.

If Anthony and John talking amongst themselves was a contrived, deviant scheme so Sophia could entice Angela, it was working. The wine was flowing faster and Angela and Sophia were enjoying each other's company more and more.

Angela picked up a piece of bread dipped in oil with a piece of cubed filet mignon on top and as she opened her mouth, a piece of the bread fell into the diamond cut-out. Without hesitation, Sophia slid her hand into Angela's dress at the perfectly designed cut-out with the pretense of retrieving the fallen morsel. She slid her hand slowly across Angela's stomach to the top of her panties, avoiding the crumb altogether. She momentarily waited on the fringe of Angela's panties for a rejection from her; it did not come. Angela's head was swooning with desire, her breathing short and fast.

Sophia continued running her fingers under her panties through Angela's pubic hair and with her talented fingers, Sophia separated Angela's wetting lips and slipped her finger inside. Angela gasped in excitement, her heart—beating faster. She slid slightly down in her chair to give Sophia unrestricted access through the cleverly designed cut-outs. Angela had never been so aroused in her life. Sophia rubbed Angela's charm with her warm juices, and then sunk deep inside again to moisten her fingers once more to stoke Angela's swollen bud. Angela moaned with pleasure. Sophia slowly pulled her finger out and raised it with Angela's glistening passion to her own lips. She tongued the tasty nectar from her finger and then touched Angela's lips. Her mouth opened and she sucked on Sophia's fingers. Her eyes fluttered like a butterfly in flight.

Peter entered the secluded room. John motioned to him as he adjusted his glasses again. Peter raised Sophia from her chair and slid the straps from Sophia's dress off her shoulders. It dropped to the ground. She was completely naked. Peter cupped her breasts from behind as Sophia rubbed up against him. Reaching back, she unzipped his pants and grabbed his hardening manhood. Bending over, she let him slip inside while she kissed Angela.

Sophia teased Angela with her perfectly manicured nails. Her hands never stopped moving—rotating softly around Angela's nipples. Gently, Sophia released the clips on the two chains that held Angela's dress together. She slid the spaghetti-straps from Angela's shoulders and let the dress fall. She guided Angela to stand in front of her so she could watch Peter slowly move in and out of her. Angela admired Sophia's naked body and her smoothly shaved mound. Each time Peter came out of her, he brought her sweet juices dripping from her inner passion. Sophia brought Angela even closer. As their bodies touched, Angela felt the motion of Peter going in and out of Sophia. Sophia placed her hands on Angela's shoulders and directed her slowly down her body, stopping her momentarily at Sophia's wanting nipples. Angela toyed with them, only temporarily abandoning them as she continued kissing Sophia's silky body down to her soft stomach. Momentarily looking up at Sophia's accepting smile, she ventured farther and found Sophia's waiting flower.

Guiding Angela's hands to feel Peter slipping in and out, Sophia arched her back so Angela had a perfect view of her swollen petals. She moaned with pleasure as Angela touched her with her tongue. Angela was in a fantasy world. She took Sophia's juices and slid up Sophia's body to her red edible lips. Their bodies pressed together; Peter started to buck, transferring the sensation through to both of them. They followed Peter's intensity as Sophia rubbed Angela's swollen bud. They all gasped with satisfaction.

The two men who obviously enjoyed the coterie, remained quiet while watching.

John, adjusting his glasses, softly said, "Well... gentlemen and ladies... why don't we take this party back to our home? I'm sure Sophia would enjoy more privacy. And you, Angela, would you like to explore more with Sophia?"

Angela's head was still spinning. She held on tightly to Sophia.

"Come, my love, let's go back to our house. If just to let the wine wear off before you return home... or you can stay; we have plenty of room. We just live around the corner and up the hill. We have a beautiful view of L.A.," enticed Sophia with a selfish agenda.

Angela could not say a word, only gathered her dress from the floor and then tried to straighten her hair the best she could.

"We will see you later, Peter," remarked John, not asking a question.

The four took leave to the waiting white Cadillac. Angela leaned her head on Sophia's shoulder as they wound up the twisty road to the top of the hill. The gate slid open; they drove in.

Even from the driveway, the view was spectacular. An elevator transported them to the main floor's balcony and as it rose, the view kept getting more surreal with the blending of the Los Angeles lights and the stars in the distant, clear sky. It was magical. The air was warm and as John turned the pool lights on, an aspiration was realized in Angela's mind. Money! And the power and influence it carried.

"One day, I will have this," exploded Angela in sheer delight.

As Angela marveled at the cityscape below her, John approached with a round of brandies.

"What's this?" she asked.

"As the French say, a *digestif,* meaning an after-dinner drink, which helps your pallet digest some of the rich food we've had tonight," informed John. "Cheers to our new friend. Angela... Welcome!"

"And hopefully, if Angela likes me, maybe my lover," said Sophia, seducing Angela in a very sultry voice.

They downed their drinks and John poured another.

"Come, Angela, let's jump in," said Sophia, dropping her dress and coaxing Angela to do the same.

Her slender body dove in and as she surfaced, the water beaded off of her naked body. The pool lights illuminated her every curve as she floated. The moonlight cast a foreboding spirit upon Sophia's face that Angela could not resist. Angela followed with her enticement. She had never gone without a swimsuit. It felt liberating and at the same time, daring. She was mesmerized by this taunting woman. Sophia knew how to pull at each cord of Angela's sexuality, not offensively, but with just enough compassion to arouse every passionate sense in an endearing way.

John tempted Angela and Sophia with another drink from the pool's edge. They swam to his persuasiveness. A clink sounded resonating off of the glasses and down the sweet nectar went, warming their insides down to their loins. They swam to the semi-circle lounge pool and lay in its shallow warm waters of the swirling jets. The ladies watched the streaks of light in the sky fly by, while Sophia caressed Angela's soft skin. Tenderly and slowly, she fondled Angela's stomach in a circular motion and so slowly she maneuvered lower and lower. Angela grabbed her hand—directing it to her waiting passion. Angela cupped her own breast and pinched her nipple as she guided Sophia's hand. Slowly Sophia slipped into the water and cupped Angela's moist awareness in her mouth. Angela arched and gasped, in a dream state; she had longed for this sensation. Sophia's tongue played with her bud and sucked back and forth like a temptress. She slid up against Angela and whispered into her ear. They got up out of the pool hand in hand, walked past Anthony and John, and retreated to the bedroom.

Angela's vision and reasoning were blurred, and as she laid in her passion she sensed the eyes of others. She felt something hard slip inside her and the weight of a body, the pumping action, as earlier, with Peter and Sophia. She heard an "ugh!" and then felt someone rubbing lotion over her breasts and then another entered her. The soft lips of Sophia caressed her mouth as she whispered softly to her.

Tabula Rasa – A New Beginning

Angela, with wet hair and a draping towel, ambled over to the open door of Irma's room. Irma was sitting at her make-up table, and upon seeing Angela's reflection in her mirror standing in her doorway, immediately swung around and looked closely at her. Getting up, she went over to Angela and wrapped her arms around her.

"My poor, baby... what did he do?"

"I don't know," she said, solemn and confused. "We met a lovely couple, had drinks and food... and then, everything started to get fuzzy. It was like... it wasn't me. I completely went gaga over this woman. I probably totally embarrassed her, but I couldn't stop myself from touching her... in the restaurant! I guess I got her so excited, that the waiter came in and he had his way with her... the poor lady didn't know what was happening. I remember we went back to their place and I think I was swimming naked in their pool. I have NEVER done that. Then things got even fuzzier and then..." Angela paused trying to reflect on the past evening events. Her hands slid down her stomach where Sophia had touched her. She looked at Irma with vagueness in her eyes, and said, "I'm not a virgin anymore!"

Irma rocked Angela tightly and said, "Shhh, my baby. You will be all right. You'll see."

"I'm fine, Irma. I'm a little older today and hopefully a little wiser. It's a new beginning for me," Angela said, downplaying any trauma and accepting her new-found sexuality.

"Uh-huh. I understand. Tabula Rasa," declared Irma.

"A what?"

"Tabula Rasa. 'A new beginning'. A clean slate."

"I like that, Irma. Tabula Rasa! Yes... that's it."

Angela's Promise

In the passing months, the only streetlamp in the neighborhood that could influence Angela's room flickered with a green cast, not conducive to putting on make-up in her otherwise dimly lit room. The peculiar knock of Reverend Michaels only warned the girls that he was entering, not acknowledging his presence at the door.

"Can't you wait for a 'Come in'?" Angela stated, boldly.

Letting the remark slide, he started to turn on the charm.

"My little angel, there is no need for this kind of talk."

He walked over and put his hands on Angela's shoulders as she sat at her make-up table. She shrugged him off. He drew back slightly. His demeanor changed. His brow tightened—his eyes beady.

"You are a fucking temptress! You might get away with that with your johns... but not me! You are provoking the wrong man," declared an extremely perturbed Reverend Michaels.

"Go to hell... Father," she sarcastically retorted as she met his eyes in the mirror in front of her.

At that moment, Reverend Michaels lost what little patience he had. He grabbed Angela right out of her chair and threw her onto her bed. Her make-up brush flew from her hand, crashing into her mirrored armoire. Holding her down, he straddled her and looked straight into her eyes.

"Now, look here you little bitch. I've got a lot of money invested in you." He slapped her face. "I own you! You understand?" he said, shaking Angela repeatedly on her bed, his spit escaping on every word. "When I say fuck, you better open your legs." He slapped her again. Her hair flew across her face. "This is business, honey. And you are my product. Got it!"

He relaxed his grip on Angela. Her face was reddening and swelling. She fought back the tears as she had done before.

"Now that we understand each other, fix your face. I've got a rich boy waiting for you at his apartment," ordered Reverend Michaels.

He left Angela's room slamming the door shut. After several moments, she slowly turned over and tried to calm down. She stared at the ceiling. Her fear transformed into rage—her body charged with adrenaline. Her mind swirled with thoughts of killing him. She promised herself—never again would a man strike her.

Irma, upon hearing the argument and the slamming of Angela's door, quietly checked for nosey onlookers before she slipped into her friend's room. She went to Angela's side to console her.

Irma, in a whisper of a voice said, "Listen, my child... That man is crazy. He would rather kill you than have you disrespect him in front of the other girls."

"I'll see him rot in hell first. I've got to get out of here," she said gritting her teeth.

"Where would you go? He'd find you... you know that. And then he'd lay a beating on you so hard, child."

"What am I to do?"

Fear punctuated Irma's voice. "Listen. I've got a friend; we used to work at the same studio together. She went through a tragedy, left the studio, and got her own place. It isn't much but let me call her. Now don't do anything stupid until I can talk to her. You understand?"

"Yes."

"Pardon me?"

More enthusiastically, Angela replied, "Yes Irma. I promise I won't do anything until you talk to your friend."

"Now, don't mention anything to the other girls, understand me?"

Angela nodded her head in compliance. After helping Angela to her make-up table, Irma gave Angela a hand at covering the welts on her face. Done up and looking just fine, Angela slipped into character with her friend, Sapphire, a dress she had copied from Sophia who wore the original at their restaurant meeting some months prior. Time was an irrelevant commodity; her life revolved around Reverend Michaels' schedule. He had her working more than the other girls, almost combined. Although her clients were all top-level, it didn't matter. Most of the time, they still believed, they had to get what they were paying for.

~

Joseph was waiting downstairs in Reverend Michaels' brand new white limousine Cadillac. He opened her door, outstretched his hand to steady her as she got in. He could tell something was up. Her usual politeness and friendly demeanor to him were missing. This time he kept the security window lowered just enough so he could keep a watchful eye on her. She was special.

Introduction to George Stanza

The twenty-fourth floor comprised of only one penthouse. George Stanza was the registered owner of the floor and the building. It was very posh inside with all the right colors and furnishings designed by the top Italian studios in Milan. His penthouse actually extended two floors on top of the roof with walk-around gardens and expansive views. The condos on the first floor started at two million dollars and it went up from there, with a waiting list if a resident did decide to sell, which was unlikely. George was well respected as a real estate mogul and businessman. No one questioned his diversity or income; as powerful as he was, he kept a low-profile lifestyle.

Carl, Mr. Stanza's confidante, put down the intercom phone after the concierge informed him that a young lady was on her way up. The bell rang. Carl looked quickly around the room to make sure everything was perfect—it was. He opened the door and greeted Angela with a warm smile. As she stepped into the room, the aroma of plush leather lent to the showcasing of expensive paintings and unique sculptures. Even Angela, with her limited exposure to fine art, could see the value in this collection of fine works.

"Please, come in. Mr. Stanza will be with you momentarily. My name is Carl, would you like an aperitif?" he asked.

"No thank you, Carl. I'll wait for..."

Together they nodded and said, "Mr. Stanza."

"Thank you, Carl. My name is Angela."

"It is a pleasure, Angela. Please make yourself at home while I inform Mr. Stanza of your arrival. The views are lovely on the terrace."

Carl left Angela in the living room. As she looked around at the beautiful white leather couches and glass tables, and to one side of the heavily-stacked shelves of books, a marble sculpture of a voluptuous butt was cast on a rotating stand. As Angela turned the piece, even the female's vulva was cut into the stone. George Stanza quietly entered the room. He was very distinguished with dark, silver-tipped hair, in his early-forties with a youthful appearance.

"Feel her," he remarked.

"Excuse me?" replied Angela, a little startled.

"Feel her. Jack always told me to tell people to run their hands over her shapely ass and slowly reach around to feel her vulva," explained George. "It is quite amazing... the sensation that is. My name is George." He extended a friendly hand.

"Hello, I'm Angela. You have beautiful art work and a gorgeous home."

"Thank you, Angela. Not many appreciate some of life's challenges of collecting art, not for the bragging rights but just for the appreciation of its beauty. Would you like a cocktail?"

"Whatever you are having, thank you."

"Scotch it is. Just a little something to cleanse the pallet."

"Yes, I have heard that before."

Angela spun around looking at the display of books shelved in polished Rosewood cabinets inset into the wall.

"Have you read all of these?" she asked.

"Most, not all. Some I will have to leave for retirement," chuckled George. "Do you read much?"

"Not like I used to. I have been reading one that a dear friend gave me."

"What's the title?"

"Oh, you probably haven't heard of it," said Angela.

"Try me," enticed George.

"Okay... *Les Juenes Filles*," she replied in a very correct French accent.

"Very good pronunciation. Have you lived in Northern France?"

"No."

"Your pronunciation has a hint of Flemish influences from the border of southern Belgium and Lille, France," informed George.

He detected he caught her a little off guard by the look on her face.

"The book... possibly follows the lesbian adventure of two young school girls who met at a French boarding school in Paris?" stated George in fact and not conjecture.

Pleasantly surprised, she said, "Yes... but why would you read a book like that?"

"My older sister gave it to me to read so that I could understand her choices," explained George. He paused, letting what he had just said sink in. "Carl has created a feast for us. Shall we dine on the terrace?"

"That would be lovely, George."

They stepped up onto a marble floor where a fashionable twelve-person table occupied the main dining room. To the right and through the French doors leading to the terrace, was a table for two with fresh cut flowers, sparkling stemware and two lit candles. The view over the heavily-planted balusters was magnificent. Jasmine scented the air and their white petals added contrast to the night sky.

Carl brought in a tray of appetizers and placed them on a highly polished, hand-carved table.

"Angels-on-horseback?" offered George.

"Pardon me."

"Angels-on-horseback. Oysters wrapped in bacon. Fancy name, but they taste great. Here, try one," tempted George in a very relaxed manner.

"Mmmmm, they are delicious!"

"Don't worry, I would never steer you wrong. Do you like fish? I guess I should have asked the agency before Carl suggested it."

"It's quite all right. Yes, I love fish. I had it a lot back east." Angela caught herself before she said anymore. But, George seemed different. He was a gentleman—not pawing at her as soon as she walked in. And, interested in what she thought.

"Good. Carl makes a fabulous Flounder *a la grecque*. Sounds foreign but it's just fish with oil and spices."

"I believe... oil with lemon, fennel, sage, thyme and crushed coriander... or does he use it whole?"

"I'm impressed," said George. "And how do you know this dish?"

"A friend was trying to cheer me up and widen my worldly knowledge many moons ago in a faraway land," reminisced Angela missing her friend, Gilles.

"Well, a toast to him... or her. I guess we are one for one," delightfully remarked George.

Carl was ready to serve his main course. The two sat and continued with their enchanting conversation over dinner. Angela had never felt so at ease with a man, other than Gilles. It was a lovely night and the company was even better. Carl returned to gather their plates.

"Carl, that was delicious. I did detect a sweet intoxicating taste."

"Yes, ma'am."

"Wine?" she asked, curiously.

"No, ma'am. Just a hint of cognac," said Carl as he flashed a smile.

Angela bubbling with the flavor of the evening congratulated Carl on his delicate pallet. "Most awesome!" came out and she immediately put her hand to her mouth and apologized for her impetuous rudeness.

"I take that passionate foray as a compliment, ma'am."

"Thank you for your compassion, Carl," replied Angela in a more dignified manner.

With a smile, George said, "Would you like to relax on the loungers?"

He offered his hand as they removed themselves from the table. Angela sauntered over to the terrace railing and turned to face George.

"I'm sorry, George. I don't know where that came from. You are right though, Carl is an excellent chef... even though..." Her face had a curious grin. "... he doesn't look like one."

"No, he doesn't, I have to agree with you there. He is not an employee, a friend really. A trusted comrade in crime, you might say. We have been together for a long time. A brandy, my lady?" courteously offered George.

"Thank you... Maybe just a little one," shyly replied Angela knowing she needed to take care of business.

After George returned with two brandies, they shared a clink and a sip, and then Angela put her glass down on the edge of the terrace's wall. She stood close to George and started to unbutton his shirt.

"That's not necessary," he said, softly grabbing her hands.

"But..."

George gently touched Angela's face.

"How often does he beat you?"

Angela caressed George's hands and held them to her cheek. She looked up into his concerned eyes.

"It's been getting worse the last few months," she wistfully said.

"Why do you stay?"

"I have nowhere else to go. If I try to run, he would pass the word around and he would find me, and then, it would be worse," replied Angela. Her eyes started to mist.

"How old are you, really?"

"Seventeen almost eighteen," she said with a twenty-five year-old voice.

"How long have you been working for this guy?"

"Almost two years," she said horrified at how the time had flown by, in spite of her treatment.

"Do you have any money saved?"

"Yes."

"How much? $500...a $1000?"

Angela pulled away. She retrieved her drink from the railing and stepped over to the lounger and sat down.

"No. I've got a lot more than that. I'm not stupid. I know what I want," she said defending herself.

George sat alongside her on the lounger.

"I didn't mean any disrespect. I was hoping you were as bright as you are beautiful."

There was a slight lull, and then George continued, "Why don't you come and work for me?"

Angela looked straight into his eyes.

"No strings attached. You are your own boss. I'll set you up in your own condo. I know a lot of influential people who fly into Los Angeles and they are looking for some side pleasure. These are big-buck people. We split 50/50 after expenses. What do you say?"

Confused, Angela replied, "Well... I...I don't know." Her mind was spinning with this offer. *Finally, a chance to leave that bastard Reverend Michaels before I killed him.*

"I thought you said you were smart? And that you knew what you wanted... but do you? Well, here is your chance to see the world and live a glamorous lifestyle with the rich and famous. And if you want, I could invest some of your earnings in high-risk venture capital companies. The return on the dollar is enormous, and, if you know how to play the game right, the risk is minimal," reassured George.

"What about Reverend Michaels?"

"Let me handle him. Look, if you've been giving him trouble, he'll jump at the chance to make some extra cash."

"That sounds so cheap, George. Buy and sell me... to the highest bidder," said Angela offended.

Angela got up and walked over to the terrace's wall and looked out at the sparkling lights of L.A.

"It isn't any different than what is happening now in your young life, except you will be in control. You will gain. It's a win-win situation."

George paused as he studied Angela. He stepped to her side.

"Nice view isn't it? It is waiting for you," George said softly, encouraging her.

"I promised a friend today that I would not make any rash decisions until I talked with her. As you trust Carl, I trust Irma... with my life. May I sleep on your offer?"

"By all means, but don't leave it too long." George's manner changed to more impending doom. He saw something in her and didn't want her to endure anymore pain. He had to convince her. "I don't want to fish you out of the river."

Angela turned to George, her thoughts collecting, swirling, and an image of being fished out of the river. An image that was too personal. She shook her head and put her arms around him. She felt his warmth, his sincerity, but why should she trust him?

"George, may I ask you? Why me? There are dozens and dozens of other girls you could have made this offer to and they would have jumped on it faster than a corner trick?"

"Ahah... You do have a way with vernacular phrasing. But seriously... networking. You know, through a friend of a friend type thing. Someone mentions certain qualities that I find admirable while others find them troubling. You, I find admirable with a possible troubled past."

"But you just met me."

"Correct. I just met you face to face. But, as our acquaintances go, I have known you longer than you think. Come, I will have Carl drive you home."

"I have someone waiting for me downstairs," said Angela.

Irma and Angela's Plan

Angela took another sip of her coffee, swirled the cup around the saucer's rim and then replaced it in its groove. Irma gathered Angela's hand in hers from the other side of the booth as the morning sun shone through the scratched and initialed window film of the café.

Anxiously, Angela asked, "So, what do you think?"

"I don't know, child. It sounds too good to be true. I mean, he acted like a real gentleman all right, but they all do when they want something and then *wham*, they have you in their control," said Irma hitting the table.

Startled, Angela said, "I've gotta do something!"

"Look, angel, I've been in this business a lot longer than you..."

"Yeah, and look where you still are..."

Irma was taken aback.

"I'm so sorry, Irma; I had no right to say that. I guess I just want this so badly to be real."

"I know you do, but you got to use your head. Didn't you tell him you would sleep on it?"

"Yes."

"Well then, sleep on it. A day or two should not make any difference if he is sincere. I phoned my friend. She said she would be glad to help out. She's a good woman. She... she had a break like yours once."

Irma paused.

"Well, what happened?" asked Angela, noticing the hesitation in Irma's voice.

"I've said too much. Maybe she'll tell you. It's not my place."

"Ah, come on, Irma. What happened?"

Irma ignored Angela's plea.

"Tonight, we get dressed like always. Don't bring anything with you that doesn't fit into your normal shoulder bag. That way, he won't suspect anything is wrong. He'll think you're out turning a trick."

"Thanks, Irma. I..."

"Don't thank me, child. I could be getting us both killed. We're not home free just yet."

Stanza's Office

The outer office was quiet on the 16th floor of Pride of Destiny, Inc. The exposed, multi-geared clock sculpture that hung on the back wall behind the highly-polished granite-top receptionist's desk indicated 6:13. Another geared display showed the 'PM' as it rotated around. A crack of light under the heavily-sculpted door of an inner office disappeared as the door slowly opened. A posh leather chair rotated around, revealing George Stanza carrying on a conversation on the phone. Carl entered.

"Look. I said tonight..." a little irritated, "...and I mean tonight. They're new customers. Yes, they have references. I don't know exactly..." putting his hand over the receiver, he asked Carl, "What do you think...? Columbian?"

"Argentinian, I believe."

"Carl thinks Argentinian," informed George, continuing his phone conversation.

Carl inserted a loaded magazine into a Glock 17 and pulled back on its slide. Click—click. He placed two more full magazines next to the gun and slid them over to George. Pulling out another, he checked its magazine and replaced it into his shoulder holster.

"Yes... say 10:00 p.m. No, that's fine. We're meeting them at midnight. That gives us plenty of time. Right, ciao."

Carl was dressed in all black and looked extremely intimidating. Quite the contrast from the white dinner jacket he had on when Angela had graced their presence.

"Everything ready, Carl?"

"Yes, sir, Mr. Stanza. Precautions have been taken care of," reported Carl rather formally as this scenario was about business, not pleasure.

"Good. Let's go get a drink."

The Kindness of Eileen

The creaking stairs of the old building were an annoyance to most of the residents. Only two more flights of the four-story walk-up before they would arrive at Irma's friend's third-floor apartment.

"You don't need a bellman announcing someone is coming with these stairs," said Angela.

"Hush, child."

The two women ascended the other flights in silence. Finally, they faced room 314.

"Someone must be superstitious... they missed 313 after 312," said Angela, trying to keep their sleuthing light.

Whispering, Irma said, "Child, this is serious. You better be watchful. You never know who is going to stab you in the back."

Irma knocked lightly on her friend Eileen Cortez's door. They heard a shuffle of feet and then an eye piece slid to one side. It quickly returned and the door opened.

"Eileen, this is Angela. Angela, this is my dear friend, Eileen."

"It's a pleasure," remarked Angela, noticing a scar crossing Eileen's otherwise very pretty face. Eileen was tall, at least 5'-9", Angela thought, and all legs. Her dark complexion made her blue-green eyes pop. *She should have been a model.*

"Nice to meet you, Angela. Please ladies, come in. I have tea brewing if you would like some?"

"Thank you, Eileen. That would be nice," accepted Angela.

"I'll take a stiff drink," said Irma.

"Make yourself at home." Eileen stepped into her small kitchen. She returned holding a tray with two cups, a hot pot of tea, and a small glass with a bottle of Jack.

The apartment was not luxurious but it was decorated in fashionable taste with a display of local art. Angela looked around and remembered the first time she was able to open her eyes and saw Gilles' cabin. Even this seemed upscale to his appointments. They watched as Irma downed a glass of Jack in one gulp.

"AH, that takes the chill off of things," she said with a shake of her head.

Laughing, Angela said, "Irma, it is 75 degrees out at nine o'clock at night. Hardly a chill."

The three laughed together.

The night was very pleasant and the ladies got along just fine. Irma decided she better head back, otherwise Rev. M's suspicions would get the better of him. Thinking ahead, she even brought some of her savings to give him so he would think she was working. A small price to pay for her life.

"Don't worry, Irma. I'll take care of her."

"Thank you, Eileen. She is special. I'll see ya later."

Closing the door behind her, Eileen leaned against it and looked at Angela, concerned.

"You'll be safe for now but long-term might not be possible."

"I know. But thank you for this short time until I can figure out my next move."

"Well, child. It is 11:55. If you feel like talking, we can do that. But if you are tired, we can make up your bed?"

Stanza Meets Valdez Brothers

The warehouse was mostly in darkness except for the reddish glare of several EXIT lights. George Stanza and Carl stood beside their car waiting for their guests.

"How much talent do you have?" asked George.

"Four heavy breathers equipped with night vision."

"Good."

A low vibration had Carl pulling his phone from his belt.

"They've arrived."

Outside in the alleyway, an older van proceeded slowly towards the designated warehouse. Stopping at 903A, they flashed their headlights off and on. Carl pressed the remote button for the large cargo door to open. Security lights turned on as the van drove in.

"Two in the front. Nothing in the back," informed a voice over Carl's ear piece.

Carl dropped the cargo door. Two men dressed in late eighties-style suits stepped into the light cast by the security system's spotlights. One shielded his eyes while the other pulled his white fedora down further.

"Relax, gentlemen! We are just waiting for the overheads to charge. We are all friends here," said George Stanza.

"OK," announced one of the visitors.

The overheads were casting an eerie orange glow but within minutes, the warehouse started to brighten up and the security spotlights dimmed.

"My name is Stark," said George, introducing himself.

They all walked over to a folding table in the middle of the room.

"Eis a plazure, Meester Stark. Thees eis mi hermano, Enrico. Mi name eis Emmanuel Fernando Maria Valdez, but chew can call mi Chico."

Enrico, Chico's brother, just nodded with little expression.

"Right, Chico. Now these are the rules of the game. You will have the lower east side. That is your territory. You set your prices. You handle your own distribution. No one from our organization will interfere. If there is a problem you feel uncomfortable handling, the organization will. This business is like any other. You have to keep your customers supplied and happy. Keep your stuff clean. Lastly, you buy from us only. If there is a conflict with this... trust me, you will lose. Do we understand each other?" asked George.

The two brothers looked at each other. Enrico was anxious. He grabbed Chico's arm to return to the van. Chico pulled him back and whispered in his ear. Chico put on a big smile.

"Yeah, sure Meester Stark... we understand."

"Everybody...?"

"Sure, Meester Stark... he's OK," reassured Chico.

"Fine. We will be in touch to set up a drop," said George.

"Ah wait... Meester Stark. Mi thought we was to get a kilo tonight?"

Mr. Stanza looked straight into Chico's eyes.

"We will be in touch, Chico. Goodnight, gentlemen," commanded George Stanza.

Chico grabbed his brother by the arm and they headed back to their van. As they settled inside and started it, Carl hit the remote for the cargo door to open. The van tires squealed as they turned on the cement floor and they slowly exited through the large, opened door.

Inside the van, Enrico declared angrily raising his fist, "Mi spit on him. He tells me *nada*. We are Valdez!"

"*¡Silencio, mi hermano. Espere!* We play hees game... *por ahora,*" stated Chico, resetting his fedora.

Waiting for the brothers to disappear, Carl expressed to George, "I don't like them or trust them."

"Neither do I, my friend. This business is not noted for its more scrupulous people. They just better be smart. Call in your talent; we'll set up a drop tomorrow. Have some heavy backers when you meet them and wear a vest. Not taking any chances until we get a better feel for them," instructed Mr. Stanza.

"Yes, sir."

Stepping into their Mercedes S600, they roared out of the warehouse. Its red taillights burned in the darkness. Carl made one call to his men. "Good night!"

Irma's Sacrifice

Reverend Michaels had burst into Irma's room in a rage looking for Angela and demanding answers.

"Where is that little bitch!?" he cowed.

"I don't know. I haven't seen her since the other day before I went out. Look, here is your money."

Reverend Michaels grabbed the money out of Irma's hand.

"I don't know how you do it! Who would want to fuck you? You better ask around. I want to know where she is... hear me?"

He raised his hand as to slap her, but hesitated.

"A thousand bucks to whoever rats her out. Pass the word," voiced Reverend Michaels in a crazed tone.

"Yes... yes, of course," replied Irma, fearfully.

"The bitch is bad for business. I didn't mean when you felt like it. Get up you lazy whore and get out there now... Find her!" he blathered.

He threw her clothes and boots into her face. The heel caught her just under the eye and split her skin open. She screamed, "You bastard!"

Rev. M. spun around and slapped her to the ground. His eyes instantly flared wide open as he saw her squirming. Without provocation, he started kicking and kicking like a deranged mad man, sweat beading on his forehead as he lashed out in his rage. She lay there barely moving; coughing, blood trickling from her mouth. He left her on the floor and slammed the door behind him so hard, it swung back open. Her fingers lingered in a pool of blood. Her eyes glassed over and rolled back into their sockets. Her face became morbidly still—she sputtered.

Shocking News

Angela and Eileen sat on the couch glued to the TV—horrified; their cries fell on deaf ears as their tears soaked the sheets that cradled their bodies. Their dear, dear friend was found in a dumpster, beaten to death.

"That fucking, fucking, fucking bastard!" cried Angela uncontrollably, rocking back and forth, pounding the top of her leg with her fist. "I will kill that fucking bastard... Irma! Irma! I will kill that fucking bastard, for you, for me, for all of us!"

The news people were not very sympathetic. It was just another prostitute playing a dangerous game of chance, and she lost. The police had no leads and were asking the locals to cooperate with the investigation. A call line was flashed on the TV screen for anybody with information; no matter how trivial they thought it might be. They used an old picture of Irma when she was in her glory as a studio make-up artist. She was beautiful.

Angela's Daring Escape

A week passed before Angela was able to function after hearing the news of her dear friend Irma's demise. She had saved Angela's life and in turn, had lost hers. Angela didn't dare go to the police with information—that would be like signing her own death sentence. She could not stay with Eileen any longer; almost two weeks was pushing it. It was too dangerous for Eileen. Angela could not handle another friend to be found that way.

Eileen had an old black-shag wig that she used from time to time and thought it would be a good disguise for Angela. She would be able to leave her building without anyone noticing the long blonde locks that she had a reputation for flaunting. Her stylish clothes were ditched at a Salvation Army in exchange for faded cut-off shorts. Some dark makeup plus a pair of brown contact lenses would add a little more deception. There were plenty of girls who fit her description that came and went daily from Eileen's apartment building. Angela thought of the two ripped girls in the bus station when she first started out on her journey. Now she looked just like them.

Angela's personal effects amounted to $6,874.00 buried in a sock, a couple of pairs of panties, and her diary with the letter from Gilles. Her total sum of two and half years of running: about fifteen hundred dollars more than when she began her journey. *How sick*, she thought. *This is my life?* She had one other thing—a phone number.

Eileen had left for a couple of hours to do some shopping, so Angela took the time to gather her things and clean the apartment meticulously as she does. As Angela finished packing her shoulder bag, she heard the unmistakable sound of creaking floor boards as hurried footsteps, more than one, were coming up the stairs. She instinctively opened the kitchen window and went out onto the fire escape. She looked around. She decided to go up knowing she would not have enough time to go down the fire escape and run through the alley before someone spotted her. The roof was only one floor up—and her only hope. She quickly scampered upward.

A peculiar knock echoed through the whole apartment of Eileen Cortez. Michaels shouldered the door open, peeling the wood from its jamb. He thoroughly looked around for any telltale signs of his missing property. Nothing, not even a strand of hair. He checked the bathroom—one tooth brush, one set of towels; in the kitchen—one cup dried on the rack. He hastily opened the fridge—barely enough food for one. He slammed the door frustrated with his overzealousness of wanting to find some clue. His eyes drifted over to the small kitchen window. He opened it and peered out. He looked down expecting to see someone and then up. Nothing. Rev. Michaels shut the window bewildered, and thinking.

He turned to his snitch Jasper, and asked, "Who said they thought they saw a blonde come up here?"

"Shaky Charlie..." replied Jasper.

"You mean the guy that sits down on the corner with his face buried in a brown bag?"

"That's him..."

"How did you ask him?"

"I asked him if he had seen a blonde girl around here and that there was twenty bucks in it if he knew anything," logically responded Jasper.

"And it never occurred to you he only wanted the twenty bucks? How fucking stupid are you? Get out of my sight, jerk-off."

Reverend Michaels scanned the room one more time satisfied the information was bogus and the lady, whoever lived there, would probably report a break-in to the cops. He hesitated in the hallway and walked back into the apartment. Pulling out a handkerchief from his sport coat, he wiped down the bathroom door and fridge. He did the same to the front door knob as he exited.

~

Angela waited until the white Cadillac pulled away from the building. She sat on the roof top, knees to her chest, her arms wrapped around them gasping with anxiety. The air stuck in her throat, so thick she could eat it. Her Irma was gone and she had put Eileen in danger. She felt sick to her stomach.

She sat there for hours. Her mind spun with possible scenarios. She remembered Gilles saying, "The only thing to fear is fear itself. Turn that negative energy into something positive. Fear is a great motivator to re-start your thinking pattern." She stood up, *I'll wait until dark*, she thought. *Then I'll cross over to the next building and down their staircase. If anyone sees me, they will think I was visiting there. I'll call Eileen and tell her she better find a new place and that I am so, so sorry.*

Angela's butt was getting sore from the stone and tar roof, but only another hour or so and darkness would disguise her movement even more. After sizing up the distance to the opposite building, she wandered over to a pile of debris. Wood left in disrepair from what looked like a makeshift aviary was strewn over the roof. There were several pieces that appeared strong enough to support her weight but not long enough. On the other side of the aviary were strands of clothesline wire. She gathered what she could from the twisted pile of wire and picked up three of the longest boards, placing them end to end. On top of them, at their joints, she placed shorter boards, which she then wound with the clothesline and then twisted the two ends together like twist ties on bread bags.

Now to test it. She propped one end up on the parapet wall that surrounded the roof's perimeter. She bounced up and down—a little creaking but it supported her. She re-tied a couple of the wires tighter. Now she only had to lift her make shift-bridge into position without the other end falling over the edge with the weight.

Gilles had shown her all sorts of things and ways to accomplish momentum, single-handedly. But he had at least 150 pounds on her; things moved for him much easier than for her. She had no other alternative. She had to do it.

The board's stationary end had a nail jutting out of it. She thought that *if* she relieved it slightly out of the board, wrapped the remaining clothesline to it, and tied it off to one of the many protruding vent pipes, she could then heave her bridge to the other building without fear of it going too far and her not being able to hang on to it if it did drop. She was four stories up. It would hurt, if not kill her if she fell.

"Think positive," she kept telling herself out loud so she would believe it. "You can do this. It's not rocket science, merely geometry or something."

Standing the bridge straight in the air, it wavered like a flag pole in a storm. Valiantly, she side-stepped it in a fanning motion to position it at the roof's edge. Looking around, she pushed her bridge in the direction of the next building. It started to slip backwards on her roof when it hit her parapet wall. She quickly forced her foot against the end of the board and held onto a protruding vent pipe. The boards teetered and then down it came, bouncing on the other wall of the opposite building.

Jumping up and down excitedly with what she had accomplished, she looked closely. One of the support boards had slipped partially out of her wire loom. "Fuck," she said out loud. Frustrated, she started walking in circles with her hands on her hips...

"What did Gilles tell me?" Thinking, she recited to herself, *the tip of a woman's spiked heel exerts more pressure per square inch than a refrigerator over its surface. And then something of force and pressure.* "God, I can't remember."

Angela looked at her bridge. "If I crawl over it rather than try to walk over it, my weight would be distributed across a greater span with less deflection. Yes! He said something like that!"

Excited with her revelation and foggy memory, she tossed her bag to the next roof, positive that she would retrieve it. She mounted the boards on her stomach and slowly began to shinny across. First, she crossed her legs tightly around the board for support as she moved her arms ahead, where her hands clamped on like two mini vises. She then slid her legs up just like she had done climbing trees. The first joint accepted her weight faithfully but the sharp strands of exposed wire scraped her like a horror movie.

Six feet out, the boards started to deflect. She hung on. Carefully, she edged further, eyeing the dislodged board. If she could get to it, she could slide it back into place enough to support her. The main board was still tethered. She continued ever so slowly. As she reached the middle, the boards had only deflected about six inches. *I'm still good*, she thought, *another six feet and I will be able to reach the last joint.*

Sixty feet up from the alley below, had her suspended in midair on boards made out of a discarded bird cage. She thought of the humor of it, if she lived. She inched further, an arm's distance to go, and then, from behind, she heard, "Crack!" She froze. She buried her face into the board, waiting, listening. She cautiously looked back. The first board had split length wise at the edge of the roof expanding almost to the first joint.

"For fuck's sake, give me a break!" she screamed muffling her inflection through her gritting teeth.

She had no recourse, she had to go on. With her adrenaline pumping, she maneuvered the dislodged board good enough to slip over. The first board cracked again and now, it was two, held in place only by the twisted wire. She couldn't stop.

Reaching for the inner edge of the parapet wall, Angela hung on tightly just as the split board let loose. Down they all fell, clanking off of a waste receptacle bin sounding like a bass drum announcing Macy's Parade.

She dangled for a moment—her arms ached as she held on to the roof's parapet. Mustering every bit of strength she had left, she pulled herself up onto her stomach—her feet trying to grasp onto any kind of foothold. One more grunting, *"harrumph"*, and over she went, safe on the other side. Her heaving chest sucked the air from around her. Collapsing on her side, she rested while envisioning what might have happened—the sound her body might have made.

Finally rolling over onto her back, she looked up into the night sky. Tears blinded her eyes—she cried out in despair, "I just want to be a lady... I don't want to be Wonder Woman!"

A Call for Help

Angela looked like she was coming down from a crack high— her mascara ran down her face in black streaks. She entered a greasy spoon restaurant and walked past the losers who she never wanted to look like or be. No one lifted their heads as she swayed through the aisle towards the restrooms and the only operable telephone for blocks. Straight ahead of her, looming like a mirage between the separated bathrooms, her fate awaited. Pausing, she looked at this black box. It was covered with scratches from unsteady fingers trying to deposit coins, and dents from the receiver used as a hammer when their dealer refused more credit. It was all there, like a *Who's Who* of losers. She was about to grab the receiver and then hesitated. Searching in her bag, she pulled out one of her panties and wrapped the receiver with them. Carefully, she deposited her coins. *Clang, clang, clang*, and then she dialed.

"Hello," said the voice at the other end.

"It's Angela. I'm in big trouble..." She paused as she peered through the marred window film to the lit street outside. Appearing unannounced, the unmistakable white Cadillac cruised slowly by and glaring eyes scanned everyone walking, sitting, or lying on the ground face down in their own vomit. No one was overlooked. It stopped suddenly. Another pair of eyes glared out the lowered tinted window, clearly looking her way. She tried to move carelessly as if she was talking to a john or her dealer. Her arms moved expressively, not at all like she was trying to hide from anyone, and her middle finger jabbed into the phone, disrespectfully. The car moved on. Angela backed up against the wall, faintly relieved, letting out a mild exhale.

"Hello... Hello, Angela. You still there?"

She raised the receiver back to her ear. "Yes... Please, I need to get out of here."

"Where are you?"

"In a diner at Washington and Olive, between the 110 and the 10 Interstates."

"We will be right there."

"Please hurry. I'm not sure how long I can hang out in this disguise without being harassed."

"Stay inside, around people. Don't single yourself out."

"Thank you," she whispered.

She hung up the phone.

Act II

Angela - Remembering Her Past

The brightly adorned room shared soft whites and pale yellows dancing with the filtered light coming through the floor-to-ceiling shear-covered windows. A polished white grand piano faced inward from the expansiveness of that view. Intricate oak casings surrounded the windows and doors; their honey-oak finish added warmth against the contrasting balanced whites and yellows. A Van Gogh, a gift, was centered on the wall next to the fireplace, as a collage of photographs from art openings, theater events, fashion shows, and friends' parties were grouped on another wall. A framed picture of a man in a white uniform, her father, sat beside another waiting to have its displayed picture removed for another of sentimental meaning.

A delicate unwrapped gift, a dancing ballerina, sat on a glass coffee table, while Wilhelmina Fernandez, the unmistakable voice from the French film, DIVA, softly played in the background. Wilhelmina's coloratura was interrupted by the ringing of a phone.

"Hello," answered Angela somewhat misty. "Oh, Eileen, no I am fine. I was just relaxing, re-reading my old diary, thinking of the old days when I arrived in L.A. Fifteen years sure flies by fast."

"Where were you last night? I tried calling you," asked Eileen.

"Oh, the senator was in town with his wife, Allison. He is such a gentleman. Always brings me something unique."

"How is Allison? And more to the point, I thought that part of your life was over?"

"Allison is doing great. Her cancer is in full remission. And yes... that part of my life has ended. It was such a unique situation to learn about both of them in that caring and fostering way. We had a nice night out, drinks, lively conversation, toasting our successes, and then I came home. Alone. It's a little difficult to carry on a tryst with three security agents following you everywhere. So unlike the old days before Richard became a senator."

"Life moves on, my friend. You really cared for Allison and I believe you gave her the strength to continue on. She must have taken a page out of your book," said Eileen.

"Well, I don't know about that, but we did share a beautiful thing."

"I won't keep you, just concerned. Now, about the art show..."

"I wouldn't miss it, I promise. I'll see you later. Hugs... ciao, hon."

As Angela stood, she put down her phone and diary onto the glass coffee table next to the ballerina, where an aging newspaper clipping revealed headlines: 'Anthony Micholanetti Charged with Murder!' She picked up her ballerina, walked over to her stereo and turned down the music. Her silk lounging gown clung to her shapely body as she crossed the living room to her piano. She twisted the delicate knob of the dancing ballerina and set it down. She began to play along with the idyllic tune.

Jeff – A Modern Gumshoe

Jeff Malardo, a 5'-10½" strapping man with sandy-brown hair and light blue eyes, was a gumshoe aficionado; born, as he said, *three decades too late*. One of his favorite crime drama movies was 'The Maltese Falcon', which he bought on a remastered CD, and then had it transferred to 16mm so he could hear the ticking of the film as it fed through the projector's gate. He felt it added to the nuance of the film noir.

After putting in ten years with the LAPD, he was frustrated with the lack of discipline, the scores of stacked cases, not enough manpower, and of course, not enough resources to be really effective in closing cases in a timely manner. He now worked for a private firm, Straight Up Communications, that located whomever and whatever, for a contracted price. This vocation allowed him to drive a new car and wear nice suits, if he wished. He was, however, a throwback in time, still using his flip phone and still driving his 1967 Firebird convertible, which was two decades older than him.

His workspace was the complete opposite to Hollywood and Jeff's imaginary sleuths. His firm used up-to-date and experimental equipment re-designed from military applications by friends of friends of his boss, Harry Peters. At times, they dialed into the NCIC (National Crime Information Center), while, at other times, they used their own investigative protocol and procedures. Some of Jeff's best contacts were old gum-shoes that couldn't let go of a case.

They studied, re-read, and asked new questions on old cases with new results. Jeff thought they were an amazing bunch of guys.

Departing work early this day, Jeff headed to a florist to pick up a jasmine plant as a gift for his over-worked, over-ambitious, undergraduate girlfriend, Teresa. His over-priced Pasadena brownstone apartment had all the characteristics of days gone by with its restored façade, but inside, the renovations were definitely beyond Jeff's eccentric taste. Teresa, however, fell in love with the blending of the character of old and the convenience of new. Jeff liked the old but was not excited about the new. Yes, it was nice, and yes it cost a lot less than a simple walk up on the west side, but the magic was gone with the ceramic stove tops, stainless steel appliances and earth-toned tile. "What happened to emerald green bathtubs and black-and-white checkered tile?" he would ask Teresa.

Rounding the corner in his top-down 67 'bird, the sweet mellifluous sounds of Christina Aguilera, crooned over his Bose speakers. He loved her soulful side and likened her to Etta James. Pulling into a curbside parking spot in front of his brownstone, Jeff saw his neighbor, friend, and newspaper boy Josh.

Greeting him, Jeff hailed, "Hey Josh, my man. How you doing?" He turned off the car and the music faded. Stepping out, he walked toward his little friend.

Looking up, Josh pulled out his ear buds and switched off his iPhone. He ran to his friend, excitedly.

"Give me five, Mr. Malardo."

"How's your day been going? School good?"

"Great! Next week our baseball team is going to New Jersey for a tournament," said Josh more than enthusiastically.

Jeff put his hand on Josh's shoulder as they walked to the steps and said, "Fabulous, dude. Are your mom and dad going too?"

"Mom has to work at the hospital, but Dad is taking time off."

"Ah man, that sounds great. You and your father are going to have a great time. I can feel it."

"Thanks, Mr. Malardo. Here's your paper."

Fumbling with his newspaper and plant, Jeff asked Josh, "Hey, you got your key? I don't know where mine is."

"Sure, Mr. Malardo."

Josh waited at the mailboxes inside the hallway for Jeff while he searched through his pockets.

"Here, hang onto this plant, will you? Where is that key? Okay, I got it. Thanks Josh, see you tomorrow."

"Good night, Mr. Malardo."

Josh ran up the stairs to finish delivering his papers while Jeff continued to fumble with his mail and his way into his apartment.

"Teresa, you home?" shouted Jeff as he entered.

"In the bedroom!" she replied.

Jeff walked over to his answering machine that sat on an antique hall table—the light was blinking. He pressed the message button, it clicked and started to re-wind. Clicked again and then the voice of one of his co-workers, Allen Travers, said: "Jeff, you really need to get voice mail. It's Allen. It's 6:25 p.m. on Wednesday. Um... hey I won't"... click, click, click... "Harry wanted..." click, click, and then a long busy signal.

"Damn!" Jeff tried to re-wind and fast forward, "Shit. Got to get this fixed."

As Jeff dropped his mail on the hall stand, he noticed a linen-rag envelope with a fancy gold script from E. Cortez & Associates Galleries Inc. in his stack. He put it down and continued to walk down the hallway, past the living room towards the back bedroom. He had to dodge a couple of packing boxes and several suitcases blocking the entrance to the kitchen before he arrived to see Teresa. Her skimpy tee top and shorts were perspiration-spotted as she attempted to squash down a medium size suitcase.

"Teresa, what's going on?" said Jeff concerned.

Teresa looked up with her beautiful deep brown eyes. She didn't want to get emotional, but as soon as she saw Jeff standing there, she started to get weepy.

"Baby, let me speak before you say anything," she said pulling aside her long hair from her sweaty face. "Professor Strong has asked me, and others... not just me, to join his team on a dig near Iquitos, Peru. I'll be able to use this as my thesis for my masters'."

Jeff stared at her. Eight months ago they had talked about starting a family and now, all of a sudden this... She's packing! He felt a flush of betrayal come over him.

"I didn't know you could get your master's by keeping a professor's sleeping bag warm," blurted Jeff.

"Jeff, you know that's not it," defended Teresa.

Jeff's face contorted—his brow creased, his eyes flared into the depths of a deep blue sea. "I've seen the way he looks at you. That pompous bourgeoisie egghead wants to get into your pants. I saw it when we were all down at the pub two months ago."

Teresa teared up. "Jeff, that is not true! I don't want to leave, but this is a once-in-a-lifetime opportunity. Not just to go to Peru, but to participate in such an important dig with scientists from all over the world. I can't pass it up. If you love me as I love you, you will understand."

Jeff searched her innocent eyes. She had always been truthful with him. She never gave him a hard time when he worked nights on the vice squad or when he came home with the smell of cheap perfume. He told her it was all part of the job and that nothing would interfere with their relationship. The all-night stake-outs didn't seem worth it to Jeff after a while and that was one of the reasons he left—for her. He had missed cuddling in bed with her; her excitement when she talked about decaying teeth and spectrograms and laser analyzers. His stupid side jokes usually culminated into a wrestling match and then they made incredible love. He started to calm down.

"I'm sorry for that condescending remark. I... I just feel like we are..."

Teresa cut him off. "Shhh, baby." She stood in the light of the bedroom window. Her perky nipples poked through her jersey top as she swayed to his side and touched his hand.

"Jeffery..."

Aha... here it comes. Only when she wants something, does she call me Jeffery. He waited for her reasoning.

"I know we have talked about our life together, and I want that too, but you know how hard I've worked for this. I am the first in our family to even go to university, and I know you had a lot to do with me being able to continue. That is why you have to understand my decision, baby."

He rolled his eyes and thought, *Oh, such reasoning. How did the Mexicans lose California? Ah, they didn't have Teresa bargaining for them. If not for her brain, her beauty would have persuaded Kearny to turn his men around and head back to Texas.*

"I think you should have gone into political science rather than archaeology."

"Ah, baby, you understand me," seductively swooned Teresa as she did when Jeff gave in to her charms.

"When do you leave?"

"The university is picking my stuff up at 9 a.m. tomorrow and I leave at 2:45 p.m." Holding his hand, Teresa whispered into his ear. Her breath was warm. "So we have all night, baby."

Teresa cleared the bed of her suitcase, and said, "Come, baby, lie beside me."

Jeff kicked off his shoes and slid beside her. She removed her tee. Her nipples stood erect on her adolescent-size breasts. Jeff turned down the waistband of her terry cloth shorts revealing her nakedness. She was so beautiful. Her toned, olive skin complexion glistened from her struggling with packing. Her sweat was so sweet to his taste. She nuzzled into his neck as he caressed her body, searching for that spot that sent her wild with passion. He lightly touched her and she whimpered with delight, her body stiffened with anticipation and her toes mingled with his. She raised her foot dragging it against his leg as she waited for that soft touch. He obliged, teasing with sensitivity, his hand upon her sweetness, his fingers dancing with her passion. She withered with his touch and let out a long, "Siiiiiii."

They played long into the night, arousing each other with their kisses and dalliance of body parts. Finally, just before midnight, they collapsed in each other's arms, exhausted. Teresa rolled to her side, and rested her hand on Jeff's chest, replaying their wonderful night in her mind. Jeff, with one hand holding hers and the other behind his head, looked up at the ceiling and asked, "Where do you think I can get my answering machine fixed?"

"Jeffery!"

Early Morning Stir

The residents of north-side Beverly Hills had barely stirred by the time George and Carl pulled up to Angela's luxury condo in his new Audi A8. George's dark blue pin-striped suit contrasted with an air of influence against the sleek light-grey leather interior—a fusion of many business dealings and fundraisers. He was a man of style and dedication to what he believed in and what he offered to his diverse clientele.

Angela had adopted his sophisticated mantra into her businesses and personal life. She had transformed a scared young girl into a multi-million dollar enterprise. She was the money behind her girlfriend's very successful art gallery located on Rodeo Drive. She was also a proud clothier-designer and President-CEO of an up-and-coming label, AD Fashions. She had created a desirable and much-in-demand interior design studio, Fournier Designs during her early twenties, which she ultimately sold to finance her clothing line. Although Angela and George had remained best friends, business partners in some dealings, and visible companions at special events, their private life had been just that—private. He had never asked for anything from Angela and maintained being a perfect gentleman. He was only the third man that she had truly loved in her life.

His eloquent Italian-made shoes soothed the cold concrete steps as he ascended toward the carved oak door, and brushed past the dracaena, which was still covered in droplets of morning dew. Entering the code, the door clicked open revealing the marble entryway. Approaching the elevator, he pushed the ivory button proudly displayed by the polished brass backing plate. The elevator door opened and he stepped inside. It smelt of lavender. Arriving, he stepped out and walked over to one of the two condos on that floor. He pressed Angela's doorbell of apartment 401.

~

Just across town, at a familiar brownstone—

"Jesus! What's that?"

"The alarm, Jeff. I got to get ready."

"What time is it?"

"Six."

Jeff grunted, "Six? Like before the sun comes up, six?"

"Come on, sleepy head. I'll get the coffee," whispered Teresa after she partially uncovered his pillow from his ear.

Teresa, in her nakedness, walked past the parted curtains, down the hall, and disappeared into the kitchen...

~

"It's open, George..." said Angela from her dressing room. He stepped inside. "...I'll be just a minute."

"Not a problem, sweetheart. We have time." George sauntered over to the piano. On top was a dancing ballerina. He turned the knob.

From her bedroom, Angela said, "Thank you, George. I just love it. Where did you get it?"

"France."

"When did you go to France?"

"When you were in New York. I had to finalize some paperwork."

Angela ambled out from her dressing room wearing a chic business suit, while putting in the last earring. "You still haven't taken me to France like you promised." She softly placed a kiss on George's cheek. "Good morning..."

George had not aged at all. His silver-grey hair complimented his distinguished appearance.

"You look ravishing as always."

"I feel like a hag," she said jokingly. "We should have made this appointment later in the morning."

"Steinburg has a flight at noon. Only time. You will feel better after breakfast."

The lights dimmed in Angela's apartment as they took leave. Across the blonde-oak floor to a slightly opened window, the breeze directed the sheer curtains to one side. Looking closely through the open window, perched on the fifth floor on the opposite side of the street, a scope spotted George and Angela coming out of her apartment building. Carl, who was standing by the car, opened the rear door for them. He rounded the front of the Audi, stepped in, and they drove off. The scope disappeared and the curtain slowly closed.

Breakfast with Steinburg

The eight-foot-tall French doors were opened to a sunny terrace where Justice Gerald Steinburg was sipping on coffee. Angela and George were escorted through the maze to his table. Upon seeing Angela, he put down his cup, stood, and graciously welcomed them.

"Good morning, you two. It's a glorious day today and even better now that our sunshine appears. Please, sit beside me."

"Judge, you are making me blush," said Angela kissing him on the cheek.

"Welcome, George. Please sit."

"Good morning, Jerry."

"Sorry about the early morning, but I have to be in Washington this afternoon. Do you have what I need George?"

"Yes, I do."

"Good. Let me see."

George handed the Judge an envelope. He opened it and pulled out a French passport. He looked at it carefully. The judge looked at Angela and then back to the passport. He then said, "I've already had my staff verify signatures and legitimize the letters from the French consulate. I believe this is what you require."

The Judge handed Angela a U.S. passport and a French passport.

"My dear, you are official," happily announced the judge.

"What? I don't understand."

Angela looked at the Judge and then back to George.

"What is this?" Angela was even more confused when she opened them and saw her picture, officially stamped as a citizen of France and the other, a citizen of the United States.

"Believe me, lovely Angela, George has a lot of explaining to do, if this is the first that you have heard of this. But it is official. No monkey business. I would not be part of anything like that. I would say at this time... 'Congratulations to you!' Sorry there is no band, but I do need you to cross your heart and raise your hand and pledge that everything in these documents is true."

The Judge affirmed Angela's true identity right there on the spot, at this beautiful restaurant, on this glorious day.

Goodbye Teresa

The neighborhood was alive. Jeff had Teresa's belongings staged at the curb, waiting for the university's van. They faced each other, foreheads touching, and holding hands.

"No changing your mind?"

"Jeff, that's not fair."

"Yeah, I know."

Rounding the corner, a white van with a university seal on the door pulled up to where the two were standing. The driver got out and opened the back doors for the luggage and then slid the side passenger door open.

Jeff looked at Teresa with a solemn face, "Well, I guess this is it. This is goodbye."

Teresa, with tears in her eyes, and still holding onto Jeff's hands, said, "Jeff... I want you to know... I will miss you." She then threw her arms around him. "I love you even more for letting me go."

Jeff understood all too well what she meant.

"You better get going. The driver's waiting. You're sure you don't want me to take you to the airport?"

"I wouldn't trust myself to get on the plane. It's better here... in front of our home. Our last stand together. I promise I'll write..."

"Go... get out of here, crazy. You got some rotten teeth to find."

Teresa smiled at his comment and even now, longed for his stupid jokes that always made her laugh. She stepped up into the van and sat down. After sliding the door shut, Jeff watched as the van drove down the street and then turned left at the corner disappearing from his sight.

Head down, he quietly went back to his apartment. The jasmine plant was still sitting on the floor and unopened mail lay beside his dated answering machine. His car keys, with the Pontiac Indian face, stared up at him. He brushed the tears from his eyes and headed down the empty hallway to the bathroom. It had never been so quiet. Teresa was always talking about something. Sometimes in Spanish, sometimes just humming, always there, always comforting. The silence...

Ravel's Sapphire Dress

The Judge had to excuse himself and left George and Angela at the restaurant. She leaned over the table and spoke softly as she questioned George of what had just transpired.

"I don't understand this, George?" said Angela, more than curious as she held onto two passports.

"Well, you wanted to go to France," he said with a passing chuckle. He looked at her with a more serious face, "It is a long story. I'll explain everything later. I've got another meeting at the office. Where are you going from here?"

"I want to go Ravel's to see what he has."

"Why would you go there when you can design your own? Yours are much more provocative, in a somewhat sensible way, than anything you can buy."

"Thank you. Maybe true, but it is nice to spread the wealth around. Perhaps, it will give a new designer a chance at breaking into the biz. It's like a collaboration and respect between designers, you understand?"

"Yes I do. But your designs are sooo... delicious, shall I say."

"Oh, George, you have always been a fan and I truly adore you for that."

"Thank you. Are you ready? I can have Carl drop me off at the office and then he can take you where you want to go. Where's Joseph, by the way? How come he is not chauffeuring you around?"

"He's doing something with the Mercedes. He asked me if I would be okay without him today, since we were getting together."

"He has always been devoted to you. You touched something in that ice heart of his. He would die before he would let anyone harm you. You know that, don't you?"

She nudged closer to George and in a whisper she said, "Ever since the conviction of you know who, he has changed. He is very sweet in a rugged, 'don't fuck with me' kind of way." Angela laughed.

"Maybe so, I know Carl had something to do with that, so you can thank him as well. Not just my doing. Carl has a history with him that I don't know about. Shall we?"

George side-stepped another truth—they were adding up. The two friends took leave and joined up with Carl. He dropped George off at his office and then turned to Angela.

"Where to, Miss Angela?"

"Ravel's, please. I want to see what he has for Christiansen's opening at the gallery."

Carl had Angela at Ravel's Shoppe within twenty minutes. She asked him to come in with her so she could get a man's perspective on an outfit if she found one. He pulled up front in the 'Valet Only' spot. He opened the door for Angela and closed it with a click of the lock. The valet nodded without saying a word and ran to the street side to help another customer. Putting her arm into Carl's, they walked inside the popular shop. It had been a long time since he had a beautiful woman on his arm.

As they walked in, Ravel, who had been checking a stock sheet, looked up and saw Angela.

"LaLa, my darling. How are you? You look marvie." He looked at Carl, "And how are you, sir?" he said in a lowered voice.

Carl nodded.

Ravel, looking at Angela, could only guess. Clapping his hands, he said, "I know... I know, Christiansen's opening. It's all over town."

"Why, yes. You are so intuitive, Ravel."

"No, no... It's just... everybody has been coming in here lately," he said slightly boasting. "It's been like a beehive with everyone who is anyone buzzing around."

Carl just stood there, listening.

"Well... Do you have anything left for me?"

"Ya know, Miss E. said you might be by, so I held onto one just for you."

Ravel put his arm into Angela's and led her to another room.

"LaLa... I saw this dress and immediately thought of you. I found it in a small out-of-the-way studio in..."

"Paris?" interrupted Angela.

"North Hollywood. Sorry, hon. But... this cut... this color... I guarantee you, you will bring the curtains down."

"Okay, where is it?"

Ravel went behind a curtain and brought out this slinky Sapphire dress, with a unique cherub pinned to its shoulder. Angela gasped. She recognized her old friend.

"Who did you say designed this?" Angela's tone was more than troubling to Ravel and as it was expressed, Ravel was not prepared.

An Invitation Sealed in Wax

Jeff had a horrible first weekend without his lover, Teresa. He decided to take a week off and just hang out at the beach. Having lived in Redondo Beach on Calle Miramar years ago, he knew the area and decided on Manhattan as a soul-searching resting spot. They always had good volleyball and he could also pedal his bike almost the whole way up the coast to Santa Monica. A little detour around Marina del Rey would land him in the middle of the craziness of Venice. Too much for him right now, but the beach and the sun would do him good—sort of returning to his roots. Actually, he was living down there when he joined the force. Amazing how time flew by.

And it did at the beach as well. Not wanting to fight the weekend crowd, he left on Thursday night for home. Settling in, he cracked a beer and ordered pizza delivery. Sitting, shuffling through his mail, he had forgotten about seeing the fancy envelope, but this time, it caught his attention. The envelope was sealed with wax. *Cool,* he thought. It excited his imagination.

The envelope, inlaid with gold-leaf inscription read: E. Cortez & Associates Gallery, Inc. *They all sound so exotic.*

Carefully, he opened it. Pulling out the engraved invitation, he couldn't believe what he read. This gallery was hosting an art opening for a long-time friend, David Christensen. *Too much*, he thought. "Wow, that is so cool for David," he said out loud.

He put it down. Next—bills, insurance for his car, and a Visa bill. The rest were advertisements for smart phones, tablets, high-speed this and that—junk. He took another sip of beer and picked up the invitation again.

"Shit... old Dave. It would be good to see him."

. . .

The next morning, Jeff went to work. He barely squeezed in before the elevator door closed on him. Adjusting his tie, he watched the numbers flicker by. Everything was speedy he thought. Eighteen floors in twelve seconds, smartphones that woke you up, took your picture, and sent emails. Too fast! The door opened and he stepped out and turned to his right, where an arched security gate scanned everybody going through. Throwing down his papers, car keys, and spare change into a dishpan, he walked through and thought, *So high tech, they still use a plastic dishpan.* He chuckled, the first time in a week and a half.

Beyond the gate was a set of heavy glass doors. He saw the receptionist sitting busily talking on her earphone while shuffling papers for other agents. He pushed his way in using his butt to open the door.

"Good morning, Mr. Malardo. Did you have a nice time off?" she said casually after admiring his butt pressing against the glass door.

"Ah, good morning, Adriane. No, not really."

"It looks like you got some color. At the beach?" asked Adriane respectfully but what she actually thought was, *If he was only free, I would be on him in a heartbeat.*

Jeff just smiled.

"Here's your mail." She returned to typing and as Jeff passed by, she raised her eyes and watched him walk down to the main office. Gritting her teeth, she muttered under her breath, "God, he is so handsome..."

Jeff walked into the main office where computer terminals were singing, binders with photos and information of missing people were flopped open and more coffee cups than a Starbucks convention lined the room dividers. *Yes, I'm home. Who could not love this?*

Jackson "Goody" Thoroughgood, a 6'-2", 260 pounds of solid muscle, senior investigator and one of Jeff's closest counterparts and friend, sauntered over to him with a steaming coffee. Jeff plopped his butt into a swivel chair.

"Heads up, buddy, it's hot. For a week off, you still look like shit."

"Thanks for the reassuring vote of confidence. She kicked my ass. I thought she was the one, you know... marry, raise crazy ass kids. Did you say anything to Adriane?"

"No man, no one. It's your business. Why?"

"I could swear she seemed nicer to me than usual." Jeff blew on the hot coffee and took a slight sip.

"Maybe you are over sensitive, right now. It all takes time. You guys had been together for a long time," said Goody.

"You have talked... Georgette? I know you. Those are not your words, my friend," said Jeff, catching Goody in an awkward position.

"Come on buddy. She pressured me. She could tell I was worried about you. She jumped all over me until I gave you up," he said apologizing as buddies do, blaming their wives. "You know she loves you, man... and Teresa, too. She told me to be sensitive... if I knew what that was. She was hard on me, man."

"Okay. Okay. I got it."

"Good. Now let's get down to business." Goody changed from his sympathetic tone to his usual military-ish manner.

"She's hot though."

"Who?" Jeff asked as he braved another hot sip of coffee.

"Adriane."

"Goody? Where is that nice sensitive guy?"

"Just sayin'..." he said as he raised his hands up careful not to spill any of his coffee.

"I got an invitation to a gallery this Saturday night. It's hosting a show for an old friend."

"You going?" Goody asked, sipping his coffee before he spilt it.

"Not sure."

Just then, Adriane buzzed, "*Jeff you have a call from someone saying he is an old friend. A Dave Christiansen.*"

"Thanks, Adriane. Patch him through, please." Jeff hit the white flashing button for the outside line.

"Hello. David."

"Jeff, old buddy. How the hell are you?"

"I should ask the same."

"Get my invitation to my show?"

"Yes, looked at it last night."

"Am I to assume you are coming? It's going to be fabulous. I have been promised a good showing of very selective art enthusiasts who have lots of money. It will be a blast. My first time back to L.A. since, forever."

"Sounds great. Wouldn't miss it," said Jeff, not really wanting to socialize with a bunch of black jacket men and silver hair ladies.

"It's black tie. Got a tux?" asked David, knowing his buddy used to live in flip-flops.

"Of course I have a tux, man. This is L.A."

"Fabulous, Jeff. Can't wait to see you. Ciao, buddy. See you tomorrow night." David hung up.

"You own a Tux?" asked Goody, curiously.

"No. Know of a rental place around here?"

Goody laughed at him.

"You and Georgette want to come?" Jeff asked.

"You couldn't pay me to get into a monkey suit. Don't tell Georgette; she'll have my balls," said Goody, meaning it.

Jeff crossed his heart.

"Why don't you ask Adriane?" digged Goody.

"Will you get off it, for fuck's sake? Don't you have something to do?" said Jeff trying to sound annoyed at his best friend. Goody, with a big grin, patted Jeff on the back and with coffee in hand headed toward his office.

Jeff annoyed with his friend's pestering picked up the phone and dialed Adriane. "Adriane, can you find me a tux rental near my house?"

"Sure, Jeff. Taking Teresa someplace special?"

"Just the tux place, please, if you don't mind." Slightly irritated by his buddy, Goody, Jeff's tone was a little harsh.

"Yes, sir, Mr. Malardo."

Before Jeff could barely open a folder, Adriane buzzed him.

"Yes."

"South Lake Ave."

And before he could thank her, the line went dead.

Is this woman on speed? How did she do that so fast? I really need to be nicer to her. Goody is right. She is hot, she's nice, and maybe when I'm more attentive. God, Jeff, get it together.

Jeff picked the top folder from his pile and opened it. He dialed a phone number. A man's voice answered.

"We have him, Mr. Jacobs," said Jeff. "No. He is fine. At an ashram. No, not hash... It's a religious cult. I have a Marshall escorting him home. You should see them tomorrow. No, my secretary will send the bill. You are very welcome. Give the Mrs. my best, sir. You are quite welcome, sir. I know it was trying for you both. All right, Mr. Jacobs, take special care with him. He needs some loving. Will do, sir, goodbye."

Jeff threw his arms up around his head and leaned back in his chair. He felt empowered. This was the best part of his job, a 'positive release' as they called them. This was not always the case and on those dark days—the L.A. sun wasn't bright enough. From beside him and across the hall, a very excited Goody screamed out, "YES!" Jeff knew he just solved a case too. *It's these mornings that make my whole day.*

A smile broadened on Jeff's face. He had seven more cases in front of him, but now, he could attack them in a better frame of mind. He decided he owed Adriane an apology. Picking up the phone, he pressed the private intercom button. She answered immediately.

"Adriane, I want to apologize for my abrupt and rude behavior earlier…"

"I'm sorry for hanging up on you. Not very professional."

"Still friends?" asked Jeff.

"Yes, Jeff. Still friends," Adriane said warmly.

Angela's Misgivings

Angela purchased the dress from Ravel but also got the address of the shop from where this creation was supposedly conceived. Carl knew she was upset but not why. The dress was beautiful and she would look stunning in it, he thought. Angela was determined to find out what was going on. She knew of two other dresses like this one. One worn by that woman who seduced her—Sophia was her name—and the copy that she made. Who knew where her Sapphire friend ended up after she split from Anthony; and now this one, popping up fifteen-plus years later. *No, this is no coincidence*, she thought. She couldn't expect Carl to recognize it; especially since she did not try it on. But she knew something was up. *Someone is trying to get to me… But who? And why?*

She had Carl circle the block before she asked him to pull over, a tactic George had used on many occasions.

"Miss Angela, what's going on?" asked Carl. "You look like you have seen a ghost from the time we left Ravel's."

"Do you remember this dress?" she said, lifting it up in her fist.

"Ah, pretty color, but I can't say I do. You wear so many beautiful dresses, ma'am."

"Around fifteen years ago, the first time we met at George's penthouse, I wore a dress just like this that I copied from one other," she explained, but it wasn't registering with Carl.

"This one is exact! Right down to the cherub on the shoulder," she stated. "To me, this is my friend, my Sapphire, my escape...my Tabula Rasa."

"Do you still have yours? Is this a copyright issue or something?" asked Carl, trying desperately to understand.

"I have no idea where the one I made is... she is lost, and I have no idea where the woman is that wore the original."

"Could that one be the original?" Carl asked naively.

"Carl, this is new. It has never been worn."

"Hmmm... I think we need to pay this shopkeeper a visit," said Carl. Missing pieces and questions that need to be asked—yes! He loved this type of work. It brought back his youth but without the hazard of dying. He had been through enough of those black-op nights.

Carl pulled up to 'Gina's Alterations'. Exiting the car, Angela left the imposter behind on purpose, neatly folded on the back seat. The little bell dinged as Carl opened the door for Angela, to a small but customary-looking alteration shop. Bolts of material, spools of thread in cabinets, plus several racks of plastic-draped dresses with price tags hanging from them, and a pretty, mid-thirties redhead wearing half glasses sitting on a stool, was busy sewing with a needle and thread.

"Good morning," she invited with a beautiful smile as she laid down her work and eased off of the stool. "May I help you?"

"Hello... Good morning. I just came from a boutique where I saw the most beautiful Sapphire dress and I was wondering if you made it and if I could possibly get it in a crimson shade?" asked Angela innocently.

Carl was proud of her, indirect, almost politician style.

"Yes, the one I put on consignment with Ravel. It was special order but no one came to pick it up," said the shopkeeper.

"What do you mean special order?"

"Years ago when I was struggling to open my own dress shop, I used to... let's say... 'model' as well. And sometimes I would create my own dresses with the hope someone would see them and magically ask me to head their design studio. I know childish idea... so here I am. Well, someone must have seen my design and remembered it, down to the 'T'. I should say, down to the cherub. They put $500 dollars down on the $3000 dollars I was going to charge for that re-creation, but then they never picked it up. This is L.A. Who knows what happened," shared the shopkeeper openly—smiling.

"Cherub? Yes, right. Are you Gina?" asked Angela.

"Yes, I am," she said politely, offering her hand to Angela.

"And you are?"

"Angela," she said, watching for a reaction, but Gina didn't seem to recognize her. *Why should Gina recognize me? That tryst at that restaurant was many years ago.* Angela had grown up from a scared young girl into a very prosperous and respected member of the community.

"Please forgive me for my 'cloak and dagger' tactics, but here is my card," offered Angela.

"AD Fashions!?" she said out loud, and then, it dawned on her. Her face flushed. "Oh my, you are THAT Angela! I am so honored to have you in my shop! I just don't know what to say now."

"Perhaps it is I that has something to say to you," shyly said Angela.

"Yes?" Gina waited for Angela's confession—instead.

"I love your designs and your technique. I don't want to offend you, but would you consider working with some of my designers and seamstresses? You could keep your own shop, but maybe spend a few hours a week with my team? I would pay you handsomely for your talent," tempted Angela.

"I... I... I'm speechless!" Gina stood there with a glow about her.

"Please say YES! You are so talented. We would complement each other," further taunted Angela.

Gina clasped her hands together and nodded her head up and down like a 'doggie' sitting on a rear-window package tray. In her excitement, she was able to blurt out, "When?"

"Monday, if that is good with your schedule. I want you to meet my staff. I will set everything up. I'll have my driver come and pick you up here, say around 9:30?"

"Okay then..." Gina leaned forward, reached out and hugged Angela. "You are a dream come true! I just can't believe it after all these years," said Gina.

"Neither can I, Gina. It will be great to mingle our minds. Your perfume... it has a very memorable scent." It was an intoxicating smell that had lingered in Angela's mind, throughout all of these years.

"Oh... thank you. I have been wearing this brand for years. I think I've bought the last bottle in the world. Some perfumes just accent who you are, don't you think?"

"I think you are absolutely right, Gina. It works very well on you. Oh, by the way... I know it is short notice but we are having an opening for an up-and-coming artist from New York at our gallery, E. Cortez, this Saturday night. If you would like, I will put your name on the guest list?"

"That's very nice of you. Unfortunately, I have been swamped and I'm a little behind, but I will try. It would be nice to do something fun for a change," confided Gina, looking into Angela's eyes. "Lately, my Saturday night date has been a martini and a movie in my apartment... Boring, right?" She shrugged her shoulders and rolled her eyes.

"Well, it would be nice to see you there if you can make it." Angela reached out and softly squeezed Gina's hand. She turned to the door.

Carl nodded goodbye and the two took leave. Just as the doorbell finished its charming *ding-a-ling*, Gina's shop phone rang.

"Hello," she answered politely. "You are kidding... For how much?" Gina's eyes widened and she repeated the caller's words, "$6000 dollars!?" Gina let out a scream, "YES!" She couldn't believe it, two miracles in one day.

Carl held the car door open for Angela. She paused and looked at him straight in the eyes. She knew he wanted to ask her something. Angela just smiled at him and stepped inside. Approaching a freeway, Carl looked at Angela through the rearview mirror and without saying a word to Angela, she calmly remarked, "Her nails. She has worked her nails to the quick." Angela looked out the tinted side window.

Carl smiled proudly as he knew there was some history between the two, even if Gina didn't remember. *Angela is such a class act*, he thought, lovingly.

Mysterious Glare

Saturday morning had Angela busy on the phone. Sitting on her couch with legs draped along the length of it with her cell phone in one hand and scribbling notes into her planner with her other, she had a quick conversation with the caterers going over the final details for that evening's event. Finishing that conversation, she checked it off in her planner. Then a short exchange with her secretary regarding Monday morning's meeting—check. And last, on a more personal note, she dialed her best friend and business partner, Eileen.

"I am positive, Eileen. There could be no mistake. Her perfume lingered on me after she gave me a hug. I felt like I was seventeen again. She said she used to, in her words, "Let's say... model". Do you think that whole night was a set up? But for what gain? No, nothing... just this dress. No, I didn't ask her but we are getting together at my office on Monday. I would feel more comfortable approaching that subject in private. I invited her to the opening tonight. She said 'maybe'; she was swamped with work. Oh, her poor nails. They used to be so beautiful. Yes, I'm going to wear that dress tonight. Let's see if anyone comes out of the woodwork. No, I don't know what her reaction will be if she sees me in it and then remembers our soiree. Play it by ear, I guess. Okay, hon, George has a brief meeting and then... hey, I just had a thought, do you want us to pick you up and then go for a quick bite at Sammy's before the chaos? Okay, then I will send Joseph over in my car. I don't know. It's a guy thing... something about safety issues. Okay, love, see you later, about 6. Joseph at 5:30. Okay, ciao."

Eileen had always been supportive of everything Angela had done. She even volunteered George to impersonate a lawyer, and her as a social worker in order to remove Angela's mother from that house and that jerk of a stepfather, Stephen. Angela's mother was now under constant care in a private nursing home. There were so many things Angela just couldn't thank Eileen enough for.

Still sitting on her couch with phone in hand, she dialed her friend and chauffeur. "Joseph, it's me. Can you pick Eileen up at her house at 5:30 tonight, please? If you want, Joseph, you are my family... It's black tie. Hmm, I would say no on that one. I like your single-button jacket; it has a sexy cut to it. The other one makes you look like a tree. Okay, I promise. I will not try to set you up with Delores again. She's sweet though. Okay... Okay. Love you, too."

Joseph really needs to get laid. Sometimes he is so uptight. I wonder what the safety issues are with my Mercedes; it's brand new. I didn't get any recall notice. Maybe he said something to Carl. Hmm, those two are a pair. Neither will open up about their past but I know they share something. Who else do I need to call? Her thoughts were wandering as she flipped the pages of her planner.

. . .

By noon, the L.A. temperature had reached 97 degrees. This kind of heat made people do weird things, somewhat like how a full moon brought out the wackos. Heat waves generated off the asphalt appeared to melt tires in a wispy ripple. The freeway traffic crawled along. Road-rage vented through open doors and rolled-down windows. Los Angeles waited patiently, always changing, never stagnant, moving with inertia as its citizens aligned with the stars and stars were made with the stroke of a pen while others signed their death warrants.

George and Carl picked Angela up at 4 p.m. at her apartment. She was wearing a cute light-weight sun dress so as not to leave any elastic marks on her body before she slipped into Gina's Sapphire dress. Carl placed it carefully in the Audi's trunk, laying it flat. Upon closing the trunk, he spotted a reflection—a glare to be precise, in the rear window from across the street. His stride remained consistent as he opened his door and maneuvered inside. He adjusted his rear-view mirror and his outside mirror before they left the curb. George caught Carl's intent, but Angela was unaware. She continued her conversation with someone on the phone about their upcoming event. With a huff, she hung up.

"The search lights are stuck in traffic," she said. "They promise they will be there by 7:30 and then a half hour to set up and charge the lights."

"The show doesn't open until 8:30," said George, figuring that should be enough time. "Besides, it will still be light out."

"Not the point... People expect to see them in the mix of things. It's part of the hype," explained Angela.

Carl readjusted his interior mirror and flashed a quaint smile. George acknowledged his gesture and said, "Any tags?"

"Not apparent," informed Carl. He knew what George was going to ask next, "Glass... Hi-tech."

"Let's keep an eye out," calmly stated George.

"Yes, sir."

"What are you two talking about? You make no sense."

"Nothing, my dear..."

Angela, cutting George off, said, "Joseph was talking about glass as well."

George looked at Angela trying to imagine her calmness, if only she knew. Concerned, George asked, "What type of glass?"

"I don't know... Safety glass for the Mercedes, I think. No, sorry, he said safety issues. My car is brand new. Why is he concerned about safety issues? I think this heat is making everyone overreact. L.A. does have a history with summer drama," said Angela, confident nothing was wrong with her car.

"If you are concerned, ma'am, I could speak with Joseph," offered Carl.

"Please... He seems very tense..." Angela started to laugh, "...that is, if you can tell, more than usual. He even asked if he could attend the event tonight but made me promise, not once, but twice that I would not try to set him up with Delores. I think you boys need to get laid. I can give you a couple of phone numbers of some very nice ladies if you want."

"Thank you ma'am. Maybe later," shyly responded Carl.

George had a big grin on his face.

"What?" she asked looking at George, and then she gave him a dig in the side. "You too."

"Next street, Mr. Stanza," announced Carl, very seriously.

The street was quiet as their Audi pulled up to the front of a once-busy warehouse. Fences had been half ripped down, empty barrels had leaked out whatever was inside years past, and newspapers fluttered in the heat of the day. Not an enticing venue to be parked outside of.

"Angela, wait inside and lock the doors. Carl and I will only be a few minutes. You know where the gun is."

"I've been in neighborhoods like this before, as you well know. I will be fine," she said rather stubbornly.

George stepped out onto the stained concrete. Carl slipped on a white fedora and together they walked to the small walk-in office door. They knocked—nothing. They banged harder. Hearing footsteps, the door finally opened to a dimly-lit hallway strewn with old bills of lading, ripped file folders, and blank perforated printer paper. They followed the figure in front of them through another door into the large warehouse space that was filled with bales of unusable newsprint. On the outside of a wire-gaged employees' lunchroom, stood Chico Valdez, looking much older than the years indicated. His infamous fedora sat lonely on top of an abandoned desk next to him. His brother Enrico walked to his side.

As George and Carl approached the two, Carl slipped off his hat and laid it next to Chico's fedora.

"Meester Stark. How ya doin? Eis been a long time, no? How can we help ya?" inquired Chico.

His English was getting better but the white suits and black t-shirts just didn't cut it in L.A. Maybe Miami, thought George.

"I didn't come here to socialize, Chico. We understand that you are trying to use your muscle to expand your territory into Centavos' area. You know the rules. Everything has been going smoothly. Why upset the organization?"

"Meester Stark, we don't wanna make for you any trouble... but the neighborhood es changin'. They are rippin' down our territory and doin' redevelopment, causin' our population to re-locate. We jus' gotta move with them."

"So what do you want, Chico?"

"Maybe the organization can giva us a new line into Centavos. Besides, hesa wimp. A baca bone like a jello fish. Wez can do better. You knows that, Meester Stark."

"We will need a sit down with everyone..."

"Excusa me, Meester Stark, but we done real good for you. No problema por anos but eis time we expand. We are no ants to step on," said Chico.

"No movement into Centavos' turf. If you want war and more territory, go after the Terranados. They'll give you a run for your money, but leave the Centavos alone. Got it! Otherwise, you will be cut off and we will be dividing up your territory."

"If you cutz us off, wez will have no food to feed my people. Wez then gonna have ta shop at another groceteria."

"The food is no problem. The territory is! It remains."

"Ok, Meester Stark. We do like you say. The Terranados," agreed Chico. Cupping his hands around his crotch, he flashed a big smile, and said, "Terranados nuts." He then laughed, showing off his gold-trimmed teeth.

"You are being smart, Chico."

"Ah... Ya right, Meester Stark. Friendly business. We hava shoppin' list and of course the monies for you mañana."

"No. Tuesday."

"That many days?" asked Chico.

"Yes, that many!" George turned to leave and Carl followed backing out cautiously after retrieving his hat from the desk.

Enrico leaned into Chico and whispered something. Chico remained smiling as Carl disappeared into the dimly-lit hallway.

"Listen, mi hermano... eis won't be long before we control every thin. Hesa gettin' old," threatened Enrico.

"Why chu think Stark thinks we dona no hesa real name?" contemplated Chico. "Hesa man gotta good taste in hats."

The rattle of the closing warehouse door overpowered George's footsteps as he approached the Audi. Angela was waiting patiently in the backseat. Carl quickly caught up. Holding his hat, he opened the car door and then placed the hat carefully on the seat beside him. Angela peered out looking at George's strained look. He stepped inside.

"Here's a drink," she offered. "Everything all right?"

"Yes. Sure. A little labor problem but nothing to worry about," insisted George.

As soon as Carl buckled in, he whisked them away from this devastated warehouse graveyard to the other side of town where the Hilltop Restaurant awaited their arrival.

George had been quiet for most of the drive. Concerned, Angela leaned next to him.

"George, is there anything wrong? You look tense."

"No, not really, Angela. Just a couple of little problems that need to be handled before they turn into big problems."

"At that warehouse?"

"Not for you to worry."

Angela, troubled by George's vagueness added, "George, We've been friends for a long time. We have certain business arrangements, and if one of our investments is in trouble, I want to know."

"Honest, Angela, this has nothing to do with any of our investments. It is one of mine that is getting to be more of a headache every day. But one I can't drop, just yet."

"Okay, George, I don't want you fretting over me. I'm a big girl now."

Pulling into the Hilltop's valet parking, Carl allowed the valet to assist Angela from the car. Before George exited, he nodded to Carl who spoke briefly with the Valet, who then permitted Carl to pull his car into a parking spot next to the front door. Sitting there, Carl picked up his cellphone, and as the patrons arrived, he scrutinized each guest thoroughly.

~

Joseph had dropped Eileen off at the gallery but had to excuse himself for a short time. He promised he would be back later. Eileen thought he looked handsome in his tux.

A Black Tie Event

Jeff approved his stylish look in the mirror, flipping from one side to the other, watching the flow of his tux jacket open and then buttoned. It had been a long time since he had worn a monkey suit. *Too bad it didn't come with a fedora*. The mirror reflected his distorted face as he tried to emulate long-time heroes who had been lost in the dust of speedy foreign cars with paddle shifters.

He was fine with his faded red Firebird. Sort of a Rockford look—except he had a Camaro. He admired Rockford's style and cunning maneuvers, even though he was only a TV character. He still had a kind of 'live and let live' attitude. Maybe even the earlier James Bond. *Yes that's it... smooth, sophisticated but deadly when provoked*.

On his bed lay the empty box of his new Android. Earlier, he had managed to program Goody's name, Allen Travers' name, and the main office phone numbers. In the limited book, it said he could use it for navigation, email, text, browse the web and the list went on, but no instructions; everything was online. He still couldn't bear to throw out his answering machine, not just yet. It had been a trusted friend—that is, until just recently.

He looked at the hands of his Timex and thought it would take at least an hour to get to Beverly Hills. Luckily, the heat of the day had passed, and he thought it would make for a nice drive with the top down, cruising to Christina Aguilera's bluesy mix. He gathered the gallery's invitation and headed out the door. Outside, he ran into his little buddy, Josh.

"Hey, dude. Wow! Who you impressing tonight?" mocked Josh.

How do these kids get so smart? Jeff wondered.

"No one, my little friend. I've been invited to a gala event," Jeff responded, waving the impressive invitation in the air, "...in Beverly Hills."

"Whoa, go gettem', Miiiister Ma-lar-do!" said Josh, sporting fingers in the air, pumping like a pair of guns.

"I'll do my best. You getting excited about your trip?"

"Yes, sir. Can't wait!"

Jeff rounded the front end of his car.

"See you tomorrow, my friend."

Josh remained seated on the concrete steps and waved goodbye.

Jeff turned the key and the engine fired right up. It purred with a deep-throated growl. The man Jeff bought it from said his son had done some engine work, adding a Holly 4 barrel carb, an MSD ignition, and he had forsaken the power glide transmission for a 4-speed Hurst mounted on the floor. His son had been killed in Iraq and his only stipulation, if he sold it to Jeff, was that he had to leave the car *as is*.

Jeff shifted it into first and idled down the narrow street. Neighbors waved as he passed by and a few cat calls hollered out from the neighborhood pub's outside seating. He loved his neighborhood—interesting people and friendly. He and Teresa were lucky to find this place. He felt his buddy, Josh, was safe delivering papers as everyone had a watchful eye.

. . .

The traffic along the 210 out of Pasadena was fairly smooth, but when Jeff came close to the 101 South, it was backed up. He decided to take Laurel Canyon, although winding and slower, there was no way he was going to sit in that traffic. Enjoying the curves and the wind in his hair, he finally arrived at Sunset Boulevard, then down to Santa Monica. He saw the faint beams of two searchlights crisscrossing in the darkening sky.

Arriving at this extravaganza, he waited in line watching the frenzy as limos and expensive sports sedans dropped off their affluent cargo. On the steps, they mingled wearing their designer dresses, and their flashy jewelry shimmered from paparazzi's flashes. He wondered what he was doing there. Nothing of this appealed to him. The valet approached his car.

Excitedly, the valet voiced, "Wow, nice car, sir. A sixty...?"

"Sixty-seven," informed Jeff.

"A classic, sir. I'll make sure it gets a safe spot." The valet sat inside. "A four-gear!"

Jeff watched the valet as he gingerly idled the Firebird past Audis, Mercedes, and Jaguars like a child in a candy store who finally found that one special treat. Jeff smiled as he tapped the valet ticket in his hand.

The crowd was amazing; buzzing with excitement and the offering of half-hearted cheek kisses. He slipped between the glamorous to the opened doors of E. Cortez & Associates. A pretty attendant, elevated with high heels, wearing only a tux vest with a white collar and cuffs, and skin-tight satin shorts, checked his name off the invitation list.

"Welcome, sir," she added with a pretty smile and handed him a program. "I hope you enjoy the show."

"Thank you," he said, trying not to gaze too long at her bulging breasts.

Over to one side, he spotted the sign: BAR. He made his way through the crowd, excusing himself as bodies pressed together. There were three bartenders. The two male bartenders had long black pants, cuffs, and bowler hats while the female was wearing the same outfit as the girl at the entrance.

"Can I help you, sir?" asked one of the gentlemen.

"Martini please. Two olives, straight up," announced Jeff with the authority of one of his debonair characters.

"Vodka or gin?"

"Grey Goose!" said Jeff as if there were no other.

"Yes, sir. Grey Goose, straight up, two olives," repeated the bartender as he handed Jeff his drink.

"Thank you." Jeff turned and took a sip.

Where to begin... He looked around at all of the made-up faces and as he did, out of the corner of his eye, he spotted Goody and Georgette. She looked fabulous in this clinging silver something or other that accented her deep brown skin and incredible body. She had a big smile returning Jeff's gaze. Goody, however, didn't share that overwhelming joyous look. Jeff pardoned himself as he snaked through the crowd.

"Jeff... Jeff. Wow, babe, you look great in your tux," complimented Georgette.

"And you look..."

Goody cut him off.

"Don't be staring at my wife," he grunted.

"...you look beautiful," said Jeff, finishing his adulation.

"We need to talk," said Goody, bending to whisper into Jeff's ear.

"Don't mind him, Jeff. Don't you think he looks handsome?" prodded Georgette.

"Absolutely, Georgette. But how did you hear about this event? I know grumpy here wouldn't have said anything."

"I overheard you talking on your phone. I called out but you didn't respond," informed Georgette.

"Ahhh... When I was programming Goody's number into my new phone. Sorry, buddy, not my fault. You wanted me to get a new phone, remember that."

"...so I told this big beluga he better take advantage of this dress because pretty soon it won't fit," happily shared Georgette.

"Yeah, and my new Camaro is now going to be transformed into a bigger house," sternly interjected Goody.

"What are you saying? You are pregnant?"

"YES!" shared Georgette with a huge smile jumping up and down.

"I told you... Don't be looking at my wife," said Goody trying to remain the stern, insensitive guy.

Jeff wrapped his arms around Georgette giving her a big, warm hug.

"I am so happy for you! Come here big guy." Jeff gave Goody a big hug as well.

"You're going to have people talking... Stop that," said Goody, looking around the room.

"Too bad. My best friends are going to have a baby. I am so excited for you."

As he pushed through the unaware crowd, David Christiansen spotted his old friend, immersed, in what David thought, was a rousing conversation.

"Jeff!" he shouted out over the noise of the crowd.

Jeff turned around upon recognizing his old friend's voice, "Hey, David!"

The two men embraced as old friends do, patting each other on the back.

"I told you that sort of thing is catchy around here," snorted Goody with a straight face.

"Hey, David, don't mind him. His bubbly exterior and over-the-top inner excitement are due to him finding out today that he's going to be a father."

Jeff introduced them to each other. The men shook hands and David gave Georgette a kiss on the cheek.

"Well, congratulations to you both. You must be very excited!" exclaimed David. "And look at this. Who knew L.A. would be so receptive to a New Yorker."

"It's your artwork. It is so sensual without being vulgar, foreboding but with sensitivity. It is amazing," said Georgette with an air of understanding.

Goody's eyebrow half raised listening to his wife.

"Thank you, Georgette. That is very kind and perceptive. Listen, I have to get back to Angela. She is going to introduce me. I just wanted to say hello before it gets more chaotic in here. Right now, no one knows who I am. I like it like that. It gives me a chance to eavesdrop," laughed David. "I will catch up with you later. Enjoy the spread."

One of the lovely ladies roaming the crowd with champagne stopped in front of Jeff, Georgette, and Goody. Jeff removed three champagnes from her tray. They clinked their glasses to the excitement of the night. Goody flashed a smile and a teardrop sprouted from the corner of his eye. The three formed a group hug. What a fabulous night.

As the sound of a handheld bell began to ring, the three friends nudged their way closer to the stage. Eileen Cortez had the microphone and was thanking everyone for attending. She elaborated on the fare, the open bar, and the courtesy of buying the art. She handed the microphone over to her partner, Angela Fournier. The crowd cheered with overwhelming excitement. She had to wait for them to stop, trying several times to calm the patrons down. Finally, they finished their accolades.

Jeff and his friends arrived at the edge of a semi-circle that had formed around her. Jeff looked up at her, and—as if a hammer had hit him on the head—Goody had to steady him. She was radiant beyond anyone he had ever met or seen. She spoke but he couldn't hear her words. He felt like when he was a child at Grumman's Theater, before they changed its name, and he had pushed his way in to get an autograph of Lauren Bacall. *He was mesmerized by Miss Bacall's stature and her smile as she looked down at him and asked his name.* Goody nudged him.

"Buddy, you all right?"

"Uh… yes. I think so."

"Jeff, you want to sit down?" asked Georgette.

"No, no. I am fine," he reassured his friends.

The crowd was laughing along with Angela. She was wearing the most incredible sapphire dress. If there were any less material, she could have been arrested. It melted with her movement—blue waves fondled her skin as her long blonde hair flowed with the air of a movie star. Jeff was mesmerized!

"...and now, my friends, let me introduce you to the star of tonight. His works are incredible... laced with sensitivity, allure, and provocativeness. Enjoy and let your imaginations lead to your checkbooks. Please welcome tonight's star, here he is: David Christiansen!"

The crowd cheered with elated jubilation to finally meet this artist that displayed such understanding of his subjects and their plight, with empathy and compassion. David blushed as he accepted their approval. He bowed, he waved, and he threw kisses.

"Thank you. Thank you," he said many times. "Thank you so very much. If you are tempting me to move to L.A., you could possibly be successful!" he shouted.

Angela elegantly grabbed his hand and with Eileen, they led him to the waiting masses. The decibels in the gallery seemed to rise by ten points as all gathered in their cliques to wait for their introduction.

Delightful delicacies and champagne were freely passed around by the attendants. The guests shuffled through the gallery, stopping at their favorite images, and then motioned to the staff of their intent to purchase. A red dot was placed by the name of each piece as the staffers were barely able to keep up with the demand. David, with Angela at his side, spotted Jeff and his friends. He whispered to her. They walked straight toward them as Jeff choked down an appetizer.

"Angela, this is one of my best long-time friends, Jeff Malardo."

Angela offered her hand to Jeff as he wiped his hand on his jacket from the sweating glass of champagne. She noticed.

"Ah... thank you... I mean, it is a pleasure, ma'am," stumbled Jeff, embarrassed.

"Don't mind him, Angela. I think he got hit in the head tonight," said Goody, extending his hand. "And my wife and future mother-to-be, Georgette," stated Goody proudly.

"It is such a pleasure to meet friends of David. Do you live in L.A.?" asked Angela, politely.

Jeff reached into his inside pocket and offered Angela his business card.

"Why thank you, but, where would you like me to put it... in this dress?" humorously implied Angela as she flowed her hands down her body.

Jeff realized, too late, what a fumbling fool he had been. They all laughed, that is, except Jeff who was still in a state of awe. Angela and David left the three for further introductions to some other patrons who were gathered around a pretty redhead wearing a very sultry dress. David turned around and mouthed to Jeff, "Hang around."

"Jeff, old buddy, you have made my night. If I had not seen you play such the fool, I would not have believed it," laughed Goody.

"Stop that..." insisted Georgette. Compassionately, she said, "I think Jeff has just met his fantasy."

Jeff watched as Angela mingled with her guests. The redhead turned and seemed to be delighted to see Angela. They embraced. Introductions were passed around and then Angela put her arm in Gina's. Together, they took David around the room. *She knows how to work it*, thought Jeff as he watched. She passed a man who looked like he stepped out of a Coppola movie. Rugged, a scar on his face and he was looking right at Jeff. *What's his deal?* he thought.

What Jeff failed to see was Joseph's reaction when Jeff reached into his jacket's inside pocket to get his business card for Angela. This man, Joseph, Angela's chauffeur and bodyguard, was in flight to her side and only stopped short of neutralizing Jeff, when he saw the business card produced.

Angela and Gina dropped David off with a benevolent patron. Arm in arm, they slowly walked the floor talking privately. Their perfumes' fragrances mingled inspiringly. They turned to face each other. Gina raised her hands to her mouth, partially stifling a gasp. Angela placed her arms around her in an endearing hug.

Jeff turned back to Goody and Georgette.

"Are you with us, buddy?" asked Goody.

"Hmm... What's that?"

"Do you want to go dancing?" asked Georgette.

"Oh..."

Goody snapped his fingers.

"Get over it, buddy. She is way out of your league."

"Goody, that is not nice. He's confused. You know..." rolling her eyes, she said, "...Teresa and all."

"Oh, yeah. Right, honey."

"Thanks, guys. David wants me to stick around. We haven't seen each other in a while. Lots to catch up on."

"Okay, baby... Give me some sugar. I'll take Mister Personality home," Georgette said sarcastically.

"What'd I say?"

"Hey, good night, buddy. You look good in a tux. Georgette needs to dress you more often," said Jeff with a smile.

Jeff watched his friends leave and as Goody stood even with the Godfather man, he noticed Goody was wider at the shoulders but the Godfather man had a couple of inches on him. Jeff imagined a Marciano versus Joe Louis match-up.

By midnight, most of the crowd had left, leaving Jeff sitting at the bar talking with a very pretty dark-haired attendant who had served Jeff and his friends four times. She had only carried on small talk as they were told to serve and not to engage in personal dialogue. She did, however, manage to slip her phone number under a napkin for Jeff. He responded by placing it into his jacket.

Jeff sensed that David, although very excited, was totally drained. But that blonde, Angela, was still going strong. *What stamina she must have... she undoubtedly works out.* He thought he needed to hit the gym the next morning himself. It had been over a week since he had gone, but with everything that was happening in his life, mainly Teresa leaving, he needed that break.

David wearily trudged over to Jeff.

"I am beat up. I have never talked so much, listened so much, and been propositioned so much in my life. Is it the air here in Los Angeles?" joked David.

"Probably..."

"There is an intimate after-party at Angela's friend's place. I hear it is awesome. Top two floors with unbelievable views. Are you interested?"

"What do you mean by intimate? Small or anything goes type of thing?" asked Jeff.

"Ahahah! You crack me up. You haven't changed a bit. I believe *small* was the indication."

"Who asked?"

"Angela mentioned that maybe my friend might like to join us," replied David.

"Did she say it with 'Let's see how he can embarrass himself some more', or a sincere, 'Please ask your friend to join us?'"

"What?"

"Sorry, champagne talk. I think I will pass," said Jeff, regretfully and a little embarrassed.

Walking towards Jeff and taking up more carpet than a 747 jet at the Bob Hope Airport, Gina flashed a big, beautiful smile. Extending her hand with beautifully sculpted nails, she said in a sultry voice, "You must be Jeff."

"Ah... yes. And you are?" responded Jeff, less clumsy.

"Gina," she replied with a smile. "Some of us have been cordially invited to join Mr. Stanza at his apartment. Would you be available to join us?"

Jeff said with devilish humor, "Am I the late show entertainment?"

Gina, not taking no for an answer or any excuses, placed her arm in his and together they walked over to where a delegation of the in-crowd were milling around.

"Angela did tell me of your card trick."

Jeff enjoyed the humor of it now and started to relax.

"I designed that dress she is wearing. Isn't she beautiful? She reminded me tonight of the first time I wore a dress similar to that one," shared Gina, openly.

"I bet you had the same intoxicating effect."

"So I am told."

The After Party

After the group discussed the driving arrangements, Jeff had the duty of escorting Gina to the after-party. She was given a special invitation with directions on the back. He warned her that his car was not on the same scale of luxury as most that had arrived. She laughed at him and said, "But I am with the most handsome." Jeff thought she might have a couple of years on him but not many. She was still very much a cougar.

David had gone with Angela and Eileen in her car with her driver, Mr. Godfather himself. The night was swirling with innuendos and one-liners. Jeff knew every tagline an old gumshoe had up his sleeve. Gina had tears running down her face listening and laughing to Jeff. He gave her his card and without looking, she placed it in her purse.

They arrived in old Hollywood style, with several cars waiting in line to drop off their fashionable patrons at Mr. Stanza's building. They, too, were greeted with the same respect. Tossing his keys to the valet, Jeff warned, light-heartily, "Easy on the clutch, she'll get away on you."

"Got it, sir."

The building had been expertly remodeled and looked like its days of glory. The brass knobs were highly polished, the marble floors almost squeaked they were so clean, and the wood-molding inlays cried South American import. The bellman waited as they entered the elevator. An inserted, special key bypassed the common floors transporting them directly to the penthouse. There was plenty of time to carry on a conversation—admittedly, a small conversation. Jeff loved the nuances. This was his era.

The elevator slowed and then the bellman opened the metal gate as the door slid open. They stood in the hallway staring at a massive wood-carved door. A man wearing black tails and white gloves stood out front. He gathered their invitation and ushered them into the mix. Stepping inside was another sensory manifestation. Beautiful people and some not so mingled in the luxury. White leather couches welcomed guests to sit and relax, artwork eyed their viewers with interest, and a wall of books cried out their verses. Gina excused herself as Jeff spun like a ballerina, taking everything in. A sculpture, with the appearance of polished marble, sat on a stand, turning as guests ran their hands over it. Jeff stepped up to it and placed both hands on its smooth roundness. Unaware of anyone watching him, a soft voice confided from behind.

"Feel her all around. Jack always told me to tell people to run their hands over her shapely ass and slowly reach around to feel her vulva," instructed Angela.

"Excuse me?" questioned Jeff, shyly.

"It is quite amazing... the sensation that is," remarked Angela, extending her hand. "Shall we try this again? I'm Angela."

Her voice was refreshing and encouraging.

"Jeff Malardo," he countered with assurance this time, meeting her hand. "You throw quite the party at the gallery. I haven't seen anything as glamourous as that since the Oscars."

"Oh, I don't believe it was that extravagant but it was a nice crowd," pleasantly replied Angela. Their hands were still locked.

"I feel a little awkward here not knowing anything about you or..." Jeff looked around, "...or the man, your husband perhaps that owns this place?"

"No husband, if you are inquiring?" teased Angela.

"Are you always so..."

"Forward? I can't answer that. I'll plead the fifth."

She laughed and tucked a wisp of hair behind her ear.

"Gina tells me you are quite the humorist," she said, finally letting go of Jeff's hand.

"I'm not sure I qualify for that title. I enjoy laughing with friends, not at them," replied Jeff in a more serious tone.

"Really, I could hear myself saying the exact same thing, Mr. Jeff."

Jeff looked past Angela's shoulder and saw Joseph starring back at him.

"Mr. Godfather, the guy over there burning a hole in my brain, he's your driver?"

"Ahahah! You are funny. His name is Joseph, and he looks after me shall we say."

Jeff shifted his weight to avoid unwanted stares.

"I bet not too many have the nerve to talk to you with that gorilla standing over you."

"But you seem to be doing just fine."

"Ohhhh..." Jeff rolled to the side with a childish grin. "I feel very fortunate to be able to, and still have my bones where they were when I walked in."

"You are funny and charming... and different," said Angela with a flirting smile.

An attendant interrupted their conversation as they still stood at the Jack Lambie sculpture. "Excuse me, drinks or hors d'oeuvre?"

"Nothing for me," said Angela.

"I'm good, thank you," added Jeff as he continued with his life's perception. "I'm pretty much me, 24/7. Not here to impress, just want some finer things in life."

"Like what? Big house, nice car, fancy jewelry?"

"Sure, any house would be nice, if I had someone to share it with. Maybe some little Jeffs and Jeffettes running around. Not into the fancy jewelry."

"You know, when a fellow mentions kids on their first date, it usually sends the girl running."

"Is this our first date? If so, I don't see you running," charmed Jeff.

"Oh, you are the witty one, aren't you?"

"Not into games with different playing fields," cleverly, responded Jeff. Their eyes were locked, oblivious to the room around them. Sharing, laughing, and enjoying this immediate connection.

George Stanza, with Gina on his arm, walked over to Angela for introductions to Jeff who were carrying on an intriguing conversation. A nudge from Gina brought Angela into the here and now. She turned to her friends and grabbed onto Jeff's arm for balance—her friend, the Sapphire dress flowed with her curves—Jeff noticed.

"Sorry, Jeff for my clumsiness. My heels are a little taller than what I am accustomed to," she said smiling and then continued with the introductions. "Jeff, this is George Stanza, my mentor and best friend. Undoubtedly, my best male friend," giggled Angela.

Holding out his hand, George said, "Jeff, it is a pleasure. I hope you have enjoyed tonight's festivities?"

Jeff's hand met his with equal bonding. George reminded Jeff of one of his classic actors, Gregory Peck. Suave, debonair, and assured but with kind eyes, much like Gregory Peck's character in 'To Kill a Mockingbird'. He had the same feeling of being on trial.

"Yes, sir, and the pleasure has been all mine. I hate to admit it, but tonight has been magical. I've watched an old friend climb to stardom, I've made a fool of myself, and now I have the chance to redeem my ill-fated ways. I believe that is magical," declared Jeff with a humorous touch.

George, patting Jeff on the back, said, "Then, well done, my friend. It is not usual that us mortal men can lose and regain our standing all in one night." He laughed. "Come, let me steal you away from these intoxicating women and buy you a drink."

As George took Jeff away, the ladies slipped out the terrace doors, and as Jeff observed, without any issues with balancing on those six-inch spikes. George and Jeff sat down at the bar where Carl was pouring drinks. The other guests were milling around in different groups, talking, laughing, and enjoying the ambiance. George welcomed some private time with this fellow who was monopolizing Angela's time.

"Bourbon, Jeff?"

"Yes, that is fine," Jeff replied smelling the sweet butterscotch aroma. They took a sip and replaced the glasses on the bar.

"So, Jeff, you have had an interesting path so far."

"I'm taking that comment as a fact and not a question."

"Do you think I would let just anyone into my home without knowing who they are?"

Jeff's facial expression changed from happy to a little concerned. "I don't understand, sir?"

"We are family here. Angela is our pledge, whom we have come to love very much and with that promise, we are dedicated to protecting her from anybody. She is tough as nails on the outside but deep down she is still a little girl waiting for her Prince Charming. Are you that Prince Charming, Jeff?"

"Well... I..."

"Exactly, Jeff. You have a lot on your plate and some healing to do as well with your current live-in gone to Peru and all."

"How do you know that?" Jeff said, tightening his brow.

"I told you... No one comes through those doors without me knowing who they are. I understand you met David when you were a bouncer waiting to get into the police academy. Not quite what you hoped for, so for the last few years you have been on the private side finding mostly, confused children and re-uniting them with their families. I commend you on that, but here it is... Angela is going through some troubling times and we don't feel she needs to be involved with someone who cannot give an affirmative answer. If I were you, Jeff, I would heed this conversation and stay away from her."

"You know, Mr. Stanza, that's what is so intensely marvelous about life. There is only one me, and with no disrespect, sir, you are not me," candidly finessed Jeff. "I believe our conversation is over, Mr. Stanza. Thank you for your hospitality and I will just bid good night to Angela."

"Jeff..." George stopped mid-sentence; he nodded at Joseph who stepped to the side. Jeff went up the marble stairs to the massive terrace doors where he had last seen Angela. He opened one side and stepped out. He saw Angela and Gina; their bodies were pressed tightly together and their dresses draped around their stiletto shoes. He closed the door quietly—maybe another time.

Jeff, standing with his arm outstretched, leaned against the ornate casing of the elevator door waiting for the bellman. His head hung, spinning—wondering what was the purpose of tonight. He clammed up again—with the wrong person; a powerful man and obviously influential, to have gathered information about him in such a short time.

Who the hell is this guy? Who is Angela? Characters from one of my old-time movies... no, this is real life. This is their world looking down at the rest of us. In Jeff's mind, George had now turned into the beady-eyed character Norman Bates of Hitchcock's Psycho. The bell dinged, the door opened and the bellman slid the gate. Jeff, feeling very vulnerable, stepped inside. He needed to get away from this madness, at least for now.

Lucifer's Set Up

A dimmed lamp sat on the warehouse desk, illuminating the dial of a black phone, as a hand reached to disable its ring.

"Hola... Quien? Lucifer, mi morning star? Que? OK, I listen."

A voice on the other end spoke. "We have a mutual acquaintance that has caused us both lost time. He needs to be removed for our future expansion. His dominance is affecting our growth; this needs to be dealt with. Your territory is at risk and you know it, mi amigo."

"What chu got in mind, Lucifer?"

"Something to send a message to all like Stanza, comprende?"

"Si... but why donna chu handle it?"

"You have more to gain than I. Let's say I point you in the right direction that cannot compromise your stakes. A sleight of hand that sets up your competition."

"OK... but why do chu need me?"

"To draw him out. Let's meet to discuss this further."

"Chu seems to knows mi number so I suppose chu knows where I be? Sura... Today, Domingo, si ata twelve. Adios."

"Whosa that?" asked Enrico.

"Lucifer!" replied Chico.

Sunday Morning Workout

Jeff tossed and turned throughout the night trying to get Angela out of his mind. Stanza and his goons were a piece of work as well. And Angela, pressed against Gina that could have been hot if he wasn't so surprised. The whole night replayed in his mind with 'what if' scenes replacing the reality. Why had she been so nice if she had no interest? Why invite him to the party? Why didn't Stanza step in before he was invited? He wasn't part of the in-crowd—a nobody to them, a mere divergence from their movie star lives. But—it was an incredible night. He got to hold her hand, the softness of that delicate hand. *I know she felt something—it couldn't have been just me.*

Jeff cleaned up his apartment and had allotted time to wish his little buddy a good trip before he hit the gym. Goody was probably down there, so Jeff felt he would have someone to help him figure this all out.

With a series of high fives and a big hug, Josh and his father caught the cab to the airport. Mom had tears in her eyes as she watched them pull away. Trying to be a sympathetic neighbor, Jeff put his arm around her to console her, and said, "They grow up fast, don't they?" This didn't seem to help. He needed Georgette with her sensitive nature; Teresa would have just cried with her. He chuckled to himself at the sheer thought. Jeff bide his farewell, and then jumped into his 'bird. It was hot with the top down but the wind through his hair seemed to refresh his messed-up mind.

Goody had already completed a set before Jeff got there. As he signed in, he saw Goody pushing, at least 275 pounds. He's a monster, thought Jeff as he picked up his bag.

"Hey, man. How's it going?"

Goody, recognizing his buddy's voice, put the weights back into the cradle.

"Hey. How you doing?" he acknowledged, wiping the sweat from his brow.

Jeff sat down on the bench next to him.

"I held her hand. And then she faked a fall and grabbed my arm for balance. And then she apologized."

"What?"

"Last night. I held her hand and looked deeply into her eyes like her Prince Charming."

"Is that before she swung at you?"

"No, man. She invited me to an after-party. I tell you, I was on my game. One-liners... I had her laughing."

"We know she can laugh at you, but with you? You still got that hammer mark?"

"What did Georgette ever see in you?"

"My obvious good looks. My charm."

"Ahhh, now who has been hit in the head with a hammer?"

"Okay, okay. I am just dying to know how your evening turned out. Oh please, oh please tell me," Goody jest sarcastically.

"Fuck you..."

"Okay, okay. Yes, I am curious to know how you pulled this off," relented Goody.

"We were getting along amazingly that is until her mentor bullied his way in between us and then under false pretense sat me down at his bar and proceeded to squash any progress I had made. He knew everything about me, even about Teresa leaving. How could he know that?"

"I don't know. Other than Georgette, no one else knows. CIA? NSA? Are you bugged?" Goody reached over the weight bench and did a body search.

"What the fuck?" Jeff pushed his hands away.

"How else would he know?" asked Goody.

"I just met him!"

"Think about it, Jeff. What do we always say... follow the trail, the paperwork, the money; it always leads to something or someone." He paused, and then added, "Your invitation?"

"Yes, the invitation! He didn't just find out about me; he knew everyone that was at the gallery. He made it sound like within minutes he had my whole life story. The bastard!"

"Charades, my friend. People believe what they perceive to be the right path, which as we know, can be a disguise for the truth or the right direction to follow."

"When did you become so philosophical?"

"When you denied your logic from seeing the truth."

"So, what's the truth?"

"She called you her Prince Charming?"

"Umm, no. It was George."

"So, he's baiting you."

"How much coffee have you had? Where are you getting this shit?"

Goody picked up a couple of hand barbells and started doing some crunches. Jeff sat with his elbows on his knees, watching.

"Look, man. You asked. He let you have a taste then stepped on you like a bug just to see what you were made of."

"For what reason?"

"I guess we will have to wait and see. What else happened?"

"Not much. Angela and Gina were naked on the outside terrace, hugging each other amorously.

"What!?" exploded Goody, slamming his weights to the mat.

"I'll let you mull that around, then tell me the psycho reasoning of that."

Jeff picked up some weights; Goody looked dumbfounded. *Monday*, Jeff thought, *I'll pick up a bug-sweep wand and ask Allen Travers about a program to check my computer.* A smile lit his face as he imagined Angela next to him, lifting weights—getting sweaty.

Jeff's Dream

The coldness of the steel casing surrounding the flat doors resembled nothing of the grandeur Jeff had the pleasure of rubbing up against in Beverly Hills. His building was stoic and stunk of hurried figures wearing cheap suits. Seven fingers pushed at the same button not uttering a word, even though, every day the same scenario with the same players. A broken cast without a script, improvising in different directions as their lives intermingled, and then disappeared without a rolling credit. Jeff got off at his floor and looked back at the blank stares.

He forged through his 'Orwell' gate, stopped by security to empty his pockets of loose change from buying today's paper. He gave up his brand of toilet paper while the security guard looked straight ahead without even cracking a smile. He pushed on. Butting the agency's glass door open, he now stood before Adriane, stripped of his weekend buzz. It's Monday.

"Good morning, Mr. Malardo," she announced in a sultry voice. "Did you have a nice weekend?"

"God, do I have to answer that? Should I tell her? Yes, it was fucking awesome... Just met the woman of my dreams. We are going to have babies and live in a shoe..."

Rrrrrrrrinnnnngggg ... *Rrrrrrrrinnnnngggg.* "What the fuck?" groaned Jeff as his annoying alarm on his new cell phone went off.

"Dismiss... dismiss!" he stammered as he hit the button. He fell back onto his bed and looked up at the slowly revolving ceiling fan. He reached over to his imaginary vision. He felt the ridges in the sheets, warm from whence she laid.

"God, get out of my head!"

A Package of Importance

Jeff looked at the people on the elevator at his high-rise office building. No one spoke. He got off at his floor. He passed the security, dropped his change in the dishpan, and searched for a smile. He stood before Adriane with her painted-on lips and luminous eye shadow. She pleasantly offered him his mail—he smiled at her. He then retreated to his sanctuary.

The office buzzed with scurrying people who were exchanging ideas and developing new ones. The coffee machine beeped with a new brew as phones rang in alternating patterns...

"Yes!" Jeff exclaimed out loud with only a few looking up from their terabyte terminals.

Goody, as the man he was, approached Jeff with two steaming cups of coffee.

"My man... You are a godsend."

Sitting on the corner of Jeff's desk, Goody bent down, and in his quietest voice, said, "So, I was thinking about Angela and the red-head..."

Jeff burst into uncontrollable laughter.

"What the fuck are you on, man?" questioned Goody, pulling back.

"I'm so sorry. I had the weirdest dream this morning and that just capped it off. Anyways, thanks for the coffee. Hey, have you seen Travers lately?"

"No. Actually, I was wondering that myself. No one else seems to know anything either. What do you think he is on to?"

"He tried leaving a message on my answering machine a week ago and I haven't heard from him since. Does Peters know anything?"

Adriane broke their conversation over his speaker phone.

"Jeff, there is a strange man with a package waiting for you. You need to come out."

Jeff and Goody looked at each other and both headed to the reception area. A short, older man sat in one of the chairs and as soon as the two men rounded the corner, he immediately stood up.

"Are you Jeff Malardo?" he asked, in an anxious manner.

"Yes. I am."

The man handed him a manila envelope. "I was told to personally hand it to Jeff Malardo," he said, shakily.

"Who is it from?"

"I don't know. I was paid to give it only to you. That's all I know."

"Okay, thanks," replied Jeff, looking at the envelope—and before he raised his eyes to ask another question, the man walked into the elevator and disappeared.

"Do you want me to go after him?" asked Goody.

"No. Let's see what's in here."

They took the package back to Jeff's desk.

"Be careful opening that," cautioned Goody. "Remember... bait, bug, the Godfather."

"Get off it..."

Jeff carefully slid his letter opener around the edge. It opened. He pealed the edge back and slowly looked inside...

"BANG!" shouted Goody, making Jeff jump. People looked up momentarily from their desks. Goody started laughing his ass off.

"Sometimes you are such a jerk."

"Just made *you* jerk," he said laughing harder.

Jeff emptied the contents onto his desk. A #10 envelope was addressed to Jeff Malardo and a peculiar piece-meal collection of cut-out newspaper headlines fell beside it.

"What the fuck? Open the envelope," prodded Goody.

Jeff peeled the flap of the envelope open. A letter on their company's letterhead revealed it was from Allen Travers. It read:

Jeff,

I received this note several weeks ago. I know I am being watched. I tried leaving you a message on your answering machine but not sure you received it. Lots of players, but at this time not sure who is who. Sweep your apartment, car, computer, and anything else you have. They are heavy hitters as far as I can tell and connected. See what you can find out about this missing girl. I'll be in touch.

Regards, Allen Travers

"Let's show this to Peters," insisted Jeff.

Harry Peters, the bureau chief, was sitting in his office reviewing expense reports when Jeff and Goody knocked on his door. Looking up, he motioned them to come in.

"Morning, Boss," announced Jeff.

"Morning. What's up?" responded Harry with an urgency in his voice.

"Sorry to bother you but we... I just received this from Allen."

He looked up again from his paperwork.

"This is such bullshit. As if we are trying to pad our accounts. Congress is such assholes. What do you have?"

He picked up the letter from Allen and scanned the piecemeal note resting on his desk.

"I suppose you did not wear gloves when you picked this up?" questioned Harry regarding their procedures.

"Um..."

"Never mind... See if you can still lift prints, including your own. Where is Allen?"

"We don't know. We haven't seen or heard from him for over a week," said Goody.

"Send it to the lab and if it looks legit, get on it, Jeff. Goody, what are you working on?"

"Smith's case."

"And?"

"The guy seems real enough. DNA has confirmed his ties to John Adams, so now it is up to the courts to do their thing."

"Good. Tie up whatever you need to submit our case and then give Jeff a hand... *if* this pans out. It sounds like Jeff might need some brawn. Be smart on this... Follow protocol... Do the paperwork and then follow the money. There is always money involved, somewhere."

"Yes, sir," acknowledged the two.

Harry reached for the button on his intercom, "Adriane, get Marsha in here, please. You guys still here?"

Jeff picked up the note using two pens like chopsticks. He delicately carried it back to his desk where he slipped it between two vellum sheets.

"Sometimes Harry can be right on," said Jeff.

"Yeah... But most of the time he is a pain in the neck! It's his FBI training. No sense of humor," remarked Goody.

"What do you make of Allen's comment 'heavy hitters'? Do you think this is a drug thing, slave trade, or a related matter with the missing girl?"

"I don't assume anything, Jeff. Not until we can get some evidence."

Jeff inserted the covered note into a plastic bag and headed down to the lab. Goody returned to his desk to finish his notes for their submission to the courts. When Jeff returned and passed through the security arch, he looked up at the security officer. He wondered, *He must have trained with the Queens Guard; this guy never cracks a smile.* Adriane hailed him as he passed by her.

"Jeff, I transferred a call to your voice mail from a woman with a very sexy voice," informed Adriane with a slightly jealous tone.

"Probably my mother," said Jeff, smirking.

"Hot Momma!" replied Adriane tongue-in-cheek.

Jeff, arriving back at his desk, picked up his phone and dialed his voice mail.

"Jeff, this is Gina from the other night. I just looked at your card and didn't realize what you actually did for work. I guess work wasn't on the menu that night. Anyway, I have a personal request... I don't know what you charge, but I am hoping in an hour's time, after I have my meeting with Angela, I will be able to hire you to find my daughter. She is eighteen and has all the right to leave, but I just want to know that she is safe and that she knows I love her. Please call me at 555-1029. Thanks, Jeff. Oh, by the way, Angela asked about you disappearing? Toodles."

Jeff, under his breath said, "I'll tell ya, Gina... She had her hands full."

Jeff saved the message and turned his concentration back to Allen's note. He'll call Gina later. Her daughter left of her own free will. He had no jurisdiction other than being a messenger boy.

George Plans with Carl

George Stanza sat in his plush office leaning on his desk, having a serious conversation with Carl.

"So, what did Joseph find?" he asked Carl.

"There was nothing in the apartment but he did notice three indents in the carpet that could have been from a tripod by the window that overlooked Angela's place."

"From a camera, binoculars, rifle?"

"Not a rifle tripod. The pattern was an equilateral triangle; too small and didn't extend back into the room. I think, from the reflection I saw in the rear window, it was from a high-speed lens used in surveillance," said Carl.

"Okay then, if they wanted Angela or me dead, it would have happened by now. That would have been a perfect vantage point. So let's sort this out. The CD we received two weeks ago of Angela, obviously drugged, having sex with Gina in that restaurant and then later at that rental house in the 'Hills' was meant in the beginning to control her. But now, as a calling card to bring her down... socially, I presume. Otherwise, why not distribute it when it was made as another smut film of an underage kid?"

"The call last night from the Valdez brothers insisting on a meeting today could be associated. There have been one too many coincidences lately," said Carl.

"Yes, you are right, but never assume. Where's Joseph?" asked George.

"Picking up Gina..." he looked at his watch, "...just about now. And then he will be free for a while."

"Good."

"Do you think all of our planning will work?" queried Carl, hesitantly. "Joseph isn't too happy. You know how he feels."

"It has to. What Joseph informed us of would precisely account for all of this. I know it has its consequences but we need to button this up. I don't like being the prey... and yes, I know what you are going to say, but if we play our cards right, everything will turn out the way it should. Angela is smart, tough, and intuitive. We have to rely on that... agreed?" asked George, looking for an affirmative from Carl.

They clasped hands. "Agreed, my friend."

Gina's Recounting

Monday morning as scheduled, the offices of AD Fashions awaited the arrival of Gina Durham. Angela's chauffeur, Joseph, had picked her up and brought her to the underground entrance. Stepping out of the driver's seat, he first looked around before proceeding to open Gina's door. He then escorted her to the elevator, placed his hand on the biometric scanner, and punched in the floor code to Angela's office. He bid his farewell as the doors closed. The elevator by-passed the darkened buttons of manufacturing floors and stopped at the penthouse offices. She stepped out.

'Miss Angela... Gina Durham is here to see you', announced Delores, sending a message over her tablet. Angela typed back, *'Please, have her come right in and thank you, Delores.'*

Gina stepped into Angela's office wearing a modest pinstriped suit with large sapphire lapels and a skirt cut to just above the knee. Her laced chemise offered a business look with a hint of naughtiness. She looked very chic for a fashion interview. She noticed glossy photos on the walls of models wearing AD Fashion designs walking the ramp at different fashion shows in L.A. and New York. Carefully framed sketches of original drawings were placed neatly next to them. A photo of a group attending an awards ceremony sat on Angela's desk as the floor-to-ceiling windows offered little space for displaying much else. On the opposite wall was Angela's personal drafting table. It was strewn with water-colored designs marked with red pencil circles. A small group of people sat in a semi-circle in plush barrel chairs—a vacant one faced them. Angela stood from behind her desk wearing a black satin form-fitting dress with a camel-sashed collar crossing her body from the shoulder to just past her waist—very stylish for the president of a fashion house. Angela extended her arms to welcome her friend. They hugged.

"Everyone, this is my friend and designer I told you about, and hopefully, if we can persuade her, she will be part of our little family. Please, sit over here Gina," offered Angela in a business tone.

Angela's team sat excitedly, waiting. Toni, a tall, short-haired spikey brunette with piercing blue eyes was the head buyer who worked closely with the design team to gather the right fabrics for each creation. Mattie headed her chosen domain—the actual production department. She knew the machines and the talent of each person that ran them. Sitting next to her was Jeremy, head of sales and marketing and several other key players. They all wore several hats and worked closely together sharing the same high standards that it took to be a number one company.

"As you are all aware, I plan on taking AD Fashions global, and with that it will mean lots of work both here and abroad. Gina, I know at your shop the other day I mentioned only a few hours a week, but you know and I know, together we can set a mark on the fashion world, which has been held by only a few houses. My team has had a chance to view some of your other works, and they are all in agreement that you are very talented and that we need to acquire that talent to propel us to the top.

"Regardless of our friendship, past, present, and future, if you agreed to incorporate your designs with ours, teach your creative stitch-work to our seamstresses, and help establish a design center for up-and-coming designers, we at AD Fashions wish to offer you VP of Productions." Gina's eyes widen and she was about to speak, when Angela said, "Shhh, let me finish. We can start you at two hundred thousand a year with a fifteen percent bonus over ten million sold with a contract in perpetuity," graciously offered Angela.

Each of the team sat on the edge of their seat, waiting attentively for Gina's reply. Watching Gina, Angela quickly changed her tone, "What do you say? You on board for some fun?"

Gina could barely hold back the tears of joy. She just nodded her head affirmatively, blotting the corners of her eyes, and flashing intermittent smiles. Angela stepped to her side, bent down to her, and held her until she regained her composure. The team members jumped to their feet and joined in on a group hug welcoming Gina to their family.

Angela softly said, "Don't change, Gina. Your heart is your imagination. I saw it at your shop. We share that. We can do this... We will do this, together."

The team left the ladies with smiles on their faces and jovial conversations about the impending expansion. They allowed Gina and Angela to bond in privacy.

"Angela... Thank you. You have no idea how much I have wanted to be part of something like this. With a child and trying to hold down two jobs *plus* occasional acting gigs, it has been difficult. Thank you for this opportunity," cried Gina as she wiped tears from her eyes.

"You have a child?" asked Angela.

"Yes. She's eighteen. It's been hard without a father for her."

"So, who was that man when we first met? I thought you two were married?" questioned Angela, a little more than a bit confused.

"I don't know. I had never met him before."

"What about Anthony? It sounded like you were longtime friends. If I remember correctly."

"I had never met him either. I was given a script to learn, told to be the lead in seducing you, and was paid a thousand dollars for it," informed Gina.

"That house on the hill? It wasn't yours?" Angela asked, getting irritated that she was duped.

"I'm sorry, Angela, I thought you had been given the same script. I didn't realize you didn't know they were filming it?"

"Filming!?" screamed Angela.

Angela walked around her desk and slumped down into her chair. Her hands cupped her forehead. Her thought process spinning... *Why? For what?* She looked up at Gina who had an astonished look on her face.

"I remember you whispered something into my ear. What did you say?"

"I said, 'I wish we weren't acting; I could love you forever.'" sniffled Gina.

Angela reached out to touch Gina's hand. They held on tightly.

"I need to call George. I'll get Joseph to drive you back to your shop," said Angela, dismayed.

The look on Angela's face had Gina concerned. Questions swirled in Angela's mind.

As Gina walked toward the closed door, she turned around and looked at Angela, and said, "Angela... It was Joseph who paid me the thousand dollars for my part."

Jeff Runs Sweep

Jeff ran several debugging programs on his computer and found no Trojan virus or possible eavesdropping connection.

His phone was new and had not left his side, so other than NSA; he felt he was safe with that. He still had to sweep his car and apartment. *If Josh were here*, he thought, *he would know of any strange activities or shady characters hanging around. The kid was on top of things.* He still needed to call Gina about her daughter, but was a little hesitant in getting involved. He wasn't sure of Gina's connection with George and the likes.

Jeff had to wait for forensics before he could move forward with Allen's request. He needed the lab to do a digitized photo enhancement of the attached picture so he could show it around to some of his contacts that still worked the streets. He had his car swept at the office and then armed with some equipment and a couple of trained cyber-investigators—they headed to Jeff's apartment.

Within two hours, the cyber team had come up empty-handed, which was good news for Jeff. Since he had some time to kill, he decided to call Gina and set up an appointment even though he still thought it was against his better judgement.

"Hello," she answered very politely.

"Gina, this is Jeff."

"Yes. Hello, Jeff."

"You okay? You sound like you have a cold?"

"No... Jeff, I am fine. A little light-headed but elated. Angela offered me a job today that is 'a dream come true'. I guess I am a little saddened that my daughter could not be here to experience this with me."

"That's great news about Angela's offer. I am happy for you, Gina. Do you have time today to see me?"

"Of course! Would you like to stop by my shop in North Hollywood?"

"Sure... Okay, North Hollywood. I'm currently at my apartment, so in about half an hour depending on traffic."

"Okay, Jeff, see you soon."

Unwanted News

Angela pulled into the underground parking structure of George's office. She was visibly upset. She rushed through the parking structure sending echoes of her quickened footsteps bouncing off cold concrete. George and Carl saw her coming towards them as the throaty Audi slowly navigated through the aisle. Before Carl could stop the car, she had the door open and jumped in.

"Thank you, George, for meeting me."

"Angela, calm down. What is wrong?"

"I had a meeting with Gina today and she informed me that the first night we met was all a set up... And they filmed it!"

"What do you mean?"

"She said someone had given her a script and she thought I, too, had been given one. She never realized I didn't know they were filming the whole night. She thought I was an upcoming porn star. George, what am I going to do!?" shrieked Angela with tears in her eyes.

"Who do you think put her up to it?"

"I don't know... maybe Anthony? But she said she had never met him. There was this guy I called Mr. C. because of his smile that I had met with Anthony, but Anthony told me they weren't interested because they thought I would be too hard to handle."

"Okay, calm down. Carl, take us someplace to get a drink, please. So, let me get this straight. Gina had never met Anthony but he was there, is that correct?"

"Yes."

"But you had met some guy with a smile previously who was also in the porn business?"

"Yes, but that was a dead end as I said. Gina did tell me, however, that it was Joseph who gave her a thousand dollars for her part."

"Where is Joseph now?"

"I don't know. He has been very sullen the last couple of days. You know him; he is tight-lipped," said Angela.

"Joseph used to work for Anthony. Maybe he didn't know what was going on, and probably didn't, if I understand the way Micholanetti worked. He used many people to do his dirty work so no one could connect him with anything. Now, you said they filmed it. Has Gina seen it?"

"I don't think so. She didn't seem to know anything more than that," explained Angela.

"Not that I like to assume anything, but let's hypothesize that it was Anthony and he filmed you to control you, but then when he was indicted for murder, he had no recourse but to hide this tape to use at a more appropriate time?"

"But, he is in jail," said Angela.

"He is out," informed George, calmly.

"What!" exclaimed Angela, surprised.

"Yes. For good behavior."

"Why didn't you tell me?" questioned Angela as she stared into George's eyes.

"We just found out." George reached out and put Angela's hand into his and then with his other hand, his fingers softly caressed the back of hers.

"Is that why Joseph has been acting strangely?"

"Possibly?" said George, trying to calm Angela down.

"Jordon's, Mr. Stanza," announced Carl.

"Thank you, Carl. Come, let's have a drink and talk about this."

George had an analytical way of seeing any and all angles to any problematic situation. He had a calming manner and Angela could tell the wheels were spinning. The lounge was nicely decorated with plush barrel seating and small glass tables, which could be arranged depending on patrons' wishes. George ordered two double Scotches. He pulled the chair out for Angela—a true gentleman. The friendly waitress delivered their order promptly. Angela took a sip and savored the taste, just as George had taught her. She relaxed back into the chair.

"Listen, Angela. I have to go away on business but while I'm gone, listen to Carl. He has your best interest at heart. You know that, right?"

"Yes, of course, George. But why do you have to leave now?" fretted Angela.

"Angela, believe me when I say this, you have friends that love you more than you know. Trust your intuition to guide you."

"George, you are scaring me. What is going on?"

George looked at his watch.

"Angela, I've got a meeting in an hour. We'll drop you off at your car. Go home and just relax. Think about that expansion to Europe you are planning. We'll handle any problems here," insisted George.

Angela hated it when George was so vague with her. What he really meant was 'stay out of my business'. She had been around him too long to not heed what he said. She was not a push-over, but right now, time alone to detail her expansion was what she needed to do. Having Gina on board relieved some of Angela's pressure; she could transfer some of the workload to her. *Life is so awesome and precious; George is right, I have the gift of loving and trustworthy friends around me,* she reminisced as she looked out the tinted side window.

. . .

In North Hollywood, Jeff pulled up to Gina's alteration shop. From inside, she watched as Jeff's classic car pulled to the curb. She wondered if Angela would take the time to nurture a relationship with him. He was a handsome man who was also quite witty. She opened the door for him and he stepped out of the heat into the coolness of her shop.

"Hello, Jeff. Thank you for coming."

"Hello, Gina. I wasn't sure if I should with the likes of Mr. Stanza," commented Jeff being half serious.

"Oh... Yes, well... but trust me, he's a very loyal man who protects those he loves," she said to hopefully reassure Jeff.

"We haven't reached that level yet," joked Jeff.

"Please, come in. You must be boiling with the top down?"

"It does feel good in here," he said as he fanned his shirt.

"Would you like some iced tea?"

"That would be appreciated, thank you."

Jeff looked around as Gina went to the back room to get a couple of iced teas.

"Does your daughter have a computer?" Jeff asked.

"A laptop, but she took that with her," she replied, stirring the two iced teas.

"How long has she been gone?" He asked, loudly.

"Almost four months." Gina put down the spoon on the counter and returned to the main shop catching Jeff in mid-sentence and in a louder voice.

"Have any friends called her... oh sorry. I was distracted by your beautiful dresses and didn't hear you." He repeated his question again in a more civil voice. Have any friends called her since she has been gone?"

"No one has called me. Here you go. Cheers."

Jeff took a refreshing sip.

"Mmmmm, good. Your blend? Because this is not store-bought."

"Yes. I mix different herbs with the tea, so thank you for the compliment."

He took another sip—longer this time and he let the coolness massage his throat. He smacked his lips, and said, "So four months and nothing?"

"Nothing. She is very talented. She has a flair for design and is an excellent seamstress, but I think her artistic joy is painting," added Gina.

"Paints what? Flowers, landscapes, tribal artifacts?"

"Mostly seascapes. She likes the way water forms unique compositions."

"So, she could make a living sewing to support her painting?"

"I suppose so. What are you getting at?" asked Gina.

"There are a few communities up and down this coast that devote all their time to nature and try to capture it every day in its changing form, whether painting, sculpture or clay reliefs. Sometimes, they don't have time to mend things. Just a thought."

"Do you know of such a place?" excitedly, asked Gina.

"Northern California, parts of Oregon and Washington State all have these small communities that are exposed to naturally wild seascapes. I'll see what I can find out."

"Thank you so much, Jeff."

"Is this a picture of her?"

"Yes. Please take it."

"No need." Jeff pulled out his new phone and took a picture of the picture. "I can send this electronically to the bigger agencies and they will run it through their systems to find any hits on the internet. It doesn't take as long as it used to," explained Jeff with a smile. "So you said you got the job you were talking about with Angela."

"More than that... She offered me VP of Productions! I was speechless. Her team welcomed me with open arms. It is like one big family," said Gina, glowing.

Angela IS special. I knew it. Jeff chanted in his mind.

"I'll let you know what I find out, Gina. By the way, what is her name?"

"Mira. Short for Miracle."

"Okay, Gina. If you hear anything, let me know; otherwise, I will talk to you soon." Jeff took one long drink of the remaining iced tea, handed the empty glass to Gina, smiled a reassuring smile, and took his leave.

Gina stood at the closed door and watched Jeff slip into his car. She was feeling hopeful.

An Unexpected Hit

Finally escaping the mid-afternoon heat, the Audi pulled past an unassuming rival to the back of Angela's parked car. George stepped out with Angela, whose car sat at the end of the aisle. Going to the front passenger window, George instructed Carl to go park the car. He then gave Carl a reassuring pat on the arm. He disappeared out of sight.

Angela looked at George. Hugging him, she said profoundly, "George, you are my savior. Thank you for everything... Thank you for my life."

"Be strong, girl. Everything will be all right. Trust me."

"Okay, George. I love you."

"I love you, too." George looked at his watch—calculating. "Now, I've got to get to that meeting. I promise, I'll talk to you soon."

George watched as Angela unlocked her door and slid inside. Turning, he walked down the main aisle of the parking structure. When he was halfway between Angela and the elevator, a white Cadillac pulled around the corner. He continued to walk. Angela dried her tears and was touching up her make-up in her rear view mirror—George slowly shrinking in the distance. As she applied the last stroke of mascara, she saw George standing opposite the back end of a white van, only steps away from the elevator.

Suddenly, from the window of the white Cadillac that was slowly straddling the middle of the double aisle came a shotgun blast booming like a giant balloon had been poked, throwing George against the parked van's doors—blood splattered as he hit. The unmistakable repercussion of the shotgun blast sent shockwaves rippling through the concrete building. Angela sat in shock—shoulders crunched against her neck, trembling. Through her rearview mirror, she watched George slither down to the cold concrete floor.

Tires started to squeal—smoke bellowed from the wheel wells. As the car sped towards her, she noticed something white being thrown from the car. She slinked down into her seat, closed her eyes tightly, and braced for an impact. The car careened into hers—she let out a scream, *"Ahhh!"* Angela opened her eyes as the Cadillac momentarily rested against the backend of her Mercedes. She stared into the driver's eyes through her mirror before it, once again, sped off, down the ramp and out of the structure.

She immediately tried to get out of the car but the door wouldn't budge. She pounded on her door with her fist to open it—then she used her shoulder. Partially open, she managed to raise her leg and used her foot to kick it far enough to squeeze out. Kicking off her high heels, she ran barefoot down the aisle, jumping over black tire streaks, to her friend's side. He lay in a pool of blood, motionless. Angela screamed in horror. A screech from another car fleeing down the next aisle exited the parking structure much like the one before it.

On her knees, Angela bent to her friend. She wanted to hold George, but instead, she just touched his leg, frenzied, fulminating with expletives. Angela cried in a rage for revenge as she stood and ran towards her car fearing she might be next. She squeezed back into it, pulled the door close to the best of her ability, turned the key and started the engine—it revved, and she threw it into reverse. The tires squealed like a butchered pig. Angela slammed the shifter into drive and sped toward the exit. Jumping the sidewalk that surrounded the parking structure, she swerved out into the street forcing another car to veer off.

She raced towards her apartment.

~

Six blocks away, a Chevy with Chico and his brother Ernesto who had just witnessed a murder—hightailed it through the streets.

"Jesus Cristo, what the fuck did that guy do?" shouted Chico. "Eis supposa to be a meeting, not a hit. We gotta get outta here. I need time to think. We gotta find that girl; she saw us."

~

Racing erratically through the streets to reach home, Angela screamed into her Bluetooth, "Carl! Car! Pick up Carl... Please!"

~

A few blocks away from George's office building, in a rundown warehouse district where a drop-off point had been previously set up, Reverend Michaels said, "Joseph, pull over, let your buddy out. Here's the fifty grand. Don't ever call me, Carlson." Carl stepped out.

Reverend Michaels, laughing in the back seat, said, "Fuck... Did you see that bastard bounce off of that van? Fucking awesome, the motherfucker! That'll teach him for framing me for that putana's murder. That's the best 50 G's those crackheads ever spent. Just like old times, right Joseph?" Proudly, he laughed. "I remember following you twenty years ago when you flushed out that pair of DEA maggots. With one shot I took out both of them. That little bitch, she had it coming more than her goon partner. My only regret is I never saw his face. Sorry about having to shoot you, Joseph, but I couldn't let them think you worked for me. Now take me to that little whore's apartment."

Joseph gripped the steering wheel tight—his knuckles were white. He looked at Anthony Micholanetti, sans his reverend get-up, in the rearview mirror; a tear bud formed at the corner of his eye. As the battered Caddy rounded the corner after dropping off Carlson at his car, Anthony lowered his window just in time to catch flashes of orange light bouncing through his interior, and then, the sonic boom of an explosion echoed between the buildings from the direction they just came. He smiled and raised the window.

. . .

An anonymous tip had Channel 8 News only moments away. When they arrived, the police had already cordoned off the area, pictures for the crime lab were being taken, and police with dogs were walking the aisles. An ambulance nosed its way past the news crew as a couple of policemen removed the barricades to allow it to pass. The news crew set up the camera and as they were about to roll, a policeman carrying a plastic bag, with a white fedora inside it approached the crime unit's van.

"Are you getting this, Matt?" asked the anchorman.

"Got it."

. . .

Carl felt Angela's anxiousness.

"Angela... Calm down, I know. Are you home? Call me when you get there. Trust me," said Carl.

Moments after Angela talked with Carl, she slammed on her brakes and came to a screeching stop in front of her apartment building. She kicked her driver's door farther open, and jumped out in a furor. She raced through her apartment's complex doors to the elevator. Once inside her apartment, she turned on her big screen TV, searching for a channel that might be covering this nightmare. Finally, Channel 8 news played the scene of her best friend and mentor, covered in a blood-soaked sheet. She stared in disbelief. Her remote, dangling precariously from her fingers, dropped to the floor startling Angela back to reality. She picked up her phone and called Carl.

"Carl!" she cried, "What am I to do?"

Calmly, he said, *"Go to your safe behind the Van Gogh..."*

She rushed over to the wall safe and threw the Van Gogh to the ground. Through her tear-filled eyes, she fumbled with the combination and had to start the sequence over again.

"...take the envelope and new phone. Destroy your old one."

Angela hurled it onto the marble floor and stomped on it with her bare foot, cutting her heel. Her new phone rang.

"Angela, listen. You got to get out of there. Do you hear me?"

Angela looked around in a daze. Her beautiful apartment—her life was here. She scurried to her bedroom and frantically threw some clothes in a small bag. She turned and headed for the living room and was about to open her door when she heard the elevator's *ding*.

"Get out now, Angela ... NOW!" yelled Carl into his phone. *"Your back door... GO!"*

The elevator door opened as two men screwing on silencers stepped out. They crossed the hallway to her door and listened. It was quiet. One of them kicked at the door and then again. The jamb split when he put his shoulder into it, finally releasing it. The door swung open.

"Check down there," ordered Anthony Micholanetti as he rushed to the entry of her bedroom. He scanned the room. Drawers were open and clothes were strewn about. He came out and saw the busted phone on the floor—blood droplets lay beside it. A safe had been opened but had been clearly emptied. He looked up at the TV; it was playing the same scenes over and over again like it was on a loop of a bloodied body lying motionless. He arrogantly smirked. Outside, he heard the breaking of glass. Rushing over to the window, he accidentally knocked over a ballerina music box that was sitting on the piano. It began to play as it crashed to the floor—its broken leg stopping it from completing its chime. It started and stopped and started again.

Swatting the curtain open, Micholanetti saw Angela running through the alley and the shattered window of a parked car down below. He ran from the window, through the mangled doorway of the apartment, and punched at the elevator's button. He waited impatiently—pacing. A bell dinged. The doors slowly opened and he jumped inside and hammered at the main floor button. Arriving at the main floor, he burst through the elevator's half-opened doors knocking down an elderly couple, displacing their groceries throughout the atrium. He eyed the front door of the building, hatred boiling inside of him.

Angela ran around the corner trying to catch the bus that just drove by the alleyway. As the bus started to pull away from the curb outside of Angela's building, it had to weave its way around a smashed-up car. She screamed at the bus driver at the top of her lungs to stop before he could fully engage. The driver upon hearing a high-pitched outcry looked in his side mirrors and saw a woman running towards him. Stopping quickly with a jerk, he opened the door as a big man entered the street from the same alleyway. As soon as Angela stepped onto the bus steps, the driver floored it as he watched another man through his large side mirrors crash through an apartment building door brandishing a gun. The heavier man from the alleyway was bent over obviously trying to catch his breath. The bus driver looked at Angela and didn't say a word.

As Angela walked down the aisle past two elderly gentlemen to take a seat, she noticed a mid-teen girl to her right and a young couple with a baby at the back of the bus. The baby was smiling as it played with shadows cast from the light reflecting off the chrome handle. Angela looked at the young girl across from her, perhaps half her age. As Angela took refuge, she rested her head against the back of the seat. She felt the smeared mascara lying in lines, announcing her despair.

The Frantic Call

As Jeff pulled off the ramp heading back to his office, he noticed his cell phone had lit up with Gina's number flashing across the screen. He turned down the soulful ballad of Ms. Aguilera, tapped the button on his earbud, and answered the call. "Hello."

The frantic screaming from Gina was unintelligible.

"Gina, calm down. I can't understand you."

"Angela... It's Angela! She is in trouble. George has been gunned down!"

"What?"

"George has been killed and they are after Angela," she said, hysterically.

"When did this happen?"

"Angela just called me saying, 'they are after me... I have to get away', and then said that she would keep in touch. That's all. She hung up!"

"Gina, I am almost at my office. Let me check it out. What's Angela's address? Okay, I got it. I will talk with you soon."

Jeff slid his Firebird into his parking spot and jumped out. Running for the elevator he called out, "HOLD IT, PLEASE!" He vaulted inside to the amazement of the other riders. Patiently, he waited seemingly for hours before this rapid elevator reached his floor. As the doors slid to the side, Jeff bolted to the check-in desk of 'Straight Up Communication' and hastily dumped his car keys and change into the dishpan. He rushed through the security arch and upon retrieving his wares, pushed through the glass doors. Adriane looked up from her desk. Concerned for Jeff's intense expression, she let him pass without her usual casual banter. Jeff headed straight to his terminal. Goody knew something was wrong and rushed to his side.

"What's up, buddy?"

"Gina just called me, in a frenzy. She told me Stanza has been murdered and now they are after Angela."

"What?"

"See if you can find anything on the news or streaming videos. I'm going to call my friends at LAPD."

Goody rushed back to his terminal and searched for information. Jeff reached out to one of his friends at his old station.

"Jim. It's Jeff Malardo. Yes, it has been some time. I'm fine... Um, Teresa? Look, Jim, I'm in a bit of a hurry. Do you know anything about a hit on George Stanza? No... Today. I don't know, maybe an hour or so ago? Nothing?" questioned Jeff, astounded. "Okay, thanks, Jim. Yeah, together. Yep, the four of us. Good talking with you, Jim." Jeff hung up the phone and leaned back in his chair, and thought, *what the fuck?*

Goody hollered out from his office, "Nothing, Jeff! Are you sure that's what Gina said?"

"She was frantic," replied Jeff, bewildered.

"There was a car fire earlier down by some old warehouses, but that's it. No reported bodies," informed Goody as he approached Jeff's desk.

"Then what the fuck is going on? I am going to Angela's apartment. Want some fresh air?" asked Jeff.

"Let's go, buddy. Hey, got your piece?"

~

The freeways were starting to back up but that didn't faze Jeff as he weaved in and out. He barreled down off-ramps, ran red lights, and went back up onto the freeway. Goody was sitting quietly as Jeff wheeled his Firebird, down shifting, slamming on brakes and sliding his car around corners. The car burned through the streets. As they approached Angela's apartment, they passed a car hauler with a dented-up Mercedes turning to get onto the freeway. Jeff slid his Firebird to a screeching stop out front of Angela's building. They jumped out and rushed inside.

Stepping into the elevator, Jeff noticed a dented faceplate and a cracked 'down' button—he pressed number four. The elevator dropped them off at the damaged door of Angela's apartment. They cautiously stepped inside with their hands resting on their weapons. It was obvious that someone was in a hurry because other than an empty safe, an original Van Gogh lay haphazardly on the floor. That alone ruled out theft. Goody walked over to where a smashed phone lay on the marble floor. He bent down and noticed it had smears of blood on it. Carefully picking up the phone, Goody slipped it into a plastic bag. Jeff stepped over to the piano to where a broken figurine, spasmodically, tried to complete its tune. This also indicated someone was in a big hurry. Jeff picked up the figurine and placed it back on the piano. It started to play its tune but the winding ran out—it came to rest.

Moving over to the window, Jeff pulled aside the sheer drapes and looked out and down to the alley below. A car parked next to Angela's building had a shattered back window.

The TV, mounted above the fireplace, played a continuous loop of a covered, bloody body. Its clarity was suspicious to Jeff, more like a downloaded signal transmitted from somewhere else.

A couple of pictures remained on the mantel. One was of a man in a navy uniform but enlarged to where Jeff could easily detect grain. And just above the right corner, he could make out a pen stroke, as if an uncropped version would have had less grain and possibly an inscription. Jeff picked up the other photo frame. It still had the stock photo image of a couple that you see in any frame or gift shop. *Peculiar?* he thought as everything else seemed to have a purpose in the room. He started to replace the framed picture back onto the mantle just as Goody appeared from the rear of the apartment.

"They went out there," he remarked, pointing behind him.

"They?" questioned Jeff.

"There is an over-turned chair and it's pushed aside. Marks on the carpet show four indents that are not aligned with obstructing free movement to the door. I think Angela tossed the chair in front of the door to slow down whoever was chasing her," speculated Goody.

Jeff turned to Goody and as he misplaced the frame on the mantel, it fell to the hearth and broke.

"Shit," said Jeff. As he bent down to pick it up, a half-burnt and ripped photo-booth photo fell out from behind. Goody joined Jeff as they scrutinized the photo. It was not of Angela but an arm around this girl in the picture must have led to someone else at her side.

"Do you think an old friend of Angela's?" asked Goody.

"I don't know. It looks old. I'll have the lab test it," said Jeff, wondering as he put it into his shirt pocket.

"Do you want to knock on doors?" asked Goody.

"Yes. Let's see if anybody heard anything. I'm going to check out that broken rear window in the alleyway. Meet you out front."

"Okay," agreed Goody.

Jeff slowly descended the private back staircase. He looked at everything and anything that offered any clues. There were some scratches that could be caused by a gun handle, but without forensics to take samples, it could have been anything. The alley relinquished nothing of significance either, except when he stopped at the car, he noticed someone had dug out the bullet from the dashboard. *Definitely professionals*, he thought.

As he proceeded out to the front of the building, he looked down at the curb. There were skid marks on the asphalt and scuff marks on the concrete curb. Walking further past from where he parked his car, near a bus stop, he found more tread marks, but they were much wider, like a big truck or possibly a bus in a panic.

Goody came out of the apartment building holding his notepad. He walked over to Jeff.

"Definitely something went on. An older couple said a man crashed into them, knocking them to the ground and sending their groceries everywhere. Whoever he was, he was definitely in a hurry and didn't even apologize or try to help them up. Very rude, they said."

"Do they have a description?" asked Jeff.

"No. They say it all happened too fast." Goody folded his notepad closed.

"Okay. Let's go back to the office and try to piece this together. First, I want to take photos of the tire marks."

"Anything else?" asked Goody.

"Let's check with LAPD to see if anybody phoned in a disturbance complaint," suggested Jeff.

"Did you catch the name on that car hauler?" asked Goody.

"No. Did you?"

Goody shook his head negatively. They returned to Jeff's car and headed back to the office.

Four blocks down from Angela's apartment, a street-sweeper darted in and around parked cars as the cool spray refreshed the kids running down the hot sidewalk. Its massive brushes turned erasing everything in its path.

Sanitized

By the time Jeff and Goody returned to the office, it was already 7:25 p.m. Jeff dropped Goody off at his car. "See ya tomorrow," he said.

"Yes, sir. Bright and early," Jeff replied. He parked his Firebird in his designated stall, stepped out, and headed to the elevators. It was late—no one to disturb him as thoughts swirled in his mind. The elevator stopped and he stepped out onto his floor. A different security guard was already settling in for the long night. Standard protocol insisted all employees had to scan their employee card, no matter what time of day, to be allowed access. As he passed Adriane's desk, he detected the fragrance of her lingering perfume. *She did smell good,* he thought.

He reached his desk, turned on his desk lamp, and emptied his pockets. The picture of a mid-teen girl, obviously very popular by her grown-up look, stared up at him. "Who are you?" questioned Jeff out loud. Next, his phone. He sorted through his photos and downloaded them onto the computer. With a push of a button they were transferred to forensics. Last, the plastic bag with the blood and cell phone that Goody procured from the marble floor. As it was late, he'd have to wait until the next day to hand over that evidence.

He sat down at his desk and pulled out a packet of 4x6 recipe cards—he called them his 'cheat sheets'. Each bit of information was transcribed on its own card and then logically displayed in a methodical order of deduction. It helped with the displacement of time for occurring events. He wrote:

3:56 p.m. Gina called. That was easy—right off his phone.

4:15 p.m. Goody and Jeff left office.

5:23 p.m. arrived at Angela's apartment: blood, scratches on staircase, removed bullet, skid marks-1, skid marks-2, photo of unknown girl, Channel 8 News Reel, broken figurine, rude man.

He had twelve cards so far. Shuffling back to Gina on card 1 (3:56 p.m.) he wrote: Angela just called her, George dead, 'they are after me...I have to get away'.

He scribbled that card out, scrunched it up, and tossed it into the trash can. He re-wrote and re-numbered another:

Card 1 – George is dead

Card 2 – 'they are after me'

Card 3 – 'I have to get away'

Card 4 – Angela just called Gina

Card 5 – Gina (3:56 p.m.) called me

"I have to assume that on Card 3 she is already running and relating what has happened when she speaks to Gina," he said aloud to reassure his mind.

He picked up Card 1: George is dead. He wrote: Angela saw killing—why not KILL her NOW if she was a WITNESS? Why chase her?

He wrote another:

Card 6 – Professional – removed bullet. *Why would a professional stop to remove a bullet before he has whacked a witness? Possibly, after she got away he returned to the car with chance of being seen and removed the bullet.* He parenthesized (Professional???) and added three question marks.

He cupped his head into his hands—thinking. He wrote:

Card 7 – broken figurine

Card 8 – rude man

Card 9 – rude man looked out window – assuming he did what I did because of broken figurine

Card 10 – rude man went to elevator – waited – slow elevator

Card 11 – rude man knocked over elderly couple

Card 12 – rude man ran out of building

Card 13 – Professional has NO hit

Card 14 – they leave – cannot stick around –

He went back to Card 13. He wrote:

Professional had plenty of time to chase witness but stopped to remove bullet, then joined his partner as if he just arrived. WHY??? Why let her live? Who was chasing Angela?

He picked up his phone and called Channel 8 News to ascertain who covered the murder of George Stanza. A line editor returned to the call and said they had no such footage. The only thing that came in was a car fire; not newsworthy enough to send out a crew. Jeff thanked the editor and hung up.

Card 15 – Channel 8 News on Angela's TV – <u>A LIE</u> – someone setting her up or wanting her to think George was dead. He scratched that out. She saw him killed.

Card 1 – George is dead.

Card 16 – NO police report of murder

Card 17 – Car fire only several blocks away

Jeff looked up at the clock. It was 11:15 p.m. He picked up his phone and speed-dialed Gina.

"Hello," answered a sleepy Gina.

"Gina, it's Jeff."

"Whoooo?" she said, her voice quivering.

"Jeff... Jeff Malardo... Gina, you there?"

"Jefffffy," she wearily replied.

"Yes. Are you all right?"

"Jeff... Oh, Jeff... Did you find my daughter?" questioned Gina, incoherently.

"No, not yet. This is about Angela."

"Yes... Angela is my friend," she blathered. "Someone wants to hurt her."

"Yes, Gina. Please, stay with me. What is Angela's phone number?"

"Um... um ... 5 ... 5 ... um 5 ..."

"Gina!" shouted Jeff. "Stay with me! 555 *what*?"

"19 ... um ... 7 ... 7." The phone hit the ground.

Jeff desperately called the number—no answer. He decided he was going to go back over to Angela's apartment. At midnight, the traffic was calmer, which allowed Jeff to arrive in decent time. He noted it was 12:23 a.m. Reaching into his glove box, he pulled out a 9mm and a flashlight. Stepping out of his car, he searched for the skid marks that would have been visible by the ornate streetlamps of the neighborhood. What he noticed instead were swirl marks left by a street cleaner that so coincidentally had driven by.

Jeff eclipsed two stairs at a time and entered the building timing his steps, the wait time, and then the elevator ride up. As the elevator door opened and he peered out at Angela's apartment door, he stepped back into the elevator and took a double take, making sure he pressed the right button. The smell of fresh paint permeated the air as he approached the reconstructed door jamb. He tried the handle. The door was locked. He reached into his back pocket and pulled out a small set of twisted hooks. He inserted them—the door clicked open. He looked around to see if anybody was watching him before he stepped further. All was quiet. He stepped inside.

He shone his flashlight around, then down and around again. Jeff darted into Angela's bedroom. The place was empty. Nothing! He scanned the floor in proximity of where the smashed phone had laid and where the blood was found—nothing. Not a piece of glass, plastic, a chip, or blood. Nothing. He scrambled over to where he had dropped the picture on the hearth. Putting the flashlight on the floor to cast a shadow, he found nothing there either. The place was sanitized.

Not giving up, he went through the kitchen to the back door and headed down the stairs. He didn't have to go all the way down—he knew. The tacky texture that he felt was from someone refinishing the wooden banister. In a whirlwind, he headed back upstairs to the living room window where he carefully looked out and down. The alley was clean, the car gone.

"Who the hell are you people?" he growled in a low contemptuous voice.

Hello, Anyone Live Here?

Goody tossed and turned throughout the night, so he decided at five in the morning to get up and go straight to the office. Usually, at this time of day, he'd stop off at the gym, but something was eating at him.

He placed his pleasantries with the security guard who scanned his employee badge. As he entered the 'war room', he noticed a small light on over Jeff's desk. Lying face down amongst his cheat sheets was his buddy, Jeff, sound asleep. Nudging him, Goody startled him awake.

"What?" he jumped, with one eye still closed. His hair looked like he walked through a static chamber at a weird science fair. He sported a two-day growth on his usually clean-shaven face. His head bounced back to where it had come—the middle of his cheat sheets. Goody chuckled and went to brew some fresh coffee. On his return, he blew the aroma of a freshly brewed batch next to Jeff's face. The other eye opened.

"Good morning, sunshine. Did we sleep well last night?" teased Goody in his best sultry voice.

"Oh shit, Goody. Is that what Georgette has to wake up to?"

"You never mind Georgette... What the hell are you doing?"

"What time is it?"

"Six," answered Goody.

"Six? Like before the sun comes up, six?"

"Jeff, that's old. Get up."

"Man, where is your compassion?" asked Jeff, wearily.

"What are you doing man?"

Jeff looked at his notes. Moving his head side to side, cracking his neck, he reached up and grabbed the cup of coffee from Goody. He took a sip and a long breath.

"Her place is clean," declared Jeff.

"Whose place?"

"Angela's. It has been san-i-tized," announced Jeff in a long draw. "No furniture, no million dollar Van Gogh, no piano, no couches, no bed, no phone, no ev-i-dence. Nothing... Nada."

"When did you find this out?" asked Goody, mystified that someone could sanitize an apartment within hours.

"Last night. I went over there about midnight. Even the tire marks have been cleaned off the street."

"What?" Goody had seen a lot in his service but even the CIA wasn't that good. He took a sip of coffee.

"You heard me... We have nothing," shared Jeff.

"What are you doing with your cheat sheets?"

"Trying to put the pieces together. It doesn't make sense. Card 13 - a hitman who doesn't hit. Card 15 – news reel that's not real, but only on Angela's TV that is no more. Card 16 – no reported murder with the LAPD. Card 17 – a car fire that no one cares about. Oh, and I called Gina, man she was out of it. Anyways, she gave me Angela's phone number and nothing on that as well."

"Move over." Goody rolled Jeff's chair aside. "Okay, let me look at this. Your 5:30 p.m. card, you didn't mention the smashed phone."

"What? Shit... I re-numbered them and must have left it out."

"Card 3 – you said, Angela called Gina, but her phone was already smashed. We saw it on the floor, which means she has another. What number did Gina give you?"

"555-1977. She could barely speak."

"Then, if Angela called Gina, her new number should be on Gina's recent call list. Come on... Get up! We're going to see Gina. Good work, though... except the missing phone thing," teased Goody.

. . .

The red-orange sun glowed through the filtered early morning smog. Freeways were moving relatively quickly in spite of the number of vehicles on the road at 6 a.m. Gina had given Jeff her home address when they last talked, in case he found anything out about her daughter, Mira. They arrived at the palm tree-lined street where Gina's second-floor walkway was located. Its central walkway opened up to a small pool, which was outlined with colorful gardens and beyond that, a concrete sitting area. It was nice, not overdone but clean. By the looks of the arrangement of the doors, it contained single and two-bedroom apartments. The upper balcony entertained garden chairs and still gave enough room to walk by.

Gina's apartment, 214, was at the end. The two men walked along the ground floor sidewalk, excusing themselves as some tenants were already watering their outside plants. The back staircase had them walking past one other apartment before landing at Gina's. They knocked—they waited. They knocked again. A neighbor stuck her head out.

"You might have to knock harder. She was pretty upset yesterday when she got home. I gave her a couple of sleeping pills," said the neighbor politely as she scrutinized the early morning guests. Not willing to leave it at that, the neighbor inquired, "You here about Mira?"

"We are working on that, ma'am. Just need to ask some more questions, but thank you for your concern," answered Goody in a police-type tone.

Gina finally dragged herself to the door.

"Yes...? Who is it?" she said wearily from behind her closed door.

"Gina, it's Jeff and Goody."

"Jeff... Just a minute," she replied with a more cognitive tone.

The lock slid open and the deadbolt threw back.

"Good morning. Come in, please."

The neighbor tucked her head back into her apartment, apparently satisfied that Gina knew them and she was safe in their company.

"Morning," offered Goody.

"We've met, haven't we?" asked Gina.

"Yes. At the art opening. I was with stutter-mouth here," quipped Goody.

"Yes, and your very beautiful wife, if I recall."

"Yes. Georgette."

"She was wearing a lovely, handcrafted dress. It really complimented her figure."

Goody looked at Jeff with a *"don't say a word about my wife"* look.

"Gina," began Jeff, "...when we talked last night, you gave me Angela's phone number..."

"We talked last night?" questioned Gina, confused.

"Yes. Around eleven. You don't remember?"

"Sorry, Jeff, no. I was a little out of sorts yesterday and when I got home, my neighbor gave me some sleeping pills."

"Yes, we heard from your neighbor already," said Goody.

"The number you gave me, 555-1977 that's Angela's, correct?"

"Yes."

"We found her phone, that is, we believe it was her phone, smashed on her living room floor. And according to our time factor, she could not have used that phone to call you. May we see your phone, Gina?" asked Goody.

"Of course," she said, confused by receiving this information.

Goody checked her recent call list. He held it up so Jeff could take a look—a series of 1's and 0's.

Gina looked at their faces. Concerned, she asked, "What is it?"

"They blocked her number," said Goody.

"What do you mean...'THEY'?" asked Gina.

"Whoever is running this charade knows what they are doing," informed Jeff.

"What do you mean... charade? Angela isn't in trouble?" she asked in a hopeful tone.

"He didn't mean that, Gina. We aren't sure what is going on. You said she was in hysterics when she called you about watching George get shot?"

"Yes, Jeff. She is a strong person, and for her to react that way, she had to be telling the truth," said Gina, compassionately defending her friend.

"There is no record of any crime being committed per the LAPD. The news people have no footage of filming it either," informed Goody.

"I don't understand...?" said Gina, starting to tear up.

Jeff put his hands on her shoulders.

"Look, Gina, we will do everything humanly possible to find out what is going on. If she calls you again, give her my number."

"Gina, do you know of any reason why someone would want to harm her?" asked Goody.

"Angela is so sweet. I don't have any answer for you; although, when we first met..." she paused, "...let me rephrase that. When she came into my shop a week ago, her intent was to ask about that Sapphire dress that she wore to the art opening."

"Go on," coaxed Jeff.

"Look... I don't want to bring up old dirt or demean anyone, including me... I love Angela and have for a very long time, secretively, I suppose. She asked where that Sapphire dress came from. I told her I designed it years ago hoping someone would see it and promote me as a fashion queen. That didn't happen. A little over a month ago, I received a call describing my dress right down to the cherub on the shoulder. I knew right off which dress he was talking about. We discussed price and I received $500 down in cash. They never picked it up, so when I had a chance to consign it to Ravel's, I did. Angela saw it and came by."

"So, Angela liked the design, or are you saying she knew that dress from the past?" asked Jeff, confused.

"I wore it years ago for a filming of... of adult nature. Angela was there. She told me that she liked it so much that she had made a copy of it as well. I guess I should be flattered." shyly, informed Gina.

"You did a porn flick?" asked Goody.

"I had a two-year-old and was struggling to open my shop. I picked up some quick cash doing a few movies."

"So, why was Angela so surprised to see this dress at whoever's?" queried Jeff.

"I believe now that she was drugged that night and had no idea what was going on."

"She didn't know she was being filmed?" asked Jeff.

"Not a bit. I only found out yesterday that she didn't know."

"Have you seen this film?" asked Goody.

"No... Usually you get a free copy of the CD, I guess for prosperity, but I didn't receive one."

"What happened to the original dress that you made?"

"I can't remember, but probably cut it up for something else."

"Okay, let me get this straight. You and Angela were in a porno but Angela didn't know she was being filmed. No one has seen this flick, and now, your original design of this dress surfaces and she is running scared," said Jeff, methodically summing up the past events.

"Pretty much," acknowledged Gina.

"God... This sounds like a game. Sexy blue dress, the candlestick, the waiter did it," scoffed Goody.

"Joseph was the one that paid me my thousand-dollar fee after the gig was over. That night seems so far away stuck in the past," sighed Gina.

"Whoa! The Godfather, Joseph. Her driver?"

"Yes... I was surprised when he picked me up for my interview with Angela. And then again, I saw him at the art opening. They are very close, I found out. He would give his life to protect her."

Goody and Jeff looked at each other. The puzzle just got bigger, but players were starting to settle into place.

"Just off hand, what kind of car does Angela drive?" asked Goody.

"A Mercedes. Beautiful. An electric blue color. Very pretty color," said Gina.

The two men got anxious. Jeff gave Gina a surprised kiss on the cheek.

"Thank you, Gina. You are marvelous. Come on, Goody, we got some surveillance tapes to look at. Gina, we will be in touch. And again, thank you for trusting me...er... us."

The two left Gina and rushed to their car.

"I'm calling Harry to see if we can get ahold of the footage from the on-ramp where we saw the car hauler," said Jeff.

"Good idea. Let's pay another visit to that elderly couple at Angela's apartment building," insisted Goody.

~

Forty-five minutes later, they rounded the corner, to just outside of Angela's building. A brightly-colored A-frame with a bouquet of balloons tied to it, announced: 'Grand Opening'. They pulled up across the street.

In the entry, there was now a security station with a guard as big as Goody. And behind him were newly-installed surveillance cameras pointing at the elevator and at the door. They watched themselves approach the desk.

"Yes, gentlemen, how can I help you?" asked the burly man.

A little confused, Jeff said, "This wasn't here the other day, or the cameras." He waited for some sort of explanation.

"Quite right, sir. They just installed this today and they are finishing off the cameras on each floor. Would you like to speak to the rental agent?"

"Yeah, sure."

"One moment... Jason, there are a couple of gentlemen wanting to see you," announced the security guard over an intercom.

"Rodger dodger, I'll be right there," replied the voice.

Goody looked at the guard. The guard shrugged his shoulders. A little man closed the door of apartment 101 and hurried to their side. He extended his hand. Goody just nodded.

"Hello..." said Jeff with his hand extended.

"Ja-son," said the agent. "Well gen-tle-men, what is your pleasure?"

Jeff answered him, "We would like to speak to the couple in apartment 202, please."

"Whooo?" the agent said looking confused.

"The elderly couple in 202," offered Goody in his throaty voice.

"I'm sorry, gentlemen, but there is no one living in 202. In fact, they just finished construction... That's why all the balloons," said Jason, delightfully throwing his hands in the air.

Jeff offered his business card to the agent. "Can we see 202, please?"

"Cer-tain-ly," said Jason.

The security guard handed Jason a master key. The elevator opened and the three stepped inside. Goody looked around and spotted four mini cameras in the elevator. They arrived on floor two.

"Down here, gentlemen."

He opened the door to an empty apartment. Blue protective polyethylene still covered the ceramic stove top and heavy paper was laid on the wooden floors to protect them from possibly getting scratched on viewings. The paper was brand new, without a footprint. They looked around.

"For the two of you?" questioned Jason.

Goody ignored the question and then asked, "Anything on the top floor?"

"They're all available," relayed Jason. "Cometh, I will show you the one I like."

They took the elevator up to the fourth floor.

"I like this one, 401. I know it is across from the elevator, but only having two apartments per floor... There shouldn't be any impact by foot traffic."

He opened the door with a click. Jeff stopped at the door jamb and took a better look at the framework. He also noticed a camera at each end of the short hallway.

"This is so beautiful with the ceiling-to-floor windows; it makes the room come alive... Don't you think?" raved Jason.

"It certainly does," said Jeff. "Probably a lot of history in here."

"Yessss. If only the walls could talk," Jason said through a smile.

Goody slapped Jeff on the arm.

"Come on, we got work to do," said Goody with an air of authority.

"Here's my business card, gentlemen, in case you would like another tour."

As they were set to leave, Jeff turned to Jason, and asked, "Jason, who owns this building?"

"Pride of Destiny, of course. The workmanship screams their high standards."

"Yes it does. I have seen others," said Jeff.

Back in Goody's car, Jeff, sitting in the passenger seat looking out the window, shared with Goody, "George Stanza owns that building."

"Really! How do you know this?"

"Pride of Destiny... I looked them up after I was at the after-party. Same beautiful workmanship as Stanza's place."

"Back to the office?" asked Goody.

"Might as well. Nothing here for us to look at," said Jeff, a little disheartened.

Goody felt his friend's pain, "Be positive, buddy. We'll find her."

"I know... I just hope we find her in one piece. And still breathing, and not at the bottom of a river."

Enhanced Security

Gina arrived at AD Fashions and was escorted to Delores' desk, which was located in the atrium of the administration suite. The two executive offices shared a wall and offered L.A. views on one side and their doors facing the atrium on the other side. Delores showed Gina to her new office and then wasted little time in explaining protocol and issuing Gina a temporary password for signing in. She also handed her a packet for her to sign with disclosures and confidentiality clauses, the whole nine yards sent over from the attorneys. Delores informed Gina that the paperwork must be completed in her presence, as she was also the company's notary.

Delores, although briefly meeting Gina, inquired about her sullen spirit, as the day before she was as bright as a shining star. Gina told her of her concern about not hearing from Angela, especially it being her first day on the job.

Gina asked Delores if Angela had contacted the office. Delores reported that the day before at noon was the last time they had spoken.

"Has Angela ever not checked in by 9 a.m.?" asked Gina, not wanting to sound too concerned that Angela was in trouble.

"No... I usually get in just before 8 a.m. and Angela is always here before me. It's her quiet time before everyone starts interrupting her day. She ponders over her design table, scribbling down different things. She won't let me clean it up. She says it's 'her dreams unfolding'."

Gina forced a smile and a little laugh. "That's Angela," she said trying to keep it light without giving away her real concerns.

"I just have to get my fingerprint pad and I will be right back," informed Delores.

Within a minute, she returned with a pad but not the usual-looking black ink type. She placed it on Gina's desk.

"Now, just hold your hand steady on the pad," she instructed.

A light beam underneath scanned her fingerprints.

"Thank you. I will be right back with your ID card."

"Wow..." Gina said. "You don't mess around."

Delores returned once again and with a smile on her face, she handed Gina her ID card. Gina looked at it.

"Where is the black stripe to swipe?" she asked.

"No black stripe. It has an embedded chip. All the information is in that chip, including your fingerprints. It's the same type of card used in Europe at all their banks. More secure than our outdated ones. You can't steal anyone's identity with this type of system," shared Delores.

"Why don't we use them here?"

"Don't know... Maybe the banks consider it too expensive to remodel their format without the government demanding it?"

"How did Angela come by this? She has never been to Europe as far as I know."

"Mr. Stanza is a bit of a security aficionado, shall I say," remarked Delores with a smile. She showed Gina how to access the data base of clients.

"Thank you, Delores...for everything."

"I suggest you enjoy this time because..." she looked at her watch, "...in about 5 minutes, you will be deluged with people wanting answers all at the same time. Would you like some freshly brewed coffee?"

"Do you have iced tea? Oh, one more thing, Delores. I have a private investigator looking into the whereabouts of my daughter. If he calls, can you patch him through right away? His name is Jeff Malardo."

Delores hesitated then turned to Gina.

"What a coincidence, I remember seeing Angela scribbling his name on one of her sketch pads a few weeks ago. Interesting, isn't it?"

"Interesting in which way?" asked Gina curiously.

"How paths cross in the universe."

Possible Link

Jeff and Goody had already set up the big board with more cheat sheets added, including the photo of the unknown girl that Jeff found at Angela's apartment. The lab had sent up a report regarding the authenticity of the article regarding the explosion of the tanker and the reported disappearance and assumed death of Gloria Jackson. The picture on the piece-meal collage also matched that of the missing girl. Harry Peters had already signed off on opening the case. Once in a while, their firm handled Pro Bono cases; it was good for their image and their 501c3 status. Congress, as well, liked to see these cases on their books; especially when it came to under-the-table financing.

A case number C-49-088-423 was assigned for charging expenses. Peters was a stickler for keeping exact expense logs. Mainly in question were travel, lodging and meal expenses; although, they did maintain a slush fund for miscellaneous occurrences that needed to be kept off the record. Regardless, he knew too well that on the spin of a dime, things could turn ugly when you were least expecting them.

Jeff rotated the board on its axis and as he did, the photo of the unknown girl fell to the floor. Not realizing it, he pinned it to the other side—Gloria's side.

He also stuck up on Gloria's side a photocopy of the collaged note, the letter from Allen Travers, and then started to break them down.

Card 1 – presumed dead – bloodied clothes – hair strands

Card 2 – Tanker driver – Peter Rogers – alive

Card 3 – location – Carroll, NH.

Not much to go on, he formulated to himself. *But let's start with Peter Rogers at location—Whitefield.*

Goody stepped over and looked at the board Jeff had set up and instantly pointed out a flaw.

"You forgot the obvious: 'Police say' and the 'News people'. I have missed the obvious as well, my friend. Don't disallow what you see in front of you but dig down and peel away the layers like an onion."

"Thanks, Goody. Always appreciate the extra eyes and twisted mind of yours," jest Jeff.

"What are you doing with the photo of the girl?"

"Ah, shit! It fell on the floor and I must have pinned it on the wrong side," explained Jeff.

Goody stopped him from removing it.

"Wait, my friend. I know this is a long shot and probably has nothing to do with anything, but look at the two pictures side by side. What do you see?"

Jeff looked closely. It was like those games where you had two photos beside each other and you had to search for missing details from one to the other.

"Age is approximate..." said Jeff.

"Good. Go on," coached Goody.

"Long hair..."

"Yes," prodded Goody.

"I don't know..." relinquished Jeff, throwing his arms up in defeat.

"If I take a picture of a fifteen-year-old today with long hair and we look at one taken twenty years ago, how do you automatically know they are not taken at the same time?" said Goody encouraging his friend to delve deeper.

"I don't know... We just can," replied Jeff, frustrated.

"Make-up, lighting of the photo, processing, hair style as you already established... But what is the same here?"

Jeff looked closer and then Goody moved him back further.

"Clarity... They are both old and faded, which establishes time. I found this at Angela's apartment. Obviously, she was hiding it because it was near to her heart, so she wanted to keep it. A KEEPSAKE!" he shouted.

"One more thing," said Goody. "Look at the way this unknown girl has an arm around her. Perhaps someone who cares about her."

"But we are talking about Angela... I mean Gloria," stumbled Jeff.

"Exactly!" praised Goody. "Angela is a loyal friend. She just made an old friend that she probably didn't know for more than what... a couple of hours, her VP. Why? Because she had a connection. It doesn't matter to her the what for or why not, she just knows. Instinctively or intuitively... she is a friend... she cares. End of story," explained Goody, of course, hypothetically.

"But you are assuming Angela is Gloria. That this picture in the note is actually Angela, but a younger-self that being Gloria. That is only an assumption not fact," said Jeff.

"True, but I am confident we will know for sure when we get that DNA results from forensic."

Jeff took a photo of the photo booth picture with his phone. He also took a close-up of the girl in the note, Gloria Jackson. He went over to his desk and buzzed Adriane.

"Adriane, can you book me a flight to somewhere close to Carroll, New Hampshire, as soon as possible? The town doesn't even have a dot."

"Sure, Jeff. Give me a minute."

"So, Goody, you think there is a connection between this note of a runaway and Angela disappearing?"

"They are both runaways. History repeating itself. If they are the same, I would say we are going to have our hands full in finding her. She has experience. Remember, she has been in hiding for one and a half decades. She knows how to hide," stated Goody.

"You are missing one very huge fact. She is out there in public more than most movie stars. She has two successful businesses that we know about. I would not consider that hiding," said Jeff.

"What a perfect place to hide, but out in the open!" exclaimed Goody.

Jeff's intercom buzzed; it was Adriane.

"Jeff, there is a red-eye leaving at mid-night tonight. I booked you. Sweet flight."

Angela Escapes Again

Angela had remained out of sight until she was absolutely positive no one was watching. Her past experiences of what had happened to her friend Irma had her fearful of contacting anyone close; especially her friend Eileen.

With only one room available, a family suite for $923.00 on the Amtrak departing for Chicago at 6:15 p.m., Angela secured passage and boarded at 6:10 p.m. She felt delaying until the next day's express to Boston wasn't worth lingering longer in Los Angeles. Besides, the larger family suite gave her lots of room to stretch her legs without leaving her chamber, and room to plot out her next move. In the large manila envelope from her safe was plenty of money to go anywhere in the world, her two passports, plus a sealed letter with the words *'Last Resort Only'* scribbled on the front in Gilles' handwriting. She had a few days to figure out if this was her last resort or not. She just needed time to think and piece together the events. She had bought a simple notebook at the station's confectionary that any school kid could buy to make her notes.

She started to jot down important names, and beside each name, she added numbers:

Sapphire dress – 3, Rev. M – 2, George – 2, Gina – 2, Joseph – 2, Carl – 2, Eileen – 1, Jeff – 1.

Alone, none of them had added up to 3, the number of times, her friend, the Sapphire dress was part of her life. She thought for a moment... *"If I combined any other two people except Eileen and Jeff, I can come up with three."* Again, she paused for a moment, drew a line through that number under Joseph, and changed it to 3. *"Joseph saw Gina the first night she wore the Sapphire dress to that deception of a dinner party, and then, the first night I met George at his apartment, he had dropped me off while I was wearing the copy I made, and then, once again at the Christiansen art opening. My poor Joseph, what is up?"* Then she started to re-think Rev. M. *"He saw Gina because he was there at the restaurant, then he saw me in the copy after he hit me and then... but he wasn't at the art opening... What if it was Anthony who commissioned Gina to re-make it? Okay, Rev. M. you get 3 as well."*

She leaned her head against the thick upholstered backs of the seat. She closed her eyes. Her mind was racing but her energy was drained. George was one of the best men she had ever met. *"Trust me,"* he had said to her, *"everything will be all right. I promise."*

My father promised me, too, and he left me. Now George. I know it was Joseph chasing me, but why did he stop after he fired that shot that took out the car's rear window? It was nowhere near me. He could have turned around backwards and fired a shot closer. And then, when I saw the other guy through the side mirror of the bus, barreling out the door,

Joseph pretended he was winded. What a crock... He's big, but he can move. No way was he winded. What is going on? I wish I could have made out the other guy. It might have been Anthony, but I didn't get a good look. Her eyes were heavy as she nodded in and out of sleep. She jerked herself awake and inserted another scenario in her notebook. Finally, it fell out of her lap like a limp doll propped halfway against the bottom of the seat, half spread out onto the floor. She slid down the seat and let the sleep angels protect her.

She didn't hear the steward knock on her door for the last dinner call. He respected her privacy without repeating his knock. The room was not so big that a little tap could not be heard. He went on to the next.

Looking for Trouble?

Jeff's red-eye flight landed in Chicago's O'Hare Airport at 6:30 in the morning and then, he had to kill several hours before catching a connection to Boston where he lost another hour. Adriane had pre-arranged a rental car for him, which he picked up without the usual bantering back and forth. When all was said and done, Jeff finally got on the road at 11 a.m. EST. He had a fairly straight shot from the airport through the Sumner Tunnel. From there, he picked up Interstate 93, which would take him all the way up through New Hampshire to just short of the Vermont border to a little town called Carroll. Gloria's last known whereabouts.

He was running on an alternating diet of canned energy drinks and coffee. Falling asleep the night before in his office hadn't helped his sense of humor or the strain in his back. His happy-go-lucky attitude that he usually displayed driving in L.A. traffic was diminishing with the number of drinks he had—or was it his lack of sleep? His rental was equipped with

GPS, cruise control, a sun roof, and a decent radio with CD capability. He slipped in Christina Aguilera's CD, turned it up and set the cruise at 74 mph. He had picked up a couple of Sabrett hot dogs, fully loaded. He was on a mission. In less than three hours, he determined he would be sitting on the Sheriff's doorstep asking questions.

It was a pretty drive once he passed Manchester and followed the Merrimack River. Lots of points of interest along the way kept his drive stimulating; not like driving to Vegas up the I-15. Ski resort signs dotted the highway as he cruised up into the White Mountains; also cooler temperatures. *How could L.A. be so stifling hot and here still be in the low 60's?* he thought.

The Interstate wound through passes and riverbeds and at some sections along the way, it felt like he took 90-degree bends to the left and then to the right. He now understood how the accident of the tank truck traveling on a minor road could occur. Without a well-maintained major Interstate, a torrential downpour could definitely impede visibility.

A sign for Twin Mountain—Hwy 3 took Jeff past another state historical site, the *'Old Man of the Mountain'*, which—according to the placard—was a *'rock face'* before it collapsed a few years back. It sure was pretty country. He followed Hwy 3 left at Twin Mountain and then turned off onto a county road to the little burg of Carroll.

As he pulled up to the address where his GPS indicated the police station was located, the building now housed a doggie boutique, a florist, a small real estate office, and the last, a locksmith. He looked around. Other than the few vehicles out front, he might as well have been in the middle of Kansas. He was too tired to go searching for the new location of the Sheriff's office, in whatever town it might have moved to, so he decided to head back down the road where he had passed a small single-story motel that posted a *'Kitchen Open'* sign.

The lady at the desk was very obliging and allowed Jeff to check out the room before he paid for it. It had old-fashioned décor with faux wood desktops covered with glass, wood paneling, a new flat-screen TV, and avocado-green bathroom tiles with matching tub and toilet, but it smelled clean—bonus. Jeff threw his bag on a barrel chair and laid down on one of the doubles—just for a minute.

~

A horn honking and some chit-chat woke Jeff at 10:05 p.m. He sprung to his feet in the dark room and immediately stubbed his toe on the metal frame of one of the doubles. "Ouch... Fuck!" He limped to the front door and switched on the ceiling light that blared brightly two 100-watt bulbs partially enclosed with a four-sided, frosted glass shade. It reminded him of his college dorm room. He took a deep breath and sighed. He looked at his watch. *"Six hours... Shit. I need a drink to wake up and something to eat,"* he muttered to himself.

With quick fingers through the hair, he brushed his teeth, added a scrape of deodorant, and donned a clean shirt. He headed over to where the 'Kitchen Open' sign remained lit. As he opened the door, he was immediately smacked in the face with cigarette smoke. He coughed and continued to forge into the misleading, local bar. A bruiser of a bartender with four days of growth on his face stood behind the bar serving the locals.

"What's your pleasure, mister?" he asked politely enough as Jeff stepped in.

"Tall rum and cola, please." Jeff looked around at the drawn looks of the ten or so patrons sitting at tables. Two others were playing pool.

Jeff leaned on the bar and said, "Happening place you got here."

"Thursday we have music, so it will be full up." The bartender placed Jeff's drink on the bar top.

"I thought the sign said Kitchen Open?" questioned Jeff.

"It is... That's the name of this place."

Jeff snorted a laugh, "Oh, you got me."

The bartender didn't smile. He bent over the cooler, grabbed a couple of beers, cracked them open and placed them at the end of the bar for the two playing pool. One of the patrons who were sitting at a low table got up, stepped up to the bar, and stood beside Jeff.

"You from New York?" he asked in a slurred tone.

"No. Los Angeles."

"You a cop?"

"No. Looking for a friend."

The man laughed, "Hell, I can tell you right now there ain't no friend here from Los Angeles."

A couple of the locals joined in on the joke.

"I didn't say my friend was *from* Los Angeles," replied Jeff, not backing down.

"What are you a P.I. like Magasin?" stumbled the man.

"I believe you are referring to Magnum, a TV character, which was filmed in Hawaii, not Los Angeles," corrected Jeff.

"Dalton, you're daft, man," said one of his friends at another table.

Jeff, keeping his cool, eyed the reflection of the men who were sitting down through the large mirrors behind the bar— only the pool players were out of his sight.

"So, who's your friend?" asked the daft calling man.

"She's a missing teen from around here, possibly fifteen or sixteen years ago?" said Jeff as he watched their reactions.

From over at the pool table, one of them spoke up.

"What's her name, friend?"

"Gloria Jackson," said Jeff, casually sipping on his drink.

One of the men that were playing pool angrily slammed his cue down on the felt and said, "Mister, we don't like strangers coming in here and dragging up ancient history."

Jeff turned to the man who offered the slamming of his pool cue down on the felt. Jeff had seen this more times than he could count. The effect was lost on him. And as if script in the pool hall rules, the man quickly picked it up and used it as an extension to his finger—and possible manhood.

"I don't want any trouble here, gentlemen. Just asking some questions, if you don't mind?"

"Maybe we do mind. She was a friend of ours that got killed in a truck fire. Let her lie in peace and don't be bothering her daddy either," threatened the cue-carrying man.

"Rodney, settle down," intervened the bartender, Jake Kitchen.

"Jake, you knows very well what kind of pain that brought our community. We don't need a pussy boy from Los Angeles coming in here and stirring things up. You know I'm telling the truth."

"Maybe so, Rodney... but I want no trouble from you or any of you boys in here. You all understand me?" demanded the bartender in a raised voice. "Now, you all settle down and drink your beers. Mister, you best be on your way. The town has had enough grief."

"Thank you, Jake, but after I finish my drink, if you don't mind."

Jake bent over the bar and said in a lowered voice, "I'm telling you nicely. These boys have had a few. For your sake, you better get out of here. The drink is on the house."

"Thanks for the warning, Jake; I appreciate your concern. See you tomorrow," said Jeff.

Jeff turned and left his spot at the bar and walked to the door but stopped short of it. Turning back, he eyed the room and said politely, "Good evening, gentlemen. Thanks for the conversation." He had lots of experience with drunks when he bounced while waiting to get into the police academy. He knew how to calm things down, but he also knew how to set a seed of irritation. His polite salutations just set the seed.

He slowly walked back to his room and as he predicted in his mind, one by one the town boys staggered out of the Kitchen. One of them made a comment.

"You got yourself a pussy nature for a boy with a big mouth," slurred drunk number two.

Not all of the men in the bar had an attitude problem, but five stood outside of the Kitchen hurling insults at Jeff. Jeff laughed it off and continued to walk toward his room and with another seed, he said, "Sleep it off, gentlemen, and I'll see you in the morning."

"You ain't seeing nothing, pussy!" screamed drunk three as they all start to run at Jeff.

Jeff calmly turned, and as one tried to tackle him, he simply pushed him aside. Another took a wheelbarrow swing, missed Jeff by a yard, and fell to the ground by his own inertia. The other three, Rodney, carrying a pool cue, Dalton and Mr. Daft calling man, came toward him like the fight at OK Corral, poised and ready to do harm. They might have been scrappers between themselves but they weren't trained goons. Jeff purposely took his time crossing the parking lot so he could position himself with the bright motel sign behind him. He faced his challengers. They charged him. Rodney swung his pool cue, but daft man came across in front and took the crack of the pool cue in the head. He dropped to the ground. Rodney, stunned, looked at his friend on the ground, which gave Jeff that split second to roundhouse Rodney and sent him sliding on his ass along the gravel lot. Jeff, with hands raised, poised to do battle, turned to Dalton—and as he also expected—he cowered away, looking for support from his buddies. What Jeff did not expect was to get clipped in the head from behind by a baton.

The next morning, Jeff awoke with a sore head and the uncomfortable and unmistakable feel of a jail-house bed. The mattress stunk of years of disinfectant mixed with vomit and urine. He sat straight up. He felt the road rash to the side of his eye where he must have hit the gravel after being knocked out. He was not amused. He hollered for someone on duty.

From the outer room, he heard the rustling of keys. A deputy sheriff walked in and opened the gate to his cell. He was scrawny and chewing gum. Jeff brushed against him as he took leave, forcing him to fall back against the bars.

"You better control your attitude, mister," confronted the deputy.

"I don't like being hit on the head by one of our own," responded Jeff.

Jeff entered the outer office and saw the sheriff sitting in his office. He wasted little time in knocking on his open door.

Politely, Jeff asked, "Sheriff, can we speak?"

The sheriff looked up from his paperwork and over to Jeff and his anxious deputy. He motioned him in. Jeff closed the door behind him, shutting out the deputy.

"May I?" asked Jeff pointing to a chair in front of the sheriff's desk.

"What's on your mind?" coolly asked the sheriff.

"Other than the bump on my head from your deputy, a couple of questions," said Jeff.

"Go ahead."

"I'm Jeff Malardo..."

"I know who you are," interrupted the sheriff, tossing Jeff's wallet at him.

"I've been assigned a fifteen-year-old case of a missing girl, named Gloria Jackson. Can you tell me what happened during that investigation?"

The sheriff tapped his calendar pad with his pencil.

"Sheriff Turner was in command and I was a young deputy at that time. She was a runaway that met her end... and... not too pleasantly," he informed Jeff. "Why now are you opening a closed case?"

"We received some information that she might still be alive. You never found her body," stated Jeff, not asking a question.

"The troopers handled that accident over at Salmon Falls. We weren't involved, jurisdiction and all," claimed the sheriff. "I imagined they felt they had enough evidence to presume her demise. I know they held that case open for several years but finally concluded it needed to be closed, for family sake."

"Yes. It is nice to have closure so the ones left behind can go on; especially dealing with one so young," said Jeff choosing his words carefully. "Do you have a file I can look at?"

"At the courthouse, maybe. We had a flood come through here that destroyed a lot of our paperwork over at the old jailhouse in Carroll. There wasn't much anyway. We questioned her friends; we searched her room and found no evidence of misconduct. Her backpack was missing and some clothes; she was a runaway. Unless you can find a body stating otherwise, I think our conversation has reached its limit," stated the sheriff.

"One more question, if I may? Where is Sheriff Turner? Is it possible to talk to him?"

"He left the force just after that incident. And, no, I don't know where he went. Just picked up the family and left."

"What about her parents? Are they still alive?"

"I believe that makes two questions." The sheriff took a long breath and said, "The step-father is still at his old farmhouse; don't know where they took the wife."

"Who took the wife?" asked Jeff, curiously.

"Don't know. A highfalutin lawyer with some sort of paperwork came here and took her away. I don't know anything more than that. We weren't involved."

"Where's the farmhouse?"

"The old Miller Road off of the 115," replied the sheriff, nodding his head in the general direction. "I would be very careful going by there. Old Stephen isn't so welcoming as the rest of the town folks," chuckled the sheriff.

"Yes, I do feel the warmth here," jest Jeff, touching his bruised head. "Thanks, Sheriff... for everything. Can your deputy give me a ride back to the motel?"

"No need, your belongings and rental are outside."

Jeff relinquished a quick smile and headed out the door. The deputy handed him a large manila envelope with his car keys and phone. The deputy added, "Just tried to save you from a beating."

Jeff looked straight into his eyes. "Obviously you were not standing there long enough to make that assumption correctly."

At least the sun felt warm through the chilled air as he stepped outside. *Nice, friendly place*, he thought. He programmed his GPS for Old Miller Road. Nothing came up.

They probably call it that because years ago, a guy named Miller lived there and has since died. Great.

As Jeff was driving out of town, to his right he spotted a hardware store with a 'Post Office' sign displayed. He parked his car in one of the angled spaces out front and went inside to ask the postmaster where Old Miller was located. He got: "Down a piece on 115 and before you cross a small bridge turn left and a quick right at the red barn. Stephen's house is the second lane on the left."

"Of course... The red barn." He thanked the postmaster and got back into his rental.

A little ways down the road, Jeff noticed a pick-up in his rearview mirror was maintaining the same pace as he. He followed the given directions and turned right at the faded red barn. Two lanes down, he turned in slowly. In his mind, he could hear the banjoes playing like a scene from Deliverance. On his left, he approached an old car and beyond that, a two-story farmhouse with a wraparound veranda. A split oak tree to the right looked like it got hit by lightning and was never cut down. Jeff stopped his car near the front steps. A man with a stubble beard wearing a sleeveless tee-shirt, brandishing a 12-gauge shotgun stepped out onto the porch. The man looked through the car's windshield at Jeff sitting there. Jeff stepped out and rested his left arm on top of the door frame and his right on the car's roof. Jeff wanted to appear non-threatening.

"Good morning," said Jeff. "Are you Stephen?"

"Who might you be?" he asked, nudging his gun towards Jeff as if it was an extension of his finger. Jeff chuckled to himself at the thought of the similarity of the Carroll men.

Jeff remained casual and respectful and said, "Jeff Malardo, sir. If I may, can I ask you a couple of questions?"

"What about?"

"Your daughter, Gloria Jackson."

The man didn't flinch, but just stared at Jeff.

"She's not my kid. She belonged to my wife," stated Stephen, somewhat belligerently.

"Sorry, I didn't mean to imply anything. So she never contacted you or your wife?"

"She's dead, mister. What do you want?"

"Your wife perhaps? Had she spoken to her before the accident?"

"No telling... she's gone too."

"What happened to your wife, if you don't mind me asking?"

"I don't give a shit. Some fancy lawyer and a social worker came in here like they owned the place and took her. Too bad about the woman. She was pretty; except for that scar near her eye."

Jeff immediately thought of Eileen Cortez, Angela's partner at the gallery.

"When was that, sir?" sympathetically, asked Jeff.

"No need for your dribble, mister. Maybe ten years or so. Best day of my life," informed Stephen. "Now you best be on your way. I got nothing else to say."

"Thank you for your time, sir. I'll be on my way."

Jeff got back into his car and thought, *Well, that didn't go too bad. No bullet holes.*

~

Next stop for Jeff was Channel 12 News in Whitefield. He was starving but thought time best spent would be to get as much information as he could in the morning before people started disappearing for lunch.

He was led into a viewing room at Channel 12 News where an assistant set him up to watch the old footage. He saw the wreckage of the truck at the bottom of the ravine, a trooper finding something, putting it into a bag, and then the men started frantically looking for something else while a few stayed with the truck driver. He also noticed that the sheriff's department and state troopers were involved. Why did the sheriff say they hadn't participated? It was a horrific crash indeed. The driver was lucky he hadn't died. Jeff rewound the tape and took another look.

"Okay, this is when they find strands of Gloria's hair"... the reel continued... "they find half-burnt and bloody clothes... and now they look towards the river. What's the dog doing? Fuck!" The camera swung back to the truck as they began to pull the driver out of the wreckage.

"No help," exhaled Jeff. He thanked the assistant and returned to his rental. The same truck he saw before was parked down a little ways from him. Nonchalantly, he adjusted his rearview mirror and started his car. His stomach was crying, *Feed me, feed me!"*

Main Street, Whitefield was bustling compared to where he had just recently been. On the right he saw a diner and quickly pulled into a diagonal parking space. The windows were large with booths angled at 90 degrees. Stepping inside, he noticed a sign stating: 'Seat Yourself'. Jeff picked a booth where he could look out at anyone who approached or entered the diner. A pretty waitress in her early thirties walked over to him carrying a pot.

"Coffee?" she asked pleasantly.

"Yes, thank you," said Jeff.

The waitress flipped over his cup that had been staged on the table and poured the coffee into it. She smiled and turned to replace the decanter back on the burner.

Sitting on a shelf across from him and to the left of the cashier, a collection of magazines and old high school yearbooks were on display. Jeff got up and wandered over. He pulled out several randomly and brought them back to his booth. He took a sip of his coffee as he slowly flipped through. The waitress came back with a menu.

"That's my old high school," she added with delight.

"Oh yeah?" responded Jeff with sincere interest as he examined the individual pictures.

He paused on one page.

"There I am," she said pointing at her own picture.

"Beautiful, as you are now. Pretty sweater."

"Thanks."

"You could have been a model," he charmed reading her name, Carol Follett.

"I was. I went to Europe, traveled around with the..." holding her fingers up, she made quotation marks in the air, "...jet setters. But after a year I was bored with all the phony crap and I missed everyone here, so I came home."

"It is magnificent here, if you fit in." Jeff pointed to his scraped face.

Before Jeff could say another word, his admirers that had been following him walked in. Jeff stood up. The waitress looked around and saw Rodney and Dalton had walked through the door.

"Is this the guy you told me about?" she declared loudly to Rodney.

Rodney and Dalton stopped in their tracks.

Looking at Jeff's physique, she turned again and glared at Rodney, and continued to berate him.

"Do you have paper between your ears? You should thank this man for not sending you home in a body bag instead of a little rosebud butt. What were you thinking? Don't answer that; you obviously weren't. Go home, mister."

The two men turned and left—just like that.

"Friends of yours?" asked Jeff.

"My dumb-head husband. I apologize for their small-town mentality."

She sat down at his booth. She turned the next page to where her best friend Gloria Jackson's picture resided.

"This is who you have been asking about," pointed Carol. "My best friend in the whole world." A tear started to form at the corner of her eye. She wiped it.

"I still can't believe she is gone. Sometimes, I will wake up in the middle of the night and feel her standing there looking at me... whispering to me that everything is all right. It has been over fifteen years." She took pause and looked up at Jeff. "Why are you here?" she questioned with a hint of sadness in her voice.

Jeff reached into his pocket and pulled out his phone. Searching through his gallery, he found what he was looking for. He enlarged the photo and turned the phone to Carol. She gasped.

"Where did you get this? No one knows of this picture!"

She got up and quickly ran to a framed photo of her and a group of people in front of the diner, cutting a ribbon. She opened the back. She pulled out a ripped photo booth photo. She matched it to Jeff's camera image. It fit perfectly. She looked at him with tears in her eyes.

"I don't understand."

"It was by accident that I came across this. I don't know for certain..."

Carol cut him off.

"That's Gloria... She's wearing my sweater," she insisted. "Look..." as she turned the page back to herself... "Here I'm wearing it before we asked the school photographer to take our picture together. After that, we went down to the old arcade and took these pictures. She is still wearing my sweater. How can you say that is not her?"

Wow... he thought... *Rodney definitely has his hands full with her.*

"I didn't say that is not Gloria. I am saying I am not sure if she is my friend, Angela," said Jeff.

"She's alive! She changed her name?" grilled Carol.

"We are still investigating the possibility."

"I can't believe it," Carol shook her head. "Why wouldn't she get ahold of me? Why would she keep that a secret?"

"When did you go to Europe?" asked Jeff.

"Not long after her accident. I needed to get away."

"Maybe she tried and found out you were in Europe, modeling," consoled Jeff with his usual logic.

"Yes... That must be it," accepted Carol, still bewildered. "What are you going to do next?"

"I don't know. Probably go down to the accident site."

"It's been over fifteen years. What do you think you will find that the state troopers didn't?"

"I don't know... That's why I need to look around and see for myself. I was a cop for a time, but not until I started with the agency have I discovered a whole new way of looking at things. Things that seem trivial or obvious are not always what they appear to be, if that makes sense."

"I can get Rodney to go with you."

"Ah, no thanks. I need to do this by myself. Thanks anyway."

"Trust me, he knows this country; it's his backyard. He's not as dumb as he acts... Well sometimes," she added lightly. "Please, let him help. This is my friend we are talking about... It is the least we can do to help her," insisted Carol. "You don't know this area. You don't know how quickly a storm can come up or how to talk to the locals..."

Jeff interrupted Carol this time.

"I talked with her father without getting shot."

Her eyes grew wide and she grabbed the table top tightly. "You talked to that bastard? When?"

"Before I came here," said Jeff.

"You know, I always blamed him. That is, until now, for Gloria's disappearance. I truly believed he killed her and buried her somewhere."

"But they found evidence at the accident scene that she was there."

"I thought the cops planted it. I don't know; he is such a bad man. I thought Sheriff Turner and Stephen were in cahoots."

"He is colorful, let's say. Why did you think the sheriff and Stephen were in on Gloria's disappearance?"

Carol laughed, "Colorful???" She shifted her position on the bench seat and clasped her hands together, reminiscing. "Well, shortly after the accident, all of a sudden, the sheriff picked up his family and left. Like everything! House, furniture, his job, and no one has heard anything from them."

"That is more than a little unusual behavior. I can see why you thought that about them. But Stephen stuck around. I need to call my partner to give him an update," said Jeff.

"Do you want a hamburger or something?" asked Carol, wanting to put this all behind her.

Jeff almost forgot he hadn't had anything to eat since the day before. He answered affirmatively. Picking up his phone, he called his office.

"Goody... What's up man?"

"Hey, buddy... DNA came back from our lab and it definitely matches Gloria Jackson. But we are waiting for confirmation from NCIC to see if their files match," informed Goody.

"I met the girl in the picture as well. Angela's mother was taken away from here by someone, who I believe to be George Stanza and Eileen Cortez. I don't know where they have her," explained Jeff. "I'll probably be heading back soon."

"Okay, buddy, talk later." They disconnected.

Carol brought Jeff her best-selling double cheese, double meat burger with homemade fries.

"Smells delicious," said Jeff. "So you own this place?"

"Yes. I bought it with the money I saved from modeling. So, what is your friend Angela, my friend Gloria, doing?" curiously asked Carol with a gleam of light glowing from her eyes at the notion her friend may indeed be alive.

"Let's say... I know of two businesses. Partners in a successful art gallery in Beverly Hills, she also owned an interior design studio, which according to records, she sold, and put that investment into her fashion company," related Jeff.

"Really... what's the name of her fashion company?"

"AD Fashions."

"What!" exclaimed Carol.

"Oh no", thought Jeff. He started to cringe.

"I received this gorgeous sapphire dress a little over a month ago. There is no way I could ever wear it around here but a typewritten note with AD Fashions was inside. There was no return address," said Carol.

Jeff just about coughed up his cheeseburger. He immediately picked up his phone, but then, hesitated. He asked, "Did it have a cherub on its shoulder?"

"Yes... a gold one, very cute."

Jeff redialed his buddy in Los Angeles.

"Goody. We either found Gina's missing dress that she told us about, the one she couldn't remember what happened to it. Or there exists a possible third dress. One of them was sent to her friend, Carol, anonymously. Goody... someone is one step ahead of us. I'm staying a little longer. Okay... talk soon. Yes, I will be careful. Thanks, man." Jeff looked across the table at Carol who was getting teary-eyed again.

"Carol, I don't want to get you involved with this, but maybe if Rodney can help me out with some gear, a rifle and some information about the lay of the land, it would be greatly appreciated."

Carol dabbed her eyes with a napkin and said with a hopeful smile.

"Trust me, he would love to," declared Carol.

Claire's Sanctuary

The Amtrak that Angela was a passenger on pulled into the Chicago station—as far as she knew—undetected. Flashing her pretty blues, she had persuaded an agent to rent her a car without securing the contract with a credit card. She had said that she needed to get away from a jealous boyfriend who had connections, so it would be wise not to get involved. She gave the young man a few extra dollars to process the deal. Besides, she was only going to be a couple of days visiting her elderly mother and father and promised she would be good.

She had driven all night, driving past the Great Lakes on I-90 all the way to I-91. From there, she headed north through Vermont to where the 302 crossed and shifted down to Highway 112. It wouldn't be long now before she would gaze upon her old, dear friend, Gilles. He had lovingly told her to use his last name, if she wished, and that everything would be all right. How many times had she heard that, and now here she was again, running for her life. She had dropped off her rental car in a shopping mall parking lot and picked up a 4x4 SUV in Albany, New York, the same way as the last rental. Strictly cash... no paper trail. She knew the long road to Gilles could get very nasty. She wanted to be prepared.

When she slowed, preparing to turn onto what she remembered to be Gilles' road, a sign beside the entrance sculpted out of thick lumber declared, 'Claire's Sanctuary'. She crept along the one-mile stretch, watching everything, trying to acclimate her mind, overlaying what she was seeing with what she remembered. The road wasn't paved but it was smoother than before, with an oil and stone topcoat. She approached her hide-away with caution as the driveway opened up to a parking lot with log railings encircling the designated area.

What has happened? Where's Gilles? she wondered.

Angela parked her 4x4 and got out. Several families were milling around, while their children took advantage of the great outdoors, jumping and playing as kids do. A young Cowasuck girl, Bernadette, who was the curator of the sanctuary, as indicated by her name tag, pointed to different areas of interest in reference to the map held by a man wearing hiking boots.

Angela stepped into the wood cabin and suspiciously looked around. Most was as she remembered but her privacy blanket was gone, including the bed she slept in. Over on the other wall was Gilles' bed, neatly arranged with an extra folded blanket. The wooden table still sat on a colorful woven mat and a single serving was set with tin pans and a cup. The cauldron where Gilles made his rabbit stew still swung from its perch, but behind the solid door where the wash basin once stood, was a slanted tray filled with pamphlets. She picked up one and read the legacy of 'Claire's Sanctuary'. On the back was a picture of her dear friend with the dates 1918 to 2015. She broke down in tears. She was so busy making a name for herself that she completely ignored the people who she cherished the most.

At the mid-point of the brochure, a tribute from the current CEO of the Fournier Foundation, Jamison Starkney, announced his lifelong friendship with one of the greatest men he had ever met. '*As my friend and mentor, it gives me great pleasure and privilege to declare Claire's Sanctuary, as a place of eternal light and life, to the ones that went before us, who suffered horrific defeats and personal sacrifice, to be now enjoyed by all, for all time in peace*'. Strangely, at the bottom, the pamphlet indicated: Printed in France.

The young curator stepped inside as Angela was about to leave. She looked through the tears into Angela's eyes. She gently reached for her hand and guided Angela outside and then a short walk up to a lookout. They stood for a moment not saying a word, overlooking the thousand-acre preserve. High in the sky, two birds circled as if they sighted their prey hidden in the shadows of the pine trees. Screeching, they descended down in a spiral, closer and closer, and finally landed on their perch with their wings fully extended, just ahead of the two women. The young curator let go of Angela's hand and placed it on the log railing in front of her. She left the woman with the aging brother and sister hawks, known as Jettie and Claire. Angela slipped down to the ground, crying in despair as the two hawks hopped to each side of the railing next to her, screeching as protectors, flapping their massive wings.

Jeff Follows Her Path

Jeff and Rodney had geared up at the local sports store with what Rodney anticipated they might need. A pair of rifles with scopes and 50 rounds each of ammunition, dried food, lightweight bags, bright-colored jackets, and canteens, among other supplies.

Dalton had dropped them off at the location of Gloria's tragic accident. Jeff and Rodney spent an hour just at that site and didn't find anything worthwhile, just as Jeff had thought. He suggested they go southwest, the opposite direction of the flow of the river and of Gloria's little town. The underbrush was thick, making any forward progress almost impossible. They hacked their way through, it seemed for miles. Rodney picked the route that led them, at times, bouncing off trees as the incline increased and then leveling to a more welcoming trail.

They stopped at a fallen tree and sat upon it for a rest. Rodney was okay, maybe a little misguided, but definitely a good guide and a devoted husband to Carol. As they were sitting having an energy bar, the sun streamed through from behind a tree where upon Jeff noticed a shiny object.

"Rodney, come here and look just to the left of that tree to where the thicket is," said Jeff pointing towards an object.

Rodney came and sat beside Jeff and looked at where he was pointing. Spotting the shiny object that Jeff mentioned, Rodney reached for his pack and pulled out a small machete, and unfolded its handle. He began to whack his way through the briar and retrieved a tarnished but recognizable round, metal grommet.

"What do you think?" Jeff asked as Rodney produced the object to Jeff in his hand.

"Could be off of anything. A drawstring jacket, a backpack..."

And before Rodney could say another word, Jeff blurted out, "Gloria's backpack!"

"How do you know?" questioned Rodney.

"The Sheriff said today that some of her clothes and her backpack were missing when they searched her room. Do you know what that means, my friend? We are following her path. Come on; let's get a little further before we have to make camp."

"You really think she is alive?" asked Rodney, almost apologizing for his behavior from the night before.

"I have hope, Rodney... I have hope."

After another hour of strenuous hiking, Rodney stopped. Looking at his compass, and cross-referencing with his map he realized, "You know, I think we are on the back side of Claire's Sanctuary."

"What's that?" asked Jeff.

"Old man Fournier..."

Jeff, startled by Rodney's statement, cut off Rodney, again, and exclaimed, "Who?"

"Fournier. He was an old timer up here that created this thousand-acre preserve for hikers and the like. You can't hunt on it, man—they'll throw you in jail. Put the boot over the barrel of your rifle and clip it."

"You did say Fournier... Are you sure?"

"Yeah man, why are you getting so intense?"

"How far?" shouted Jeff.

"Just over there," he said pointing through the maze of trees and underbrush. "We should be able to see the hawks' perch with binoculars," replied Rodney, wondering what had Jeff so agitated.

They trudged a little further until they were in sight of a higher rock formation with its jagged plateau protruding. Rodney nudged Jeff to get out his binoculars.

Longing in despair, Angela looked up from where she had collapsed. Overlooking the serene valley, she suddenly noticed a glare of light being reflected. She ducked down and slid her way off the plateau and ran back to the cabin. She shouted to the curator, "Do you have binoculars?"

"Yes," she replied in wonderment. Bernadette opened the drawer underneath the pamphlets and handed them to Angela.

Angela grabbed the binoculars out of Bernadette's hand and rushed through the door of the cabin to the knolls edge. Crawling on her belly, Angela edged to the look-out's point. Two men, one of which was using a rifle scope to search the rock formation. The young curator walked up to where Angela was lying.

"There are two men with rifles down there," frantically said Angela.

"No ma'am that's not allowed. No man to hunt here. Everyone knows that. Big fine and jail time," stated Bernadette.

Angela tossed the young girl the binoculars.

"Then look for yourself," she bellowed.

The hawks felt Angela's tension and took to flight.

"Look Jeff, aren't they beautiful," remarked Rodney searching the skies with his binoculars.

"You got me there, Rodney. Magnificent," replied Jeff, following their graceful movement.

Angela ran to her 4x4. Bernadette followed, concerned.

"They are after me!" she screamed. "How did they find me? When they get here to question you, don't tell them

227

anything about me being here. Do you understand? Your life could depend on it," said Angela, passionately.

The young curator stood, amazed, as the blonde lady turned her 4x4 around and headed in the wrong direction, away from the main driveway, through over-grown fields.

The Elusive Spirit

The following morning, Jeff sat in the privacy of his motel room making detailed notes including Rodney's insistence on securing his rifle. He also included the accounting of their arrival at the cabin of Claire's Sanctuary, and the apparent madness several hours prior of a paranoid blonde lady who drove through a corn field. The young curator, Bernadette, knew Rodney and she told him that when the crazy lady saw their rifles through the binoculars, she flipped out, babbling all sorts of things like, *"They are after me"* and not to say anything because she would be at risk, as well. Bernadette did add that the blonde lady's spirit lived at the sanctuary. The hawks protected it.

Jeff wrote in his notes: "I picked up a pamphlet and noticed that Angela shared the same last name as the man honored. Possibly her grandfather on the mother's side, as the father, Stephen, possessed little spirit other than the bottom of an empty rum bottle.

"Rodney and I have acquired a mutual respect for each other, as his abilities for tracking and his concern for the environment and protection of the animals have raised my expectations. I suggested that he might be the one to lead guided eco-tours through the sanctuary... added note—it might help with his misconceptions of people from other areas; sort of an inside joke we share. After talking with

Carol, Angela's high school friend, I am going to head down to Portsmouth." End of report.

Jeff picked up his phone to call Goody just as his phone rang. Goody's name appeared with his picture.

"Hello," answered Jeff. "Hey, my man, how's it going?"

"Good," replied Goody. *"I have some news for you. The DNA that we found at Angela's apartment matches that of Gloria Jackson according with what NCIC had on record. So my friend, you are looking for the same person."*

"Jesus ... Goody. What the hell is going on then?"

"I don't know. A long web of interwoven lives. Also, a rental car was found abandoned in a shopping mall parking lot in Albany, NY. The young rental agent said a pretty blonde lady rented it with cash, in Chicago. We also have a look out for a white SUV 4x4 rented the same way. Bear with me, it gets better. I also found out, while you were on your nature hike, that a guy called Anthony Micholanetti, alias Reverend Michaels, was released from prison two months ago. Now this is where it really gets good. Forty years ago, he lived in New Jersey and as a fifteen-year-old, got involved in an auto accident killing a young female tourist from France. He and his buddies were intoxicated. Because of his age, authorities could not prosecute him as an adult and I believe with his family's ties, he escaped without jail time. He was sent to Vegas to live with an uncle where he had a few minor run-ins with the law and then moved to Los Angeles. Years later, he developed a reputation for drugs, trafficking, and a harem of 'Ladies of the Evening'. The murder of one of his prostitutes finally landed him in prison, but then, was paroled early from his twenty-year jail term for good behavior... preaching the word is what a friend told me."

"So, what are you saying, Goody... that Angela was part of his stable?"

"Perhaps, young Gloria. I don't believe Angela would have put up with him," said Goody.

"Do you think it's this guy, Anthony Micholanetti who has been baiting everyone to get at Angela?"

"I would put my money on it. He has had sixteen years to plan his revenge."

"Nice work, my friend. I'm going to take a trip down to Portsmouth and then come home. I still have contacts in the LAPD vice department and a few acquaintances on the street. I'll follow that lead of Gloria working for Micholanetti. See you in a couple of days."

"Okay, stay cool," said Goody.

"Hey, one other thing. My nature hike, as you called it, ate me alive. I got horse-fly bites the size of quarters that I would gladly share with you if I could."

Goody laughed, *"What's that song... oh yeah, Love Bites."*

"I think it is, Love Hurts, but nice try... Ciao." Jeff chuckled to himself as he hung up.

While Jeff was preparing to pack for his trip to Portsmouth, a knock on his motel room door echoed out. Upon opening the door, Rodney stood partially blocking the early morning sunlight from blinding Jeff.

"Hey, mornin' Jeff."

"Good morning, Rodney. Come on in; I just finished packing."

"I ran into Bernadette at the hardware store this morning. She didn't know if it mattered but a man of the cloth came to the Sanctuary just after we left and was asking strange questions that a man of his calling, according to Bernadette, had no reason to ask. He picked up a pamphlet and left. She said he was not very nice in his tone, not like Pastor Perkins."

Jeff hesitated for a moment, then said, "Rodney, here are a few of my business cards, and if you can distribute them to a couple of your friends, the diner, and maybe at Kitchen Open and tell them if anybody starts asking questions about me or Gloria, to let me know. I'm going down to Portsmouth and then I'll be heading back to L.A. Trust me; we will get to the bottom of this."

"Will do... and thank you Jeff for giving me a second chance and us all hope for Gloria's survival. By the way, I took your advice and Carol made me some flyers. I talked with the elders of Bernadette's tribe and it looks like we are going to jointly offer guided tours and historic recounting of the spirits living in the Sanctuary. The tribes' young men will provide the history and Dalton and I will lead the hikes and over-night campouts."

"That's fabulous, Rodney. I know you will do well. You have a magical feel for that land. Good luck to you."

They shared a sincere handshake and then Jeff jumped into his rental car. He had a smile on his face as he took leave of this little town of Carroll. He hoped their faith in him finding Gloria would lift that veil that had been shading the community from losing someone so young. He headed to the gravesite of Gloria's father, with the help of Carol's directions.

. . .

Several hours later, Jeff passed through the gates and stopped at the Portsmouth Cemetery's office for further directions. In the distance, and unbeknownst to Jeff, a yellow cab caring a weeping female passenger slowly wound its way out of the cemetery's grounds. Jeff followed the mosque-lined roadway to near the end of the last row. He pulled to the side and stepped out. Instinctively, Jeff looked around at others visiting their past loves and at cars that might be hesitating in their approach. Nothing seemed to be amiss. It was easy to find the grave of Gloria's father—freshly-cut flowers were arranged neatly. He sat for a moment looking at the grave trying to feel the presence of Angela. He could smell her lingering perfume and imagined a little scared girl crying over the loss of her father.

He felt a swell of emotion and promised on the grave of her father that he would find her and protect her, forever.

Adulation and Abduction

The familiar look of its passive passengers disembarking at their chosen floors and the stoic look of his security guard reassured Jeff, he was home. As he pushed open the glass doors, his attractive receptionist Adriane looked up and beamed when she saw Jeff enter.

Very sweetly, Adriane welcomed Jeff.

"Good, good morning, Jeff. I'm... we are so happy to see you. We all missed you," she confessed.

"Good morning to you as well, Adriane. You look very pretty today... I mean you always look pretty, but today you have a glow about you. A new man in your life?"

"Nooo." she said, emphasizing her answer. "Just happy to see you," said Adriane.

"Thank you. You are very sweet," commented Jeff as he headed down to his cubicle.

He stopped short and looked around at the empty room. By now, the office was usually buzzing. *Where is Goody? What's going on?*

He turned around and looked down the hall towards Adriane. She was carrying a cake with lit candles and as if in slow motion, he turned to see all of his counterparts jumping up from behind their desks and shouting, "Happy Birthday!"

Goody stepped forth as did his boss, Harry Peters, who was holding a ceremonial gold key. Jeff had completely forgotten about his birthday nor had the time to celebrate. But his friends had clearly remembered—and—with enthusiasm.

As the birthday wishes reverberated throughout the office, Adriane brought the cake to Jeff's side. With friendly coaching, he bent down to blow out the candles. Her precarious positioning of the cake left Jeff with no alternative but to claim his view of her very noticeable cleavage.

And as she caught his eyes, she couldn't help herself and happily blurted out, "Teresa called from Peru," she said, "...and wished you a happy birthday and hoped you would take time to find someone who could make you truly happy."

Jeff smiled at Adriane and figured out very quickly what she was up to with this new information about his lost relationship. Harry Peters shook his hand gratuitously and gave him the ceremonial key to his new office and a promotion to a Senior Investigator position.

He stood there mystified; *I haven't solved anything, so what's the deal?* Goody approached him seeing the wonderment in his eyes and informed him that Congress had given them $10 million because of the hard work their agency was doing. Jeff was listed as one of the congratulatory recipients. Jeff was still suspicious of what was going on, and of his promotion.

"Come on, buddy... lighten up. You just got back; time to celebrate a little," insisted Goody.

"Yes, Jeff, have some cake," offered Adriane with a plastic fork full hovering over a paper plate.

He accepted graciously and within fifteen minutes, all returned to normal. Adriane rushed off to answer the switch board, Harry Peters returned to his office and closed the door, and Goody made himself at home in a chair across from Jeff's new desk.

"You know, Adriane has been walking around here with a perma-grin after talking with Teresa. She arranged everything in your office for you."

"Well then... I'll have to thank her. But right now, my head is not into fueling another relationship."

"You mean, not until Angela has another chance at your heart strings," joked Goody.

"Look," said Jeff in an austere tone. "You of all people should know that this case could be a huge feather in this agency's cap. I have missed Angela twice now. There is not going to be a third, just so some crazy man can execute his revenge."

"Okay... my friend. I know how serious you are taking this." said Goody, holding up his hands in surrender.

"Sorry, buddy... I have been so close and now the Teresa thing... just wasn't expecting all this, this morning, that's all."

"Hey, no apologies needed. I understand when someone slips through your fingers and you have to start all over again. You know I have been there before. It's part of it; we can't let it get us down. So, what's your next move?"

"We need to update our board," said Jeff, pulling a small clear bag from inside the breast pocket of his suit jacket and emptying the contents of the plastic bag onto his new desk. "Here's what I believe to be part of Gloria's backpack." He held up a rusted grommet. He then picked up the pamphlet. "And this brochure from the Sanctuary." He pinned it to the board.

Already on the board were the two photo-booth photos pinned together that he had sent to Goody over an email and a cheat sheet with a photo of the infamous Sapphire dress—

sent to Carol. Another cheat sheet had Gilles Fournier – possible 'Grandfather???' written on it.

"I took a photo of Gloria with my phone from Carol's high school yearbook that I can show around, so I think I should start there," said Jeff.

"What do you make of the pamphlet? You said it was printed in France?" Goody asked, staring at the handout.

"Yes, the Fournier Foundation owns the sanctuary, and although I don't like to assume, I am assuming the Foundation is based in France."

"I can run that for you, buddy, while you do the foot work with the photo," offered Goody.

"Excellent. Do you want to do dinner tonight with Georgette?" He paused a moment before adding, "...I was thinking of asking Adriane to join us."

A slow smile spread across Goody's face. "I'll call her, but I don't think there would be a problem," said Goody. "Why the change of heart with Adriane?"

"I don't know... maybe you are right. Angela is a fantasy, out of my league. Who knows where she is now? She is a case number; I can't make this personal," rationalized Jeff.

"Now you're talking buddy. Welcome back!" laughed Goody.

"Okay, now, get out of my office!" said Jeff in a joking manner. "Geez that sounded good."

Jeff settled back into his new office chair and looked around. Wood-encased glass windows with pleated blinds looked out over the maze of room-divider walls. He shared an interior door with his pal Goody and at the far end of the double-wide hallway sat Adriane to the left. His office was big enough for a twin-sized couch that sat under the windows, two chairs in front of his desk, a four foot by five foot reversible whiteboard and wood shelving unit behind him. This is where Adriane had placed the picture of him and Teresa. He pulled out his keyboard and sent a message to Adriane requesting that she join him in his office.

. . .

Chinatown was always a happening place no matter time of night or day. It was full of interesting people if you liked to observe and cast them into different characters. The two couples, Goody and Georgette, and Adriane and Jeff, were enjoying a very restful and fun time, laughing at different scenarios, each pitching their own version. Adriane glowed with her long wavy deep-red hair and freckled face. She was as pretty as Rita Hayworth and just as voluptuous. *Why have I been side-stepping her attention? She was fun, intelligent, and got along well with Georgette. Not a pretentious bone in her body—her luscious body,* he thought. He was trying to think of the last time he felt a warm body next to his. *Maybe tonight, if she was up for some casual sex.* The rice wine was definitely slowing the thought process down. *What the hell, I'm single and so is she.*

Midnight was approaching fast, so Goody and Georgette bid their farewells. Jeff and Adriane walked among the shops arm in arm, laughing and occasionally holding the other up. They were having a surprisingly really good time looking at all the paraphernalia on display. A rice paper umbrella looked charming against her hair as she twirled it behind her like a geisha from a Glenn Ford movie, and then she offered a flirtatious wink. As she released the latch and folded it, Jeff caught a stare from someone watching them from a far corner. Jeff placed his hands on Adriane's hips and pulled her close.

"Oooo, Jeff... You're making my body tingle," she whispered to him.

"Don't move Adriane... Someone is watching us," he said as he nuzzled into her.

"They're probably jealous thinking we are lovers," she said with a laugh.

"Not that kind of voyeuristic watching. More like someone is tailing us. I thought so at the restaurant but so many people were coming in and going out, I wasn't sure. Come on, let's go," insisted Jeff.

"Back to your place?" she questioned with delight.

"No... Your place."

"Alrighty then," smiled Adriane as she rested her head on his shoulders. Jeff maintained their saunter while they left Chinatown so as not to spook whoever was watching.

. . .

Jeff wasted little time cruising on over to the 101 to Interstate 10 to Alhambra where Adriane's little house lay waiting for her return. He walked her to the front door.

"You're not coming in, are you?" queried Adriane to Jeff's obvious concern for whomever was watching them.

"Not tonight, Adriane, regretfully I might add. I'm going back to Chinatown. I don't want you getting involved with whatever is going on. Lock your doors and don't let anyone in. Understand?" insisted Jeff in his down-to-business voice.

"We had fun though, didn't we Jeff?" asked Adriane waiting for a reassuring answer.

"Yes we did, Adriane. It was the best birthday I could've hoped for."

Adriane leaned over and kissed Jeff on the cheek.

"Don't wait too long Jeff. Life can pass you by before you know it. Goodnight, handsome; I'll see you tomorrow," said Adriane respectfully but warmly.

"Goodnight, Adriane. Lock your doors."

Jeff waited until he heard the double throw of the lock and the slide of a chain. She was safe inside. And he had work to do.

. . .

Roaming around Chinatown didn't generate any definite observations. He decided to head to the Hollywood strip. He knew of a couple of places that would be hopping with the paid-for-love crowd. He parked his Firebird outside a busy café and pushed his way past pimps and their ladies that were hanging outside. As Jeff leaned over a patron to order a coffee to go, a voice from the back called out his name. Straightening up and scanning the direction of the voice, he heard his name again and spotted a wave of a hand. He saw one of his informants, Rita, a pretty lady of color with big beautiful eyes and a perfect white smile, sitting with a couple of friends.

He squeezed by a table of lavishly-dressed drag queens and a couple of street musicians, to the outstretched arms of Rita.

"Come here boy, give me some sugar," she boisterously said.

"Hey ya, Rita," he said, returning her a big hug. "How have you been?"

"Well, and you? You have been such a stranger. How's the lost and found business going?" she asked.

"Been busy. You are looking great," complimented Jeff.

"I've been off the juice coming up to three years, thanks to you."

"Not all me, Rita. You had the guts to stay with the program. I admire you for that."

"Jeff, this is Rishonda and Miriam, friends of mine."

"Nice to meet you, ladies. How's your little girl?" asked Jeff as he turned his attention back to Rita.

238

"She is getting so big." Rita hunted in her purse and proudly displayed a picture. "Look at her."

"She definitely has your smile," said Jeff.

"I look at her every day and thank Jesus I am clean. So are you trying to tell me you had nothing to do with the courts in getting my baby back?"

Jeff laughed and held up his thumb and finger, "Maybe this much, but you did the rest, girl."

"What brings you down here, honey?" asked Rita.

Jeff pulled out his phone and showed Rita and the other ladies Gloria's picture.

"How old is that picture?" Rita asked.

"Maybe fifteen to sixteen years old," stated Jeff.

The girls started to laugh.

"Jeff, seriously? You expect to find a missing kid from over a decade ago."

"Oh, I found her, but lost her. And now it is dire that I find her again," said Jeff fervently.

"Then what are you doing with the old picture?"

"Trying to fill in the pieces. Maybe a background of friends or places she used to visit. Maybe if she had a pimp or worked solo, her area, anything actually."

"Jeff, you have a kind spirit. If anyone can find her, you will," reassured Rita. "I'll see what I can find out."

"Thanks Rita, I'll owe you. Goodnight, ladies."

"Jeff, yours is the only credit I'll accept," laughed Rita.

Jeff smiled, left the ladies at the booth, and pushed his way through the confusion of the café.

The air outside was a mixture of pot, cigars, and cigarettes. A couple of late twenties' gentlemen were eyeing Jeff's ride.

"Sweet!" exclaimed one of them as Jeff stepped to his driver's door.

Jeff nodded with acceptance of the fellow's compliment and they stepped aside in a stumble, allowing Jeff to open his door. The two men continued talking trash to each other when one said, "Ya, man, just like it!"

Jeff picked up on the conversation just as he was about to step inside.

"Excuse me... You have seen a car exactly like this one?" he asked.

"Ya, mon," replied the high gentleman.

"Impossible... There aren't many cars like this one," said Jeff, coaxing him to elaborate.

"I'm telling ya, mon. I was getting a set up over at East 12th and Santa Fe. It was under a tarp," relayed the high gentleman.

"When?" questioned Jeff.

"This... um... yeah, this afternoon," remembered the gentleman.

Again, Jeff emphasized, "Just like this one?"

"I told ya, mon, orange, white top, white interior," described the man.

"It's red," corrected Jeff.

"You call it any color you want. It looked just like that one," said the man as he pointed.

Hustling to unlock his car door, Jeff jumped in, fired her up, and squealed out from the curb. Grabbing his cell phone, Jeff dialed the Alhambra Police Department and asked if they would send a car over to Adriane's house. He tried to call Adriane, but there was no answer. He called Goody.

He answered, *"This better be good..."*

"Goody, it's me. Meet me over at Adriane's." Jeff hung up.

Jeff thought, *If someone wants to get close to what they have discovered, what better way than to question one of their own?* He hoped not—not Adriane.

Two squad cars with flashing lights were already sitting in the driveway when Jeff pulled up, and as he slid into her driveway, right behind him came Goody. The cops were in the house with one outside and one looking around the grounds with a flashlight. Jeff jumped out of his car and rushed to the door. The cop stopped him and Jeff showed him his ID. While inside, he heard Goody rush pass the cop and with his deep voice, "Get out of my way, rookie!"

The two inside cops were still looking around but had not found anything other than a flipped over chair near the door and a note on the table addressed to Jeff Malardo. They said they had not touched anything. Goody and Jeff stared at the note.

"I'm calling forensics," said Goody.

"You guys want us to stick around? We didn't find any force of entry. The door was slightly opened when we got here," recounted one of the police officers.

"No. Thank you. Our boys will be down here shortly. Thank you gentlemen, have a good night," said Jeff.

"What got your panties in a twist to assume this?" asked Goody.

"This guy said he saw a car just like mine around East 12th and Santa Fe. He called it orange, like you did. If Adriane looked out her window, she might have assumed, in the darkness, it was me coming back for some late night fun," speculated Jeff.

"I'll call Peters and have him use his clout to send the cops and a forensic team to the warehouses on East 12th," said Goody. "The perp won't think we will be onto him this quick. He probably thinks we won't notice until tomorrow morning when she doesn't show up for work."

"Great idea, Goody. Thanks, my friend, for being here."

Within a half hour, Jeff got a call from the LAPD that they found a Camaro convertible with a white top and white painted interior. The engine was still warm and they were waiting for forensics to show up.

Meanwhile, Jeff's team just finished dusting the envelope and found no prints, in or out. The note read:

"I have what you want. Now find what I want."

"The motherfucking bastard. If he hurts Adriane in any way, there will be no trial!" Jeff exclaimed wildly.

"Calm down, buddy... We all care for Adriane. As long as he thinks we still have something to go on in finding Angela, Adriane will be all right... albeit scared to death, but she knows how things work and she knows our determination," reassured Goody.

"I should have taken her with me. I've underestimated this guy. No more, Goody," stated Jeff.

"Where did you go?"

"I saw someone watching us after we left the restaurant, so I brought Adriane home and went back to Chinatown; found nothing so I went to the strip and talked with a friend of mine about young Gloria," related Jeff.

"Anything?"

"No, but she said she would keep her ears and eyes open."

They both sat down at Adriane's kitchen table while their forensic team searched for more evidence.

"Any thoughts on how this guy knows our moves?" asked Jeff.

"I have been thinking about that as well. Does he really know our moves or has he planted a seed to anticipate our moves? In any investigation there are protocols we must follow in case we uncover something; it has to be admissible in court. I could name you a dozen websites where anyone can find information on our investigative procedures," factually stated Goody.

"So, he is just following us... using us like a tracking dog."

"Basically, yes," responded Goody.

"Tracking dog... Tracking dog..." said Jeff repeatedly. "Tracking dog! When we arrived at the outpost, Bernadette said Angela saw two men with rifles." He paused a moment, then continued, "Goody... By the time we could see the bluff, Rodney ordered me to put a protective boot over my rifle's barrel and clip it. It would have blended into our backpacks and surrounding foliage. The only thing we had out was our binoculars. Someone else was there... following us. And, if Angela had seen us, she would have recognized me, I hope, or at least Rodney who was a friend of hers."

"So we are basically leading them to Angela?" said Goody, summing up everything that had gone before.

"Yes. I saw a truck following me and assumed when Rodney and Dalton came into the diner that it must have been them. But when Dalton dropped us off at the accident site, he had an older truck. They can't afford new, not like the one following me," stated Jeff, excitedly.

"Could you see the plate?" asked Goody. "Think back."

"I... I... No. I can't remember even if I saw a front plate."

"We are going to need a diversion so he thinks we are doing one thing but actually doing something else."

"Okay, but what?" asked Jeff.

"I don't know. Let me think..."

"I feel sick to my stomach sitting here... useless. I'm going to the office. I won't be able to sleep now anyway," remarked Jeff.

"That's it!" exclaimed Goody.

"What's it?"

"Get sick, preferably outside for the enjoyment of whoever is watching. We have an argument, I instruct you to go home and stay there until you are feeling better. You leave the curtains closed, your car in the parking garage, and you sneak back to the office," explained Goody.

"Good plan. But it was only an expression... being sick to my stomach," retorted Jeff.

"It might be, but still, let's look around and see if we can make you sick," said Goody calmly.

"You're kidding, right?"

"No." Goody looked through Adriane's cupboards and muttered, "What sets off Chinese food?"

Allen's Contribution

Jeff, sitting in his office feeling a little tepid from his fifteen minutes of vomiting on Adriane's front lawn and under the watchful eyes of her neighbors, was re-arranging his cheat sheets. The weatherman was calling for a major rainstorm that night. Jeff thought the rains would provide good cover for him to slip between the warehouses, where the LAPD found the fictitious replica of his car. A hat and trench coat seemed appropriate—plus his 9mm concealed in the inside pocket.

Goody came into the office around 7:30 a.m. with news that the LAPD had impounded the car and were thoroughly checking it out. *It's amazing how much clout Harry Peters had,* thought Goody. The two sat in silence studying their board, each taking a turn at re-arranging the cards.

Annette, on loan from 'special procedures', was staffing the phones during Adriane's abduction. The usual buzzing had somehow lessened as everyone waited for any news. Meanwhile, Harry was immersed in a meeting with a couple of suits, one older, grey-haired gentleman and the other who looked like he should be playing video games in a mall somewhere. This case had become very personal. Kidnapping one of their own was one thing—but then ransoming her life for another—was totally unacceptable. This guy, Anthony Micholanetti, was a wanted man—and as far as Jeff was concerned, he was a dead man.

Annette approached Jeff's office with a small, padded envelope. He opened it and found a flash drive. He put it into a special receiver to see if it was safe to open and when the green light flashed, he transferred it to his computer. Listed were two files, both MPEG-4. Jeff clicked one open and proceeded to click the play arrow. It was a static shot of an elevator and next to it was a parked white van. A man walked into the frame, who Jeff recognized right away as being George Stanza. A white car pulled up into the frame only displaying the hood and roof because of the angle of the camera lens. George Stanza stopped at the van and turned to face the car. When he did, a shotgun blast threw him against the rear doors of the van. The car pulled away and something white slid underneath a nearby car. Moments later, Angela ran into the frame, bent over George, and by the look on her face—fear, sorrow, and revenge all collided together. She ran out of the frame. Jeff and Goody sat back. Within minutes, police cars arrived and an ambulance pulled into the frame as a news crew set up. A police officer had a white fedora in a plastic bag that he retrieved from under a car next to George's body. The video stopped.

Jeff clicked on the next file. It was from a high vantage point looking down at an alleyway. They saw a woman, who appeared to be Angela because of her long blonde hair and known location, running from her back stairs through the alley being chased by a man who slowly took aim and shot out a car's rear window at least fifteen feet away from the running woman. Jeff thought it was Joseph because of his size but the high vantage point made it impossible to make out faces. Then the man stopped, pulled out a pocketknife, and removed the bullet from the dashboard. Sticking it into his pocket, he started running again, stopped at the corner, and bent over like he was out of breath—a mere fifty feet away from the parked car.

"What the fuck!?" exploded Goody.

The two look at each other more confused than before after receiving this footage, but it confirmed their suspicions of Joseph not trying to kill Angela.

Before they could come up with any kind of rebuttal, Annette buzzed Jeff's office and told him Harry wanted to see them both in his office. Jeff removed the flash drive and put it in his top drawer and locked it. When Jeff and Goody arrived at Harry's office, he introduced the two men, the older one as Tom and the younger as Todd. Jeff thought they could have at least come up with something original like Tom & Jerry. No affiliation was mentioned, and when Goody approached the issue of which affiliation they belonged to, Harry replied, "It is of no concern. Sit down and watch."

The young man, Todd, directed them to Harry's larger wall monitor where he played the same footage that Jeff and Goody had just watched. *How did they get it?* thought Jeff.

The young man, Todd, translated the sequence.

"As you can see, this man stops at the back of the van and appears to say something, and then he is shot down before he can say anything else."

"We got that," interrupted Goody.

"Quite right," Todd said a bit shyly. He continued, "Now let's re-play it. The man comes into the frame, he stops, we see a shotgun blast, and then he is thrown against the van by the force."

"Yes. We get it," said Jeff, annoyed at this kid's insistence.

"Okay... One more time. The man comes into the frame, he stops... Ask yourself, gentlemen, why not take cover? Why not run to the elevator or take the stairs...? Watch." He operated the footage in slow motion. "He is showing no fear in his face and then, gentlemen, the coup de grace, he is shot but the blood does not splatter until he hits the back of the van. A shotgun with any type of load that close would have opened him up," stated the young man.

Jeff jumped up to his feet. "Play that again," he insisted.

Todd re-set the sequence and played the scene again.

"Fuck me, he is right!" declared Goody.

"Now that I have your full attention, gentleman," Todd said with more confidence. "Watch after the girl is at the dead man's side. Light, dark, light, dark showing through between the aisle of parked cars. Another car was there. They possibly witnessed the killing and were obviously in fear of repercussions, sped away along the opposite aisle. Now watch the counter, the video has not been altered with any time elapsed. Okay... mark. That was four minutes before the cops showed up, five minutes before the news crew was on the scene, and five minutes and twenty-five seconds before the ambulance arrived. I don't know about you, gentlemen, but I don't know of any service from any branch of government that could operate that quickly," theorized the young man.

"Who are you people?" queried Jeff, staring at the young man.

"Sorry, sir, we cannot divulge that information."

"Give me one second," said Jeff. He ran to his office and opened the locked drawer. He pulled out the flash drive. He looked at it intensely. In the encased rubber were the initials 'AT'. He rushed back to Harry's office.

"We just received this from Allen Travers. It is exactly what you just showed us. How did you get the same footage?" questioned Jeff with his new authority.

"Sorry, sir, we cannot divulge that information."

"Whether you can say it or not, you were spying on either Allen or George Stanza. Which one?" demanded Jeff.

"Jeff," said Harry. "It doesn't matter at this point. We know Allen is still with us as you just received your information from him and that this George Stanza is presumably still alive. Now, where does that leave you with the Gloria-Angela case and where does that leave you in finding my receptionist?" Harry asked authoritatively.

He then turned to Tom and Todd and calmly said, "Thank you, gentlemen; we will be in touch, no doubt."

Back in the privacy of Jeff's office, Goody was re-arranging the cards once more. He interrupted the silence with, "Where do you think we stand?"

"Fuck the cards," said Jeff as he paced the room frustrated. "Gloria's father died at an early age. They moved, mother and child to Carroll, mother married an asshole. When Gloria was in her mid-teens, she ran away from home and somehow found her way to the Sanctuary. She obviously cared for this elderly man who also cared for her. He gave her his name, possibly related. She then leaves, for whatever reason and goes to L.A. She meets up with this Anthony Micholanetti character that has, in a previous life, caused the death of old man Fournier's wife. So who does she meet first... Gina, Eileen, or George Stanza? Then there's Joseph, arm and leg man for Micholanetti and now chauffeur for

Angela; except he now hunts her, but not really... Fuck!" said Jeff exasperated, flopping down into his chair.

Goody had been sitting on the other side of the desk in one of Jeff's client's barrel chairs, swaying side to side, following Jeff's summary. He stopped. "Back up, Jeff... YOU, my friend," stated Goody. "You were brought into this for a reason. What is it?"

"I do not know, Goody, and that is the truth... I don't know," insisted Jeff.

"Look, buddy..." Goody hurriedly wrote on a card 'JEFF', got up, and rushed to place it in the center of their whiteboard. "We are looking at this the wrong way. If I put you in the center, everyone revolves around you. You know all the characters. Maybe you are not the director but you are the eye of the pyramid, the one that sees it all. The only other one is Angela; she is your tagman," enlightened Goody.

Jeff stood and stared at the wheel that Goody had created. He then stepped farther back and reevaluated the time-plot list.

"Where has Carl been and where has Eileen been in all of this. We know where Gina is... at AD Fashions, George dead, maybe; Joseph, we are not sure whose side he is on but I would gather by his actions, he is on Angela's side and only pretending to be siding with Micholanetti... Joseph, the inside man? Who is Joseph reporting to... Carl? Stanza?"

"What about T&T? They look military to me," remarked Goody.

"I would agree. That kid had a stick-up-his-ass look and every time he revealed something, the other T nodded," prudently offered Jeff. "They have to be tied in with Stanza somehow. The kid never mentioned his name, only referring to him as 'the man'."

"Maybe, he is the Man! The Man in charge, the top dog. Who else could pull this off? The cops, the ambulance, and the news crew were all for show. A Hollywood production," said Goody.

"A Hollywood production. That's it!" Jeff's eyes lit up. A new energy flowed. "They were probably actors. It was staged for whoever was watching and to scare Angela to get out of town while they took care of business without her being involved or getting hurt."

"But, that business, Mr. Micholanetti might not have fallen for, so you are their backup. If they fail to get to him or... let me run with this... Maybe, *you* are the one that has to take him down to protect their identity," said Goody, beaming with enthusiasm.

"You are delusional... You know that. How could that possibly work? Who could possibly come up with that, other than YOU?" said Jeff, rejecting the idea.

Goody chuckled and said looking around the room as if it was a spook house, "Hey buddy, if I thought of it, more specialized minds in Black-Ops probably have. Don't count it out. These guys got ears everywhere. They are probably listening to us right now."

Jeff stared at Goody and motioned him to keep talking. He quietly moved closer to his desk and looked around, lifting books, intercom, lamps—and then Jeff spotted it. A wave of memories flooded through his brain as he recalled that Goody had said that Adriane even placed the picture of Teresa and him on the shelf. Goody continued his babbling as he watched Jeff. Slowly, he lifted the frame and turned it around—and there it was. Tucked neatly into the crease of the fold-out arm laid a wire with a tiny microphone. In a rage, he threw the frame to the floor and smashed it, grounding the mic into it with his foot.

"Motherfuckers!" said Jeff. "Is this office a plant? What about Harry? Is he in on this as well? Is that why Allen hasn't shown up for work? Has Adriane really been kidnapped? What the fuck, Goody?"

Goody, sitting with arms folded tried to hide a smirk as he attempted to calm his buddy down.

"Stay cool, Jeff. Are you over your fit? Our main focus is finding Adriane and then Angela. Are we cool with that?" Goody asked, calmly. "Jeff?"

"Yeah, yeah. My fit? Sometimes my Italian blood just boils; especially when the safety of my friends is involved," replied Jeff, not too happily.

"Take a nap, you look like shit. I'm going to see what I can find out about Joseph," said Goody.

Goody is right, thought Jeff, *I am beat*. He didn't get any sleep after Goody made him sick at Adriane's place and then after returning home, he quickly showered, snuck out of his apartment to avoid another tail, and then ran four blocks before hailing a cab. A nap sounded good. He laid down on his two-seater couch; his legs dangled over the arm. Tonight he would scout the warehouse and use the rain as a diversion, *if* the weatherman was correct.

Who were these people? And what game of cat and mouse were they playing? Allen Travers was right. These were big boys, which usually meant high stakes and big money. Yes, he thought, *big money. How did that old hermit buy a thousand acres?* He started to fade. *Truck, license plate, tracking dog, rifles, that blue dress... Yes, that blue dress.*

The sleep bandit was slowly being driven from his body. He let himself relax...

Precise Extraction

Jeff was sprawled out over his office couch sleeping peacefully. Goody was on his way home but felt compelled to wake Jeff up before leaving. Jeff needed to get organized if his plan of staking out the row of warehouses where the cops found the alleged kidnap vehicle was going to happen. Goody tapped on his door.

"Jeff! Hey man, it's time to get up."

"What? Oh, yeah." Jeff stretched his legs out and arched his back. "Thanks, man. What time is it?"

"Six-thirty and my dinner time. And lucky you, it's pouring out."

Jeff swung his legs over and sat up on his couch. His head rested in his hands, his mind processing.

"Raining? Good. Okay." He looked around. "Where are you going?"

"Home, man. You know, I still have one; wife and such waiting for me," said Goody.

"Yeah, yeah, I got it."

"I got some info on Joseph from an associate of mine. Hearsay has it that he was compromised in a shooting of two DEA agents. Allegedly one of the agents was his sister and the other, a guy named Will Carlson. They were all shot by an unknown assailant. The female agent died, and Joseph obviously survived, but there is no data on record of the other agent's injuries or whereabouts; not unusual if the guy was undercover. Joseph was cleared of any wrong-doing and has pretty much stayed in the shadows ever since. From what I was told, again not documented, Joseph took it pretty hard and swore, if it took a lifetime, he would find the killer. That's all I could find out about him so far."

"Thanks, Goody. I wouldn't want to piss Joseph off, and I wouldn't want to be the guy who shot his sister either once he does find out," said Jeff.

"You up?"

"Yeah, man... Thanks, I'm good. See you tomorrow."

. . .

Jeff had set, with the help of the permit office of LA County, a perimeter of warehouses he wanted to scope out. Not all would be desirable candidates but there were still quite a few in the area. He had already secured a non-descript car from their surveillance team, so donning his Wallaby hat and Drover oilskin trench coat, he was on his way.

For a change, the weatherman was right—it was pouring out! He arrived at the warehouses around 8 p.m. and with the black skies looming overhead, it seemed much later. He dropped in and out of doorways, sometimes disturbing their inhabitants and getting a "fuck off!" remark. *Oh, how he missed the good old days*, he briefly thought. But not really. It was a thankless job that took its toll on many guys. He was one that had to make a decision between having a real life or living in the gutters busting petty crimes. It would have taken him more than ten years on the force to work his way up to the big busts.

He crouched for a short time in a double doorway scanning each floor and looking for anything when he spotted a modest halo of light emanating from a top-floor window of a building across the street and two warehouses just north of him. He swaggered along his side of the street to the middle of the sidewalk and back again, bouncing as if the building violated his space. He looked very convincing as a character of the street until, almost at the corner of the building, he passed a doorway, and all of sudden, the figure lying in wait tripped him, sending Jeff face down onto the wet concrete sidewalk.

From the top floor of the building that Jeff had been observing, a figure was briefly silhouetted and appeared to be talking with another who was out of sight.

"Looky that, my little redhead. Two fucking drunks battling for a doorway. A bunch of fuckin' losers," said the silhouetted man. Turning away from the window, he looked at his hostage who was tied to a chair. A small goose-neck desk lamp that sat on the rough-cut wooden floorboards shone upward illuminating her blindfolded eyes and duct-taped mouth. He walked over to her.

"If your boyfriend doesn't do what Lucifer wants, you are going to become fish bait, my loveliness." He ran his hands along her cheek to her chin, missing her taped mouth.

"So you thought I was him when I pulled up, didn't you? All dressed pretty for him in your slinky robe. Too bad for him, now I get to admire what he gave up. Stupid fucker, isn't he. Leaving all this..." His fingers dallied on the lapel of her robe opening it slowly as she whimpered. "...yes, it's too bad to waste such beauty."

On the street outside, one man lay in a doorway and the other was face down on the street.

"Don't move, Jeff. Top floor, a hundred yards north on your right. Watch and learn," said a familiar voice. *Tom from Harry's office? Why is he here?* thought Jeff.

Above the roof, two helicopters hovered in stealth mode. Six men in SWAT gear, with no apparent insignias, from each helicopter on each side of the building fast-roped down to the roof's edge. They waited momentarily. Suddenly, with exact precision, they all pushed off, swung out, and lowered themselves simultaneously with a burst of suppressed firepower. Only the disengaging glass crashing to the ground emanated a thunderous noise of exploding plate glass, which was heard above the drenching of rain from the street below.

The shattered upper windows now made easy access for the rescue team as they swung through. "Come on!" Tom commanded. Tom and Jeff got up and as they ran across the street, six police cars with flashing lights all pulled up. Also, one agency car with Harry Peters peering out of the sedan's rear-quarter window slid to a stop.

Out of the shadows, two figures, also dressed in all black, rounded the corner of the building, one with a battering ram in hand. He cocked it back and swung it hard, knocking the lock and chains flying off the warehouse entrance handles freeing it from its bondage. A minimal passage lock was no match for the second SWAT member's raised boot that followed. Jeff, running a step behind Tom towards the freed doors pulled out his ID from inside his trench coat to identify himself to the team of avengers who stood on either side. The two men, Tom and Jeff, took two stairs at a time for the complete six floors, adrenaline pumping as they anticipated their capture of the man known as Lucifer.

When they arrived at the top floor, the SWAT team already had the assailant handcuffed and face down with one of the commandos resting his foot on the perp's back; his military-style rifle pointed down at him. Others were securing the premises with the cries of "CLEAR, CLEAR, CLEAR" coming from abandoned offices. Another was removing the tape from the woman's face whilst another cut off her bondage.

As Jeff reached the top step, he was halted by a team member until Tom waved approval. Jeff looked around him and saw Adriane being freed, he shouted out, "Adriane!"

She looked up through her teary eyes towards that welcoming voice and screamed back, "Jeffery!"

Approaching, he side-stepped other members until he reached their emancipated hostage. The team leader who was last in line stood down and let Jeff pass. Jeff quickly removed his trench coat and placed it over Adriane to eliminate any further embarrassment to her. He hugged her like he had never hugged anyone. He sighed with relief as he held her tight. She was one of theirs, his team, his friend—and no one fucks with his friends.

Tom stepped to Jeff's side after a quick conversation with the commando leader.

"Jeff, I know you would have caught him but we needed him alive," stated Tom. "Your boss is waiting downstairs. And, by the way, you owe us a microphone," remarked Tom with a very slight attempt at humor.

"Thank you, Tom... I owe you more than that," said Jeff as he offered his hand to Tom.

"Glad we could help," said Tom sporting a smile of relief.

"Tom, was this Harry's doing or someone else's?" queried Jeff.

"You know I can't answer that," he said. "We'll take care of this guy and will let you know what we find out."

"Promise?"

"I promise, Jeff. Take your delicate friend home. I am quite sure Harry will handle any questioning of the lady."

As Jeff and Adriane approached the stairs, the young kid, Todd, who was carrying his laptop under his arm, breathed a sigh of relief after reaching the 6th floor. He looked at the traumatized woman and said, "I am so sorry, miss." He took another long breath, "I thought that was Mr. Malardo's car..."

"TODD!" hollered the commander. "Get over here!"

~

After enduring two days of intense drama and a precise extraction of a visibly shaken young woman by a team of unknown origin, Jeff's brain was swirling. He held on tight to Adriane as they approached their waiting boss, Harry Peters who sat patiently anticipating the safe return of his receptionist. Harry's driver opened the sedan's rear door for

Adriane and Jeff guided her to the rear seat where Harry had a blanket waiting for her. Jeff's phone rang with an annoying ringtone that sounded like two competing hip-hoppers. She momentarily held on tight to Jeff's coat, but then relinquished it to him as she looked up at him with appreciative eyes. Jeff fished for his cell phone in the inside pocket, which nestled against, his 9mm, and dismissed the annoying sound. He clicked on the three dots and opened the text message. It was from Rita asking him to call her.

"I'm sorry about that screech, but I need to take this," said Jeff.

Harry leaned over Adriane and said, "Don't worry, Jeff. I'll take Adriane home with me. My wife will take good care of her."

"Thanks, Harry. I don't want her to be alone tonight," insisted Jeff, compassionately.

"Jeff!" called out Adriane. "Thank you for being there for me..."

"Shhh. Go home with Harry and get a good night's sleep. We'll talk later," he reassured.

"Jeff, I want to see you and Goody in my office tomorrow morning," ordered Harry.

"Where is Goody? How come he didn't come down here?"

"He wasn't informed. I got a call only an hour ago telling me to get my driver and head for the fashion district. From there, we were given this address and as you saw, we arrived at the same time as the police," related Harry.

"You had no knowledge of this?" asked Jeff.

"I'll see you in the morning," said Harry as he tapped his driver to take them home.

Jeff watched as the taillights dimmed through the rain. Soaked to the bone, he looked around and the only thing he saw was a couple of police cars that remained nose to nose while the officers removed the yellow barrier. Tom and his crew vanished as quickly as they had appeared; only leaving the rain dancing to its own metered rhythm on the broken glass that lay on the water-soaked street. Jeff threw on his trench coat, warmed by his friend Adriane, over his wet, drenched body and headed off.

He was uneasy about using his cell phone. If *they* could bug his office, a cell phone would be simple. He got into his company car and drove to the nearby bus station where he knew of a restaurant that was located across the street. He had gotten take-out on many occasions when he was working late on stakeouts. The wet weather had brought the hordes inside. He eyed everyone before dialing on the pay phone.

"Rita... Jeff here."

"Not over the phone, Jeff. How about I meet you? In an hour. Our diner." She hung up. Jeff stepped to the counter and ordered a coffee to go.

He headed down 7th to Figueroa, a right turn and then a left on Wilshire to Vermont where he circled around back and parked the company car. He looked ominous in his Drover trench coat with pitched hat and long stride—a man on a mission.

Rita had seemed anxious when he called her back. Jeff arrived early. It gave him time to observe anyone he felt looked anywhere close to being suspicious. He was hardening fast—*"watch and learn"* kept echoing in his mind, as if that guy was a purveyor of the unorthodox, a sleuth among sleuths, a teacher of calculating reason with a thumb on illogical perceptions. Jeff was gaining enormous respect for this man called Tom, a man of decisive mannerisms; a man who deserved the title 'Sir'.

He recognized Rita outside the diner as she lowered her umbrella and watched as she stepped in. No one seemed to bother with anybody entering their domain—conversations remained fluid. Jeff gave up his location with a short wave of familiarity. She weaved her way through the talkative crowd to his table. Standing out of respect, he studied her as she slid into the booth.

"My God, it is wet out there," she said.

"Yes indeed, but it only rains once in a while. It has to make up for lost time," jest Jeff, taking his seat.

"Wasn't that a song by The Mamas and Papas?" asked Rita as she settled in across from Jeff.

Jeff tapped on the table and began to sing... *"But girl, don't they warn ya. It pours, man it pours."*

"That's it... You got a pretty good voice," complimented Rita. She reached for a napkin from the metal container that sat next to the ketchup, mustard and glass sugar dispenser, and attempted to wipe the droplets of rain from her face.

"I guess singing in the shower does prove fruitful," laughed Jeff.

Rita leaned towards Jeff, and in a low voice said, "There's a lot of shit going down. I heard about a major bust of the century is happening as we speak. From here to Vegas, through to Kansas, to New York, and down to Miami. The Valdez brothers headed back to Argentina, I've been told. Someone has them on attempted murder and conspiracy to commit murder charges. Someone said they looked like two white mice running from a cat." She laughed at the thought.

"I haven't heard anything?" said Jeff, wondering at the reliability of the information.

"You know, hon, the snort line is quicker than the internet. When those junkies can't get their supply, everybody knows. Someone always tries to fill the void, but not this time. Anyone with any product is lying low. So says the street," whispered Rita as she leaned back in her seat.

"Anything on that young girl I showed you a picture of?"

"I think she is ancient history. Good luck in finding her now; however, there was this pimp down here that went to jail for killing one of his girls. Rumor has it, he was looking for someone else and tried beating the information out of her. Very tragic... I didn't know her. Maybe it is your missing girl he was after?" shared Rita with a quick dubious shrug.

"Anything about underage girls being forced into making movies?" asked Jeff.

"In pornos? That is taboo in the adult industry. Everybody now has to prove who they are and their age; it's been that way for ages. I can give you the name of a guy in Chatsworth; it's like the capital of porn in the States. He would know better. There are always some bad apples spoiling the pot for others though. I am quite sure they would like to see those guys gone. The porn business has become so mainstream now. Who do you think makes all the money on the Internet? You have crews that work on adult movies shooting sex scenes for Hollywood and Hollywood crews adding technical advice for the porn industry. Work is work," stated Rita.

"Anything else I should be aware of?"

"You know, about a week ago this young snot-nose kid carrying a laptop, barely old enough to get an erection, showed me a picture of a priest and asked if I had seen him around. I laughed my ass off at him, but after I spoke with you the other day and was reminded by my friend, Miriam... you met her... about that pimp that went to jail for killing his girl. I believe he dressed up like a priest," informed Rita.

"Thanks, babe. Need a ride?" asked Jeff, getting up from the table.

"I didn't see your car out front?"

"In the shop. Got a company car around back."

"Thanks, but no. Night is still young... Still lots of traffic."

"Thank you, Rita. If you ever need a get-out-of-jail card, call me," said Jeff concerned for his friend.

"I have your card right next to the Captain of the Vice Squad," laughed Rita.

"One other thing, Rita... Ever wondered who starts the rumors?"

Jeff smiled and headed back out into the rain-soaked night. He still had one more change of clothes at his office and if he made it by midnight, he could still catch their security guard Mr. Personality before the next shift started. Jeff thought Tom should recruit him as he had a temperament more suited for covert-type operations rather than a security guard.

. . .

Jeff pulled in under the lights and security cameras at Straight Up Communications. He was getting a little gun-shy and thought it best to be as visible as he could; especially in an underground parking structure. The elevator door opened and rushed him to his floor. As he stepped out, he looked at his watch—well before midnight.

"Where is Mr. Personality?" he asked the new security guard.

"Don't know, sir. I was asked to report here and that from now on, your agency is my sole duty," informed the friendly security guard.

"Great. I am..."

"Yes, sir, Mr. Malardo. I have studied your dossier. Sorry, sir, but I still need you to scan your ID."

"Not a problem. Welcome aboard, T. Greene"

"Tom, sir," replied the new security guard.

Jeff flashed a smile, "You wouldn't happen to be part of a covert team, would you?" jest Jeff.

"No, sir. I was in the Marines, though."

Jeff held his smile as he walked through the glass doors. The automatic lighting turned on with each step as he neared his sanctuary.

Bonjour

Angela swung her shapely legs out of the taxicab and immediately commandeered a young porter to follow her with her bag. Her white polka-dot black dress waved as she strutted in her wide-brim hat and oversized sunglasses. Heads turned as she walked—"A movie star," whispered a passenger waiting in line to return to Minnesota, and another ran to get her autograph. A simple stroke of an 'A' was all it took from her long sleeve-gloved hand to raise an "Ahhh!" JFK terminal waited in suspense as the unknown movie star approached the check-in podium of Air France.

"Bonjour," Angela stated in a sultry voice to the agent.

"Bonjour, Mademoiselle," welcomed the ticket agent.

"Un billet aller simple à Paris, s'il vous plaît?"

"Économie?" he asked politely.

"Mais non!" Angela chuckled, "Première classe."

"Oui... Bien sûr! Mademoiselle. Passeport, s'il vous plaît," said the ticket agent.

Angela handed him her new French Biometric passport. He opened it to her photo and looked back at her.

"Angelique Fournier?"

"Oui, Monsieur."

He handed Angela the stamped passport and boarding pass.

"Porte A-Vingt-neuf. Bon chance, un vol en toute securite."

"Merci," thanked Angela.

The agent checked in her baggage and she headed for Gate A29. She thought she had done quite well asking for a one-way ticket, first class and not economy as proposed by the agent. She also thought it was nice of him to wish her luck and a safe flight—real customer service.

As she went through the security check-in, a familiar face had just landed from Paris and upon seeing who he thought was Angela, yelled out her name to confirm his delight. She made no acknowledgement of his gesture and continued to saunter down the aisle towards her gate.

Clean and Simple

Awakening before 7 a.m., Jeff felt surprisingly good after spending another night on his miniature couch. People were already settling down for another day of solving problems and finding whatever information their clients wanted. It was never boring and mostly satisfying; especially if it had to do with a missing or abducted child. Jeff had learned a lot lately about reading between the lines. Just because something appeared to be one way, it might not always be that way. *Tom was a trip*, he thought. *How did that old man keep up with me taking the stairs two at a time? Actually, it was more like, how did I keep up with Tom?* He was so appreciative and happy for his help, but Tom was right—he might have killed that guy trying to extract information from him. Jeff was that riled up. The perps made it personal—Jeff couldn't hang with that.

On his computer terminal, he noticed a message from Harry that he wanted to address everyone that morning. It was very seldom that he was not in at 7 a.m. Jeff started to think the worst until he looked up and saw Harry walking in, with an already growing crew following him. Goody was right behind him. *I wonder if he knows about Adriane.*

"Everybody, gather around," encouraged Harry as he approached Jeff's office. The team of agents left their desks and created a semi-circle around their boss. "It has been very gloomy around here... we all know why, but, I have great news! Last night one of your senior agents..." he pointed at Jeff, "...orchestrated an effective extraction in cooperation with local law enforcement, of our beloved Adriane."

The cheers rocked the building. Harry waved his hands to calm them down.

"That is what persistence and hard work delivers. Adriane is resting and indicated to me she wants to come back tomorrow. There is no talking her out of it, so ladies and gentlemen, I wanted to let you know that business is open as usual!"

Again the cheers deafened the office, and as Jeff stood astounded at Harry's proclamation, everyone filed by to congratulate him. The room returned to its crazy buzz once again.

"You two... in my office," ordered Harry looking at Jeff and Goody. "Not a word until I have finished talking." Jeff and Goody shuffled in and closed the door behind them. "Sit please," offered Harry.

"Sorry Goody that you had to find out this way, but it seems our esteemed colleague has some heavyweights in his back pocket." Looking at Jeff, he stated matter-of-factly, "Your report will indicate that between our agency and the local police, we were able to ascertain the whereabouts of the perp, where he was detaining our fellow colleague, and that a coordinated strike was then ordered to apprehend. Nothing else, clean... simple. What else have you two come up with?"

Goody ran his finger around his collar and forced a strained gulp. His face went from an inquisitive stare at his buddy's night follies, to his deep military power voice. He replied, "We have declared formally that the missing girl, Gloria Jackson, is, in fact, Angela Fournier. DNA supports this finding."

"Good, anything else?"

Jeff followed up with, "I was informed last night that the drug trade has come to a standstill and that simultaneous busts are happening across the country. One of L.A.'s own, the Valdez brothers, has taken flight to their homeland and probably will not be back. It seems they have been indicted for attempted murder, conspiracy to commit murder, and the list probably goes on. I believe that was one of the reasons for the staged death of George Stanza."

Harry paused and looked at Goody and Jeff before stating, "Okay. Here's what I found out. Your Angela it seems was born a couple of weeks ago. Up until that time, she had no driver's license, no social security, no identifying paperwork, yet she is a successful businesswoman. She is listed on different boards of directors, but they don't necessarily get paid for that honor, which eliminates anything from the IRS. Everything is run through a parent foreign corporation. She was issued an American passport through proper channels with supporting documentation of being a citizen of France. So, whoever is controlling her purse strings, it again seems, they are untouchable. This George Stanza you mentioned; did you check him out? Don't bother because I did, and although, his name comes up on certain documents, it is more of an alias." Harry took a moment for what he had just said to let it sink in. "Okay, gentlemen, that is what I have. I suggest you put your noses to the grindstone and fill in the missing blanks," instructed Harry.

"Somebody is directing this play, and I believe Jeff was brought in to uncover this creep Micholanetti and put him away for life. Whoever it is doesn't want any collateral damage that might affect their status," theorized Goody.

"What do you say, Jeff?" Harry nodded in his direction. "Do you agree with Goody's summation?"

"We have been hashing out all the possibilities, and Goody's reasoning seems the most plausible. I believe this, whatever you want to call it... plot or charade or covert ops... has been in the making for a long time. We have been fed enough information to pique our interest so we keep looking. And then, when we get too close to ascertain these identities, things are sanitized. Allen is right, these guys have deep pockets and are connected," remarked Jeff.

"Someone has been following Jeff that we know, and we believe they are waiting for him or us to find Angela so the bad guy, Micholanetti, can take her out. But I also think it goes much deeper... and that is what we want to find out," insisted Goody.

"You might never know," said Harry. "Let's stay on Angela; she might be a pawn as well as Jeff. Don't take any unnecessary chances in placing her in harm's way, or yourselves. I have a feeling that if it came down to it, the whole U.S. military would be covering your back. Keep me posted."

That was their clue that the meeting was over. They headed out Harry's office door and back to Jeff's office.

"What the fuck happened last night?" asked Goody, digging for some answers as he closed Jeff's office door behind him. He stood with arms folded, legs spread as if he was going to start berating a cadet. Jeff shuffled the cheat sheets on his desk into a pile, sat down, and looked up into Goody's demanding stare.

"Our old friend Tom and his team of commandos descended onto the warehouse like angels of the night from two helicopters, and within minutes had the place secured.

The precision was awesome to watch," said Jeff relaxing back into his chair, hands interlocked behind his head.

"So, how did ya hook up with Tom?"

"He tripped me," said Jeff, but looking at Goody's face, he knew he wasn't going to fall for that, which was kind of like a double entendre, he thought.

Goody shifted his weight—arms still crossed. He looked down at Jeff relaxing in his chair

"Okay," said Jeff throwing his arms up in the air. "I was going along the sidewalk of the warehouses when I saw a dim light from an upper floor of a building across the street from me. As I staggered past Tom, who was lying on the ground of a doorway, he tripped me and told me not to move. "'Watch and learn'" were his direct words. From above, these two helicopters hovered silently over the warehouse, and then six men from each fast-roped down to the roof... and then at exactly the same time, they crashed through the windows. Tom said "'Let's go'" so we took off running. Six police cars came up with lights going and sirens blasting, and then Harry pulled up. By the time Tom and I reach the top of the stairs, the SWAT team had secured the floor and were untying Adriane. They, as in Tom, took the guy away. It wasn't Micholanetti but some stooge he hired, but when Adriane and I stopped at the top of the stairs, young Todd came up and apologized to Adriane, telling her he thought it was my car. So *they* as in Tom and whomever he works for are watching everyone. And when I met with Rita afterwards, she said this kid with a laptop asked her if she had seen Micholanetti."

"Interesting."

"That's it? Interesting?" said Jeff, raising an eyebrow.

"I'm thinking," replied Goody. "Your choice of words *they*, and silent helicopters rings a myriad of bells, if you know what I mean. Where is that pamphlet you brought back from the Sanctuary?"

"Right here." Jeff stood from his chair and went to the whiteboard. He raised his hand and snapped his fingers as if a light bulb just turned on. "Okay, I know what you are thinking." Jeff pulled down the pamphlet from their board... "*Printed in France*," he read.

"She is a French citizen. I don't know by what circumstances, but nothing else makes sense so why should that? You said you missed her at her father's grave site..."

"Yes, I am assuming because of the fresh flowers and her perfume."

"Whatever... it still remains that was in Portsmouth, New Hampshire, which is not far from Boston. Maybe she skipped the country?" remarked Goody.

"Maybe, but everything we have been fed leads me to believe that whoever is controlling this wants to make it happen here in the States. And that would make sense if they wanted a U.S. conviction without years of legal battle with extradition from France," assumed Jeff.

Just then, Annette buzzed Jeff interrupting his and Goody's conversation. *"I'm sorry, Jeff. I know you didn't want to be disturbed but there is a gentleman calling from New York that insists on talking with you. His name is David Christiansen."*

"Thanks, Annette, put him through."

"Hey David, what's up? I thought you were still here in L.A.?" said Jeff into the receiver.

"No, man. I just got back from Paris with Eileen. I mean, she is still there but when I landed this morning at 6 a.m., I thought I saw Angela. I yelled at her, but she didn't respond. Have you heard from her?"

"No. Why do you ask?"

"Well, Eileen made a remark that she hasn't been able to get in contact with Angela for over a week, and that was just

before I left. She was more than just a little concerned," informed David.

"Where was this lady headed, when you saw her?"

"She was heading towards Air France terminal out of JFK. I thought she might be joining Eileen. I guess they are looking at buying another gallery and they want to showcase my work for their grand opening."

"Really! When?" asked Jeff.

"Don't know yet. Maybe in a month or two. I'm not sure if the deal has been finalized yet. That is why Eileen was anxious to talk with Angela, but too wild, isn't it?" remarked David, amazed at his success since meeting those two ladies.

"Truly amazing, my friend. You will have to send me an invitation," insisted Jeff.

"You got it. Talk to you soon," said David, hanging up.

Jeff looked at Goody. "It's about an eight-hour flight to Paris from JFK. So, if Angela had allegedly talked with Eileen right after David left, she would conceivably have had enough time to talk with Eileen, pack, book a flight, and arrive at the airport in eight hours; especially if she was holed up in New York. Whether Eileen knows or not, what do you say... Want to go to Paris?"

Angela Digs Deep

The 6:30 a.m. departure from JFK had Angela on the ground at Charles de Gaulle, Paris at 7:30 p.m., which still gave her enough time to head to an internet café. Everyone retrieved their overhead baggage, shuffled out of the plane, walked through the maze of red, white, and blue ribbons that were attached to the stanchions, and divided the lines: Visitors formed a line on one side, and the other: *Citoyens Français.*

269

She watched the citizens as they scanned their passports and upon authorization, they entered an airlock gate controlled by the border police. Next, they placed their hands on a pad that scanned their fingerprints. Angela had never been through this process. A sense of anxiousness flushed her body, forming droplets of perspiration on her brow. *How can I pass the scan? If I get out of line they will know something is up and stop me.* She had no choice; she would play it by ear and pretend she was a dumb blonde.

Angela was next in line. She stepped forward. *I should have read that letter from Gilles; maybe it would have told me something.*

"Mademoiselle... Passeport, s'il vous plaît," motioned the heavily armed guard.

She stumbled with inserting it. The guard asked for it and scanned it for her.

"Merci," replied Angela in a delicate, helpless voice. He motioned for her to step inside the airlock. Her hand was trembling as she raised it to the scanner. She placed her first finger on the pad and waited; the light remained red. The guard looked at her. She wiped her fingers on her dress and with a smile, she placed her whole hand on the pad and tried again. This time, the light blinked to green. The guard nodded at her as she passed through the other end of the gate. She almost felt giddy with relief as she passed through.

Controlling her urge to rush, she instead continued her imaginary movie star persona—sashaying with her large, brimmed hat and oversized sunglasses hiding the grimace on her face. Her apprehension eased as she approached the *Douanes et l'immigration* realizing their Biometric system would have instantly alerted any false documents. She passed by freely. Stares still followed her at the carousels while she waited for the luggage to off-load. Finally, she retrieved her bag and quickly walked to the cabbie stand outside.

The September air was fresh and welcoming. It felt invigorating compared to the heat of Los Angeles. A cabbie pulled to the curb. His friendly smile welcomed Angela as he departed his cab to assist her. His linen coat parted in the breeze and his tam sat neatly skewed to the side of his head revealing a lower band of hair. His years of experience allowed him to load her one suitcase into the trunk of his Citroen with ease.

They left the airport and skirted onto the ramp for Paris. Angela tried to relax and observed the marvelous architecture along the way. She had only seen these structures in movies and travel magazines, although, she thought, she must have looked like a tourist instead of a French citizen gazing at all the fascinating visuals.

The cabbie pulled up to an internet café on Avenue de L'Opéra where she went inside to register for service. She also grabbed a coffee and beignet to take to her table on the outside terrace. An Audi A8 rumbled by on the narrow street as she juggled her suitcase, her laptop, her coffee, and her beignet. As she settled in, she just sat and stared down the street as the city lights started to flicker on. *So this is Paris*, she thought.

Opening her laptop, the first thing she searched for was the Fournier Foundation. The company logo displayed a complete mission statement and then, what she was looking for, the 'contact us' button. A phone number and address listed indicated it was located on the Boulevard du Perini on the west edge of Paris known as La Défense. She thought it strange that there were no photos of the principals of the Foundation. She then searched Gilles Fournier and was completely aghast at the information she uncovered. She felt paralyzed as she read, without any idea, of his stature in France or his influence in the infancy of metal shipping containers and their mega vessels that carried them.

One story mentioned the tragic accident of his wife, Claire Marie Sonnet, and how that caused Gilles Fournier to choose a lifetime of obscurity and mystery. His lifelong friend and prodigy, Jamison Starkney, continued to oversee the Fournier fortune and philanthropic works throughout the world. Since Mr. Fournier's death in 2015, 47 cases had been filed as the heirs to the billionaire's fortune, with all claims being denied by the courts. The noted lineage, explained by the executor of his will, proclaimed an elderly sister-in-law who lived as a cloistered nun in Belgium, and the whisper of a daughter conceived years into his aging life.

Angela took a sip of her coffee and a nibble from her beignet. She wondered why Gilles had never mentioned *this whisper of a daughter* when he talked about his wife Claire. He had said she was pregnant but thought the unborn baby had died as well in the car accident. Angela thought it strange that Gilles had never mentioned anyone else. She was thankful to him for letting her use his family name but thought on her return to the States she might change it to eliminate any confusion if there was a young daughter somewhere. After all, it was just a made-up name.

And who was this Jamison Starkney? She couldn't find much about his past but located a story about a Deborah Ann Starkney and her younger brother, not named because of his age, whose parents were killed in a train accident and then placed in the care of family friends in Tournai, Belgium. As she scrolled down the article, she read, 'The Sonnets were saddened by the loss of their dear friends and promised to care for the young children as their own.'

Angela was feeling drained from the trip and decided she had uncovered enough for one day. *Tomorrow*, she thought, *I'll head to the Foundation and try to meet this Jamison Starkney, the friend of my friend, Gilles.* Sipping the rest of her coffee and another bite of her beignet, she stood up, closed the laptop, and while gathering her things, glanced at the table next to her where a gentleman and lady had been sitting, reading, but had left leaving the newspaper behind. The social page was folded open with a headline reading "Merci Fournier." There was an attached photo but the gentleman in the picture had his hand up across his face, waving as he was getting into his car. Angela stared at it intensely. The ring on this gentleman's finger was that of her dead friend, George Stanza. She knew it intimately as she had designed it with the help of a goldsmith in L.A. and had given it to George on his 60th birthday. She floundered from side to side and slumped back down in her seat, wobbling in disbelief.

How could this be? she thought as tears welled in her eyes. *I know George came to France a lot on business. Could this be a friend of his? But how did he get George's personal effects so soon? And Carl, he knew I gave it to him; why wouldn't he give it back to me?* She sat, wondered, heart sickened.

The barista peered out to his customer who faltered at one of the outside tables. He thought she was about to faint. He ran out of the café and approached Angela with grave concern,

"Mademoiselle... Êtes-vous de mauvaise santé? Vous êtes blanc fantomatique."

"Blanc fantomatique?" she repeated out loud while translating in her mind. *I look ghostly white?*

"Oui!" responded the barista.

"I believe I might be, I have just seen a ghost," replied Angela, in English, confused.

"Pardonnez-moi?"

Angela's Surprise

La Défense, located on the western edge of Paris's business district and glorified with la Grande Arche, a four-dimensional cubed archway, listed La Fondation Fournier as one of the corporations occupying several floors in one of the many glass-wrapped towers—quite the contrast from the rest of the architecture of Paris.

Angela was determined to unravel the mystery of this man called Jamison Starkney, who was wearing her friend's ring. As she entered the main foyer of La Fondation Fournier, the rising sun rose above the influence of other high-rises in the neighborhood and shone through the tinted glass casting Angela's image in shadow upon the imported Italian-marble floors. A pretty receptionist sat behind a stainless-steel-clad desk topped in marble of a contrasting grain to that of the floor. Her dark brown hair was haloed by the sun's reflection from the white marble walls until Angela's shadow engulfed her. She looked up.

"Bonjour, Mademoiselle," welcomed the receptionist.

"Good morning," replied Angela. "Do you speak English?"

"Yes, may I help you?" inquired the receptionist in an infused French accent.

"Yes. I would like to speak to Mr. Starkney, please," stated Angela.

"One moment and I will ring his personal assistant. May I ask your name?"

"Angela Fournier."

Without faltering, the receptionist dialed the number.

"Bonjour. Une Mademoiselle Angela Fournier de voir Monsieur Starkney," she informed the personal assistant.

"Un instant, s'il vous plaît." The receptionist swung her microphone away from her face and asked, "Monsieur

Starkney's personal assistant asked if you had an appointment as she cannot find an entry?"

"No. I was hoping to discuss a personal matter with Mr. Starkney," replied Angela.

Replacing her microphone, she said to the PA, "Non, une affaire personnelle."

The receptionist listened intently to the PA and then pleasantly informed Angela, "Mr. Starkney's assistant informed me that he was on his way to Brussels, Belgium and then from there, he would be returning to the United States."

"Merci... et Merci d'être si agréable pour moi," said Angela.

The receptionist looked astonished as Angela thanked her for being so polite in perfect Parisian French.

"Au revoir," said Angela with flair as she exited the building.

~

Next on Angela's agenda was to search out this Sonnet family who were so kind in rescuing the Starkney children. Angela hired a driver to take her to Tournai, Belgium, a mere couple of hours away. If Jamison Starkney had business in Brussels, it would be a few days before he returned to the States, allowing Angela time to explore some of the questions in her mind. The article she had read online said one heir to the Fournier fortune lived a harmonious life as a cloistered nun. It gave no indication as to where, but it did say the Sonnet family lived near Tournai. Her mind was spinning as they drove through the beautiful countryside of France. The lush green valleys were dotted with farmhouses and cattle roamed freely. *Why would Gilles not return to this serenity?* She imagined he had his reasons. *His love for his wife kept Gilles where he wanted to be, in her Sanctuary. Such a beautiful, romantic story that should be shared,* she thought.

As they pulled off the A1 to a secondary roadway, signs posted on the side, announced Belgique—26 km. She sat up straighter in her seat and gazed out the side window with great anticipation. *Finally... a sign pointing to Tournai.*

As they entered the historic city and passed through the Grand-Place, it was evident how the old adopted the new rather than the other way around. Eminent buildings of Gothic design had coffee shops and restaurants that spilled out into the streets. As they slowed on the cobble street, a young couple rested against a column in a romantic embrace, oblivious to anyone else. The Belfry Tower stood majestically on the corner as the Notre Dame de Tournai loomed over the noble square.

Angela thought that one day when she had more time, she would indulge herself with the history of this city—but for now, she had one purpose: finding Deborah Ann Starkney.

Her driver stopped at one of the schools instituted by the local Sisters to inquire of the whereabouts of one of their peers with the last name of Sonnet. She was informed that Sister Marie was retired and very frail but nonetheless, they gave Angela the Sister's address.

It was only a short distance away as the 'old city' was very small. As Angela entered the foyer of the convent, she was greeted by Sister Monique, who showed her to the gardens where Sister Marie was sitting in her wheelchair reading in the warmth of the day. Angela walked along the carved-stone walkway and approached the retired nun.

"Bonjour, Sister Marie," greeted Angela.

Sister Marie looked up over her half-glasses into the face of a beautiful blonde lady.

"Bonjour," she replied warmly with a smile. "You must be from America," she astutely queried in English.

"Yes. How did you know?" Angela asked, a little confused knowing her French was excellent.

"You called me Sister instead of Soeur," laughed the aging woman.

"Ah, I see." Angela smiled and noticed that Sister Marie was reading a detective story, assuming the book in hand might have possibly been the Bible.

Angela laughed. "You got me on my first three words. You are very astute."

"Thank you. I will take that as a compliment. How may I help you?"

"I don't know where to begin. I am looking for a Deborah Ann Starkney. Do you know of this person?" asked Angela.

The Sister was taken aback; her eyes misting.

"I am sorry, Sister if this brings you pain. I am at a loss myself and only need to clarify my friend's situation."

"I apologize for my weepiness. Deborah Ann and her brother, Jamie, were taken in by my parents after their good friends, the Starkneys, were killed in a train accident. We were impressionable girls who became instant friends. We went to school together, we traveled, we did everything together. You see..." she motioned to this young woman for her name.

"Angela... I apologize for my rudeness."

"Well, Angela... Deborah and I had been lovers since we were fifteen years young, and continued to be, up until her death ten years ago. That is when I joined the Sisterhood," explained Sister Marie.

"I'm so sorry for your loss." Angela paused. "I believe you had a sister as well if I am not mistaken."

"I chose to be called by her name when I became a nun. Her middle name was Marie," shared the Sister.

"And her first name was Claire?" asked Angela.

"Yes."

"And she married a man named Gilles Fournier?" warmly asked Angela with a slight swell of tears in her eyes.

"Yes, child. How do you know this?"

"Gilles was my friend who saved my life," cried Angela.

The Sister raised her open arms for Angela who knelt beside her and they embraced.

"Yes, my sister married Gilles and went on holidays in America. She was killed in a car accident. Unfortunately, Gilles lost all interest in business and remained at her side in the middle of nowhere," stated the Sister.

"Not in the middle of nowhere, Sister Marie, at Claire's Sanctuary," wept Angela, remembering the joy Gilles brought to her.

They held on to each other, rocking back and forth, comforting each other as much as possible. Finally, Angela, releasing her grip, asked, "Sister, what happened to Jamison?"

"Oh... Well, Gilles took to the boy right away. They became inseparable. Gilles mentored Jamie and took him to France along with Claire where they further developed the Sonnet lines and founded the Fournier Foundation. Jamison still heads that corporation to this day," informed Sister Marie.

"Have you seen him lately?" asked Angela.

"Every time he comes back to Belgium. Where do you think I get these books?" laughed Sister Marie, holding up her mystery novel.

Angela composed herself.

"Sister, I don't mean to be insensitive about this, but when actually did you see him last?"

"I saw him about two months ago, but he called me yesterday," informed the Sister.

"Do you know what he was doing here two months ago?" questioned Angela, thinking back to what George had said to her. '..."*It is a long story. I'll explain everything later.*"'

"I believe he said something to do with his passport," answered Sister Marie. "You said Gilles saved your life. It seems he had a habit of doing so."

"What do you mean?"

"Years ago, he sent Deborah and me a letter about a scared young girl whom he became quite fond of and rather fatherly towards. We knew of his and Claire's circumstance of what they had left behind in France and he told us what his intentions were and asked if we would be in agreement. Deborah's only regret was that she never had the chance to meet this phantom girl who lifted Gilles' heart. Gilles was a very forthright man. Not too many like him anymore. The world has changed, my dear."

"Would her name have been... Gloria?" wondered Angela, searching in her own heart.

"Why, yes. Do you know her?" questioned the aging nun with extreme excitement.

Angela stood, head down, unstable as she wandered to a nearby tree. Her heart was pounding, she was short of breath, and she felt like she might vomit.

"My dear, what has you so?" asked the Sister, terrified of Angela's reaction.

Angela slowly turned and looked at Sister Marie. "My real name is Gloria Jackson. No one knows that," she sobbed. "I am listed as dead and I was... until I met Gilles. He gave me strength, he gave me a will to live, and he told me to use his last name as if it were my own. He said he would alway watch over me, and I believe that he still is... Maybe through another." Angela cried.

"Mon Dieu! My child... Mon Dieu! You are her. You are my Angelique Fournier! You are the daughter of my brother-in-law, Gilles! Come here, my beauty; you are my family," Sister Marie stated emotionally with happy tears in her eyes. "You are all I have left."

Angela, now uncontrollably crying, shared an embrace with her—her aunt, Sister Marie.

"Child... You have no idea how long I have waited for this moment. Gilles wrote many letters to us about your new life and I am so sorry you had to go through what you did, but you are a fine woman in spite of your hardships."

"But Sister, how did he know? I am ashamed to say that I do not deserve to be loved like this. I didn't stay in touch... I concentrated on me, me, me!"

"I guess you have an angel, my love. You have made this woman's old heart happier than it has been in years. Gilles said you would find your way to me. He believed that; he believed in you," related Sister Marie as she held her niece tight. "He said to me, 'If there is a God in the sky, she will come by her own accord'. He was not very religious after Claire's death, by any means, so for his prophecy to come true, renews my faith in the Lord, and I believe good things will happen to you, my dear," consoled Sister Marie.

~

A car streaked down N7 to the outskirts of a town called Tournai to the rest home of the only known survivor of the Fournier fortune, and hopefully to the whereabouts of one Angela Fournier.

From the parking lot, just past the well-manicured hedges near a shade tree, he spotted her. He could tell, even from that distance, she had found her home; at least in her heart. He walked closer to her through the silent green grass and as he saw the tears in her eyes, he too felt a swell. He called out. "Angela! Angela!"

She looked up, stunned. She dampened the tears from her eyes. "Jeff?" she questioned. And then emotionally, she cried out louder, "Jeff!"

He ran to her side and embraced her passionately. She accepted his strong arms, clutching with mounting fervor. She squeezed him tighter than she had ever embraced another man. *He IS my knight in shining armor. My Prince Charming.*

From afar, a man hopped over a hedge and with discernible purpose, walked towards the couple. He reached into his jacket pocket just as Jeff looked up from the clutches of Angela's arms. As the man descended upon them...

"Angela, do you remember my partner, Goody?"

...he snapped a picture.

"Sorry, but I had to get a snapshot for posterity," beamed Goody, eating the words he once spoke to Jeff about him being out of her league.

"What are you doing here?" happily asked Angela.

"We're here to save your ass," answered Goody. He paused and looked over at Sister Marie...

"Oh, excuse me... I am so sorry, Sister."

They all laughed at Goody's choice of words.

"You must be the detective I heard about?" questioned Sister Marie.

"Excuse me, Sister?" said Jeff with more than a casual interest.

"Jamie said, if his plan worked, I would have company," stated the Sister.

"I don't understand, Sister? Who is Jamie? And what plan?" asked Jeff.

"I believe, my aunt is telling us that George Stanza is Jamison Starkney."

"Your aunt? Jamison Starkney, the CEO of Fournier Foundation is George Stanza?" questioned Jeff, astounded.

"There is no other explanation," explained Angela.

"George is not dead, Angela. We can almost guarantee that," interrupted Goody.

"I know. He was wearing his ring in a photo I saw in yesterday's paper. It was taken the day before," said Angela.

"Gilles gave me a letter..."

Jeff interrupted Angela, "When you were Gloria Jackson?"

"Yes..." Angela looked at Jeff, curiously, wondering how he had connected her with her past—she then continued. "...I have never opened it. When I fled my apartment, inside the safe was a new phone, my passports, lots of money and a letter from George. I have not opened that one either. I am afraid if I do, they will disappear from my life and then my life would not be worth living. Does that make sense?" queried Angela looking into Jeff's eyes searching for an alternative answer.

"Perfect sense to me," he said.

"So you and your aunt are the only heirs to the Fournier fortune?" asked Goody.

"Honestly, I never thought of it until you just said that. It has always just been about the men in my life who I have loved. Not about fortunes or anything else. I'm still confused over all of this. Until I read those letters, maybe then I'll have a better understanding."

"So, do you think that is why Micholanetti is after you? He knows about your financial windfall?" asked Goody.

"I think it is more personal. He couldn't know if I only just found out. Besides, I have no knowledge of any financial gain or otherwise. My mind is spinning with questions!" stated Angela.

"Sister, would you like me to wheel you in?" asked Goody, politely.

"Heavens no! This is more exciting than my detective novels," said the energized Sister Marie. "What about the butler?" she blurted out.

"The butler? Excuse me, Sister, but I think that is a game," said Goody.

"Not on your sweet tushie," added Sister Marie, humorously. "You keep your eyes open for him."

"Yes, Sister... We will," remarked Jeff.

"Okay, so what is our next move?" asked Goody.

"Jamison's receptionist said he was going to Brussels and then back to Washington. I think we should head back to the States and follow up on any loose leads," said Angela, sternly.

"Whoa, wait a minute. People are trying to kill you. You are not going back there and you are not joining in on this investigation," insisted Jeff.

"Whoops, young man, she is a Fournier. Good luck in trying to tell her what to do," interrupted Sister Marie.

Angela bent down and gave her aunt a kiss. "Thank you, Auntie. Well, you heard my aunt; you can't ignore that," proudly declared Angela.

"Brussels... There is a summit there on fighting the drug cartels and a friend of mine told me about a serious bust happening all through the States. Do you think George, excuse me, Jamison is working for the government?" asked Jeff.

"Jamison does not work for anyone but our holdings," insisted Sister Marie. "But in saying that, he could be instrumental in helping them."

"What do you mean, Auntie?"

"You will soon find out about your lineage, my child. But, we will not allow anyone to hold ransom, terrorize, or destroy anything we have built, in any country for the good of the people. No matter what!" said a fiery Sister Marie, clenching her fist.

"Damn... I wouldn't want to have dated you when you were younger," joked Goody.

"Excuse me, sonny, nothing against your manly looks or color but you are the wrong gender," roused Sister Marie.

"Whoa!" exploded Goody, laughing. "I didn't see that coming."

"Now, gather around. Here's what I think you should do next," conspired the not-so-frail, Sister Marie.

The Magic of Tournai

Angela dismissed her driver and went with Jeff and Goody after leaving her fiery aunt, Sister Marie, at her convent to mastermind, in her mind, the outcome of her niece's plight. They drove down the brick inlaid street of N7 to just past the grand square and stopped before The Belfry to enjoy one of the many outside cafés. Sipping on a glass of wine, Angela asked, "When did you find out I was Gloria Jackson?"

"Well...we weren't certain when I accidentally found your half photo of Carol, but after meeting her, I was positive. However, in our line of work, Goody wouldn't accept the findings until we had a blood match."

"You met, Carol? How is she? Where is she?" quizzed Angela, raising her hands to her face smothering a scream excited to hear news of her long-time friend.

"She is doing well, owns a diner in Carroll, is married to Rodney..."

"Rodney?!" smiled Angela, somewhat skeptical.

"Yes, he adores her. We had some time together when we hiked your trail from the accident scene and came up on the backside of Claire's Sanctuary," said Jeff.

"Oh yes. That poor truck driver. Did he survive?"

"Yes. And got married," added Goody.

"Really! So it was you I saw from the rock outcrop with the rifle pointing at me?"

"Hell no! Rodney made me put a special boot over the barrel when he realized we were on Claire's Sanctuary's land. We had our binoculars out looking at the two hawks in the sky."

"My hawks, Jettie and Claire. I helped raise them." Angela paused momentarily, recounting that day. "Who had the rifle?"

"We are assuming, Micholanetti or someone he hired," answered Jeff. "How did you escape without going down the main road? Bernadette, the young curator said a crazy white woman drove off through an old crop field."

"Yes, I understand why she thought I was crazy. Years ago, Gilles showed me an escape road that had been abandoned from the old trapping and railroad days. I really messed up that SUV. I should send them some money. I feel foolish now," confessed Angela.

"Never! Your life was in danger. I'm surprised you had the wherewithal to do the things you did," said Jeff, putting his hand on hers.

"Look, if you two are going to get all mushy, I'm heading back to the States," said Goody.

Angela smacked him on the shoulder. "Don't even think about it until we follow through with the plan."

"Yes, ma'am," said Goody, rubbing his shoulder.

"Right, in the meantime, let's toast to... new beginnings," proposed Jeff.

"Yes... Tabula Rasa!" added Angela.

"Quite right, Angela. Quite right," affirmed Goody.

They all enjoyed the developing friendships that afternoon, as this would be the last time the three would be seen together. According to their rehearsed plan, Goody was to drop back for any surprises that they hadn't counted on. Goody had already found the tracking chip in Angela's new phone and suggested she leave it be for now as he assumed it was Jamison and his crew keeping tabs on her. There were still many questions unanswered, but they felt if they ever saw Jamison again, he would be the one to clarify their missing pieces.

For now, Jeff and Angela were going to take in the sights for a few days before heading back to Paris. Goody had been in contact with their agency in L.A. and learned that Allen Travers returned to work as well as Adriane. And it seemed, as the spy train goes, Tom—the new security guard—fell head over heels for Adriane. Jeff was relieved to hear that. *Good*, he thought. *She had someone who could keep an eye out for her safety, and I wouldn't have to explain my feelings for Angela.*

Angela and Jeff checked into one of the historic refurbished hotels with adjoining rooms; Goody had one just down the hall. He thought he would have to bring Georgette there someday. *She would love it here.* They agreed that Goody would reserve his seating a half hour before theirs. And as a purely a strategic move, if he sat leisurely in the lounge with a Cuban rolled cigar, he'd have a better chance to scrutinize the patrons—Goody's idea.

Angela hadn't packed for any social occasion but managed to throw together an ensemble after stopping at one of the clothier's just down from where they had lunch.

Jeff knocked on her door at 7:45 p.m. for their 8 p.m. seating. She opened it and Jeff just stood there looking at her, speechless.

"Well, say something!"

"Uh... You look absolutely beautiful. Why is it every time I see you, you take my breath away and I am left muttering like a fool?" said Jeff, humorously.

"I don't know, Jeff. You tell me," flirted Angela.

He put his hands on her shoulders and drew her near. He gazed into her blue eyes looking for acceptance, they sparkled back at him—inviting. He bent towards her, lightly kissing her on her edible red lips.

"Look out dar-ling, I could very easily devour you," he whispered drawing out darling like a Bogart movie.

"We will have to wait and see, won't we?" she teased. "I think the last time we were this close, you were talking kids and we hadn't even kissed yet," she softly taunted, gazing back.

He bent again to her luscious lips and placed his upon hers. They embraced in a passionate kiss. He lingered in her taste, softly teasing with his lips, pecking at hers as she swooned in his arms.

"Okay... You have broken that barrier," she flushed. "Phew!" She reached to his lips and removed the lip gloss. "Not your color," she said as she laughed. "Okay, if we are heading for dinner, we better go now. Is it warm in here or is it me?"

Smiling, she put her arm in his and they headed down the hallway to the early 1920's iron gate and buzzed the bellman to raise the elevator.

On the main floor to the right of the elevator stood the Maître D' who greeted them politely. He offered the lead with his white-gloved hand and added a precautionary gesture to

Angela regarding her stiletto shoes on the cut-stone floor. They walked past the smoking lounge where Goody was enjoying a flavorful cigar to a dimly lit table for two at the opening of the terrace doors.

The night air caressed their faces as lovers strolled by on the esplanade. Not a more perfect night could have been contrived than the sweetness of the Belgium air, pierced with jasmine. Their blue eyes danced in the flicker of the candlelight as they bore into each other's soul with the pleasure of conversation. Their words matched as if they had known each other a lifetime and their laughter assured each other's delight of the immediate future. Jeff watched Angela's lips as she formed each syllable as she ordered their dinner in French. Noticing, she peered at him with a questioning stare.

"What are you looking at?" she asked, softly.

"Your mouth as your tongue licked your lips when you were ordering," he whispered across the small table.

She stroked his leg with her foot.

"I am warning you, mister. If you keep this talk up, we will have to get dinner in a to-go box," she said smiling.

The waiter approached the table and gave an excusing guttural inflection. He placed the salad on their table and inquired courteously, "Frais poivre moulu?"

"Oui, monsieur," replied Jeff. The waiter ground fresh pepper over their salads.

"Very good, Jeff," complimented Angela.

"I think that is all I know. I can ask, 'Where is the bathroom?' in Spanish, but my French is, I am sorry to say, nil," laughed Jeff as he took another sip of champagne. "Angela, why do you think George, I mean Jamison, threatened me to stay away from you the night of the after party?"

"HE'S the one who made you run off? Knowing him, he knew or hoped you wouldn't give up. He has a keen sense of people's values. I am quite sure he had you checked out before you were even invited to the opening."

"Yes, he seemed to know all about me. Who is he?"

"Jeff, I thought I knew him better than most and yet, here I am with you, wondering the same thing. I thought it might have been Gina and I out on the terrace that sent you running," shyly said Angela.

"You saw me?"

"I was... somewhat involved, but I could feel your presence."

"I didn't know what to say," admitted Jeff.

"And what would you say now, Jeff?"

Without missing a beat, Jeff offered, "Leave some for me."

Angela burst into laughter and maybe a little too much for the atmosphere, but they both took delight in the humor of his answer.

She blew him a kiss and said, "Thank you, Jeff, for accepting me as I am. I promise, I will do nothing behind your back, if... you can keep the little Jeffs and Jeffettes at bay for two years. Do we have a deal?"

"Let me get this straight... Perhaps, straight might not be the correct word. How about, let me get this right. If this is our official second date, and you haven't run off yet, *and* I am comfortable with your bi-interests, you are willing to have little ones with me?"

Angela took a sip from her champagne, looked him straight in the eyes, and then, coyly asked, "Deal?"

"Where do I sign?" passionately exploded Jeff.

"Upstairs!" she replied solicitously.

~

She was partially out of her dress as Jeff fumbled with her room key. She pushed him against the door and ripped open his shirt and pressed her bare breasts to his masculine body. The door swung open and they fell to the floor. He rolled her over and kicked the door shut as he smothered her with kisses. Their mouths grasped for each other's as their lips pressed tight and their tongues explored. Their clothes flew off as he lifted her to the bed; her round ass cupped in his hands as he lowered her slowly down. Angela squeezed his muscular arms feeling his muscles twitch with her weight. They meshed together in the mangle of sheets.

Jeff tenderly toyed with each nipple with his tongue. "Harder," she said softly. He gingerly took each one in his teeth and gently pulled as she whimpered, "Yes". Their passion was on fire as she raised her legs around him pulling her hips to his. She instructed him, "Now, baby, I want you now." He entered her silky smooth mound and as he thrust deeper, her body rippled with desire and he felt a gush of warm fluid against his shaft. "Don't stop, baby", she said as she clawed at his back. Again she flushed as her hips rammed him with his motion. "Oh my God, baby, you feel wonderful; you fill me up. Oh, yes, right there, you're rubbing my clit with your dick... Don't stop. Oh my God, yes, baby... baby... baby... cum with me, baby!" she screamed. They let out a harmonious exclamation of delight as the sweat dripped from their bodies and they heaved with multiple aftershocks.

Catching their breath, lying face up on the bed, and with their hearts beating like a well-tuned Ferrari, Angela smacked Jeff in the chest and declared, "Where have you been? Oh my God. That was so amazing." She turned onto her stomach and looked at him, and she said, "Consider that as being signed up, mister, but with one other condition..."

"What's that?" he asked, still recovering.

"It is... forever!"

The Wheeler Dealer

The next morning brought bright blue skies and if you stood at a certain angle, the wind whistling through the village sounded like the strings of a Stradivarius. Arm in arm, Jeff and Angela headed for breakfast. As they stepped out of the elevator, the sun's rays drifting through the stained glass windows painted their faces in a tapestry of color. A waiter guided them towards the dining room, past the cigar emporium. Sitting at the last table against the back wall, Goody watched the two as they surfaced at the French doors leading into the room. He almost choked on his fritter as they walked in and he saw their illuminated faces. *Oh boy*, he thought, *there will be no living with him now*.

Instead of sticking to the plan, Jeff and Angela walked up to Goody's table. He followed their intentions as they approached him.

"Excuse me, sir," asked Jeff. "Would you mind taking our picture for posterity's sake? I have a friend that will not believe our situation unless I constantly remind him with this photo."

"Yeah, sure, mister. I can understand how your friend might seem a little chastened," replied Goody.

He snapped a picture with Jeff's cell phone.

"Would you mind if we join you... that is, if you desire company?" asked Angela.

The two sat down after Goody gave them a nod of approval. He leaned into them and said in his softest voice, "Okay, you two love birds, what are you up to?"

Angela, batting her eyelashes, asked, "What do you mean, kind sir?"

"You two are not fooling anyone, especially me, or anyone else that could be watching. Okay, I'm happy for ya, even though you have known each other like what, twelve hours," sarcastically stated Goody.

"You are such a cynic sometimes, Goody," said Jeff.

"Listen, I admit it. I'm eating a lot of crow. I am truly happy for you two... really." Goody turned to Angela and added, "I'll be very pissed off if my little buddy gets hurt, missy."

Angela put her hand on his arm. "Goody, I promise you, it won't be me. Besides, we have a deal, and that deal has a clause... It's forever," stated Angela, feeling the love of Goody for his buddy, Jeff. "Our situation might be a little out of the ordinary but I know deep in my heart that we are meant to be. How did you meet Georgette?"

"Well..." Goody paused. He wondered when his answer might bite him in the ass. "I was in the hospital checking on the condition of a client that we just extracted when this vision from the heavens walked by. I turned to watch her as she passed and when I turned back around, I ran into the center post of the floor's double doors and broke my nose. Lucky for me, she was the doctor on duty and snapped it back in place," informed Goody, shyly.

"Aha, you never told me that," laughed Jeff.

"And don't let that get around the office either," he sternly said in his Goody-ish tone. "I know I am going to regret this, too, but how about a group hug?"

"You are such a teddy bear. A big masculine guy with a big heart when it comes to his friends. Thank you for being Jeff's friend," said Angela.

"Okay, you two. Have you settled your concerns? Can we get back to our plan?" asked Jeff.

"I need to get back to Paris to see Eileen so we can close on our new gallery," said Angela dampening her teary eyes with her linen serviette.

"Is that wise?" asked Goody.

"I can't hide all my life. Yes, I need to do this," said Angela.

"Okay, I guess we are going to Paris, buddy. Harry said not to put her life in danger, so I guess it is up to us to provide protection."

"You know, when Auntie said I was a Fournier, when you think about it, I have been a Fournier longer than a Jackson. I have learned the Fournier way and... nobody... is going to prey on me like a hurt animal," declared a fiery Angela, gritting her teeth.

"Yes, baby, we get it... Right, Goody?"

"Yeah man... I hear ya. We are just doing the gallery business and then flying home, right? No seeking out the Fournier fortune or anything?" queried Goody.

"I don't want to draw any undue attention to myself right now. There will be plenty of time to figure all that out and what Gilles had in mind. I have done just fine without knowing about the Foundation, so a few more months or whatever it takes to get Anthony behind bars does not bother me," assured Angela.

"All right then. Why don't we take the rest of the day to look around? Goody, you might find something nice to take home to Georgette," said Jeff.

"I could help you. She is going to need some maternity clothes soon. I saw a nice shop just around the corner on Rue des Chapeliers," added Angela.

Goody had a funny look on his face but conceded to Angela's wishes. After all, she was a Fournier; who was going to argue that point?

They spent the rest of that day dragging Goody from shop to shop. According to Angela, he needed something nice to bring home to Georgette. Angela had him buy several maternity outfits and a very sexy lace *negligée de chambre à coucher* and she made him repeat the French pronunciation of bedroom negligee fifteen times to get it right. He was putty in her hands and Jeff took great pleasure in watching his buddy succumb to her wishes.

. . .

The next day, however, was gloomy and raining as they streaked down the A1 towards Paris. Angela had called Eileen, who was relieved to hear from her and the fact that Jeff and Goody were by her side. Eileen detected an even more than usual enthusiastic tone to Angela's voice, but Angela would not say anything more until they met.

The gallery was set in a four-story building with a grand façade of Gothic design, with full glass displayed from floor to ceiling on the first and second floors. Under the stairs, they would build the serving bar and possibly a small desk, with minimal interference, keeping the floors and walls clear for display space. The third floor would be used for storing artwork for upcoming shows and packaging others for shipping. The fourth floor was truly unique with a glass pinnacle that rose in the middle of the roof, dispersing natural light throughout their office space. All floors were serviced by a freight elevator in the rear of the building with access to the alleyway.

Angela had been the chief negotiator with the French realtor and had come to an agreement of Euros 2,500,000, which was approximately $2,725,000 in U.S. dollars, a bargain for a building of this size and with its excellent location on Avenue de L'Opéra, only a few blocks from the Musée du Louvre. Goody and Jeff just sat and listened as she played her game, as she had done at her gallery in L.A. She had the realtor flustered at times and laughing at others; a true negotiator. She wasted little time in calling her bank in L.A. to wire the funds to the realtor's bank. They shook hands; the realtor handed over the keys, the purchase agreement, and he left with a smile on his face after Angela agreed to pay him an extra percentage point on his commission because of the lowered price.

Angela and Eileen were thrilled to say the least. They were in sync as they shared the same ideas for transforming their new acquisition into a masterpiece of visual enlightenment. Angela excused herself several times to Jeff and Goody for their zealousness but the two had dreamt about this day for a very long time.

"This calls for champagne, my friends," insisted Angela.

One of the key elements in choosing this building was the immediate access to the restaurant next door, which had a clientele of affluent patrons that frequented it on any given night. They could also cater the gallery's events—a win-win situation for everyone.

"I'll go next door and get a bottle and four glasses," offered Jeff.

"Thank you, baby," warmly acknowledged Angela.

Goody stood looking out the window watching the rain pouring down.

"Okay, Angela... What's the scoop on Jeff?" asked Eileen.

"He is my knight in shining armor. It feels so right... even from the very first time I met him when he tried handing me his business card and he felt so foolish. I knew, if I had a chance, it would be him," said Angela.

"You are glowing, my friend. From the minute you walked through that door, I knew something was up. I am so happy for you," said Eileen.

"It has been a long time coming. He knows my past and still accepts me for who I am. A girl cannot ask for more than that... and... in bed... he rocks my world," glowed Angela.

The two were hugging as Jeff brought in the bottle of champagne and four glasses. With the pop of the cork, he served each glass and with a toast, they *clinked* to future successes and family.

Even Goody discarded his usual insensitivity for a more accommodating nature, but not without questioning the whereabouts of Jamison Starkney.

"Who?" questioned Eileen.

"George. George is Jamison Starkney," informed Angela.

"I don't understand?"

"George led me to believe he was murdered and I ran for it not wanting to get anyone else involved. Jeff and Goody were assigned a case of a missing teen assumed dead, which led them to me, and I came here to France to the Fournier Foundation whereby I met my auntie, Sister Marie, where Jeff found me in Belgium," enlightened Angela.

"Whoa... slow down, please. You didn't come here just for the real estate deal?" asked Eileen, confused.

"No. Jeff told me that David saw me at JFK boarding an Air France flight and that he had been here with you in Paris, which led Jeff to come here. When I arrived, I searched on the internet for anything on the Fournier Foundation, which led me to my aunt who told me that we were the sole survivors of the Fournier fortune, which Jamison Starkney has been managing for years," explained Angela in a concise version.

"Why would George invent his death to scare you?" asked Eileen.

"That's what we want to know, Eileen," added Goody.

"We have assumptions but nothing concrete, until we find this Jamison Starkney to explain fully," said Jeff.

"That's why Joseph has been acting so strange," said Eileen.

"What do you mean? He shot at me!" blurted Angela.

"Baby, he loves you as much as I love you. He would not harm you or let anyone do so. I don't know this Jamison Starkney, but I do know whatever is going on has been brewing for a long time," informed Eileen.

"Let me ask this, ladies. How did you find this building?" asked Goody.

"The realtor emailed me about this space. Angela and I had been looking but not real seriously. And when I mentioned it to Joseph, he insisted I come over here right away."

"Joseph insisted. Is that not a little too coincidental that you both should be here out of the States, out of harm's way?" said Goody.

Jeff had been a little distracted with his and Angela's unbelievable connection but he was following his buddy's lead.

"Who owned this building?"

"I don't know, Jeff. It has been all done through the realtor," explained Eileen.

"I would bet my last dollar that Jamison Starkney is involved in this, one way or the other. In fact, you probably just invested back into your own company, the Fournier Foundation," pointed out Jeff with an interesting take.

Goody started to laugh but agreed with Jeff.

"Eileen," interrupted Jeff, "...may I ask, what is your relationship with Joseph?"

Eileen shied away and as she began to explain, a tear formed in her eye.

"Years ago before this..." she pointed to her scar, "Joseph and I were lovers. Anthony forced his way into my apartment and cut me until I told him where Joseph had gone. I had a career as a model... he ended that. And the next thing I heard on the news was that Joseph and two others were shot. I believe the female agent that was killed was Joseph's sister.

We never talked about it and remained as friends but Joseph was not the same after that."

"Oh my God, Eileen! I never knew. Irma said you had a story but she never had the chance to say what it was. Again, that asshole Anthony..." Angela made a fist, "...jail is too good for him."

"Slow down, ladies. People have gone through a lot of trouble to arrange for all of us to be here. This is no simple plan, more like a covert operation," informed Goody.

"Goody is right. George has played us all, and I don't mean in a bad way, but in his way. He has orchestrated each and every move, including my falling for Angela. Somehow, he knew I would not let you be hung out to dry. We have to start thinking like him," said Jeff.

"That's right, buddy. I believe I told you that from the beginning. You ladies coming to Paris are giving him and his buddies time to make a move on Anthony..."

Jeff interrupted him.

"I don't believe so, Goody. Remember what Sister Marie said: 'We will not allow anyone to hold ransom, terrorize, or destroy anything we have built.' She said 'we'; this frail old lady with clenched fist saying that. I think George or Jamison is waiting for us, Goody. We need to take Anthony down. They are just offering us the tools, the indictments, and the legal background to back us up and put him away, forever," shared Jeff.

The room quietened as they all sifted through this theory and contemplated their next move.

Angela spoke up first. "Baby, before you say anything to the contrary, please listen. Anthony wants me..." she put her fingers to Jeff's lips, "...let's give him a chance to hang himself. What if we set up a location that we have secured beforehand and, I don't know, do something to draw him out, not too public but where he feels comfortable, like down at the docks or warehouse district."

"Where has he been hiding out anyway? How come no one, including George, has found him?" questioned Eileen.

"Maybe, it is as Jeff said... or I should say as Sister Marie said... that he'll do nothing to put the Foundation at risk. He probably knows exactly where Anthony is but is waiting for us to get our shit together," offered Goody.

"Goody is right. We have certain protocol we have to follow as far as documentation and our motivating factors for doing anything we do. We are accountable for everything. George knows this; he is a smart man," insisted Jeff.

"I like Angela's thinking. He has to feel comfortable and that it is his idea to capitalize on the situation. What would you be doing down at the docks?" asked Goody.

"Signing in imported artwork," claimed Eileen without hesitation. "We do it all the time for artists from the Pacific Rim, including Canada, Mexico and South America. Port of Entry and Customs are at the L.A. docks; especially if the pieces are large and can't be transported by air."

"Is there anything else you ladies need to do here?" asked Jeff.

"Plenty! Permits, contractors, drawings, and decorating. This space is raw; it's our canvas," said Angela.

"Okay, let me re-phrase this... What do you need to do right now that would delay our flight back to the States?"

"Locking the door and walking out into the rain. The realtor is very accommodating; especially if he can make back some of that commission he lost with my frugal bartering," said Angela.

"I thought you were giving him a browbeating?" laughed Goody.

"It only sounds like that when you get adamant. I just love French expressions," said Angela, laughing.

"We can send him architectural drawings for the contractor and even have the contractor pull permits," added Eileen.

"And I would imagine if you tag a line to mention the Fournier Foundation, they would jump through hoops," shared Jeff, joining in on the fun.

"By the way, did you see Sister Marie's cell phone? I thought mine was up to date. Mine looks like it came out of the Smithsonian compared to hers. I am quite sure Sister Marie has already informed the Foundation about your visit and they know they fucked up by not seeing you when you went there. I wouldn't want to be Jamison's personal assistant after Sister Marie finished with them," said Goody, laughing.

"Are you insinuating that my auntie has a certain nonconformist attitude?"

"Ha... That is mildly understated."

"But she is so lovable, don't you think, Goody?"

"She got me... I will concede... she warms my soul."

"You know, her plan of pulling him out of hiding isn't too far off of what we are saying right now," said Jeff.

"Well then, I insist. We can't disappoint my auntie," Angela said with a smile.

They locked the front door of their new gallery and ventured out into the pouring rain with a plan in hand.

More Truths Over Cocktails

Once in flight, Angela snuggled into Jeff's arm as the four prepared for a relaxing flight back to the USA while being pampered in first class. Jeff and Goody never had the pleasure of the larger seats and accommodating attendants. "Air France really knows how to do things right," said Jeff as he looked across the aisle at Goody who sat with an acknowledging smile on his face. Eileen sat next to him sketching what she was imagining for that wonderful space they now had in Paris. Her eyes gleaming, her cheeks ballooning into a full grin.

Jeff's mind was still spinning as he wondered... *Why hadn't Joseph taken out Micholanetti if he knew Anthony was the one that shot his sister? Maybe he didn't know for sure and was baiting Anthony as George baited me. George was definitely good at what he did and connected. Maybe Tom worked for George? Maybe George had his own mercenaries to do the Foundation's dirty work? George, Jamison... the names were starting to be interchangeable. Was that part of his grand scheme? And how does Angela tie into all of this? Who is George to her? Who is Gilles Fournier? How does he really fit into all of this?*

At the moment, it did not matter because on his shoulder was the love of his life. There was no denying it; she couldn't be any more perfect for him. They shared a certain common background even if it was on either side of the fence. They both knew the streets, which was in their favor for bringing down Micholanetti. He smelt her perfume and had tasted her lips. He slipped into a subconscious sleep. Angela was on his mind.

~

After a superb lunch and an in-flight movie, the plane was about to descend into U.S. air space. Coming out of the clouds, they could see New York to their left with the Atlantic to the left of that. There was an earlier announcement about being over Newfoundland, Canada, then the Province of Quebec, and now, New York State. Home at last—well, the U.S. of A. Still another five hours to get to L.A., not counting layover time.

They shuffled through the lines of passengers; Angela had shown her U.S. passport in France so they all stood in line together. Angela and Eileen went through first, followed by Jeff. Goody brought up the rear and was the only one stopped with something to declare. When asked what he had, he shyly informed the customs officer that he had bought lingerie for his pregnant wife. The officer looked at Goody and saw the bead of perspiration forming on his forehead. The officer said, "Very expensive lingerie you are claiming."

"Not my fault, officer. That blonde lady you let through first made me buy it," replied Goody, very embarrassed.

"That little blonde lady made you?" questioned the officer with a hint of a grin knowing he was getting this passenger's goat.

He stamped Goody's passport and waved for the next passenger, still sporting a smile.

"Fucker," said Goody as he caught up to his friends.

Jeff had to keep looking away as he knew his friend was pissed. Angela grabbed his arm and didn't say a word but brandished a larger smile than Jeff.

They transferred terminals and waited three hours before the next flight to L.A. To kill some time, they went into an Irish pub as it was advertised outside with faux trees and little green leprechauns. Fortunately, no one on the inside vaguely resembled what or who they were advertising.

As soon as they sat down, a pretty red-haired waitress approached their table. In a heavy Irish brogue she asked, "What's your pleasure?" This seemed funny to them, but very appropriate. Eileen and Angela both ordered a Guinness; Jeff and Goody both opted for a rye and water.

Goody, who had calmed down from the customs official, had a smirk on his face as he looked at Angela.

"What?" she questioned.

"You don't seem like a beer-drinking girl," elaborated Goody.

"You have a lot to learn about me, don't you?" replied Angela with a smile. "I am a survivor. I had to put up with an abusive stepfather, I survived a terrifying accident, a winter storm, and a bus ride across this country before the age of sixteen. I think I can handle a stout beer."

"I didn't mean that..." backtracked Goody. "...it's more, your looks, I guess. Too beautiful for a working man's pleasure."

"Oh... God, I wish I had a tape recorder," laughed Jeff. "Since my dear friend bridged the subject, what else should I be aware of?"

"Let's see... If you are questioning as to whether or not I can take care of myself. I can shoot the center out of a target at 50 feet with my 9mm, I can take down a 250-pound man with two kicks without breaking a nail, and I can drift a car around a track in under two minutes. Anything else, gentlemen?"

"Ah, you got me," said Goody, raising his hands.

"Who taught you all this?" asked Jeff, somewhat miffed.

"Carl."

"Fifty feet is pretty impressive, but it is a lot different when the target is moving," explained Jeff.

"Boy, are you a Doubting Thomas. Carl took me once to a practice range where they had targets coming out of different buildings and such," said Angela.

"How did you do?" asked Goody in a ho-hum voice.

"Nine of out ten, smart ass," answered Angela. "And if it wasn't for the family guy with the wife and child looking like my stepfather, I might not have emptied five rounds into him."

"Where was this?" asked Jeff.

"Not sure. Up in the hills someplace."

"A police range?"

"There were no signs. A couple of guys were in fatigues but no one had insignias, army-type guys," said Angela.

"We are talking about Carl, as in George's butler slash driver, whatever he is?" asked Jeff, surprised.

"Your aunt's comment of the butler perhaps?" asked Goody.

"Oh, he is not George's butler... more like a good friend who enjoys cooking and I guess a certain intrigue that their business dealings allow," informed Angela.

"Which are what?"

"That I don't know, Goody. George has always kept his line of work secretive with the exception of our real estate interests."

"He certainly demands first class work on the buildings I have seen," remarked Jeff.

"Which, by the way, your apartment is non-existent," informed Goody.

"What do you mean?" asks Angela.

"It has been sanitized," offered Jeff.

"Where is my car?" asked Angela, getting a little upset.

"Your pretty blue Mercedes?"

"Yes."

"The last we saw of it, it was on the back of a ramp truck that doesn't exist either," relayed Goody.

"Did you ever wonder how you managed to drive your car back to your apartment, smashed in the back end like it was, without the automatic gas shut off and the air bags deploying?" asked Jeff.

"Why would I wonder that?"

"Because any other new car, like yours, would have been disabled at the scene of the accident, yet you were allowed to escape in that damaged car," said Goody.

Angela sat quietly—thinking.

"Joseph had taken my car a few days before all of this went down and said he had to handle some safety issues, which I didn't understand as it was brand new."

"Part of the grand scheme, I would bet," said Jeff.

"Okay, so where is all my stuff?" she asked, sitting back and lacing her arms across her chest.

"Don't know. Another question to ask George or Jamison depends who comes out of the woodwork," said Goody.

"If you are worrying about where you are going to stay when we get back to Los Angeles that is not a concern you have to worry about."

"You can stay with me," said the quiet Eileen as she adjusted her beer before leaning in forward to join the conversation.

"Thank you, Eileen for your offer but Angela will be staying with me at my apartment. I had it swept before I left and I will have our team do it again before we return. I want to know where you are at all times. Is that understood, Angela?" stated Jeff emphatically.

Angela dropped her arms back down onto the table, batted her eyelashes and said, "Yes, baby." She then leaned her head against Jeff's strong shoulder, smiling.

She Dances For Angela

Jeff had called the agency and had his apartment and Eileen's swept for any listening devices and arranged for surveillance of Eileen's apartment, the gallery, and AD Fashions. Allen was very pleased to hear from Jeff and accepted his request as an honor. He had devised a tracking system that changed every 10 seconds to avoid anyone from monitoring his information. He was pissed when he found out someone had tapped into his feed. "Never again," he said. This was a challenge that he lived for—superspy versus superspy. It wasn't about good guys against bad guys, no. This was good guy versus good guy and who was a better sleuth.

The flight to L.A. seemed to be wearier than the one from Europe, possibly the time difference was setting in and the adrenaline had slowed. They dropped Eileen off first, but before leaving, they checked out her apartment and made sure Allen had his ears on. Goody was next. Georgette was waiting outside flashing a big smile, and the tell-tale signs of a baby bump. The limo stopped out front of Jeff's brownstone to let the remaining two off.

Sitting on the steps of the brownstone, Josh watched as this monstrous car pulled up to the curb. The driver assisted Angela in getting out of the car to Josh's delight. First appearing were her shapely legs, followed by all this blonde hair with a starlet's face. Josh was beside himself wondering who this vision of beauty was that graced his neighborhood. Jeff appeared next, to Josh's surprise. He ran down the steps to Jeff's side, screaming all the way. "Mr. Malardo, Mr. Malardo!" Jeff bent down and gave him a big hug.

"Mr. Malardo... Who's the babe?"

"The babe is Angela. Angela, this is Josh, my little friend I was telling you about on the plane."

Angela bent down and offered her hand. Josh bypassed it and gave her an equally strong hug around her neck.

"Well, thank you Josh for the warm welcome."

"I knew Mr. Malardo was up to something. There is a package addressed to Angela Fournier, care of Jeff Malardo that I saved in my apartment for you," said Josh, excitedly. "Did you get married?"

Angela looked at him and lightly grabbed Josh's chin. "Not yet. He hasn't asked me," she informed him with a sulking voice.

"Mr. Malardo, what are you waiting for, man? She's a dish!"

"Josh, you are going to have to stop watching my movies with me."

"I think he is adorable," said Angela, glowing.

Josh grabbed her hand and escorted her to the apartment.

"Come on, Miss Angela. Be careful on these steps with those shoes," insisted Josh, gleaming with his new friend.

The limo pulled away leaving Jeff standing at the curb to carry the bags up the stairs to his apartment. Josh had already opened the door for Angela and held it for Jeff as the true little gentleman he was. Excusing himself, Josh left them at Jeff's door and ran upstairs to retrieve the package addressed to Angela.

Angela and Jeff stepped inside. The apartment was much smaller than Angela's but she noticed a woman's touch had, at one time, adorned the place. Jeff had never mentioned anyone close in his life. She walked around. In the bookcase in the living room sat a picture of Jeff and a pretty brunette, the only photo displayed that she could see. She picked it up.

"My ex," responded Jeff.

"Anyone I should be concerned with?" questioned Angela.

"Not at all," insisted Jeff as he put his arms around her. Looking down at her and as her eyes met his, he said with a grin, "Ancient history."

At that moment, a knock resounded on the door. Angela put the photo back onto the shelf and the two sauntered over and opened it. It was Josh with Angela's package; he offered it up to her. Jeff nervously took it from her hands as Josh watched. Jeff instructed them to stay where they were. He went down the hall to the kitchen and placed it gently on the counter. Carefully, he unwrapped the package one corner at a time. A box, approximately 5" x 5" x 7" high sat on the brown paper before him. Its decorative design was similar to what he had seen in Belgium.

He lifted the top off ever so cautiously and pulled out the white tissue paper, placing the figurine on the granite countertop. He wound it; it played a familiar tune. Angela rushed down the hall to the kitchen and saw her figurine playing her song. Jeff looked up at her as she started to tear. Delicately he said, "This one is new. Your other one had a broken leg."

"Jamison?" she replied in shock looking at Jeff. "George gave me that... George and Jamison must be the same person. But why hasn't he contacted me? He must know that I am worried sick."

Jeff texted Goody about the dancing ballerina and the reply read: *"Not now."* Jeff smirked. He turned to Josh who was still watching the dancing figurine and Angela who definitely seemed upset.

"Josh, has anyone been around here that you think doesn't fit into our neighborhood?"

"No, Mr. Malardo... Not that I have noticed. Just the package from a delivery service."

"Any interruptions in cable service or phone?"

"Oh... like in that movie we watched where the bad guy crawled up the pole to spy on the good guy?"

"Yes, something like that."

"Nope. Been quiet since you have been gone." Josh hesitated. "There was a white Caddy that drove by slowly. I watched it, but it didn't stop, and then it was gone."

Angela looked at Jeff.

"Anthony's car!" Angela blurted. A flush reddened her face.

Jeff held her and kissed her forehead.

"That's okay. We stick to the plan. There is no place to hide around here. My neighbors are very close-knit. Anything at all out of place and the cops are here. It's extremely safe. Even the kids play road hockey, sometimes there's a scream out of the window reminding them to watch the cars, but other than that, my little buddy here is like the sleuth of the neighborhood. Nothing gets passed him," reassured Jeff.

"Are you okay, Miss Angela? I wouldn't want anything to happen to you," he said standing there looking up at her with big, bright eyes.

Wiping her tears, she said, "You are so sweet, Josh. Tears of frustration. Thank you for your concern but my strong man here will take care of me." She felt safe with Jeff around but her life's 'modus operandi' had been self-preservation. She wondered how acceptant she would be to anyone else's wishes.

"Josh, can I speak to you for a minute?" asked Jeff, slowly directing his little friend to the door.

He talked to Josh in a low voice. Josh's face lit up and with a shaking of his head up and down in a positive manner, they shook hands.

"Got to go, Miss Angela. See ya later!" Josh hollered with excitement as he darted out the door.

"What did you say to him?" asked Angela.

"Oh, just a little insurance."

A Lesson Learned

Angela and Jeff had fallen asleep in each other's arms. The warmth of her body meshing with his had Jeff wanting her even more than he thought possible. He had been in love with Teresa, he thought, but this was totally different. There were no hidden agendas, no judgments, nothing but true love. How had he missed this sensation before? Maybe it just wasn't the right time or the right person. Teresa had made the decision, one of which Jeff was sure, she had not made lightly. But nonetheless, it was her decision that set him free.

The alarm rang. Jeff raised himself onto his elbows and swung his arm around to shut off the annoyance. Angela moaned with the disturbance. "What's that?"

"The alarm."

"What time is it?" she faintly uttered through half-closed lips.

"Six."

"Six? Like before the sun comes up, six?"

Jeff absolutely lost himself in uncontrollable laughter, so much so that tears streamed down his face.

"What has gotten into you?" asked Angela, turning over to look at her lover.

"Nothing, babe, nothing at all," he said, reaching for a tissue from the nightstand to wipe his tears.

"I could sleep for days. I guess all that travel tired me out... and your naughtiness last night also could have something to do with my state," smiled Angela as she stretched.

"Coffee?"

"Please, baby."

Jeff hopped out of bed; his nakedness highlighted by the rising sun through the partially open curtain. Angela watched him as he disappeared into the kitchen. Moments later, Jeff returned with two freshly brewed cups of Joe and placed Angela's on the nightstand. She stirred under the covers, smoothing the sheet along her body and whispered, "Come here, baby."

He sat down on the bed next to her.

"If you can excuse my morning breath, kiss me," she teased—polished nails dragged down his arm.

Jeff bent to her wishes and he pressed his mouth onto hers; their previous night's lovemaking still lingered on their lips. They kissed with even more intensity, devouring each other's taste as if it was their last. Panting, Angela came up for air and insistently declared, "Don't ever stop kissing me like that."

"Never!" he replied, smiling down at her. Hesitant to change their mood of the moment, he said, "I need to go to the office. Do you want to come with me?"

Angela, also realizing her need for contacting her office, said, "No, babe, I really need to see Gina. I have been enjoying our time together but feel a little selfish now, lying here, admiring you."

"Well, never feel selfish. It has taken some time for both of us to find someone who fits our ideal of whom we imagine we want to spend the rest of our lives with." He kissed her again. "You can drop me off and then take my car to work. I can pick one up at the office so you don't have to come back and pick me up."

"You're right, babe... and it's not a problem. Your work is on the way home."

"I like the way you said 'home'," said Jeff.

Angela smiled. "Possibly, I could say that was a Freudian slip, but babe, wherever you are, will be my home. I truly mean that."

Jeff gazed at this beautiful lady lying between his arms. Her words, slowly healing his broken heart, and he danced on each of her words that slipped from her sweet lips. He would never let go, they shared the exact same words. She was his future, the one to grow old with, but, he thought, first, his focus was on the creep that wanted to end this fantasy come true.

"Come on, babe, time for us to join the real world," said Jeff.

She exhaled and with pouty lips rolled out of his arms and said, "All right, if I must."

. . .

Jeff pulled up to his parking spot in the underground parking garage of his agency, slipped the shifter into neutral, and maneuvered out of the driver's seat. Angela swung her leg over the console and slipped in behind Jeff. She adjusted the seat forward. Jeff leaned on the door.

"Are you going to be at AD all day?"

"I'm planning on it. I have to catch up with what has been going on."

"Be extra careful, babe."

"With your car or life in general?" she said with a smile.

"Both. It has a stiff clutch," said Jeff. He bent and kissed her delicious red lips.

Angela backed out of the spot and slipped the shifter into first gear. She revved the engine just enough and dumped the clutch, leaving two black tire marks and a squealing that echoed throughout the underground parking structure.

"Watch the clutch!" yelled Jeff.

Angela waved her hand and shouted back, "Got it!"

She slammed the shifter into second and laid another patch of rubber. Jeff hung his head and shook it side to side. He knew life would never be dull with Angela.

. . .

What felt like hours later driving through the L.A. traffic, Angela pulled into AD Fashions underground garage and parked Jeff's little red hot rod. She swiped her ID card and imprinted her hand on the pad, just like in France. Everything was starting to make sense, but one burning question still swirled in her head: *Why hasn't George or Jamison contacted me?* The elevator opened to her approved identity and zipped her to her floor.

It was still too early for Delores but there was a light on in the office next to Angela's. The door was partially open. She quietly stepped closer and pushed the door ever so slightly. She knocked. Gina jumped, startled as she looked up and saw her friend standing there—glowing.

She screamed, "Angela!!!"

Gina dropped the fabric she had been studying, ran to her friend, placed a huge kiss on Angela's lips, and almost squeezed the life out of her.

"I've been so worried. Not a word from anybody! Everyone kept coming in and asking about your whereabouts and I just lied and said you had some personal matters you had to attend to," blabbered Gina.

"Calm down, lovie. I am fine. I was definitely scared out of my mind for a while there, but everything is working its way out," insisted Angela.

"Tell me... What's going on? George? I never saw anything on the news, Angela. And look at you, you are glowing. What's going on?" quizzed Gina again.

"My head is still buzzing. Please sit. We believe George is not George, but a guy named Jamison Starkney who runs a foundation out of France. He, George or Jamison, was not shot at all, but set someone up to think he was shot dead. He needed me to leave the country, for which reason we are not sure, but maybe so I could meet my auntie who is a cloistered nun in Belgium and an heiress, along with me, I am assuming and not really sure how, to the Fournier fortune. Jeff found me there and now, we are in love," explained Angela, leaving lots of questions to swirl in Gina's mind.

Looking at Angela, confused and teary-eyed, Gina said, "That is so fucked, Angela. I was so worried about you."

Angela held her friend. She bent down to kiss the top of her head, "Shh, everything will be all right. Jeff promised me."

Squinching her nose, looking very much confused, Gina asked, "Now how did Jeff, our Jeff, right...? The card guy and investigator, that Jeff... How did he know where you were?"

"He was talking to David, his artist friend, who mentioned to Jeff that he saw me getting on an Air France flight, and then he mentioned something about Eileen being there as well, looking at a gallery we bought."

"That's why I couldn't reach Eileen. I was so scared. Please do not do that again," said Gina in a weepy voice. "But, how did you and Jeff turn this nightmare into a love story?"

"It just happened. When I saw him running towards me at my aunt's retirement home in Belgium, my heart leapt into his," explained Angela.

"I thought you went to France? How did you get to Belgium? Where is Belgium?"

"I went to Paris and looked up this fellow, Jamison Starkney, online who is listed as the CEO of the Fournier Foundation, whose name I got from the pamphlet I found at Claire's Sanctuary..."

"Angela," interrupted Gina, "...you need to write this down... I am totally lost."

"I know it is confusing right now, but trust me, when this is all over everything will be laid on the table, including who this Jamison Starkney is and his involvement. Right now, how are things going?" asked Angela.

Gina wiped her tears, "Fine... Well, as good as can be expected after leaving me to fend for myself without any direction."

"Good. I guess I did make the right decision," joked Angela, realizing Gina's frustration with running a corporation compared to a simple store. "Did you fire anyone?"

"No... Why would you ask that? Everyone has been so helpful. You have developed a real team; the networking is awesome. Some do have their little quirks but in the end, everything is about AD Fashions."

"Fabulous. Well then, we shouldn't waste any more time in developing Europe. Do you have a passport?" asked the newly energized Angela.

"No."

"Don't worry, I will handle that for you. Okay. One more thing..." Angela hesitated. "There is this guy from our past that is trying to kill me, but we have a plan."

"What?!" screamed Gina. "Who?"

"Anthony Micholanetti."

. . .

From the underground parking garage of Straight Up Communications, Jeff bypassed the after-hours security elevator and took two stairs at a time to the main floor of his building. He joined the noisy masses in the foyer as they crammed into the silent elevator. He had a confident grin as he was whisked to his floor. He stepped out.

"Good morning, Tom. How's it going?" he said as he entered the security archway.

"Great, Mr. Malardo, and welcome back," acknowledged Tom, the new security guard.

Jeff gathered his belongings from the dishpan and pushed through the glass doors. He saw Adriane with a welcoming bright smile.

"Well, stranger, how was France?" asked Adriane, warmly.

"Just fine," he declared as he passed by her receptionist's desk on his way to his office.

"Jeff!" she called out. He stopped and turned to her. She stepped out from behind her desk with a tissue. She walked up to him and wiped the red lipstick from his lips.

"Not your color," she said with an endearing grin.

Jeff smiled as he headed to his office. Adriane returned to her desk but before she sat down, she blew a kiss to the new security guard, Tom. He returned her gesture.

The elevator door opened again and out stepped Goody. He went through the same ritual with Tom and then through the plate glass doors.

"Good morning, Mr. Thoroughgood," offered Adriane with her usual gracious form.

He stopped and looked at her and then back to the guard and then back to her, "It is good to see you, Adriane. And please, just Goody." He walked to his office, confident.

"Morning, buddy," said Jeff upon seeing his friend.

"Back at you. Sorry about the text, but Georgette was excited to see me."

"No explanation needed. I figured as much, my friend."

Adriane buzzed Jeff.

"Yes, Adriane."

"I left you a couple of messages in your inbox. One is from a fellow named, Swanny about a girl called Miracle and a couple from Allen, and Harry wants to see you both as soon as he arrives."

"Thank you, beautiful... I appreciate it."

"You are so welcome. Uh, Jeff..."

"Yes."

"I'm seeing someone, now," said Adriane shyly.

"Good for you. I sincerely hope things work out for you and Tom."

"Thank you, Jeff. Still friends?" asked Adriane.

"Always, love... always."

"You know, little buddy, your high can't last forever," said Goody.

"Doesn't have to last forever... only as long as I am alive."

"Oh, aren't we the jokester today," chuckled Goody.

"I do believe that I detect a softer you this morning as well," said Jeff, looking through the opened adjoining door at the smile on Goody's face.

Jeff picked up his phone and dialed a number that one of his contacts, Swanny, had left for him.

"Hello?" Jeff heard a young girl's voice.

"Is this Mira?" he asked.

"Yes."

"My name is Jeff Malardo. I am following up on information supplied to me by one of my contacts. I am a friend of your mother's," informed Jeff.

"Yeah."

"She is concerned about your well-being and she wanted you to know that she understands your need for your independence. And she wants you to know she loves you very much."

"Okay," replied Mira with indifference.

"That was your mother's message, now here is mine. Do not fuck with your mother's love for you, understand me. She loves you very much and sometimes life strips us from feeling or expressing what we must in order for others to respond with their feeling of fulfillment. Here is your mother's new phone number at AD Fashions. You will probably be switched to her personal secretary because Vice Presidents are very busy, but talk to her. She needs you. I don't want to have to call you again," insisted Jeff.

"My mother is a what?" asked Mira confused.

"Vice President of AD Fashions," informed Jeff.

"But how? She owns a small shop. How could she become VP of AD Fashions? No one knows her. At times, she could barely feed us with what she made. How could she become a VP?" said Mira, clearly shocked.

"But she did, didn't she? What, you didn't have a fancy car to go to high school so you thought you would put your mother through hell?" countered Jeff.

"Yes... well no... I just didn't want to end up like her. Wishing away her life." cried Mira, finally showing some emotion.

"What, a mother who loves their child? You owe her an apology. Your mother is an awesome, caring, and talented person. I understand you have inherited her artistic flair. Are you going to throw that away?"

"Well... no... but..."

"But nothing... What your mother paid me to find you could have put you through art school, so get your butt home. Do we have an understanding?"

"Yes, sir... Oh, and thank you. I will call her now," said Mira audibly weeping as she hung up.

Overhearing Jeff's distasteful remarks, Goody looked at his friend with questioning eyes, and said, "Holy shit, Jeff! I have never heard you speak to anyone—especially a runaway—like that. What the fuck?"

"It was something Gina had said, about a man has never been around who cared... you know, a father figure. I thought she needed to understand that life doesn't guarantee some model reality. It's the love shared around us," explained Jeff.

"Very deep, my friend." He paused, and then said, "I thought you did this pro bono?"

"I did, but she doesn't have to know that."

"You are too much, buddy. Love ya, man."

A Leaked Story

Eileen called Angela and told her a story had been leaked to their gallery trade magazine about an art show to be installed at E. Cortez Gallery for an artist from South America, whose works would be arriving at the L.A. docks in a week. And that special clearance would have to be guaranteed by the owners of the gallery.

"Good, Eileen. That is perfect. Talk soon, hon." They hung up.

"You won't be in any danger, will you?" asked Gina.

"I will have my men nearby," informed Angela.

The phone rang again in Gina's office. Angela picked it up since she was standing right beside it.

"Hello... No, this is Angela Fournier speaking. You are... pardon me, who? Mira Durham and you wish to speak to Gina Durham. Let me see... my Vice President is very busy. Hang on please." Angela held her hand over the receiver and whispered in disbelief, "Oh my God, Gina, it's your daughter!" She handed Gina the phone.

Composing herself, Gina clutched the receiver in her hand and counted to three. "Hello, Gina Durham speaking..."

"Mom, I am so sorry I hurt you... Please forgive me. I love you so much!" said Mira, breaking down, pouring her heart out to her mother.

Gina had just finished drying her eyes from Angela's news and now, the two of them fought a losing battle trying to keep back their tears of joy.

"I love you too, baby," replied Gina.

"Can I come home, Mom?"

"You are so welcome, baby. I can't wait to see you. Okay, baby, a month to clean things up there. See you soon, love you... A man named Jeff Malardo? Why yes, baby. Okay, see you soon. Be safe," said Gina through teary eyes.

You Make Me Nervous, Jimmy

For some, the trade papers in Los Angeles were what people depended on for whether they got up in the morning or signed a new deal. It was the bible of the movers and shakers; who's on top and the ones who had fallen out of grace. There were events and advertisements posted on the back pages, with sometimes a 'hearsay' note posted before it could be authenticated, but no one really cared if it was true or not. It was gossip, and in L.A., gossip was what turned the wheels. Of course, there were many legitimate ads posted; but in this particular issue, the mentioning of an artist from a foreign country to be showcased at a renowned gallery brought lots of interest and of course, questions that needed to be answered.

Anthony Micholanetti was one of those star chasers who wasn't able to break out of his hoodlum persona because, truly, he was a bad man. He had been given the privilege of receiving some old trade papers during his incarceration. He kept up with all the events after being paroled, especially with what E. Cortez and Associates had been doing. The online version of the trade paper, however, was immediate. He saw this 'hearsay' note and it was exactly what he needed to flush out his doomed prey. All he had to do was find out at which dock and a definite time of the owner's arrival. After considering all of his near misses, he knew she would not expose herself during normal business hours; too many people for her to keep an eye out for. *No*, he thought, *she will demand a special viewing where she has control.* He chuckled to himself. *She is so predictable. And with that prick Stanza out of the way, she has no one.* Anthony Micholanetti laughed out loud at the thought.

He reached for his phone and dialed thirteen numbers. A strange ringing tone followed, and then, *"Privet!"* answered the foreign man on the other end.

"It's me. Can you have a team together and over here in a week?"

"Bitter yetz, Iva got whatca need alreatie," answered the Russian on the other end. *"Mi boyz will be there whenz you need them."* Short and sweet—they hung up.

Anthony's brain was filled with delicate information on the importation of drugs and the trafficking of young girls, which had sparked the interest of an inmate who had connections in Russia. They had made a deal.

He checked the loaded magazine from his gun and slid it back into the frame... "This time, bitch..." It clicked into place. "...I'll do you myself just for the satisfaction," he vented boisterously as he planned his move. Summarizing his plan, he thought, *With back-up from the Russians, even if she pleaded for help from that kid-finder, he would be no match for what I have in store for them.* He picked up the phone again and called an associate who worked at the docks.

"Jimmy... it's me. I need information on some artwork arriving at customs later this week. No, I'm not going to heist it; I just need to know when a meeting is being set up for a viewing and signed transfer. It's coming in from South America, if that makes a difference. Good. Let me know as soon as you can, got it? How much? Ten grand sounds fair... Later." He hung up.

"Ten grand... What a schmuck. He thinks he has me, ha! He'll never see the light of day again."

That same day, Jimmy called for a meet. He suggested a diner, near the docks, where he would be waiting at noon.

. . .

Jimmy looked at his watch—12:35 p.m. He sipped impatiently on his third cup of coffee, playing with his cigarette pack, flipping it from one side to the other like a square wheel. His leg bounced in perpetual motion under the table. He started to put his cigarettes away when a white Caddy pulled up to the bay window. A man stepped out, looked around, and then entered the diner. He spotted Jimmy sitting in a booth by the window.

"Jimmy," acknowledged Anthony.

"Anthony," nodded Jimmy.

Anthony sat down. His hands formed a pyramid on the table. "Well... What do you have?"

"You got the money?" asked the nervous man.

Anthony reached into his jacket pocket and pulled out a manila envelope and slid it toward him. Jimmy quickly slammed it into his jacket out of sight.

"Well?" Anthony said, raising his eyebrows.

"They just got the paperwork. They've added two more guards and have a schedule for the viewing and guarantee to be signed at 10 p.m. That's an hour after the guards' shift change," informed Jimmy.

"Will you be there?"

"My shift doesn't start until 11:00 that night," said Jimmy.

"Okay, so if I need you, you will be close by?"

"I can be right here; the diner is only five minutes away. But why would you need me?" asked Jimmy.

"Might need to stash delicate cargo in a container. You got keys to the holding yard, don't ya?"

"Yeah, we all do. The gates have to be locked at all times," confided Jimmy as he bent forward over the table.

"Good. That works to my advantage, but I will need you to be here at 9 p.m. during the shift change of the guards, got it?"

"Sure, Anthony... Sure."

"You better stop drinking coffee. You're making me nervous, Jimmy."

Jimmy formed a slight smile. "Ya... sure thing..." he continued to nod anxiously. "... you're right."

"You still over off of Rosemead?" asked Anthony in a friendly tone.

"Yeah... for now. It's cheap. Nothin' special."

"You must have put away a nice nest egg by now with all your dealings you've made over the years at the yards?"

"A few dollars. Not enough to fly this coop," said Jimmy, looking around the dinner.

"Depending on the outcome, you might just find that perfect resting place," smiled Anthony.

"Yeah. It would be great to get out of here."

"I'll be seeing you then, Jimmy." Micholanetti stood. He looked at his nervous associate, turned, and left Jimmy at the diner.

Jimmy's leg continued to beat up and down to an unknown melody.

Girl Talk

Picking up her office phone, Angela dialed her executive assistant, and said, "Delores, Gina and I are taking the rest of the afternoon off. Have you finished programming my contacts into my new phone?"

"Yes, Miss Angela, and the numbers you asked me to check on are not in service any longer. If you give me their names I could try to find them for you?" said Delores.

"It's fine, Delores. I am certain they will contact me when they need to," assured Angela.

"Is there anything else?"

"Not at the moment, thank you." Angela hung up and looked at her friend.

"Okay, Gina, let's go apartment shopping. You will need a bigger place when Mira gets back home," insisted Angela. "I know of a really nice place now that the riffraff is gone."

~

Angela and Gina had jumped into Jeff's red-hot Firebird and arrived at a familiar four-story apartment building forty-five minutes later.

"Wow, Angela this is sure nice on the outside. I hope the inside looks just as nice?"

"You will be floored," Angela quipped somewhat sarcastically.

Angela pulled up to the front of the building and parked. After adjusting their outfits and smoothing wrinkles, the two ladies walked up the four steps and through the oak door to where a security guard stood watching revolving images on multiple screens.

"Good morning, ladies," acknowledged the security guard, looking away from the screens. "How can I help you?"

"We would like to see your apartments on the top floor, please," stated Angela.

"One moment, ladies, and I will ring the realtor... Jason, a couple of ladies to view the upper apartments," informed the guard. "He'll be right with you, ladies."

"Thank you. I like the security cameras," said Angela.

"Hel-lo ladies," greeted Jason. "How may I help you?"

"We would like to see the top floor if you don't mind?"

"Very popular lately... but still available. Shall we..." said Jason as he held the elevator door open for them.

"And how did you hear about our lovely building?" asked Jason politely.

"From two male friends of mine," hinted Angela.

"Real-ly? Would one be a handsome black fellow with a very masculine physique and an equally cute white gentleman?" inquired the agent.

"Why yes..." admitted Angela.

"Did they find a place?"

"Not yet... You know, still arguing over colors and floor plans," insisted Angela.

"Oh, sweetie... I know exactly! Those strong types and all," said Jason with a smile.

"Yes... They spend all their time in the gym when they should be smelling the roses," said Angela, leading Jason on.

The elevator stopped on the fourth floor.

"Which one would you like to see first?"

"Let's see 401, please. I'll bet there are a lot of stories hidden behind these walls," shared Angela.

"That is so funny. That is exactly what the smaller gentleman alluded to... What are the odds of that?" Gina let out a muffled chuckle.

They stepped inside. Gina's face lit up as she spun around appreciating the sun shining through the giant windows highlighting the hues of the soft colors. Angela slowly approached the wooden mantel above the fireplace. She ran her hand along its smooth edge where her father's picture once held a respected spot. She was deep in thought.

"Angela, are you okay?" asked Gina, noticing a strange look on her face.

"Yes. I'm fine."

"I love the big windows. It makes it so airy," said Gina taking it all in.

"And the master bedroom is to die for," added Jason.

Angela quickly responded, "Can we see 402? I believe it is a two-bedroom. I also understand a park is going to be constructed on that empty lot on the other side of the building." Angela stepped to the windows, pushed the sheer curtains to the side, and looked out. "And with a building across the alleyway from this apartment, it could restrict your privacy."

"Fine with me," agreed Gina, delighted to view something she has never been able to afford before.

Jason closed the door of apartment 401, and walked past the elevator to the only other apartment on that floor.

"Here we are, 402. An equally adorable apartment but a two bedroom as mentioned." Jason opened the door.

Angela walked over to the floor-to-ceiling windows and looked out. "I believe the next building is coming down as well to expand the park," remarked Angela.

"Real-ly?" questioned Jason. "Girl, I really need you working for me. How do you know that?"

"Let's say I heard through a friend of a friend that this whole block is destined for change," relinquished Angela. "And across the street, the lower floor will house a restaurant, bookstore, and specialty food market to service these apartments."

"Girl, really. I need to know your contact. I could easily push these apartments knowing all that," insisted Jason.

"I believe a scale model of the surrounding development should be arriving to put on display very soon. So don't give up, Jason... You will have your additional selling features. It's nice to see the cameras installed."

Jason stood with his mouth open in awe of this lady's backroom knowledge.

"What do you think, Gina? You like it?" asked Angela.

"It is awesome!"

"Oh... I also believe on this side of the building, larger terraces will be built out to take advantage of the park view, and French doors will give access to your private space," Angela further stated.

Jason stood with his arms crossed listening to this presentation.

"I want to buy one," he shared, enthusiastically waving his hand. "Where do I sign?" he laughed. "But I can't afford $2.5 million."

"How much?" choked Gina.

"Trust me Gina... I know I can get it for much less. Much less." She turned to the agent. "Consider it sold, Jason. I believe your commission is 2.5%, and if you sell it at asking price that would give you $62,500. I will have my... *our* secretary send you your commission check for that amount and deposit another $75,000 into your escrow account. Lock the door when you leave, please. I know the way out," instructed this shrewd businesswoman.

"Yes, ma'am!" obeyed Jason. He wondered, *Who is this woman?* He followed shortly after the two ladies left, closing and locking the door behind him as instructed. His face was beaming.

Jason, awe-struck, caught up with the departing businesswomen at the front door of the prestigious building with a balloon in hand, and waving with the other. The two ladies sauntered to Jeff's car and uncharacteristically jumped in without opening the doors, like Thelma and Louise-ish.

"Wasn't that fun?" giggled Angela.

"Yes, but what was that thing about the two men?" asked Gina, curiously.

"I'll have to get Goody to explain that to you. He had me in stitches on our flight back from JFK," said Angela. "You did like the place, though?"

"Yes, but I still can't afford $2.5 million, even on your generous salary."

"Gina... We will get it for cost. Probably between four and five hundred thousand," stated Angela.

"How do you know that?"

"Because... George and I own it," laughed Angela as she put the car in gear and pulled away from the curb.

Gina shared Angela's laughter and shook her wind–blown hair just like Angela. Gleaming with admiration, Gina said, "Angela... you are priceless."

~

The ladies sped down the 101 back towards AD Fashions so Gina could pick up her car. Angela shared with her that possibly one day that week, Angela needed to shop for a new car as her pretty blue Mercedes wasn't around anymore. She had a love-hate relationship with driving and she preferred to be chauffeured through the Los Angeles traffic but had no idea where Joseph was. Although they were having lots of fun passing up some of the more expensive European cars on the freeway in 'Jeffs-mobile', she still hungered for her independence.

. . .

Angela arrived at Jeff's agency at 4:30 p.m. slightly favoring her left leg. She took the stairs to the main floor and grabbed the elevator to Straight Up Communications' floor. She stepped out and sauntered over to a smiling security guard who was stationed just past the security arch.

"May I help you, ma'am?" he inquired.

"Yes. Could you tell Jeff Malardo that his... that Angela is here," she said with a smile as she looked around at the security system and past the glass doors to a pretty redhead who was staring straight at her. Tom picked up the security phone and dialed Adriane who transferred the message to Jeff's computer. On a run, Jeff momentarily stopped at the receptionist's desk to get a visitor's pass. Adriane handed it to him holding on just long enough forcing Jeff to look back at her. She smiled.

Jeff walked past the plate glass doors and gave the pass to Tom who was in the process of screening Angela's ID.

"Just recently got your driver's license?" questioned Tom.

"Yes... How can you tell?"

"By the number... A late bloomer?" he said with a chuckle, inappropriately.

"No... Dead chauffeur," she replied with a straight face, startling the guard.

Jeff looked at her and smiled.

"Thanks, Tom. I'll take responsibility for her from here," said Jeff, rolling his eyes.

Together, Jeff and Angela stopped at Adriane's desk for introductions.

"Adriane, this is Angela, my..." Jeff hesitated as 'girlfriend' didn't seem a strong enough of a word for what he felt for her.

"Ward," stated Angela with a quick up-turn of a smile.

"Ward... Really?" Adriane lifted the tissue from behind her desk with Angela's lipstick that she had wiped from Jeff's lips that morning.

Angela started to laugh, and with a friendly smile she offered her hand to Adriane and said, "And the mother of his future children."

"It is a pleasure, Angela. Someone had to harness him," replied Adriane, humorously.

"You two do know that I am standing right here?" objected Jeff.

"Just girl talk, baby. Territorial thing," said Angela. "Looking forward to getting to know you better, Adriane," Angela stated seriously, without any side comments.

"Me too, Angela. I am very happy for you... and Jeff. He has been glowing all day."

"Jeff told me you are very sweet..." She looked over at Tom, the ex-marine, security guard with the chiseled body; she turned to Adriane and gave her an approval wink.

Jeff dragged Angela away to his office when he noticed that she was favoring her left side. "What's wrong with your leg?"

"Your clutch in L.A. traffic," complained Angela.

Jeff smirked. "It's a man's car. What can I tell ya?"

Goody, noticing Jeff and Angela coming down the hallway, got up from behind his desk, and stepped inside Jeff's office. He gave Angela a big hug.

"How are you today, Miss Angela?"

"Very well, Goody." She looked around. "So this is the think-tank for all your extractions," she said, looking at the large board with recipe cards thumb-nailed to it.

"Not very hi-tech but it works as a problem solver," informed Goody. "We have been stalling Harry all day until you arrived, so we better have this meeting so we all can be on the same page."

"Well then, let's meet Mr. Harry," insisted Angela.

Angela Fournier - Tabula Rasa

Act III

Brutal Force

Angela was feeling apprehensive as she waited for Jeff at his apartment. He was to take her first to the gallery and then down to the docks. The meeting at Jeff's agency with Harry Peters had her head swimming with what-ifs. The difference between strategically executed operations (SEO) and mere planning was, as he said, collateral damage. "Never underestimate your opponent or let your guard down as that is the time the enemy will strike," he said. He had several clichés for everything he said. *Sounded real FBI. It would have been fun to listen to a discussion between Carl and Harry Peters*, she thought.

Jeff and Goody had their recipe cards placed in multiple scenarios on their big board. They even drove down to where the meeting for signing in the art work was going to take place. They studied the building layouts, pathways between containers, employee profiles, their schedules, and the usual chaos of a normal shipping day. Angela had previously questioned whether or not Gilles had conceived the magnitude of container shipping when he developed his first metal prototype.

Angela tried sitting still on Jeff's couch, crossing her legs one way, then the other, picking up a magazine, and then putting it back down. She stood and started to pace up and down the hallway in a slow methodical stroll. Was her choice of clothes satisfactory without giving away to Anthony their true intentions? She wanted to be free enough to move without restrictions but still had to balance her taste and what Anthony may perceive as a set up, and then possibly he would back out at the last minute. They all agreed that he must be getting frustrated with the last few misses and again, they all agreed, Anthony would want to make this hit personal.

They, however, had an ace in the hole offered up through the FBI, but even that was no guarantee. Jeff was also right about the difference in shooting at a real human being and being able to take down a sparring partner compared to a real life situation with deadly consequences. She was out of her league and she knew it, but she insisted that without her showing up, she would be constantly looking over her shoulder. Not an ideal situation when raising children, never knowing if someone would kidnap your child and hold them for ransom—or worse. She couldn't live like that; it had to be this day. Tonight would end it, one way or the other.

Angela was so thankful for meeting Jeff and loved him very much. She never thought it possible to feel like she did—for anyone. Her heart was his and together, she thought, they could accomplish anything. Her friends, Gina, Eileen, and even her old friend Carol all entered her mind and then drifted out. Strategy, planning, execution, and extraction—words that followed her every thought. "Where is Jeff? He should have been home by now," she said to the walls and any other object that might be listening. She looked at her watch again. Only five minutes from the last time she looked.

Suddenly, a knock on the door broke her concentration. She drew her 9mm from inside her stylish jacket and looked through the peep hole. She had to look way down. It was Josh. She put away her gun and opened the door. He was clearly excited.

Puffing hard to catch his breath, he said, "Miss Angela, tell Mr. Malardo everything is buttoned up on our street."

"What do you mean, Josh?" asked Angela.

"All the stairwells leading to the roofs have been locked," informed Josh. "And every roof has been checked out."

"Jeff had you do all this?"

"I gathered my friends and their fathers to make sure everything was safe," replied Josh, still panting for breath. "We all have these really cool walkie-talkies so we can communicate with each other," said Josh, showing her the hi-tech military-looking devices.

"Jeff got you these?"

"Yes, ma'am. He must really love you. These sets must have cost him a fortune," related Josh proudly.

Angela smiled and bent down to give Josh a big hug.

"I really love him, Josh. More than any words can describe."

"Don't forget to tell him everything is A-OK," commanded little Josh.

"I won't forget, sweetie. Oh Josh... Thank you!"

"You're welcome, Miss Angela. See you tomorrow." Josh turned and climbed the stairs to his apartment.

Angela closed the door and leaned against it. What was her man up to? In that same breath, she felt the rattling of the door handle behind her—and then, a scratching sound fumbling at the lock. She pulled her gun out once more and stepped back; she wanted a clear view. A draw of the dead bolt clicked with defiance as the door swung open. Staring at a raised 9mm, Jeff said reassuringly, "Baby, relax. It's only me."

She eased her arms and hung her head as she fought the emotional tension that had been manifesting inside her. Jeff approached her and Angela rested her head on his chest. She held on tight.

"Are you all right?"

"I am now," she replied. "And your little commando says everything is A-OK."

Jeff smiled as he held her.

"We need to get going if we want to beat the traffic. Anthony won't expect any trickery seeing my car; he already knows it and he saw the damage to yours. He probably thinks I will escort you, so you can bet he won't be alone." Jeff paused before asking, "Are you sure you want to do this?"

"Baby, I have never been surer of anything, except my love for you. I have spent the last few hours stressing but when you fumbled with your key and I had the thought that it somehow might have been Anthony, I was prepared to do battle," reassured Angela.

"Okay, babe, but be loose. If you tense up, your brain doesn't react as fast."

"So my sparring partner used to tell me after I got my first black eye," said Angela. "What about Eileen and Gina? Are they safe?"

"I just came from Gina's place and there are two officers inside her apartment. Eileen is also buttoned up in hers. Young Tom has Adriane fortified at his place. And just to be on the cautious side, we have another two officers with Georgette with added patrol cars at each spot. No one is getting through to harm our friends," insisted Jeff.

"Alrighty then... I guess we should do this," said Angela, her nerves surging up once more.

They were about to leave when Jeff turned to Angela.

"Where is your bag? You are always carrying a bag."

"I didn't want it to get in the way."

"No... You have to act normal. I need you to be seen searching for paperwork when the guards ask, pulling out make up and a cell phone, like you do," said Jeff.

"What are you saying? I have my priorities screwed up?" lightly joked Angela.

"Not at all, babe... just be yourself. We don't know who all Anthony might have on the take. Everyone is to be taken as a threat, no matter if they are wearing a badge or not. It's the stereotypical inflections you need to look for."

"Like what?"

"The way someone walks or holds themselves, their mannerisms, their speaking tone, even their eye movement."

"And you can tell that in a split second?" questioned Angela with doubts about her ability to perceive what Jeff was talking about.

"Only if I want to live longer than they do," he said, partially joking.

. . .

The ride to the gallery seemed surreal as Angela looked up to the beautiful night's sky with a half-moon surrounded by diamond-bright stars. If anyone were watching, they had to be convincing that the stop to the gallery was to pick up the paperwork for the customs declaration. She locked up the gallery and walked back to Jeff. He sat nonchalantly with his left arm perched on his door while his hand idly played with his vent window. She stuffed the paperwork into her oversized purse. Once again, she tied her kerchief around her golden hair as they drove off into the night toward the Long Beach Seaport.

As they approached, the truck traffic increased from intersecting roadways until they sat in line between idling diesel trucks for their turn at the guard shack. A few horns blew as Angela removed her kerchief and fluffed her hair as she sat in the red convertible.

Their turn finally arrived and as they pulled up, Angela had the paperwork ready to show the guard.

"Good evening," he greeted as he perused Angela's paperwork. "Follow the double lines around the far building to another yard check point," he instructed. "Watch out for trucks turning. It's a busy night."

"Thank you," said Jeff.

As they pulled away, Angela leaned over to Jeff and asked, "Good guy or bad guy?"

Jeff looked through his rear view mirror. "FBI."

"How do you know?" she asked with a little doubt.

"He touched his ear. A bad guy would have rubbed his nose or scratched his chin."

Angela smacked him on the arm. "Maybe grabbing his balls," she said as she expelled a much needed laugh, enjoying Jeff's sleuth powers.

They rounded the far building, driving into dimmer light than that of the main lanes from where they had just been. Paralleling the seaport dock, they drove through another area that was surrounded with metal fencing and topped with razor wire. Jeff saw hundreds of containers sitting in this area. He stopped at another check point.

"Good e-ven-ing. Purpose in your visit?" asked the heavily accented guard.

Jeff handed him the paperwork that Angela held in her hand.

"Does the lad-y have ID?" he asked.

Angela pulled out her ID to show the guard.

"Angela Fournier, very good. Park to the side of build-ing D and pro-ceed to the sign 737," he instructed.

"Thank you," said Jeff.

As he pulled away slowly, Jeff raised the top of his convertible.

"Why are you doing that now? My hair is fine at this speed," said Angela with a questioned look that begged *'Why not on the freeway?'*

"Harder to put a bullet in the back of our heads," said Jeff in all seriousness.

Angela was afraid to ask good guy or bad guy... but...

"Which one?" she uttered.

"Bad guy."

"Why?"

"No nightstick. His accent was definitely east European but I know there are a lot of Russians working here, so I can't hold that against him. Oh... there it goes..."

"What?" wildly questioned Angela.

"He's warning others on your confirmation... He just spit," said Jeff. "There are only a couple of flat roofs, so no more than two snipers. Do you have a permit for your gun?"

Angela looked at Jeff. "You are kidding me, right?"

"I'll take that as a no. Slowly slide it out of your purse and put it into the side door panel. I am assuming the guys on the inside are legit. On your paperwork, 737 is the team that handles imports like artwork. I have a permit and I will declare my gun when we step inside. Ready, my love?" asked Jeff, calmly.

"As ready as I'll ever be," grimaced Angela.

"Okay. No irrational moves. Be yourself."

"No break dancing?" she said, lightly jesting.

Jeff parked his car under the security light. Looking around casually, what he noticed and what he could not have determined when they sourced out the dock during the day were the lights mounted to the side of the tin buildings. They now cast long shadows over the shipping containers, an easy place to hide. The roadway that they were on led down to an end building. It stood taller than the others and had large cargo doors that stared right at them. *The roadway must turn to the right,* he thought. The illumination from its security light produced separation between the first row of containers and its tin siding.

They stepped out of the car, walked over to the entrance of 737, and went inside. At the desk, an official customs agent looked at the clock and then greeted them.

"Angela Fournier?" he asked.

"Yes... and my fiancé, Jeff Malardo," informed Angela.

Jeff pulled out his wallet to show his ID and permit for his gun. The official asked him to slide it through the access of the bullet proof window with magazine removed and chamber cleared. Jeff complied.

The agent buzzed them in and as they approached the warehouse door, the custom agent swiped his security card and then punched in a series of numbers. The door clicked open to the huge storage area. He instructed Jeff and Angela to take a seat on the golf cart just as another officer walked by with a German Shepherd.

"Dogs... still one of the best security systems," remarked Jeff.

The agent showed no expression nor said a word and continued to the designated holding area. He stopped the cart and stepped over to a locked cage, again topped with razor wire. It had two sets of doors, one for foot traffic and a larger one for forklifts. The custom agent scanned the markings on the crates verifying they corresponded to his paperwork.

"Miss Angela Fournier, E. Cortez Gallery and Associates, Beverly Hills, California, correct?" he asked, looking at the tags.

"Yes, sir," politely confirmed Angela.

"Very well."

The agent cut one of the wire tags and then another and with the supplied key he unlocked the crate and opened the hinged door. He slid one of the heavily wrapped pieces out of its protective slot. The agent then took it over to a table.

"Would you be so kind as to inspect the authenticity of this piece for me, please," instructed the agent.

Angela looked at Jeff in wonderment. She thought all this was pretend, not a real endorsement. She carefully unwrapped the piece of art.

"Oh my God! A Carlos Honduras original. You know how long we have been trying to get his work up here?" stated Angela, in utter surprise.

"This is your import?" questioned the agent.

"Yes, of course! I am so excited to actually be holding one in my hands," said Angela.

"Sign here, please," instructed the agent. "When do you anticipate pick up and what carrier?" he asked.

"We will self-pick up, and we usually use a rental truck," informed Angela.

"You will need to call the office with the names of whoever is going to pick up the crate and provide the truck license plate number," said the agent.

"Yes, sir. Not a problem," said Angela.

Angela wrapped the piece back up and the customs agent returned it to its protective slot. The agent re-locked it and applied a green wire tag.

Angela was so excited—she almost forgot why they were there. The agent ushered them through the locked doors into the main office where he re-issued Jeff's gun to him. Angela seemed more at ease after being surprised by her discovery of such prominent works; especially after a year and half of negotiations. To finally hold one in her hands, she was more than delighted.

For Jeff, as he opened the door, momentary thoughts questioned his ability. Was he an investigator worthy of a senior position? Was he a man of higher standards? Was he intuitive enough and was he capable of protecting the woman he loved?

The two stepped out into the shadow-cast roadway into the humid night air. Soon, the fog would creep in from the colder waters of the Pacific Ocean surrounding the coastal towns in a subtle blanket. Always, Jeff thought, when the light of the day dimmed and the air closed in, there in the shadows lurked the evil of all evils. Just like Jeff's black and white movies, the night's shadow obscured the evil that waited to pounce onto the unexpected. He could hear the foreboding music as the tension rose and the innocent approached closer, doomed.

Jeff reached for Angela's hand and together they slowly walked toward the car. He turned to face her. He held her tight as the light illuminated her angelic face against the black backdrop. He stroked her hair and whispered in her ear.

"Four men just came from around the far building, each carrying a lunch bucket held in their left hand with an 'I'm late for church' walk, with an hour before their shift change. The convertible top is blocking most of their view. I'm going to spin us around so my back is to them. Slide down me and get your gun out of the side panel. I will swing us so they can see your long hair. Do not look at them yet. When I say 'now', take out their lunch buckets on the two to your right; I'll take the other two."

Angela gulped involuntarily. Her angelic face turned ghostly white. Jeff began to laugh loudly as Angela slipped down his body and reached in for her gun. She felt the elastic of the side panel's pocket and then the cold steel.

She gripped the handle tight as her training clicked in. She removed the safety with her thumb and brought it to her side as Jeff spun them sideways to the car still laughing loudly. The men approached and as they stepped out of the shadow, the security light from above Jeff's car briefly blinded them.

"Now!" he commanded.

Angela effortlessly raised her weapon and in two rapid shots left two men clutching their hands. Jeff let off his two rounds with the same accuracy. They stayed behind the vehicle with guns drawn.

"You motherfucker!" yelled one of the thugs. A rifle shot rang out in the stillness and hit Jeff's car inches from where they stood. They ducked down. The thugs took advantage and charged at them. Two came from behind the car and two from the front of the car.

Jeff shot the first in the leg and the other jumped him with knife in hand. They rolled out from behind cover as Angela pumped two rounds into the chest of her first attacker, but his large size only staggered him from his forward thrust while the other jumped over him and grabbed Angela. She managed one more shot before her gun was knocked from her hand. The injured thug stumbled against the car and slid down to the ground. Angela and the other squared off. His left hand was bleeding but he still mustered a tight fist.

"Come on," she coaxed. Her adrenaline took over, flooding her body. "You want some of me, you slimy fuck?

You want to play with my titties and then throw me down the stairs? Come on, fucker. You are going to die tonight!" she shouted with a not-so-vague memory.

The thug lashed at her with a powerhouse swing. The wind nearly knocked her off balance.

"You got to do better than that, fat boy," she said, taunting him. "Come on fucker... you like it rough..." At that, she jumped into the air and kicked him broadside in the chin, sending blood and spit into the air.

He staggered backwards from her well-placed kick. His eyes lit on fire. He rushed at her with his massive hands pawing the air like a windmill. She grabbed his jacket collar and fell to her back bringing him down with her. She shoved her foot deep into his chest and with all her might, threw the gorilla over her. She quickly scampered to her feet waiting for his return.

Angela briefly looked over at Jeff who missed another swipe from the knife-wielding man. Suddenly, from behind, the man with the shot leg grabbed her. The gorilla kicked Angela in the stomach, which sent her retching. Still holding onto Angela's arms, the injured leg man straightened her up as the gorilla set to pummel her again.

A loud "UGH!" rang out as the knife-wielding man turned with his knife stuck in his throat. Angela quickly used her capturer as a brace and kicked the gorilla in the face as he hesitated that one second too long. She then slammed her head back and into the nose of her capturer and slipped from his grasp. Turning, she faced her capturer and squared off a kick to his groin, and as he bent forward, she slammed her open palm into his broken nose, dislodging the bone into his cerebral cortex.

Jeff tackled the giant who was set to bring Angela down. He wailed on him, each punch drawing more and more blood from the bully's already scarred face. Punch after punch, wild and powerful, but precise.

"Jeff!" shouted Angela. "It's okay, baby. He's not going anywhere." She winced in pain holding onto her stomach.

Adrenaline still pumping wildly—and breathing hard, Jeff looked at the man's bloodied face; eyes already swelled shut. Jeff stumbled off him. His shirt was slashed and blood-soaked from the wielding knife that made its contact. The two dropped to their knees supporting each other as bodies lay on each side of the car in the shadow-cast roadway.

Angela and Jeff knelt there. They cried and they laughed and they cried some more, holding each other tight in the cast of the light. The seconds seemed like minutes as they tried to help each other up to their feet. Jeff held his shirt over his open gash with his broken, raw hand while his other wrapped around Angela's waist. She gripped her aching stomach. Their long shadows wobbled toward Jeff's car and upon arriving, used it as a prop to hold them upright. The sound of a distant engine had them looking up to the end warehouse where they saw the unmistakable white front-end of a Cadillac dauntingly appeared in the light.

The Cadillac slowly made the corner and stared down at them. The headlights switched from two to four, burning bright and blinding Jeff and Angela. As the engine revved, the tires squealed with its power—smoke billowed from the rear. Closer and closer it approached, speeding faster like a freight train. Angela and Jeff lunged for their guns over two dead bodies that lay in the middle of the roadway. The car, unpassionately, headed straight for the squirming bodies. They had nowhere to run or take cover, even if they could. A hundred feet away and closing fast, they waited anxiously until the Caddy was within range. They raised their guns and fired.

In milliseconds, the air roared with gunfire, shattering the windshield and leaving a giant black hole, glass splayed in all directions on the roadway until *click... click*. They were empty. The car recklessly approached at highway speed. Jeff leaped for Angela. They rolled on the unforgiving concrete, slamming into the dogged clasps of the shipping container—pinned, waiting. Jeff's body laid exposed to the unstoppable evil. The Caddy swooshed past, missing them by mere inches. It rammed into the back of Jeff's prized possession, sending it skipping with defying chirps—it landed, rocking. The Caddy only partially slowed whilst careening off the unconscious body of the gorilla thug, forcing the wheel to turn in the direction of Long Beach Harbor. Crashing through the yellow baluster barricade, it plunged off the dock and plummeted into the cold dark waters below.

Angela and Jeff lay there in an embrace, breathing hard, anxious but thankful. Each one helped the other to stand upright. Tenderly they held on, each using the other as a crutch. They stood shivering in the cooling air. With conviction and determination, they limped over to the dock's edge and looked down. Bubbles trailed in the bright red taillights that illuminated their rise, deeper it went—and then—darkness. A gurgle followed and the ripples ceased.

Scarcely a moment had passed before two helicopters rose from beyond the flat roofs with two men strung, motionless to their tether while others scurried in the darkness and then vanished. In the far distance, sirens muffled by the foggy air perceived closer. An unmarked car sped towards them and then slid to a stop. A grey-haired man stepped out.

"Sorry about the close call on that discharged round; however, we were able to disengage any further possible threat and extracted the two snipers," apologized Tom with a serious look. "You two all right? Helluva fight, I must say. Don't piss off Miss Fournier. She can handle herself, my friend."

Jeff extended his unbroken hand. "Thank you, Tom... again."

"Our pleasure. Thank you for staying in touch. You are quite the man, sir," remarked Tom.

"You were watching all of this?" choked Angela in dismay.

"We had you covered, ma'am. Sorry, but Jeff knows the rules. I got to go, the cavalry is coming," stated Tom.

"Tom, one question. When Angela and I marry, will you be working for us?"

"Sorry, sir. I can't answer that." He paused at the car door and with a smirk, he looked over at the battered couple and said, "I thought we already were."

Angela and Jeff nodded and flashed a momentary smile. Moments later, they were surrounded by FBI, ICE, DEA and ATF agents. Following them were the LAPD, sirens screaming four abreast.

The two limped back to Jeff's smashed car where they were handed FBI blankets to wrap around their shoulders. An ambulance negotiated between the orange cones and a maze of yellow tape; it finally pulled beside Jeff and Angela. Bags were flipped open and latex-gloved men inspect every crevice of their aching bodies. The couple was helped into the ambulance. All of sudden, in her excruciating pain, Angela managed to shout out — "Fuck!"

Jeff, concerned, wincing in his own pain from his slashed ribs and broken hand, reached out to her and said, "Baby, what is it?"

"I broke a nail!" she exclaimed.

Men with fluorescent-lettered jackets were scurrying everywhere, some waving indictments in each other faces, others looking at the black waters, each wanting a piece of Anthony Micholanetti—deceased.

Emotional Strain

The physical trauma that had been inflicted on Angela and Jeff had taken a few months to heal. But the emotional psyche affecting Angela still needed more time. Angela felt a huge weight had been lifted from her shoulders and she had made good on a 'years ago promise' to a dear friend. Unfortunately, the feeling of shooting someone, to actually take one's life— even if he was scum—was not so easy to reconcile. Jeff offered great emotional support for her as did her dear friends Eileen and Gina, who tried to lighten any situation when they could see her drifting back into that nightmare of a night.

The Carlos Honduras show was a smashing hit with reviews in the trades congratulating Eileen, Angela, and the Cortez Gallery on their visional insight. "They have come into their own" was one comment, and "Nothing has been presented so uniquely to emphasize the complete visual experience, kudos." They were riding the high from this overwhelming success and now transferred that energy to their new gallery in Paris.

Jeff requested time off from Straight Up Communications to join Angela and Eileen in Paris to finalize the remodel of the new gallery and coordinate the set up for his friend, David Christiansen's debut in Europe. Jeff was an immense help, running here and there and sometimes, getting lost. They concentrated on the visuals and flow of the show. They called their new gallery 'Angileen', a combination of Angela and Eileen's names.

From all accounts, this show would be equally received as their predecessor had in Los Angeles. Patriarchs stopped by in a continuous stream of well-wishing and reporters ran articles referencing the '*lost child*' has now found her way back home. Angela still had not claimed her right to the Fournier Foundation, if there was such a thing. Her time was spent with the gallery and Jeff. She felt she had plenty of time to be introduced into that arena, and she still hadn't received any word from her friend George, alias Jamison Starkney—or was it the other way around? She believed, whatever he had gotten into, he needed more time to handle it.

Goody and his beautiful five-month-pregnant wife Georgette flew to Paris the day before the opening. They all made time for each other for a casual dinner where Goody reaffirmed his displeasure at having to coordinate all the agencies and police surveillance of Angela's friends. He wanted to be with his friends busting heads, but Harry Peters ordered him to be the point man. Peters knew well how miscommunication translated to collateral damage; he privately held previous records. Goody was his choice. Someone had to direct the other agencies so they wouldn't crash the party too soon. The whole plan could have been compromised. As it played out, it was tactically perfect. Goody still balked.

Angela noticed at dinner that Goody and Georgette seemed to be beaming more so than anyone else as if they were suppressing the confidence of someone. She asked, and Georgette's reply was only how happy they were to be part of all the excitement. But Angela presumed there was more and let it rest—for the time being.

The big day finally arrived after months of planning. The weatherman guaranteed perfect Parisian weather, which meant a mixture of rain or sun or just plain grey. When they arrived at the gallery, their newly-hired assistant, Tulaine, had already opened the doors for the staff of the restaurant next door. They buzzed back and forth prepping the bar and trays of delicacies.

Although Eileen and Angela were professionals at curating such events, they knew very well how things could go wrong in an instant. They had left a cleared area for the restaurant's set-up personnel and as soon as they were finished, the ladies replaced the artwork. "An ounce of prevention was worth more than a pound of cure," insisted Eileen.

Jeff alluded to some other errands he needed to accomplish before the opening and that he would be back soon. Angela received a text from Gina that she and Mira had arrived very late and they would catch up with Angela at the gallery that morning. Meanwhile, Tulaine had been informed by the permit department that the canopy and two search lights were endorsed and the confirmation document would be dropped off shortly. Everything was falling into place nicely.

Goody and Georgette arrived by cab at 11 a.m. and right after them, Gina and her daughter Mira arrived with arms full, carrying the evening's grand statement—their dresses.

"Where's Jeff?" asked Goody as the ladies busily opened their packages.

"Yes, where is my man? He said he had some errands to run, but he should have been back by now. I'll call him if you would like?" Angela stated.

"Let me have your phone, Angela. You have better things to do."

Goody strolled over to the plate glass window and dialed Jeff.

"Hey, man... Where are you? They're doing frilly things here."

"Be right there, buddy. It's all arranged."

"Good. Get your ass back here," insisted Goody in his usual tone.

Georgette looked at her husband and smiled, shaking her head. "Men!"

Finally, Jeff sprung into the gallery and saw Goody standing by himself.

"Where are the ladies?"

"Upstairs trying on their dresses that Gina brought from the States."

"Here, put this in your pocket. Angela has wandering hands..." he laughed. "...you never know where they are going to end up."

Jeff walked to the back of the gallery to where the intercom sat on the sales desk. He buzzed Angela in the upstairs office.

"Hey, babe... I'm back. Need anything?" asked Jeff, calmly.

"Hi, Jeff. It's Eileen. Angela is indisposed at the moment, but do come on up, please. We need your manly impressions."

"Let's go, buddy. They need our input."

"You know I'm no good at that sort of thing," said Goody.

"Come on you stuffed shirt."

Jeff and Goody took the stairs up the four levels to the freshly remodeled office-apartment. The ladies were in the bedroom as they entered.

Loudly, Jeff announced, "We're here!"

"Okay... be right out," informed Angela from the powder room.

Gina emerged first in an off-the-left shoulder marine blue polka-dotted dress with matching veil-like material filling in a deep 'V', and a flared skirt filled with layers of crinoline coming to just short of the knees.

Jeff clapped while Goody stared at him; hesitantly, he joined in.

"Thank you, kind sirs," she said as she bowed to their admiration. "We thought we would all dress in distinct colors of the rainbow with fun polka-dot infusions and full crinolines. May I introduce Ladies Mira and Tulaine who will be hosting the sales desk and accepting the patronage of David's admirers..."

The two young ladies stepped out, pirouetted, and stood on each side of the room. Again, the gentlemen applauded.

"Our next blooming lady is Lady Georgette..."

She entered with a beautiful bright smile and with the crinoline reduced in her skirt, her baby bump was barely visible; however, her growing breasts looked outstanding in the V-cut with the double shouldering material. Goody clapped with enthusiasm. He leaned to Jeff and whispered, "Don't be looking at my wife's booty," and laughed.

"Our next amazing star of the evening is Lady Eileen..."

She entered with the style of her previous life—fashion model. She looked radiant with an off-the-shoulder to the right ensemble and the two men warmed the air with their continuing support. She pirouetted to where Georgette was standing.

"And now gentlemen, our very own, Lady Angela."

Angela entered dressed in a crimson strapless bustier with the same deep V-top as the others but with deep red-wine polka-dots. She looked awesome as ever. Jeff and Goody lost their gentlemen-like fervor and threw in a couple of whistles. She sauntered to her spot, followed by Gina, to a picture-perfect frolicsome sextet.

"Ladies, you all look fantastic!" exploded Jeff in delight.

"Hands down ladies... you will knock them dead," shared Goody, still clapping.

"This is all Gina's doing and of course, help from our new intern, Mira, whose idea of the rainbow colors inspired these outfits," said Angela, endearingly as she looked at her with pride.

Goody walked over and introduced himself to Mira and placed her hand into his. "I want to apologize for the insensitivity of my partner while he was talking to you on the phone."

"No need, Mr. Thoroughgood. It was exactly what I needed. I am so happy to be part of this... and my Mom," smiled Mira, reassuringly. "Without Mr. Malardo's honest insistence, I would still be wandering aimlessly. Now, I have purpose. But thank you for your concern." She smiled.

"You have family all around you... and..." said Goody in his usual masculine authority, "...if anyone bothers you, they will have me to contend with... Understand?"

"Yes, sir," said Mira with a grin, giving the big guy a hug.

Jeff approached Georgette. "Who the hell is that guy? What have you done to my partner?" loudly jest Jeff so everyone could hear.

"Don't blame me..." said Georgette. "...he has always been like that with me. It's *your* doing, thinking he almost lost you and Angela. That's what has changed his outward manner to his friends."

"You know, I am standing right here, you two," flared Goody. He then flashed a smile.

"Well, ladies, end of fashion show. Let's all meet here around eight tonight to refit. After we change, Gaston's next door is serving lunch," informed Angela.

The Truth Revealed

A beautiful clear starry night accepted the searchlights as the Gendarmeries directed traffic around the decorative canopy. Black tuxedos and shimmering dresses swayed beneath the white opaque top. Inside the gallery, the crowd filtered through the well-placed, brightly-lit works while Gaston's staff mingled with trays of delicacies and champagne. Some of the guests indulged at the special martini bar while others enjoyed the libations served from the mixologists' unique flamboyance. Tulaine and Mira answered questions as the crowd awaited the arrival of its newest duo while listening to the sweet sounds of a string quartet. To the side of the stage, near the martini bar, Goody, Georgette, Jeff, and Gina also stood with the enthusiastic crowd, waiting for their entrance.

The crowd hushed as Tulaine rang a tiny bell. From the opened elevator door, Eileen and Angela stepped out with David Christiansen between the two. They sauntered to the newly-constructed mini stage amongst whispers of 'McQueen' and 'Vuitton' floated in the air as their polka-dotted material swished and crackled with each step delighting the crowd of *oohing* patrons. They ascended the double-steps to where Angela and Eileen commanded microphones.

"Bonsoir mesdames et messieurs," announced Angela enthusiastically.

"Good evening, ladies and gentlemen," translated Eileen.

"Bienvenue! Nous sommes ravis d'annoncer l'ouverture de notre galerie pour votre patronage et la jouissance."

"Welcome! We are thrilled to announce the opening of our gallery for your patronage and enjoyment," stated Eileen.

"Ce soir, s'il vous plaît bienvenue, David Christiansen."

"This evening, please welcome, David Christiansen," announced Eileen as the crowd shared warm applause and cheering.

The two ladies led David down the stairs of the stage to his waiting admirers. Angela translated some as most of the patrons spoke English very well. Angela left David in Tulaine's capable hands and she joined Jeff and her entourage who were standing by the martini bar. Jeff approached her as she came closer.

"You look stunning, my dear. My name is Jeff Malardo, and I would like very much to take you to bed," jest Jeff whole-heartily.

"You sweet talker, you. How can I resist your warm invitation," replied Angela in a helpless, southern accent.

She threw her arms around him and they danced to the soft sounds. The shy Goody placed his hands around his beautiful Georgette and swung her to the same sweet music. The night would be as it was meant to be.

The crowd dissipated slowly, and by almost midnight, Gaston's crew had most of the gallery cleared of their set ups. David, thrilled with the response from his French patrons, also seemed to be enamored by the young Tulaine. Jeff approached them, and not wanting to interrupt, but asked if they would like to join them on a surprise escape. David declined as Tulaine had promised to show him the Eiffel tower at midnight. Jeff patted him on the back and bid him a good evening. He then quickly joined the others.

"Ladies and gentleman, I have a surprise for you all. In..." Jeff looked at his watch, "...two minutes, our chariot will take us on our first stage of the surprise. I don't want you ladies to worry about anything. All has been taken care of. And please, trust me, you will enjoy this."

Goody, on guard at the large display window, motioned to Jeff that a black limo had pulled up.

"It is time, my friends." Jeff escorted Angela, Eileen, Gina, Mira, Georgette, and Goody to the waiting car.

"Where?"

Jeff interrupted Angela with, "Shhh... Not a question, my love."

They all entered the limo and it whisked them off to the Charles de Galle airport where a private jet was taxied and waiting. The ladies were all questioning Jeff's surprise as the jet's companionway closed.

Within a little more than an hour, the jet began its descent. Out the windows, they saw the lights of a town and a shoreline but had no clue where they were, and Jeff was not giving up anything. Even Goody was sworn to silence.

Once the plane had safely landed, it taxied to a private hangar and came to rest. They stepped out onto the tarmac where another limo awaited their arrival. Jeff attended the door and helped the five ladies enter. Goody sat at the side door opposite Jeff, with Angela in the middle. Reaching for the champagne, Jeff popped the cork, and served all except Georgette who graciously accepted a non-alcoholic beverage. Angela declined the alcohol version and joined Georgette's choice. The ladies were all excited as the limo pulled onto Avenue Francis Tonner, and from there, a right onto Bd. du Rivage, followed by a left onto Bd. du Midi Louise Moreau. It finally stopped on a dock where Bd. du Midi Jean Hilbert ended.

Their frilly crinolines crackled as they slid along the plush leather interior. This time, Jeff waited for the chauffeur to open his door. The sweet smell of sea air permeated throughout the limo as the door opened beside him. Jeff left Angela's side, stepped out and to the side as a tall large man dressed in a chauffeur's suit wearing black gloves stood waiting at her side. With an outstretched hand, a rugged-faced man began to tear.

"Ma'am, may I offer assistance?" he said with a sincere, recognizable voice. Angela looked up in disbelief into the teary-eyed big man and screamed with delight.

"Joseph!" she cried instantly, accepting his steady hand. When she stood up to his full size, she hugged him desperately. "Joseph... Joseph."

"I'm sorry for what you had to think, Miss Angela, but there was no other way. I love you and would never harm you," said the big man as his eyes continued to tear.

Goody assisted the other ladies with negotiating their way out of the limo. As Eileen stepped out, she looked over to see Joseph and Angela in a heartfelt hug. She also began to tear and she ran to their side. Joseph looked up on hearing her footsteps and opened his arms wide to encompass her as well.

"I love you, Eileen Cortez... I love you with all my heart. I always have," he shared.

"I have never stopped loving you either, Joseph," sniffled Eileen.

"I don't understand. Joseph, what are you doing here?" asked Angela as they released their embrace.

"Ask your friend. He's quite the schemer."

Angela corralled Jeff as she attempted to wipe the tears of joy from her eyes.

"You planned this?"

"Not all my doing," insisted Jeff. "Come on."

"Where are we going?"

"You are going down that dock until you find what is in your heart."

"I don't understand?" replied Angela.

"I'm right here behind you," he coaxed reassuringly.

Angela slowly walked down the dock holding onto Jeff's hand while her entourage followed unaware to what was planned. Two boats down, she spotted a multi-level mega-yacht with its stern facing the dock. As she stood wide-eyed facing the stern, the name boldly displayed: 'Claire's Sanctuary'. Angela looked back at Jeff who coaxed her to proceed. She approached and with his help, she stepped off the gang-plank into the finery of the aft deck.

One by one, they gathered alongside Angela. Jeff went to the front of the group and slid open the glass-etched doors that were prominently initialed with 'FF'. He slid the door to reveal a lush interior with white leather sofas and a teak-wood finished dining table with a place setting for thirteen that would easily have sat twenty guests. Slowly, Angela proceeded, guarding herself as if the dead would jump out at her. The galley smelt of fresh fish with a hint of bacon. She walked in deeper. From the port side of the galley, she saw a shadow of someone walking down the curved wood-lined staircase. As he appeared in the light—the face she had longed to see...

"George!" she screamed, running to his side. They embraced as a father and daughter might. And behind him stepped Carl with a big smile. Jeff bypassed the elusive Jamison, alias George, and Angela, and with an out-stretched hand, Jeff and Carl shook hands, and then the two embraced with a macho bump.

"Good to see you again, Jeff," said Carl.

"As always, Will."

Joseph brought over several tissues for Angela. She wiped her tears and looked at Jeff. "Will?" she said with a questioning look to match.

"Welcome aboard everyone. Let's go upstairs to the lounge. I know some of you have a lot of questions on your mind," insisted Jamison.

They all followed Jamison up the curved staircase to another experience of plush leather seats. Will picked up a tray of prepared 'Angels on Horseback' and served around while Joseph followed with chilled champagne and two non-alcoholic glasses.

Jamison stood at the front ready to unfold his mystery to Angela and her friends; they all sat with anticipation.

"Before I begin..." he motioned to a small circular elevator with a greenish white light revealing its rise from below. The curved teak door slid out of sight as a pushed wheelchair introduced her auntie, Sister Marie. And pushing her was a familiar face, although somewhat aged, Rodney. Behind Rodney was her best friend, Carol, wearing a stunning Gina inspired, Angela's friend, her Sapphire copy.

"Oh my God!" cheered Angela as the two friends collided in an embrace. They held on tight, spinning each around like little girls in an amusement park—boobs peeking out and crinolines cracking. Rodney quickly let go of Sister Marie's wheelchair and instinctively supported the whirling duo from toppling backwards. They finally released their embrace as the other ladies had to have Joseph fetch them tissues. Angela turned her attention to her auntie and bent down to her and gave her a huge hug.

Wiping her tears again, she managed to say, "I can't believe you are all here."

Jeff went to Angela's side and gave her a reassuring hug.

"And you..." she sobbed, lightly beating on his chest as he held her.

"Come on, babe. Let's sit so Jamison can fill us in."

"Thanks, Jeff. To begin, there are many parts to this story that have brought us all together. There has been physical pain, a lot of emotional suffering, and deaths that have touched us all. But, there have been friendships, camaraderie, and love that have held us all together in an infinite, unrealized realism of truth.

"I imagine..." Jamison paused as he looked around the room at his guests faces. "...the beginning to be that of a tragic train accident that claimed the lives of my parents in Belgium as they were on their way to a soccer match in

England. Their friends in Belgium, the Sonnet's, took my older sister Deborah Ann and me in and treated us like family. My sister and this angel, Gwendolyn, the now—Sister Marie, had been lovers for over fifty years. My mentor Gilles Fournier brought me into his life and business. When his wife Claire Marie Sonnet's life was tragically taken in a vehicle accident in New Hampshire by a heartless kid, Gilles relinquished his duties to me. Claire was Sister Marie's sister. I was barely twenty-five years old. Gilles stayed in constant contact with Sister Marie and my sister until her death, ten years ago.

"It seems a certain runaway named Gloria Jackson and my mentor and friend, Gilles, crossed paths. She stole his heart, mended the pieces, and gave him life again. And he, I know, lifted hers and gave her strength. It was Gilles who informed me and asked me to watch over her if our paths crossed, and he felt they would. But, he was adamant that I could not interfere, unless your life depended on it, Angela. He had given young Gloria a letter clearly laying out all of this, his explanation of past decisions, and his intentions for your future involvement. But, our Angela was too stubborn and wished to make it on her own, so much so that she filed the unopened letter... along with her heart... into a secretive place. I'll let Will take it from here... Will."

Will nodded and stood front and center as Jamison stepped to the side. "Thanks, Jamison. Angela, my real name is Will Carlson, hence the alias Carl. I was a DEA agent working on a case with another undercover agent named Pia Cortesse. We had secretively married and declared that the current case we were working on would be our last. Unfortunately, we were not anticipating such finality. She was shot dead as the bullet passed through her and into me. She was also the sister to your friend, Joseph, who at the time was the leg-and-arm man for a scumbag racketeer named Anthony Micholanetti. We had no proof that it was actually Micholanetti that also shot Joseph until a few months ago when Micholanetti thought he saw George Stanza get shot. It was actually me with flash bullets. 'George' was wearing a vest used in the movie industry to splatter blood on impact. We placed a van behind him for this reason. Micholanetti handed me 50 G's for shooting 'George', and I was supposed to get into my car that we had parked a few blocks away and drive off into the sunset. But, Micholanetti had rigged a bomb in it, which Joseph had seen him install and informed me. I stood behind a building and let it go off. The idiot, in his delight, confessed to Joseph, who was wearing a wire, about shooting two DEA agents and setting Joseph up as the fall guy." Everyone looked around the room at one another as the story continued to unfold.

Will continued. "It took all of my energy and strength to convince Joseph not to kill him. We needed to hook him legally. At the time of our accident and my wife's death, Jamison came to me with a plan as he knew it was Anthony who was responsible for the death of Claire in that car accident. He made it a priority and with his influence in the business and legal world, he wanted closure for Gilles. Jamison kept a close watch on Anthony's dealings and he asked Joseph to become our eyes and ears to bait this guy. The man was a walking time bomb. I will hand this back to Jamison."

"Thanks, Will. Are you all bored yet?" asked Jamison, jokingly. Heads just moved from side to side as the attentive group listened and thirsted for more.

"I should add to Will's testimony that because of Joseph, we were able to establish contact with you, Angela. Gilles was a very intelligent man, a kind man, a philanthropist... but not a naive man. When we constructed dams for water supplies and crop growing in not-so-friendly countries, we got involved with security systems as a means to secure our facilities and protect the people that worked at them. That side of the Foundation has quadrupled in size, reputation, and monetarily, but with a strict code of enforcing the welfare of citizens of the world, not to oppress.

"Sorry, I am digressing from the immediate. One of the Foundation's interests lies in the support of important findings that add value to man's existence. One such example is an important dig going on as we speak in Peru. Will and I just returned a week ago. We spent three months down there making sure they had what they needed, and nothing had been unintentionally misplaced. As I told Jeff at our first meeting, we know everything about everyone, who has been sanctioned to receive aid from the Foundation, but mainly to protect our investments. When one of the professors added a Teresa Mendez to his list of potential recruits, we checked her out and found out that she lived with Jeff Malardo, who was an investigator for missing children. Very noble, I might add. We set the seed into Angela's ear about an up-and-coming artist out of New York who had been a good friend of Jeff's. David was our bait to bring Jeff on board with the invitation to the opening at the gallery in Los Angeles. I hoped, and was correct in my assumption; especially after meeting him at my apartment."

"I wasn't so convinced," added Will from the sideline.

"Thanks, Will," said Jeff through a smile.

Jamison continued, "I knew you both had broken hearts but hoped it would have been Jeff's integrity that propelled him forward. We needed a guessing game for him and his partner, Goody. Some of their developments, we had nothing to do with; they were solely engineered by their experience and expertise. Angela was the wild card and harder to control." Pausing, he looked at Angela, and then added, "We figured the longer I was not around and the less you knew of me, the better for your self-discoveries. I am so sorry, sweetheart for the pain, but it was necessary for you to seek out the truth since you were bound and determined not to read those letters."

Angela looked stunned by all of this news and asked, "How did Jeff know who you were?"

"Ask Jeff. Your turn, buddy," said Jamison.

"Well, babe. Goody and I saw a video made by one man but interrupted by another. We knew George was not dead but truthfully not until you received the figurine. And it wasn't until I staked out Fournier Foundations that I approached the man I knew as Carl, who then brought me to Jamison, who laid it all out to me."

"What about that guy, Tom? Who is he?" quizzed Angela.

"He is part of the Foundation's security force, I believe, which has not been confirmed to me as of yet. I called him before our rendezvous with Anthony. He was the only one I trusted to have our backs. The FBI wired an informant whom they had on surveillance for a series of dock thefts for a long time, so we knew Anthony's proposed plan. And I know, baby, you have been struggling with guilt, but I just found out today that neither you nor I killed Anthony. We shot him all right and you had a perfect cluster in his heart, I am told, but the kill shot came from a distant tower and not from Tom's men. I only know two guys that could possibly make that shot..." Jeff paused.

"Who, damn it?" asked Angela, relieved but curious as well.

"Not sure I will ever find out, babe," related Jeff as he knew Will had just returned from Peru. He looked around the room casually at Goody who engaged Jeff's eyes in a cold, precise stare.

"I have a question," meekly asked Mira. "Where are we?"

"Cannes, sweet pea," informed Jeff light-heartily.

You could feel the tension in the room ease with Mira's question and Jeff's answer. A low, "Ahhh," as each breathed a little easier. Jeff walked over to the ship's stereo and placed Christina Aguilera's 'Bound to You' on softly.

"I have one other thing that I wish to add..." He stepped to Goody's side, retrieved something, and then turned to Angela.

"We all have been brought here for the craziest of reasons, but the only one that truly matters now, and the answer I hope I can trust to be a yes..." Jeff opened a tiny box and picked up Angela's hand. "Angela, you are my every breath, my sunshine, my soul, and my life..." He dropped to one knee, "... Will you, Angela Fournier, give me the honor and be my wife?"

Angela hoped one day this man would ask this question but today, was the best day he could have, and with a loud and affirmative "YES!" She buried her lips into his.

Releasing her hold on Jeff, Angela said, "And, baby, I have a surprise for you... and I hope you are as excited as I am. You know our deal...?"

~

Jeff rallied with excitement as his soon-to-be bride, confessed that she reneged on their deal of waiting two years before having children. She was pregnant. Her only discoverer was Georgette as she sat smiling at the dinner table looking at Angela the night before the gallery opening.

Jamison took Angela and Jeff aside and presented her with the one and only CD of a young girl's video mishap. He also informed them of the Russian intruders' fate. The man with the painfully sore throat did not make it. The attacker with a cluster of three shots to his heart also did not make it. The man with the buried bone in his brain now sat staring out of windows, and the huge man that survived Anthony's car running over him, would carry permanent tire treads up his back as a reminder as he sat in prison. The two snipers, the one who managed to get a single shot off and the other who hadn't, Jamison had not heard of their whereabouts.

Jamison also informed Angela that her anguish over shooting Anthony was a by-product because she knew him—it became personal. She had never mentioned the other man that she shot as he posed an immediate threat, while Anthony was a lingering distaste. Angela felt relieved and hugged her friend.

Jeff had wandered over to his buddy, Goody, and asked him one question: "Where were you actually located to coordinate the other agencies? Possibly in a crane's tower?" Goody did not reply but hugged his little buddy. Nothing else needed to be said.

As they all retired in the wee morning hours to their staterooms with the liberation of truth still on their minds, sitting on Jeff and Angela's nightstand was the original framed picture of her dad with his inscription intact.

~

The troupe enjoyed their cruise through the Mediterranean. Old stories with new twists delighted the endearing group. Past loves reunited with a promise of eternal flame as new loves planned their future and hopes for their children. As they all were basking in the Mediterranean sun, Angela added one final thought.

"My darling Jeff, as we open a new chapter in our adventurous lives together, shall we focus on the evil that exists in the shadows of 'Darkness After Midnight'?"

The Author - John F Russo

I began writing Tabula Rasa during my years living in Vancouver, B.C. around 1983, where I began to research the phenomena of missing persons in general. Back in the eighties, the incidents only numbered around the two hundred thousand that disappeared without a trace. Now, I believe it is between the eight hundred thousand to one million that go missing each year. These numbers take into account runaways, deaths, and obvious kidnappings—and we are still left with that incredible number. Just vanished!

Tabula Rasa, the first in the series featuring my heroine, Angela Fournier, was started as a screenplay written in the present tense, like all screenplays, and I continued this style of writing in the first edition. However, upon the infusion of the last line in the novel by Angela, I couldn't help but obey Angela and write more of her adventures. Also, the characters themselves were not satisfied with being a Los Angeles-based novel, but craved the adventure of a more international flair. From this first novel in this genre, everything exploded as future novels delve into the empowerment of women, the corruption of government, drugs, and the greed of corporations.

Jeff's recipe cards (alias cheat sheets), are exactly what I use to form the storyline. They are my snap-shot of personalities, names, special dialogue, and action scenes.

Angela, in the screenplay format, had no inkling of becoming an heiress to the Fournier fortune, mainly because there was no such thing. As *they* always say: *"The book was better than the movie."*

Many scenes I have lived and some embellished upon and it is up to you, the reader, to figure out which ones are which. I hope you all enjoy this novel and continue to support Angela in her next adventures.

Interesting Facts

I owned a 1967 Firebird convertible in 1983-84 and wish I still did.

My grandmother was a Sonnet, and from Belgium, which I visited in the early seventies along with Paris and the rest of Europe—a hippie thing driving a 1966 VW bought in Amsterdam.

The figurine that plays in several parts of the screenplay, I wrote the music for, as a tribute to my daughter, Nikki.

My friend, Jack Lambie—RIP—creator of the revolving sculpture, related the exact words (page 75) to me at a group art show we were in, and in turn shared by George to Angela and to what Angela relayed to Jeff. Jack was an amazing man of many talents.

The boat moored in Cannes is, at this time, only a dream, so thanks for buying my book.

Scary Facts

When Angela was being driven to Belgium, I just threw in that number of 26 km to Tournai, Belgium but when I was in Google 'street view', I came upon a sign that pointed to Lillie, France—26 km.

I also had no idea that Tournai was the birthplace of the order of Holy Union Sisters. I picked Tournai only as a relatively close location for Angela to drive to within a time frame. And now, this has become a place my wife and I want to visit.

I have some sort of fascination for 551. First, it was the address of my childhood home in Canada. Second, my wife Lori and I got married on the fifth of May at one in the afternoon. But the strangest flirt with this number is—I finished writing this novel at 5:51 p.m.

Angela Fournier - Tabula Rasa

Beta readers that have read Angela Fournier Tabula Rasa questioned the immediate love affair and commitment to each other as unrealistic. I will have you know that the love affair is taken from Lori, me, and our life together. And it is still as endearing as the minute we met.